DEPRAVED
HALLOWEEN

BRYAN SMITH

Grindhouse Press
PO BOX 540
Yellow Springs, Ohio 45387

Grindhouse Press #106
ISBN-13: 978-1-957504-20-9

This one's for Aron Beauregard

PART I

MONSTERS WITH HUMAN FACES

ONE

MEREDITH DANNER THREW OPEN THE door of the backwoods house and ran for her life, plunging into the surrounding dark forest at a heedless breakneck speed. She felt like a blind person charging through an obstacle course devised by a sadist, bouncing off trees and low-hanging limbs she couldn't see and tumbling to the rough ground over and over. Sometimes the low limbs smacked her in the face, inflicting damage. Jagged rocks pricked at her bare, bleeding feet, eliciting pain that made her wish she could stop or slow down, but she didn't because she knew it would mean death.

All day she'd waited for a chance to make a break for it, and unfortunately the opportunity hadn't arisen until after nightfall. Far from the lights of the nearest town, the only illumination was courtesy of the crescent moon hanging in the partly cloudy sky, and even that was hidden behind a heavy canopy of leafy branches. Now and then as she ran, she passed through a spot where the diffused light of the moon leaked in through a gap in the leafy canopy. When this happened, she tried her best to get her bearings and adjust her course in a direction that might prove more conducive to escape. The problem was she only had a split-second during each flashing sliver of light to assess things and make a decision. In those moments, forward motion might slow for a millisecond, but never ceased, not even when she fell. Each time she hit the ground, she propelled herself upward and got her legs churning again.

The sounds of pursuit provided all the motivation she needed to maintain the unrelenting pace. She never stopped hearing the ugly cretins crashing through the wilderness after her, cackling like madmen and making wild whooping and hooting noises. One of the men chasing her had a Viking war horn and intermittently unleashed blasts of resonant noise, stirring the air and sending disorienting vibrations racing through her body. The sound was like the bleating of some great, primordial beast.

After several minutes, she sensed they were toying with her and enjoying the chase. It was why they all sounded like they were having such a grand old time. They weren't worried about recapturing her. That was a given. She was in unfamiliar territory under the most adverse circumstances imaginable. Even if by some miracle she managed to find her way to a road, what then? It'd just be some desolate rural route with no traffic. They'd take her down there as easily as in the woods.

The situation was hopeless.

Yet she couldn't give up and accept her fate, not after what she'd seen these monsters do to Angie and Kate. They'd made her watch while doing all those vile things. The bodily violations. The beatings and the torture. The relentless process of terrorization. She'd tried closing her eyes against it, but they punished her for that, making her keep her eyes open, forcing her not to look away. The pain made resistance impossible. Her flesh was still aflame with agony from the numerous places where they'd carved into it with their blades. It was all horrible, every atrocious aspect, but it wasn't all the same. There were levels to the awfulness. For Meredith, the worst thing of all was the cracking sound of the hammer, that blunt and brutal rending of flesh and bone.

Almost as bad as what came after.

The . . . *removal.*

Several more minutes passed as she hurtled through the darkness. Her pursuers were never far behind, but they never drew much closer, either. She arrived at a section of wilderness where there were larger gaps in the leafy canopy, admitting more milky moonlight. From somewhere way off to her left, she heard the faint and distant hum of a car engine. Her heart stuttered with desperate hope. Maybe she was closer to a road than she'd thought.

Maybe someone would stop and save her after all.

She shifted course slightly, following where she believed the sound of the car's engine had emanated, but shortly after starting in that direction, her feet got tangled in some undergrowth and she again went sprawling to the ground. This time she wasn't able to regain her feet and get moving as quickly as the previous times. Kicking free of the vines in which she'd become entangled took several tries, and by the time she'd managed it, it was too late.

A whimper escaped her lips as she looked up and saw their ugly faces arrayed around her. One of the men wore a burlap sack over his head with a single eyehole cut in it. Seeing this stirred faint memories of the villain in some old slasher movie she'd seen long ago. Another one had a carved-out pumpkin wedged over his head, with slanted, drooping triangle eyes and a wide mouth with jagged teeth cut into it. The pumpkin was a reminder Halloween was only a few days away. She thought about how she'd promised to take her young niece Jamie out trick-or-treating. If things had gone according to plan, she would've gotten back home to Ohio in time to make that happen.

Now she'd never see the little girl again.

The other men, perhaps less self-conscious about their ugliness, wore no masks or head coverings. The one called Jed sneered in his snaggle-toothed way and moved closer, making her cringe as fresh tears rolled down her cheeks. Dangling from a rusted chain in his hand was the head-bracing device she'd watched them use twice already today.

Jed snickered. "It's time, little missy. Your turn to give up the sweet stuff."

Meredith whimpered again and scooted backward on her ass, shaking her head as she said, "No. No, no, no. Please."

They all laughed at that.

One of them repeated what she'd said, mocking her in a heartless tone that penetrated the hopeless depths of her withering soul. He spoke in a sharp and biting deep south twang, the kind that was far more pronounced than the warmer, more cultured tones she'd encountered in bigger southern cities. It was imbued with a deep-fried flavor of giddy derangement.

Her gaze flicked to the clear plastic bag one of the others carried, her stomach rolling at the sight of how it drooped from the weight of the organic matter stuffed inside it. She knew they weren't done stuffing the bag.

Your turn to give up the sweet stuff.

"*No!*"

She surged to her feet as she screamed and made one last-ditch attempt to get away from them. For one fleeting instant, she believed she might actually make it. The foul-smelling men in their rotting garments stood around her in a loose circle, with ample gaps between them. She was moving through one of those gaps, too fast for anyone to catch and hold her, but in the end, it didn't matter. Something came whipping through the air and struck her in the back. She stumbled and dropped hard to the ground, one of her knees smashing painfully against an embedded rock, creating another bleeding gash in her flesh.

After flopping forward onto her face, she tried turning over, but one of the men stopped her with a booted foot pressed into the small of her back. She turned her head and saw the head-bracer lying on its side on the ground. Its rusty metal frame had four legs and was shaped vaguely like a miniature oil derrick. Sharp points protruded from the bottom of each slanted leg. This allowed the legs to be driven into the ground or hammered into a wooden floor. Suspended by coils inside the frame was a metal band that could be adjusted by a small crank at the top of the device. The band was wet with the blood of her dead friends.

Belatedly, Meredith realized the head-bracer was what had hit her in the back. She squirmed beneath the boot holding her down as she watched Jed snatch the device off the ground. More terrified squeals emanated from her throat as she clawed at the muddy ground. She gave that up and tried bracing her palms against the ground, summoning every remaining ounce of strength as she tried pushing herself up hard enough to dislodge the boot from her back, but it was useless. The man holding her down was six feet tall and then some and weighed well over three-hundred pounds. She was five-two and barely more than a hundred pounds. No amount of fierce determination could turn that miserable equation in her favor, but that didn't stop her from trying.

The men tittered at her efforts, taking them no more seriously than the protestations of a misbehaving child. They laughed harder at the way she screamed and kicked out when another of the men, kneeling out of her line of sight behind her, began pulling her jean shorts off her body. All her other garments were already gone, tossed in the fire pit out back of the house, joining the already burned remnants of her friends' clothes. One of the men, presumably the same one who'd removed her shorts, slapped her ass and giggled at the high-pitched yelp elicited by the smack. She wept profusely in anticipation of the violations she knew were still to come.

Jed knelt in front of her and began moving the head-bracer into position. The evil contraption stood maybe fifteen inches tall, just large enough for the outward-protruding legs to encompass any normal-sized human head. Meredith screamed yet again and tried swatting the thing away as Jed tried lowering it into place.

The man's snaggle-toothed smirk gave way to an angry scowl. At his direction, two of the other men grabbed hold of her arms and stretched them out, holding them firmly to the ground away from her torso. These men were nearly as large as the one standing on her back. Their huge hands gripped her slender wrists hard enough to grind the fragile bones beneath her flesh.

Meredith whimpered as Jed slid the head-bracer into place and drove the sharp leg points into the softly yielding ground. Her bladder let loose, staining the ground with her urine as he began fitting the headband around her skull, working the crank to tighten it and render her head immobile. He'd turned her head so her mouth was pressed against the ground, but that didn't keep her from uttering more desperate pleas for mercy.

As always, the only reaction was more laughter.

Her eyes revolved in their sockets in search of anything resembling a sympathetic expression. She knew there would be no salvation. Not for her. Not today. Not ever. All she could hope for was some slight gesture of humanity, no matter how small or fleeting. All she found was the sickening sight of Jed's erection straining the crotch of his filthy overalls.

He met her gaze and smirked.

Then he looked at one of the other men still arrayed around her. "Get over here with that noggin cracker, J.J."

Meredith let out a wailing moan of utter despair as she heard the crunch of booted feet approaching. She continued to beg as she heard the metallic scrape of an old railroad spike being slid through the opening at the top of the head-bracer. A voice in her head yelled at her to shut up, to not give these horrible men the satisfaction of hearing her pathetic pleas, but the primal terror making her heart thud so heavily overwhelmed any attempt at stoicism.

She had no dignity left to salvage.

She moaned again when she felt the sharp point of the railroad spike press hard against the crown of her skull.

Jed held out an open hand. "Now gimme that hammer."

Meredith whined. "No. No, no, no. This can't be happening. It can't."

Jed chuckled. "Afraid it is, missy. You best hush your whinin'. Won't do you no good, no how. Besides, this here business serves a higher purpose. Like I done tried explainin' to you gals a hundred times, it's for science. Y'all's contributions to the cause will help save our old Grandpap. Console yourself with that knowledge. Now get ready to do that graveyard jig."

Meredith figured most of what he said was deranged bullshit, but she knew what he meant by that last part.

It was the same thing he'd said to her friends right before he sent them to their brutal fates.

Meredith closed her eyes tight and mumbled some last-second prayers as Jed raised the hammer into the air. They shot right back open as Jed brought the hammer down, smashing it against the head of the spike. The pain was bad. Horrendous. That awful, blunt metallic sound of the hammer striking the spike was also bad. On one level, it was so banal, the sound of a man doing work. Coupled with the sound of her skull cracking open, though, it was the soundtrack to a horror show like no other, one in which she was the star.

The hammer went up again and came down again. Meredith groaned as she felt the spike pound deeper into her skull, widening the fissure enough for her murderers to glimpse her brain. Her body spasmed as the hammer rose yet again, doing that graveyard jig.

Consciousness faded and then mercifully deserted her as Jed continued the work of opening her skull wide enough to scoop out the brain. Once removed, it went into the same bag containing the brains of her friends. After zipping the bag shut, he passed it back to Cletus. He was the one wearing a pumpkin over his head for some damn-fool reason.

After removing the head-bracer from the dead woman's skull, Jed rose to his feet. Instead of beginning the trek back to the house, the group of backwoods hillbillies remained where they were, eyeing the motionless corpse in silence. They were all thinking variations of the same thing, though for some reason no one was quite ready to say it out loud.

The silence endured until Bubba Ray, the man with the burlap sack over his head, removed the bag, revealing himself as easily the most handsome of this otherwise profoundly unattractive gaggle of madmen. "Well then . . . we runnin' a train on this dead bitch or not?"

Cletus kicked at the ground and said, "Aw, heck, she was the purdiest dang one of them all."

He sounded almost sad.

Jed smiled, nodding. "That's right, boy. I reckon that's why we saved her for last. Don't you fret none. We're just doin' what we gotta do. We got noble intentions. That there makes it right in the eyes of the lord and whatnot."

There were murmurs of assent from all present.

Jed set the head-bracer on the ground and began undoing the snaps of his overalls. "What's done is done, and it'd be a shame to let this fine piece go to waste without fully availin' ourselves of this precious gift the lord saw fit to deliver unto us."

Bubba Ray chuckled. "Amen."

And with that, the rest of the hillbillies began to disrobe.

The train ran deep into the night.

TWO

ON THE NEXT-TO-LAST day of October, after living in tranquil anonymity in one location for the better part of a year and a half, Jessica Sloan came to the reluctant conclusion that it was time to move on. Time to hit the road in search of new places and faces, fresh territory where she could again be a stranger to everyone she encountered. Truth be told, the feeling of tranquility had started eroding several weeks before arriving at this decision. She'd started feeling twitchy and restless, always looking to the distant horizon with a growing sense of yearning. For what she wasn't sure, other than just to be somewhere else. Anywhere else at all.

Articulating a clear and specific reason for the shift would have been difficult even if she'd had the benefit of a sympathetic ear to bend on the subject, which she did not. In general, she didn't talk to people at all, beyond the most cursory way when she was buying groceries or supplies from various stores in town. She had no friends, nor even any close acquaintances of any real depth. This was by design. Some people wanted to find her, even more than four years after retreating from her former life of violence and adventure. It was

8

possible they weren't searching for her quite as diligently as they had in the past. She was getting older, the strong allure she'd once held for certain powerful people and organizations might well be fading, but she knew she'd be a fool to ever fully let her guard down.

And even though she'd stringently avoided forming close relationships of any kind, eighteen months was more than long enough to become a familiar face in town. She lived in a cabin miles outside of the little city, but after so many months of seeing her around, local residents began to treat her like one of their own, smiling and nodding when crossing her path. They called her Janine, because that was the name that popped into her head the first time anyone asked her for one. She sometimes wished she could take the alias back, exchange it for one she liked better, but she became stuck with it. Not that it was a bad name. It just never felt like it fit. When she looked in a mirror, it was never a Janine looking back at her. Why it was the first name her brain had conjured out of the ether when put on the spot was something she doubted she'd ever understand.

Not that it mattered anymore.

That was one of the things she thought of after stowing her belongings in the trunk of her Nissan Versa and driving away from the cabin for the last time. She could be someone else now, could choose any name at all, finally shedding the "Janine" identity like the half-formed, ephemeral phantom it'd always been. A range of exotic names held an immediate appeal, but she knew it'd be smarter to choose something blander and less likely to attract attention. Blending in as a "Mary" or a "Lisa" would be easy. Doing so with a name that made her sound like something out of a James Bond film would be a far more difficult proposition.

Alas.

As she glanced at the Versa's rearview mirror and watched the cabin disappear from view, she felt only a mild pang of loss. She'd felt at ease for much of her time there, comfortable, like a regular human being rather than the quarry of some faceless hunter or hunters. At the same time, it'd never felt like a real home. In eighteen months, no one had ever shared that space with her. She'd taken no man into her bed, never invited anyone over for drinks and conversation. The only memories forged were of silent isolation.

Thinking about that could make her sad if she allowed herself to dwell on it for long. This lonely life was such a vastly different one from what she'd imagined for herself when she was younger, back when she'd been a normal woman living in a big city. A regular person with ordinary concerns.

Not a killer.

Not a fugitive.

She'd almost certainly still have that life if not for her fateful encounter with a man named Hoke. Her rapist. The man she subsequently kidnapped at gunpoint and drove out to the remote countryside with the intent of executing him. She thought about that a lot. All of it. If only she'd never gone to Hoke's house. If only she'd kept driving instead of stopping where she did, in Hopkins Bend, where she'd spent a night of horrors fighting not to die at the hands of the deranged locals. If only she'd gone to the police instead of taking matters into her own hands. If only she hadn't joined the Army after all that was over.

If only she hadn't become a professional assassin.

If only . . .

Two little words that haunted her so much. She wished she could go back in time and take it all back, but that was impossible. It was as useless as wishing for Santa Claus or heaven to be real. All that horrible shit happened and all she could do now was resign herself to this joyless shadow life she'd slipped into. It was better than still being a killer, better than being coerced into doing awful things at the behest of awful people.

Not that she was innocent in all of it past a certain point.

Oh, no. Not at all.

There were things she'd done, often of her own volition, she was certain would send her to hell, if such a place existed. Cruel, sometimes heartless things. Always in the interest of prolonging her survival, of course, but what did that matter? Cruelty was cruelty regardless of motivation, and she was long past the point of trying to justify things for which there was no valid justification. All she could do was try to be better going forward, so long as the universe saw fit to cooperate on that count, and so far it had.

Four years and counting, she thought.

Four years since she'd killed another human being. It was a streak she could keep going the rest of her life and she'd still never be able to clean her hands of all the blood they'd spilled.

The past. It's all the past.

You're driving into the future now.

She turned on the radio and tuned it to the nearest classic rock station, a faint signal that went in and out at the beginning of her new journey but strengthened the farther south she drove. It was comfort music that helped keep her mind off the litany of past transgressions. She sang along to familiar songs, surprised by how many she still knew by heart years after she'd last heard them. So much of it was the music of her father's generation. As a young girl, she'd fallen in love with it for that reason. Later in life, she avoided the music of his era for the same reason. For so long it'd been a painful reminder of his betrayals, but she was pleased to find she could finally enjoy it all again without that enjoyment being tainted by memories of the past.

It was revelatory to know she could pick and choose pieces of the past to carry with her into a new life while discarding all the worst parts of it. She'd spent most of these last several years believing the only way to move beyond a past colored by extreme trauma and dysfunction was to nuke it all into oblivion, but perhaps she didn't have to become something entirely new to achieve something resembling contentment in life. The good parts of who she'd been long ago could still be salvaged. Maybe.

It was something to think about, anyway, something she could maybe work on in a more dedicated way once she arrived at her new home, wherever that might be. She was driving toward Florida but did not have a specific destination town in mind. Heading off in search of a new place to live without a concrete plan in mind might have unsettled the majority of people, those accustomed to an existence anchored to the things that made society function while also making them slaves to the system. She did not need a job, harbored no concerns over credit scores or taxes, and wasn't interested in finding a man to marry. Wherever she stayed next, it didn't have to be her permanent home. It was likely to be just another way station along the way, a place to rest up and think, and that was okay. A somewhat more long-term stay somewhere was likely, but she was in no hurry to find her next temporary home. It'd happen when it happened.

She couldn't help smiling at the thought.

How very Zen of you, Jessica. The old you would laugh at what you've become. This was the absolute truth, and she didn't mind at all.

She'd been on the road for many hours and was deep into Alabama when she pulled off at an exit directing her into a town called Montclair. The radio station she'd started out listening to had faded out a long way back, but she'd had no trouble finding others like it as she'd continued driving south. The latest one was playing a song by the Rolling Stones as she pulled into a small and lonely gas station a half-mile off the exit. She pulled up to a gas pump and cut the engine as Mick Jagger was singing about not always being able to get what you want.

Taking a look around, she decided Montclair must be one of those genuinely small towns that truly deserved the label. The area where she'd stopped was missing the usual adjacent cluster of fast-food restaurants and competing gas stations. This place was called the Pump N' Go and it was the only building along this stretch of road. There were just two gas pumps and only one other car in the lot. The store's interior was lit up and she could see a fat man nodding off on a stool behind the counter.

Instead of immediately getting out, she remained behind the wheel a few moments longer, continuing to scan her surroundings. There wasn't much to see, but it was the emptiness itself that made her hesitate. She flashed back to that long ago day when her life had changed forever. Though she hadn't seen much at all of Montclair yet, she was nonetheless reminded of Hopkins Bend. The vibe she was getting was it was the same kind of nowhere backward pit of rural hell, the kind of isolated place where unwary travelers could disappear forever.

She gave some thought to starting the car up again and heading back out to the interstate. Perhaps it'd be better to press a little farther on down the road until she reached a more populous area. She was getting a bit low on fuel, lower than she normally liked when she was traveling a great distance, but not so low that it was at a crisis level. The tank was a bit over a quarter full and the Versa got pretty good mileage. That much gas could take her another fifty to sixty miles down the highway, give or take a bit. Surely that'd be more than far enough to deliver her to somewhere less desolate looking than Montclair.

Her hand went to the key still in the ignition, fingers tensing in anticipation of turning it and starting the engine up again.

Again, she hesitated.

Goddammit.

She was becoming irritated with herself. This fearfulness was a resurfacing of a part of the old Jessica she remained okay with having jettisoned. The one from before Hopkins Bend, the more vulnerable one whose years of relentlessly fighting tooth and nail to stay alive were still ahead of her. Becoming a better, more enlightened version of herself was an admirable goal, but she'd come too far and been through too much to allow fear to rule her actions. In reality, she was far more dangerous than any random person she might encounter here or anywhere else. Besides, any faint flickering of fear was rooted in baseless paranoia.

Montclair wasn't Hopkins Bend.

That rancid little shithole was hundreds of miles away and all its depraved citizens were long dead. The isolation aside, there was no hint of anything sketchy happening in the vicinity. In addition to wanting to refuel, she'd stopped because she needed a break. She was tired and in need of a quick recharge in the form of caffeine and gas station snack food. A chance to stretch her bones for a few minutes would also be nice.

Knock this pussy-ass shit off. You're already here. Get the gas. Get whatever else you need and be done with it.

Jessica opened the door and got out of the car. The bell above the door rang as she entered the gas station, the sound causing the clerk to snort and stir from his slumber. He wiped drool from a corner of his mouth as he sat up straighter on the stool and squinted at her. The look on his face wasn't openly hostile, but there was no discernible friendliness in it either. More than anything else, he looked confused, as if he couldn't believe she was in the store. It was the kind of look she'd expect to see if she'd walked in with a pet tiger on a leash. Or maybe she was reading too much into it. Maybe what she was seeing was a lingering dullness from being surprised out of sleep.

Or he was stupid.

Or both.

She gave him a nod and turned away from the counter. After availing herself of the single-occupant public bathroom in back—which was slightly less gross than anticipated—she grabbed a couple cans of Red Bull, some snacks, and headed to the front of the store. She set the items on the counter and took one of her many falsely procured credit cards out of the rear pocket of her jeans.

The clerk scooted his stool closer to the counter, glanced at her items, and started punching in numbers on the register. "Getting gas?"

Jessica nodded. "Give me twenty dollars unleaded."

She handed over her card and waited while he processed the payment. Moments later, he returned the card along with her receipt and bagged her items. After thanking him, she took the bag and started toward the door. She was halfway there when she heard the words that stopped her in her tracks.

"Stupid cunt."

She stood there a moment, staring out at the parking lot and wondering if she'd heard him right.

Then he said it again, removing all doubt as he enunciated the words with exaggerated clarity.

Jessica seethed, overcome with unexpected anger. She felt it rising inside her like poison, obliterating every trace of the peaceful feeling that had persisted throughout her journey southward to this point. Her capacity for sudden, shocking violence, dormant for so long, started to reawaken. She felt it tingling in her fingertips and the tight set of her jaw. An urge to return to the counter and beat the man to a bloody pulp was almost too powerful to resist. She knew doing so would bring her some moments of intense satisfaction. There was a catharsis that came with violence and in some situations the allure of it was almost delicious, something she savored, but it was a slippery slope and she'd worked so hard for so long not to be that person anymore.

She didn't know why this guy was being an asshole to her out of the blue but decided it didn't matter. It was infuriating, but it didn't require an act of bloody retribution. Surrendering to that impulse would ruin her mood and taint the rest of the evening. It might also have repercussions she wasn't prepared to deal with.

Just walk away. Let it go. He doesn't matter. This place doesn't matter. Walk out that door and leave it all behind forever.

She let out a breath and started moving toward the door again. Her hand was on the door handle when he spoke again.

"That dirty talk get your pussy wet, you outsider cunt?"

Jessica's hand tightened on the handle. Her jaw quivered as she felt the poison rising inside her again, a hotter rush of it this time as her face turned red with burgeoning fury. A scream felt ready to blast through her clenched teeth. Along with the rage came another feeling, a fear that dwarfed the tingling of paranoia she'd felt upon pulling up to the gas station. The fear wasn't of this man or this nowhere town. It was, instead, an almost blinding terror of what she knew she was one more tiny nudge away from doing and any of the accompanying transformation within herself that would come with the act.

Walk away, walk away, for fuck's sake, walk away!

She was still fighting this inner battle when she saw headlights appear in the road beyond the parking lot. The obnoxious clerk continued to taunt her in his bluntly profane way as she watched the vehicle slow and turn into the parking lot. It was a rusted old pickup truck of a style that had last been manufactured several decades ago, with large round protruding headlamps that made the front grille look like the ugly face of some giant monster insect.

The clerk started laughing.

The pickup truck pulled right up to the front of the store, forcing Jessica to squint against the bright glare of the big headlamps. Her hand trembled on the door handle. She told herself to open the door and walk right past the truck to her car. There was no reason to fear these new strangers, who she still hadn't seen.

Nonetheless, she hesitated.

The truck's blinding headlamps turned off and a moment later the doors opened on both sides of the cab. Two large men in ragged and filthy backwoods hillbilly attire got out and approached the store.

One was wearing a carved pumpkin over his head.

THREE

THE MITCHELL CLAN WAS ONE of Montclair's so-called "old families." What that meant was there'd been Mitchells living in the area further back than anyone living could remember. The oldest surviving pieces of documentation linked to the family dated back to a few years before the Civil War, but they were thought to have been in the vicinity of Montclair for at least a generation before that. Family lore held that the clan was of Scottish origin, but it was also said there'd been an undetermined degree of cross-pollination with early French settlers.

It was also said that a significant offshoot of the clan had moved on before the end of the nineteenth century, eventually resettling in Louisiana. This was supposedly the result of a bitter dispute within the various factions of the family, which before the split had become quite large. The dispute was long-simmering and complicated, but at its core was a conflict between a faction that aspired to social respectability and a lawless larger faction of insane degenerates, with the latter stubbornly failing to heed calls from the former to clean up their act. When it became clear the warring philosophies would never reconcile, the contingent of degenerates packed up their shit and headed out to Cajun country, where supposedly they continued to thrive and get up to all manner of fucked up shit to this day.

Well . . . that was what they said anyway, "they" being the elder members of the Mitchell clan still living in Montclair. Jedidiah Mitchell could not personally attest to the veracity of any of it, though he figured there was at least a strain of truth in the lore, which was all oral history, passed down from one generation to the next. Having recently attained the milestone age of fifty damn years, he reckoned he wasn't quite an "elder" yet, but he'd already told his kids the same stories he'd been told as a young'un.

Not once in all fifty of those years had Jed had any direct contact with anyone from the Louisiana faction of the family. He'd be inclined to believe they didn't exist at all, except that his Grandpap, still among the living and lucid at almost ninety-five, claimed to have gone off to visit them in 1955, spending several months tearing it up with descendants of the so-called degenerates before returning blind in one eye from drinking too much bad moonshine. The stories the old man told from that period beggared belief. They were insane. He couldn't imagine how anyone could get up to the kind of stuff his Grandpap described and still be alive to tell the tale, but Grandpap swore up and down it was all true.

Jed was in the shed out behind the ramshackle old family home, mixing up a new batch of moonshine. The brains of those gals from the other night were simmering in a cast iron skillet on the old stove they kept out here specifically for mixing up these special recipes. They'd previously been diced and whisked to a smooth porridge-like consistency. Judging them ready, he removed the skillet from the burner and poured the brains into a rubber bucket. After returning the skillet to the stove, he mixed the brains into the corn mash with a long wooden spoon.

The entirety of the whisked brain matter wasn't being utilized in this new batch, just the larger portion of it. Another smaller portion had been held back for stirring into jars of already distilled shine from the last batch. That was for contingency purposes, in the event something went awry during the distilling process. He was anxious to get this batch going because he'd been less than pleased with the results of his previous experiment. Taste wasn't the issue. It'd been delicious, like always. The problem was he'd failed to produce the desired results. He was trying to recreate the fabled "brain-shine" Grandpap claimed to have been perfected by their Cajun kin.

According to the old man, brain-shine was the ultimate back-woods self-improvement potion, sort of like a turbo-charged hillbilly synthesis of Viagra and various popular over-the-counter things regular folk took to improve mental acuity. A regular intake of brain-infused shine had all kinds of benefits, reputedly, amping up a man's physical strength while making his senses keener. It was alleged to boost intelligence and stave off the advent of debilitating brain ill-nesses like dementia. As Grandpap continued creeping closer to cen-tenarian status, this understandably became a source of great concern for the aging patriarch. To his way of thinking, a century on God's green earth wasn't nearly long enough. He was adamant in his belief that perfecting the brain-shine might yet prolong his time in the mor-tal realm for decades to come.

The problem for Jed was he'd yet to see any real proof of the efficacy of the stuff, and it wasn't from lack of trying. In the begin-ning, he'd followed Grandpap's recipe with exacting precision. He'd tested the first batch out on his offspring and some of their cousins. They all attested to its superior taste, but after consuming most of that first batch over three days, he'd noted no perceivable improve-ments in the strength or acuity of any of his test subjects.

Grandpap was furious, accusing him of fucking it up somehow. Jed pointed out that the boys were all young men who were already big and strong, rendering any improvements on the physical side of things difficult to gauge. Also, they were pure idiots, every one of them. Being non-participants in the public education system, their in-telligence had never been measured via any of the normal standard-ized testing methods, but Jed felt it safe to say the younger Mitchell boys were all below average in that area. Like, way, way, *way* below average. One or two of them weren't discernibly smarter than, say, a fence post. Therefore, a far greater amount of brain-shine would be necessary to even come close to transforming any of them into Mensa candidates. After stewing over this a bit, Grandpap declared that what the recipe needed was augmentation.

More brains, in other words.

Also, a higher quality of gray matter would be preferable. The first gal they'd snatched was a meth-addicted teenager from the next county over, a scrawny thing who scratched out a pitiful existence turning tricks out of the trailer she lived in with her mother, who was also a meth-addicted whore. Bubba Ray and the others picked the young one over the mother because the mother looked like a sasquatch.

That was how Bubba Ray put it anyway. What it meant in exact terms was hard to say, as Jed hadn't personally set eyes on the lady, but the clear indication was she was grossly unattractive. In theory, this should be irrelevant when the goal was harvesting brains, as should the gender of any potential involuntary donors, but properly motivating Bubba Ray and the other boys to do the dirty work of procuring required certain concessions. Among other things, this meant they only targeted women and young girls. It also meant that at a bare minimum their victims had to be at least tolerably decent-looking.

The gals didn't have to be beauty queens. In fact, it was better if they weren't, as snatching the real high-level honeys from neighboring counties would inevitably attract more attention than they could handle. The boys were happy if, after the brain was removed, they were left with a fleshy shell that didn't make their dicks shrivel up when they were ready to have some post-mortem fun with it. That first young meth-whore fit neatly into that category.

The recent trio of hot little fillies they'd had such a rousing good time with the other night—and whose brains he was continuing to stir into the mash—constituted what Jed considered the first acceptable deviation from the no fine honeys rule. What made it okay was they were only passing through on their way back home to the Midwest after a trip to Florida. October was a strange time of year for that kind of thing, being much more common in the spring and summer, but for the Mitchells it was a most fortuitous development in more ways than one. The gals were all university grad students, their more highly developed brains making them ideal candidates for contributing to a rejiggered brain-shine recipe. Just one extra smart gal would have been quite the prize, but ensnaring three of such superior quality at one time was a veritable bounty of riches. What made it even better was they were highly developed in ways beyond the mere cerebral. The girls were all long-legged and gorgeous and possessed some of the nicest tits Jed had ever seen in real life. Maybe he'd seen some that were as good in old *Playboy* magazines, but that hardly counted. Those were just faded old pictures.

These honeys were the real deal, three-dimensional flesh and blood sex dolls. They could be touched and extensively handled, even now, two days after having their skulls popped open. At Jed's direction, the boys had disposed of the first few unfortunate donors once they'd all had a chance to have a go at them, chopping up the bodies and burning them in a pit before burying the charred remains deep in the woods. The college girls, on the other hand, were still intact, save for their excavated brains.

The one called Meredith was currently rolled up in a blanket and stashed beneath Jed's bed in the house. He'd closed the jagged opening in her skull as best he could with a surgical stapler, rearranging her hair in a way that masked the ugly nature of her demise. It wouldn't be long now before she decayed to an extent that would make coupling with her unsavory, but Jed was determined to enjoy her as much as possible until then. Why, just this afternoon he'd dragged her out and given her a good what-for before beginning his distilling work.

As for Meredith's friends, they were now guests of Bubba Ray, stowed away in the mini-camper he kept parked behind the Mitchell homestead. The mini-camper was parked no more than twenty feet from the shed, and Jed could hear it rocking as he worked. He could also hear the boy's shouted exclamations of twisted passion, "Oh, baby" and "Get, get it, get it" being the most commonly repeated ones. The boy had a sexual appetite like no one Jed had ever known. He figured Bubba Ray had shown his new girlfriends a good time at least half a dozen times already today. Surely he'd be all spunked out soon.

Jed sure hoped so anyway.

He was about sick of "Get it, get it, get it."

Deciding the mash was stirred up well enough, he poured it into a larger bucket filled with warm water and stirred again. The contents of the bucket then went into an old Budweiser beer keg suspended over a propane-powered burner to begin the fermentation process, which would take a week or two depending on how impatient Grandpap got to try it out. In general, it was preferable to ferment a little longer for a higher grade of shine. This was a special batch the likes of which they might not be able to attempt again. If Grandpap started hollerin' for it too soon, Jed supposed he'd have to put his foot down.

Grandpap was easily the most aggravating human being Jed had ever known, but he loved him anyway. Extending his life by another quality decade or even longer would be a wonderful thing. If the old man made too much of a fuss, Jed planned to stir some of the held-back portion of brains into a leftover jar of shine and placate him with that.

Jed smiled as he patted the beer keg. "Dear heavenly father, please bless this mash and work your magic through the powerful elixir it'll soon yield. Me and my kin would be much obliged."

And with that, he closed up the shed and stepped out into the night. He glanced over at the mini-camper and saw that the light in the window was out and the curtain was drawn. Bubba Ray was probably taking a nap, having worn himself out from rutting with his temporary girlfriends so much.

The thought brought on his stirring of arousal, a feeling that intensified as he imagined having another go at the gal under his bed. A vivid image formed in his mind. He saw himself trembling with anticipation as he slid Meredith out and opened the blanket, unwrapping her like a birthday present. He could almost feel her cool flesh beneath his fingers as he caressed it with great tenderness before picking her up and laying her gently on the bed.

Jed rubbed his crotch and licked his lips. "Oh, baby."

Moonshine work made a man awful randy.

Jed grinned with wicked delight as he went on into the house.

FOUR

JESSICA PUSHED THE DOOR OPEN before the men from the truck could reach the store and walked right past them at a brisk pace. She sensed they were surprised and had taken no note of her presence just inside the door. The wood-framed door had a glass center, a portion of which was covered with stickers and signs she figured had partly obscured her form.

She continued walking at the same brisk pace but did not break into a sprint, even though a part of her yearned to. The men stopped in their tracks and turned their heads to watch her. The one with the pumpkin wedged tight over his large head was the closest to her as she walked by them. She'd passed within a few feet of his lanky form and had caught a glance of creepy eyes through the triangular slits at the top of the pumpkin's carved face. A shiver of revulsion went through her at the thought of those eyes assessing her, weighing her up like a particularly juicy cut of meat. The man smelled awful, as if he'd slept in manure and hadn't bathed in many months. Hell, maybe that was the case, judging from the filthy state of his raggedy clothes.

As repulsive as he and his unmasked companion were, she didn't want to give them the satisfaction of showing fear. Being in a hurry was one thing. They could think whatever they wanted about that. But she didn't want to run like a scared little damsel, which was the opposite of anything she'd been since taking her long ago revenge on Hoke. A part of her thought this impulse unwise, labeling it as stubborn pride that could potentially backfire in spectacular fashion if the men came after her. This was true enough. There was a greater level of assured safety in the relative pragmatism of making a fast getaway.

Still, she did not run.

She even slowed her pace slightly.

Complicating things was that after four years of living in retreat, Jessica was no longer in the habit of having a gun on her at all times. She did still have one, a Sig Sauer 9mm, but it was in one of her bags in the trunk of the Versa. Once upon a time, she'd had many guns, but she'd slowly divested herself of them over time, another way of shedding the skin of her former life. She'd held onto the Sig because a person of her background would be foolish to leave herself entirely unprotected, knowing her old enemies or shady former employers could resurface at any time. Fat lot of good it was doing her now, though, locked away where she couldn't hope to get to it quickly in the event of an attack.

The distance from the store to where the Versa was parked was short, no more than twenty feet, but operating in the face of a perceived possible threat had a funny way of lending physical distance a surreal elasticity, making her objective seem farther away than it was. She walked the entire distance fighting the urge to turn her head and look back, but that would also convey fear, so she didn't do it. It was ridiculous. She knew that. In situations like this, an accurate visual threat assessment was essential to staying alive, and in the past she'd never hesitated to use all tools at her disposal. That included exercising common-sense care when suspected predators were present.

Like now.

As she neared her car, she recalled the rationale that had propelled her out of the car and into the store. Just as she had no tangible proof of this town being the same kind of cesspool of corruption and depravity as Hopkins Bend, she didn't know anything about these men she'd never seen until now. It was possible they were perfectly harmless.

But, boy, that sure wasn't the vibe she was getting.

The vibe was *super creepy*, as in these guys were weird enough to give even the worst of the hillbilly perverts in Hopkins Bend the willies.

A bell sounded when she was within about three feet of the gas pumps, causing her to at last surrender to the instinct to glance backward. The big, bearded one wearing a wool hood hat had disappeared into the store, but the lanky guy with the pumpkin on his head appeared not to have moved at all since her last glimpse of him. He tilted his head when he noticed her looking and raised his hand in a strange gesture of greeting, waving slowly with just the tips of his fingers.

Then his head tilted in the opposite direction.

Jessica frowned when a giggle emerged through the carved mouth of the pumpkin.

What the fuck does this guy—

The thought was interrupted when the toe of her shoe struck the gas pump's concrete slab base, causing her to take a painful tumble. One knee hit the slab as she flailed blindly with her free hand in a failed attempt to break her fall. The giggling from the pumpkin guy grew louder, became more *gleeful*, as she hit the ground. He even clapped his hands and jumped up and down a time or two.

Jessica cried out in pain as her other knee impacted against parking lot concrete, causing her to lose her grip on her bag of purchases as she rolled onto her back, banging an elbow in the process. Pain shot through her limbs as she reflexively tried straightening her legs. Her elbow felt like someone had driven an icepick through it, a sharp stinging sensation that was somehow even worse than the pain in her knees despite the less severe level of impact. The top of her head was a few inches away from the rear wheel of the Versa on the driver's side. Grimacing in fresh pain, she turned her head to the right and saw that one of the cans of Red Bull had come out of the bag and was slowly rolling across the parking lot. The other can had popped open in the bag, soaking the snack packages.

Her only solace in this moment of profound pain and embarrassment derived from determining that no bones seemed broken. This feeling of marginal relief dissipated when she belatedly picked up on the sound of booted feet approaching. At the same time, the giggling of the pumpkin guy was getting louder. With a grimace, she lifted her head off the ground and saw what she expected—pumpkin guy stalking toward her in deliberate predatory fashion, taking long, bowlegged strides and again tilting his head in an exaggerated way that was probably in imitation of things he'd seen in horror movies. The same went for the giggling, another calculated attempt at creepiness. In less vulnerable circumstances, she'd sneer and say something scathing, but right now any insults she might sling would ring hollow.

Credit where it was due—his derivative spook show mimicry was creeping her right the fuck out.

Jessica sat up with a groan and scooted backward, putting her back against the car and heaving a breath of exertion. Ordinarily after a bad spill, she'd take her time getting up, but that wasn't an option in this case. Though he was weird and engaged in an obvious effort to frighten her, it was still possible the guy was a harmless nuisance, but she wasn't about to stake her safety on that assumption. She needed to be on her feet again before he reached her, ready to defend herself, and there was no time to waste. A few more of those weird bowlegged strides and he'd be right on top of her.

After summoning her strength and taking a deep breath, she surged up off the ground, wobbling for a moment after she was upright. A brief moment of lightheadedness made her grateful for the presence of the car right behind her, knowing she could lean back against it if necessary to avoid another fall.

The sudden way she'd sprung up from the ground appeared to have surprised him. He hadn't retreated, but he'd stopped moving forward. Though she couldn't see his real face, she sensed apprehension in the man hiding behind the pumpkin.

In another bit of good news, the swimmy feeling in her head passed within a few seconds, sparing her from having to lean against the car for support, which would've enhanced an impression of lingering vulnerability.

Jessica went into a fighting stance, showing him a defiant sneer while ignoring the throbbing ache in her knees. "What's the matter, pumpkin boy? You look a little less brave all of a sudden." She laughed. "Little factoid you should know about me. I'm ex-military, trained to kill with just my hands if necessary. I've done it, too. You're a tall drink of dirty water, but I'd take you down faster than you can blink."

She feigned a lunge, chuckling at the way he flinched.

The bell above the store's front door chimed again as it opened and pumpkin boy's larger hillbilly companion joined him in the parking lot, cradling multiple six-packs of Milwaukee's Best in his arms. His hood hat with its peaked top made him look a bit like the

Scarecrow in *The Wizard of Oz,* but any resemblance to L. Frank Baum's kindly creation ended right there because this man's misshapen countenance conveyed not even the faintest flicker of friendliness.

He scowled as he pushed the six-packs of beer into the arms of the surprised pumpkin boy, who struggled to hold onto them. The scowl deepened as he came a step closer to Jessica than his lanky friend had dared. "You say something to spook this boy?" He shook his head, snorting with disdain. "Mighty brave of you to pick on a child."

Jessica frowned.

Child? Is that a fucking joke?

The so-called "child" was well over six feet tall. She supposed the pumpkin might have obscured the face of a teenager who'd had an extraordinary growth spurt, but there was nothing childlike in the aura he exuded.

She grunted. "This child, if he truly is one, has behaved in a disrespectful, threatening manner. I'm not picking on him. What I'm doing is responding appropriately. Here's my promise to you, Fester. If the two of you don't fuck off away from me right now, you'll both be picking your teeth out of your assholes in a few seconds."

Confusion registered in the bearded hillbilly's face. "Fester? Who in the goddamn hell is that?"

The man was one of those cornfed, southern-fried boys prone to saying "hell" like "hail."

The pronunciation sparked a giggle from Jessica.

The man's dry, cracked lips peeled back, revealing gums black with rot and missing at least half their teeth. "Somethin' funny, you uppity city cunt?"

Jessica sighed, shaking her head. "Not really, but that's two of you plug-ugly Montclair boys who've called me a cunt already tonight, and I've about had my fill of it, Fester."

Her body tensed as she again edged closer to an explosion of violence of the type she'd come so close to giving into in the store. She didn't think she had it in her to pull back from the edge a second time.

Jessica felt ready for this.

She wanted it.

By this point, she even kind of *needed* it.

"Bitch, I done asked you once already, who the hell is Fester?"

Hail.

Jessica smiled. "You are, you gene pool reject. I don't know your real name, but you look like a Fester, like some inbred redneck scumfuck who crawled out of the festering, diseased cunt of some backwoods whore, so as far as I'm concerned, that's your name."

The man's hands were shaking with barely contained rage. "I'm about to shut that smart mouth of yours up forever, bitch."

Jessica's hands flexed as she shifted her stance slightly. "Bring it on, Fester."

The hillbilly looked like he was maybe a millisecond from taking a run at her, and she figured he really would've given it a shot if not for the abrupt intrusion of a sound that gave them both pause.

The approach of another car engine.

The hillbilly's eyes flicked toward the road, and judging from the abrupt way his expression changed, becoming more guarded and light years less aggressive, she had a strong hunch about what sort of vehicle was approaching. Not ready to let her guard down yet, she relaxed out of her fighting stance but did not turn toward the road to confirm her guess. She wasn't taking her eyes off the hillbillies until she knew for a fact it was safe to do so.

The approaching vehicle pulled into the parking lot and drove up to the front of the store. A moment later, a door opened and slammed shut with a heavy *thunk*.

Jessica summoned a smile of faux friendliness. She turned her head and saw that her hunch was indeed correct.

The law was here.

FIVE

EVEN WITH ITS TWO LITTLE windows open, the inside of Bubba Ray's mini-camper was getting stuffy, almost unbearably so. This being late October in Alabama, the climate outside was tolerable. Though it was maybe a touch unseasonably warm now, it was far from hot, and a slight chill would creep in as the evening lengthened.

Bubba figured he'd be pretty dang comfortable if not for two main factors, one being the lack of an air conditioner. He had a cheap window unit once upon a time, but it stopped working. Same went for the even cheaper oscillating fan he replaced it with, which went kaput after a month. He tried to exchange it at the dollar store, but they gave him guff about not having a receipt, probably because he'd shoplifted it and never had a receipt in the first place. He considered shoplifting another one, but the sons of bitches running the store made accusations and kicked him out, banning him from returning.

Assholes.

The other contributing factor to the mini-camper's stuffiness was the high level of physical exertion that came with having wild, energetic sex with his girlfriends. He'd been at it most of the day, arranging them in several different fun and exciting positions and using up a large quantity of the big tub of lube he'd purchased from the adult bookstore just past the county line. The lube was the warming kind and he'd selected it because he reckoned it would make his girlfriends feel almost alive when he was inserting his pecker in their various holes. It was quite effective in this regard, contributing immensely to the rampaging nature of his libido today. He'd had a hell of a time, going at it with such enthusiasm he more than once feared he might knock the mini-camper off the blocks holding it off the ground.

Now, though, he was pretty sure he'd used up all the spunk he had in him, down to the very last drop, at least until his body was able to replenish. He hoped like hell that wouldn't take too long. At two days dead, his girlfriends were still fresh enough for frolicking and he was keen not to waste any of the precious remaining time he had with them before that changed. The first day hadn't been much fun because of the rigor mortis stiffness, but today that had passed, meaning it was time to party. He figured they were good for maybe one or two more amazing days of good, sexy times, but after that the state of them would deteriorate to a point where even a man of his perverse appetites would start to become repulsed by them. The bugs were already starting to be an issue. Their bodies weren't overrun with them yet, but there were more than yesterday and he imagined there'd be even more tomorrow.

It was too bad.

Even in death, they were far sexier than any live girl he'd ever had. Some of the local gals weren't too bad, even kind of cute, but these fancy college ladies were on a whole different level. With their expensive clothes, makeup, and hairdos, they looked like magazine models or movie stars. Even the smart way they'd talked while still alive— often using words he didn't know—had turned him on.

He kind of wished they could've waited a while longer before cracking their skulls open and scooping out their brains. That part had been fun, no doubt, as it always was, but he found himself experiencing an uncharacteristic wistfulness for how they'd been when he first met them, so vibrant and exciting in ways unfamiliar to a simple country boy. He wouldn't admit it out loud to any of his kin, but a part of him wished he could go back in time and run away with them instead of doing what he did.

Just a stupid fantasy, yeah, but they'd liked him at first, he could tell. It wasn't just an act. They weren't making nice because he'd stopped to help them with their flat tire. That's what he'd think if he'd heard the same story from any of his cousins or brothers, but Bubba Ray was different from them in one important way. He was the only one of them who was almost handsome in the traditional sense, not just compared to the rest of his decidedly non-photogenic kin. His face was a pleasant one and he had an easy, disarming grin. If he wasn't so hefty, girls in general would probably think he was real hot stuff. Some did anyway. There was a reason he was usually the one tasked with luring in the test subjects for Jed's brain-shine experiments.

But Bubba Ray was a Mitchell through-and-through first and foremost. Family loyalty came first always. Forsaking his own kin to run off with some out-of-towners from way up north had never been a real possibility. Didn't mean he couldn't acknowledge part of him wished things could be different.

Bubba Ray heaved a big breath and sat up a little straighter at the head of his bed. A bunch of sweaty pillows were piled up against the headboard and he had his back pushed up against them. He had his girlfriends positioned to either side of him, with their shapely legs splayed over his much girthier ones. Their heads were on his shoulders and each of them had a limp hand on his crotch, which was also quite limp for the time being.

His hairy barrel chest was drenched with sweat, as was the rest of his body. The slickness of his skin meant he had to continually fight to keep the girls from sliding out of position. He didn't want that to happen yet, because he liked having them with him like this. It made him feel like a king on his throne, reveling in his excess and decadence. All that was missing was some servant of his royal court to bring him wine and fancy pastries on a tray, all the while bowing and scraping and calling him "my liege" or some shit like that.

Oh, well. You couldn't have everything.

After a while, though, the stuffiness in the mini-camper became too much and he decided he needed to step outside for a bit to cool off. He thus began the complicated process of extricating himself from the intimate cuddle with his girlfriends. This he did with some regret, loving the feel of their cool, soft skin draped all over his body, but he would return to them soon enough and again luxuriate in the abundant pleasures they offered.

"Fear not, my dears, the sweet lovemaking will recommence soon-

30

eth, but alas, I must temporarily venture beyond the sweltering confines of the royal mini-camper."

He squirmed free of the necro-romantic three-way embrace, but as he got clear of the girls, they fell against each other, their noggins knocking together. The cracking sound made Bubba Ray wince. Once he was able to heave his bulk off the bed, he leaned back over it to examine them, an effort that required digging through the rearranged hair atop their heads. In each case, the line of heavy-duty staples holding together their cracked-open skulls remained intact. Sighing in relief, he rearranged them in a sleeping lovers' embrace, with their legs intertwined and Kate's head resting between Angie's ample breasts. Bubba Ray took a moment to appreciate the visual appeal of his handiwork.

He nodded, grunting in self-approval.

Yep, it was hot as hell.

Or "hail" as his ugly-ass cousin Beau would pronounce it.

With that out of the way, he pulled on a pair of stanky-ass XXXL boxers, slipped on flip-flops, donned his Miller High Life trucker hat, and exited the mini-camper. He was careful to firmly close the door behind him, not wishing to let in more bugs and potentially hasten the deterioration of his fine ladies.

He took a can of cold Coors Light from a large cooler on the ground, popped it open with a fizz, and slurped the foam that rushed out into his eager mouth. A bigger gulp of beer ensued, followed by a satisfied sigh as he palmed sweat from his brow. The cold beer was like a little taste of heaven after spending so much time in sauna-like conditions. He chugged it down in a few big gulps and immediately cracked open another after crumpling the first empty and chucking it over his shoulder. The ground around the mini-camper was littered with hundreds of dead soldiers. He kept telling himself he'd conduct one of his occasional clean-ups soon, gathering up all the empty cans in a trash bag for taking down to the recycling center. It was worth doing now and then because that little bit of money the cans garnered went right back into his beer fund, but his generous share of the cash they'd taken off the college girls meant he didn't need to be in any hurry to take on that tedious task yet.

The steadily cooling night air felt good on his skin. He'd done the right thing in finally taking a break from his amorous activities, though it pained him not to feel the bodies of his girls wrapped around him. It really would be a damn shame to say farewell to them when the time came.

He was popping open his third can of Coors Light when the cracking of a twig somewhere to his rear caused him to turn around. A slight twinge of apprehension gripped him as a dark form emerged from the woods and started heading in his direction. Then he relaxed as the light of the moon shining down into the little clearing behind the house illuminated the slender form.

"Hey there, big sexy," a familiar female voice called out. "Got a beer for me?"

He gestured toward the cooler. "Help yourself."

Loretta Mitchell was a tiny thing with stick legs, buck teeth, and tits hardly bigger than a pair of baby tomatoes. Her long brown hair was dirty and looked like a rat's nest. Bubba Ray figured his weird little cousin had been sleeping out in the woods again like an animal, as she sometimes did when she had a little too much of her daddy's subpar shine and went feral. She was clad in boots, ragged denim shorts that looked way too big on her and a T-shirt with holes in it she'd likely gotten from a Goodwill reject bin. It said Poison on the front in green letters. Beneath that were the words *Open Up and Say . . . Ahh!*

She fished a beer out of the cooler and popped it open, taking a big swig. Wiping foam from her mouth, she said, "You up for a screw?"

Bubba Ray covered a wince by bringing the beer can to his mouth again. The girl came around asking for dick from time to time and he'd always said no up until one regrettable night a few months back when she'd waltzed into the mini-camper uninvited without a scrap of clothing on while he was high on meth. He gave in because he was so out of it and not thinking right, prompting her to try the same tactic again the next night and then the night after that as well, once again giving in each time. Each time he experienced some serious PTSD once he was no longer high. After that, he quit meth and got in the habit of locking the mini-camper. She eventually got the message and stopped coming around so much. This was the first time he'd seen her in weeks.

He shrugged after another big gulp of beer. "Afraid I can't."

She scowled. "Why the hell not?"

He nodded toward the mini-camper. "On account of the company I've had the last couple days. Been screwin' all day. I'm all out of spunk."

Her scowl deepened. "What company?"

He nodded toward the mini-camper again. "Take a look."

Loretta snorted. "Reckon I will."

She took another big swig of beer, threw the can down in a huff, and stomped over to the mini-camper, ripping the door open after ascending the stack of cinderblocks he used as steps. Some more stomping around noises emanated from the mini-camper at first, but then Bubba Ray's cousin went quiet for an extended time. He wasn't overly concerned. She was well-acquainted with the kind of highly illegal shit Mitchell boys got up to sometimes. Hell, getting necro-romantic at least once in a while was almost a required rite of passage for adolescent members of the clan. She wouldn't be calling the cops or berating him for violating the laws of nature or anything like that.

But she might be a tad jealous.

Hopefully only a tad, because Loretta could sometimes transform into a ferocious wailing banshee of unrivaled proportions when she was especially riled up. It didn't happen a lot, but when it did, no one in their right mind wanted to be anywhere in her vicinity.

Loretta was still quiet when she at last reemerged from the mini-camper. Her expression was thoughtful as she descended the cin-derblocks to the ground and extracted another dripping-wet can from the cooler.

After opening it and taking a smaller sip than before, she looked him in the eye and said, "So, you been fuckin' them dead bitches all day?"

He nodded. "Yep."

She grunted. "And you'd rather fuck them than me?"

There was an edge in her voice that made him wary. He rolled his big shoulders and did a little head-wobble as a vague way of suggest-ing it wasn't as simple as that, though in reality it was exactly that simple. "Well, now, it's just a matter of timing. They were here and I was ready. Ain't seen you in weeks till now." He shrugged again. "Just the way it is."

She smirked, shaking her head. "Whatever. I need the meat, so I'll hang around long as it takes for your sac to fill up again." She gave him a wink. "Tell you what. I might even be down for a foursome with you and your dead gals."

The suggestion caught Bubba Ray off-guard. His face twisted in a look of confused contemplation as his mind automatically started en-visioning the scenario. To his surprise, it didn't conjure the reflexive repulsion he might have expected.

"Huh."

She smiled, tittering. "Thinkin' about it, ain't ya?"

He shrugged, striving to maintain an outwardly noncommittal stance, though he already knew he'd have a hard time declining her titillating proposal.

She tittered again. "Yeah. You are. It'll be a good time, baby, you'll see."

Bubba Ray reckoned it would, but he still didn't say anything.

Loretta downed the rest of her beer and helped herself to yet another one. She watched him as she drank it, studying his expression in a quietly analytical way that was atypical for her. Bubba Ray hardly noticed because his mind was wandering, caught between fascination with the possibilities inherent in his cousin's bawdy idea and a growing sense of melancholy over the imminent loss of, face it, the greatest lovers he'd ever had.

"You know what tomorrow is, don't you?"

Once again, Bubba Ray was caught off guard. "Huh? Whatcha talkin' about?"

Loretta cocked an eyebrow. "Halloween, dumbass. What else?"

Bubba Ray frowned. "Oh. Yeah. That's right. What about it?"

There was a strangely knowing cast to her features that unnerved him. She laughed as she moved closer, putting her hand on his bare chest, which was no longer sheened with sweat. Her fingertips teased him as she fluttered them up and down his torso. "Halloween is when the veil between our world and the world of the dead is at its thinnest. All kinds of weird shit is possible."

Bubba Ray shivered at the teasing motion of her fingertips. He hardly wanted to admit it, but a stirring had started in his loins. "Again, what about it?"

She slipped a hand inside his boxers and curled her fingers around his cock, making a sound of exaggerated surprise. "Ooh, signs of life. Speaking of which, I had an idea."

Bubba Ray felt his dick grow hard in his cousin's hand. He wasn't even high on meth. It might not officially be Halloween yet, but he reckoned it was close enough. Weird shit, the kind even a backwoods freak show like himself wouldn't ordinarily entertain, definitely seemed to be on the agenda. For the first time, Loretta seemed actually kind of . . . sexy.

And it don't get no weirder than that.

He shook his beer can. It was almost empty. He downed the rest in a final swig and tossed the can over his shoulder. "What kind of idea?"

She smiled and gave him a squeeze that made him groan. "You ever heard of an old movie called *Frankenstein*?"

SIX

THE UNIFORMED MAN WHO EMERGED from the sheriff's department cruiser could not have been more different from the few other denizens of Montclair Jessica had encountered so far, at least in terms of physical appearance. He had a lean but muscled build that looked distractingly hot in the fitted dress shirt and slacks of his brown and tan uniform. The way his broad shoulders strained the fabric of the shirt briefly made her feel weaker in the knees than she already did in the wake of her painful spill. His face matched the body, with chiseled, angular planes and the slightest hint of a dimple at the center of his chin. A five o'clock shadow of dark brown stubble enhanced his overall sexiness, as did his alert and intelligent eyes, which were the same piercing blue as her own.

In addition to all that, he appeared to still possess all his original teeth, which were bone-white and aligned in perfect straightness. Also, unlike the hillbillies, he didn't reek like someone who'd spent weeks marinating in sewer water. All in all, he looked more like someone who belonged on the cover of a male fashion magazine than someone from a putrid backwater burg.

The sight of him stirred something in Jessica that had lain dormant for a long while. The strong disarming effect he had on her was like nothing she'd experienced in recent memory, overriding all her usually reliable self-protection instincts.

As he approached her, an almost shy smile came to her lips, an expression that was like another echo of the more innocent young woman she'd been before the nightmare of Hopkins Bend. She didn't realize something was amiss until he had the handcuffs in his hands and started reaching for her wrists. Her eyes popped wide in alarm and she tried jerking her hands away, but it was too late, he'd seized one of her wrists and already slapped on one of the cuffs.

Whereas another person might have crumpled in confusion or started demanding answers for why this was happening, Jessica resisted from the start, knowing there was no point in anything else because nothing about this was right. Any faith in the man's standing as an honorable upholder of the law was wiped out the instant he came at her with those cuffs. Nothing he was doing was normal protocol. He hadn't asked questions to assess the situation. She and the hillbilly she'd called Fester had exchanged verbal threats, but there'd been no physical fight in progress to break up and therefore no justification for any form of forcible restraint. If he somehow knew her true identity and she had warrants she didn't know about, it still didn't matter because he wasn't following proper apprehension protocol.

Not that she believed for a second he was attempting a lawful arrest. There was no way he knew who she was. That'd be too random a thing in so obscure a spot. No, something else was going on here.

Something *bad*.

The only thing she knew for sure was she was fighting to save herself. If she lost the fight, it might well be the end of her, and there was no way in hell she was letting herself get killed by a bunch of depraved hicks. She'd come too far and gone through too much for that.

Jessica managed to shift her body and jerk the deputy off-balance by pulling hard with her cuffed hand, creating enough separation between them to deliver what should've been a punishing blow to his throat, but her sore knees buckled, throwing off her aim. The punch glanced off the edge of his jaw instead. He was thrown further off-balance by the blow, but because he managed to maintain his iron grip on her wrist, she was dragged along with him.

The hillbillies went into a joyous frenzy as they observed the altercation, whooping and hollering and jumping up and down like a pair of deranged monkeys on meth. Jessica kept pulling at the man and steering him around in a stumbling circle as she tried to rain more blows upon his head. He tried retaliating, but it was clear he wasn't as skilled a fighter as she was. She was able to avoid most of his punches and land most of her own. Fighting through the pain in her knees and keeping her feet moving was the key. Her skill in that area was the legacy of her long-ago special ops training. He tried pulling his gun at one point, but she was able to knock it out of his hand and send it skidding across the parking lot. The same happened when he tried pulling his Taser. What worked against her was his significant height advantage and superior strength. The majority of her punches continued to land just off-target, robbing them of their power.

Even with this disadvantage, she might ultimately have managed to subdue him. The problem was she had no one on her side to shield her against perimeter assaults from the other men. When the hillbillies realized she wasn't going to be a pushover for the deputy—and she might even be capable of beating him—they ceased their antics and began creeping in close. Little by little, they forced Jessica to change tactics, adopting a more conservative defensive posture as she struggled to keep the deputy at arm's length while fending off intermittent attempts by the hillbillies to grab onto her.

She managed to keep them at bay a couple of minutes longer, but the haphazard circle she was moving in with the deputy continued to constrict at a terrible, inexorable rate. The one with the pumpkin over his head eventually managed to get in close enough to slip his arms around her waist. One of his hands slithered up to her chest to squeeze a breast. She tried launching herself backward to break the loathsome embrace, but by then the deputy had a firmer grip on her as well. A deeper sense of panic began to set in for Jessica. She could feel pumpkin boy's erect penis pressing against her through his putrid jeans. Visions of being raped right here out in the open by all these vile men set her heart to pounding. She'd vowed to never let anyone do that to her again after Hoke and had always been willing to fight to the death to avoid it. The notion of it happening like this was insane, almost unfathomably so.

Yet it seemed on the verge of happening anyway.

Then, dimly perceived through the frantic din of struggle, a faint sound registered somewhere at the blurry edges of consciousness. It was the sound of the bell above the Pump N' Go's door as it opened again.

The next sound wasn't so subtle.

The unexpected boom of a shotgun blast assailed Jessica's ears, a loud percussive thud that hit her almost like a physical thing. Startled yelps from the hillbillies followed in the aftermath of the blast. A shivering pumpkin boy relinquished his pawing grip on her and went stumbling backward, whimpering with fright.

Jessica's gaze jerked toward the store, her eyes going wide again when she saw the fat clerk had emerged from behind the counter with a pump-action Mossberg. He held the barrel pointed toward the sky as he directed a sneer at all of them.

"Now, look here, y'all," he said around a mouthful of chewing tobacco. "This rumble in the jungle wrestling smackdown ultimate grudge match nonsense has to be taken elsewhere before y'all start scaring my customers away."

A costly moment of befuddlement followed the clerk's loud and dramatic interruption for Jessica, providing the deputy with the opportunity he needed to spin her around and finish cuffing her hands behind her back. She resumed struggling against him, but he was too strong and now had her at too much of a disadvantage.

Out of options, Jessica started screaming as the man began wrestling her over to the cruiser. The back door was standing open, a thing she belatedly understood should have served as an ominous warning. It'd been open from the start, but she'd taken no notice because of her instant fixation on the deputy's good looks and impressive physique. Too many years out of the game had lulled her into a false sense of security. She'd also relaxed into an unfounded faith in symbols of authority. That she'd snapped out of it in time to put up a fight didn't excuse these egregious lapses in judgment.

Once they arrived at the cruiser, she leaned her full weight backward against him and used his body as a fulcrum, swinging her legs up and bracing her feet against the cruiser's quarter panel. She then tried driving herself backward to make him stumble and lose his grip on her. The pain in her knees flared again, but she managed to put a decent amount of force into the effort, which did cause him to stagger backward a few steps. Unfortunately, she was unable to loosen his grip on her. All she succeeded in doing was to make him angrier. He wrestled her back toward the cruiser, angling her toward the open door. This time he leaned harder into her, utilizing his greater muscle mass to maximum advantage, bearing down on her in a way that prevented her from kicking her feet up again or attempting any similar maneuvers. A few seconds later, he was able to throw her into the back of the cruiser and slam the door shut.

Jessica screamed, her eyes brimming with unaccustomed tears. The tears made her angry, but she couldn't help it. The terror gripping her was like nothing she'd experienced in a long time, mostly because it'd been forever since she'd last felt this helpless. She was trapped and effectively restrained, with no hope of getting free without help.

She seethed with fury and fear as she watched the deputy retrieve the gun she'd knocked away and confer with the store clerk and the hillbillies. The deputy did most of the talking. His voice was audible but muffled, most of his words indistinct. Much of what he was saying seemed directed at the store clerk, who was nodding along with a grin on his face. From the deputy's tone and the few clear words she could pick out, she got the impression the lawman was expressing gratitude to the clerk. She assumed this was for providing a helpful distraction at a crucial moment, though it seemed possible there was more to it than that. Reason being, she still had no clue what had precipitated this incident.

Maybe the deputy and clerk were friends. The clerk's nasty, aggressive attitude toward her as she'd started walking out of the store still struck her as strange in the extreme. Was it possible he'd summoned his lawman buddy to snatch her for nefarious purposes, perhaps as part of some ongoing arrangement or mutual understanding they had? It was a disturbing notion, one she wished she could dismiss, but could not.

The weird one with the pumpkin on his head stood separate from the rest of them as he talked. His attention was on her as he crept steadily closer to the cruiser, bowing at the waist to peer in at her through the window. He did this odd thing where he waved with the tips of his fingers. Jessica cringed in disgust, recalling how he'd availed himself of the opportunity to molest her while interfering with her attempt to get free of the deputy. He came closer still and leaned lower until the face of the pumpkin was pressing against the window.

Jessica was so focused on her feelings of repulsion for pumpkin boy she didn't realize the deputy's conversation with the others had concluded until the front door opened and he dropped in behind the steering wheel. He started the cruiser, cranked the wheel, and turned around in the parking lot. The bearded hillbilly moved closer and leered in at her, making a lewd gesture. His pumpkin-wearing companion did a weird shimmying thing with his long, lean body that resembled the herky-jerky motion of one of those inflatable air dancer things at car dealerships getting blown about in a high wind. The guy was, without question, one of the weirdest individuals she'd encountered in recent memory.

As the cruiser rolled away from the store and pulled out onto the road, her attention returned to her predicament. "You have no right to arrest me. It's not too late to stop now and release me before things go too far. I promise to leave town without a fuss and never breathe a word of this to anyone."

The deputy did not reply.

He didn't even glance at her in the rearview mirror.

As the cruiser picked up speed, Jessica noted they were headed not back toward the interstate junction but were instead moving in the opposite direction. She turned her head and watched the gas station recede behind them, catching a final glimpse of her car still parked at the pump before it disappeared from view. It occurred to her she might never see it again. The car itself wasn't anything special. She liked it and it had served her well, but there was no sentimental attachment. More upsetting was the potential loss of the things in her bags. They contained not just her clothes and other necessities but also the few remaining meaningful personal mementos from her younger days.

Nothing she could do about it now.

She faced forward and again addressed the deputy. "Why have I been detained? I've done nothing wrong."

This time she did get a reaction from her captor. He chuckled softly and shook his head but still did not say anything.

She nonetheless continued trying to engage him, calmly at first, but then in an increasingly agitated fashion as each time he again failed to offer any sort of verbal response. Her attempts to reason with him not getting her anywhere, she resorted to kicking the back of his seat. Repeatedly. At first he ignored this new tactic as well, but he at last lost his patience when her kicks became forceful enough to push him forward in his seat.

He screamed at her to stop, glaring at the rearview mirror. "Knock it the fuck off, bitch. Kick my seat one more time, and I'll have you fellate my Glock. Think I'm lying? Fucking try me."

Jessica stopped kicking the seat.

She was still shaking with fury, but there was something hard and unyielding in the man's voice, a quality she perceived as absolute sincerity. His threat was not an idle one. The urge to fight and rage against the wrongness of the situation lingered, but she was in no hurry to choke on the barrel of his gun. She wished now she'd pried it from his hand instead of merely knocking it away. If she could do it over, she'd take it from him and put a bullet in his skull. Then she'd kill the rest of them too, without hesitation. A harsh solution, no doubt, but it was exactly the kind of merciless thing she'd done several times in the distant past, when she was still active in the world of covert operations and professional assassination. Any hope of survival she was still clinging to hinged on getting that same ruthless edge back.

That was the stone-cold truth and she knew it, yet recognition of this came with a pang of regret. A little while ago she'd been reflecting on how content she was with having left that part of her past behind. There'd been a deep gratitude for no longer being that person, a happiness at no longer being a killer.

Yet here she was, ready to embrace it all again.

To throw away the vows she'd made to herself like they were nothing.

She stared at the back of the deputy's head and felt her hands tighten into shaking fists behind her back, muscles aching for release, instincts yearning once again with the need to inflict violence and pain.

So be it.

They drove on in silence for a while after that, the deputy guiding the cruiser along the sharp curves of a winding back road. It was dark, the streetlamps few and far between. At one point, they passed a sign pointing the way into the heart of Montclair, where she assumed the jail and the sheriff's office would be, but the deputy didn't take that turn.

Jessica grunted. "I'm not really under arrest, am I?"

The deputy glanced at the rearview mirror, smirking. "Not officially, but you *are* my prisoner."

His laughter then had a blatantly sinister edge to it.

A few miles farther down the road, he took a turn, steering the cruiser down a long private drive and continued for nearly another mile until guiding the vehicle to a stop in front of a nice two-story cabin surrounded by wilderness. No other vehicles were present, but there was ample exterior lighting, granting her a good look at a place she knew would appear quite picturesque in the daytime.

The deputy cut the engine and met her gaze in the mirror again. "Welcome to your new home. This is where you'll spend what's left of the rest of your life."

His smug smile shifted, becoming a sneer.

He held her gaze a moment longer, allowing her some more time to fully appreciate the depth of the evil staring back at her. She didn't need to know anything about his prior deeds to know what he was. Though he wore the uniform of a public servant, he was a predator first and foremost, an opportunistic one who preyed on outsiders because he knew how easy it was for a man in his position to make them disappear without a trace.

He would hold her against her will here for an indefinite time. Maybe a short time. Maybe a long time. She knew of women who'd been held for many years by men like this one. He would be cruel. He would torture her. Sexually violate her. Indulge all his sickest fantasies to the fullest extent.

Eventually, when he'd used her up or grown tired of her, he would kill her.

The deputy opened his door and stepped out of the cruiser. Instead of then opening a rear door to haul her out, he started walking toward the cabin. He went inside and lights came on, transforming the dark windows in front into squares of bright yellow.

Jessica stared at the front of the cabin, expecting him to return for her almost right away, but his absence stretched on for several minutes. While he was gone, she stretched out on the bench seat in the back of the cruiser and started contorting her body, lifting her legs and pulling her knees toward her chest as she worked to bring her cuffed wrists up over her ass and then over her legs. The maneuver required a lot of painful straining and for a while she was sure she wouldn't get it done. She clenched her teeth against the pain and strained a little more, her muscles stretching to their limits as she was at last able to bring her wrists clear of the tips of her shoes.

Knowing she had no time to waste, she repositioned herself on the seat, pulling her legs back again in preparation for kicking at one of the windows. The heavy-duty partition screen separating the front and back seats meant that smashing out one of the back windows was her only hope. If she could do that and slither out through the opening before the deputy returned, she'd take off running into the surrounding woods. Heading back to the road would be a mistake. He'd catch up to her in no time. The wilderness was a risky unknown. She didn't know the territory. It'd be dark. She might be leaking blood from cutting herself on shattered glass. But there was a remote chance she might be able to lose him out there in the dark and she meant to take that chance if she could.

She pulled her feet back and kicked at the window. The glass did not immediately splinter, but she expected that. It would take several of the hardest kicks she could muster to get the job done. She was grateful she was wearing boots with thick rubber soles.

She pulled her feet back to deliver a second kick.

Then the rear door on the other side opened and suddenly the deputy was looming over her, leering as he applied a rag soaked in chloroform to her face.

SEVEN

AFTER BLOWING HIS LOAD INSIDE Meredith, a sweating, panting Jedidiah Mitchell lifted himself off the woman's unmoving form and flopped over onto his back. As he stared up at the ceiling while waiting for his breathing to even out, he reached over and cupped one of her breasts. He idly manipulated the spongy nipple with the ball of his thumb, entertaining himself with thoughts of how her body would respond if she still had air in her lungs, all that moaning and squirming live girls did when they were aroused.

Or, in some cases, when they were faking arousal.

Jed had a grin on his face as he turned his head and looked at his wife. "Funny thing, even without a pulse, this gal's a better lover than you ever were. Not a lick of backtalk and she don't say no to nothin'. If she could cook, she'd be the perfect woman, but I reckon that's a bit much to ask of someone so, uh, empty-headed."

Laughter spewed from his mouth, along with a spray of spittle. His merriment was not matched by Norma Mitchell. This was no surprise, given that all that remained of her was her skull, which at the moment was resting on the little table next to their former marriage bed.

Jed sat up with a groan and swung his legs over the side of the bed, scooting to the edge and bracing his bare feet against the warped and uneven floor planks. A bug emerged through one of the narrow gaps between planks and crawled up onto his foot through the space between his big toe and the one next to it. He paid it no mind as he rose shakily to his feet and went out to the hallway, where the one bathroom in the house was located.

Aside from the creaking of the floorboards under his feet, the house was quieter than normal for this early in the evening. Most nights around this time the TV in the parlor could be heard blaring from one end of the little house to the other, often with at least a few of the boys gathered around it, swilling their cheap beers and loudly jawing off about this and that, generally making a racket and wearing on his nerves.

Tonight there was none of that. The TV was either off or muted and there was no murmur of conversation drifting in from anywhere. Jed figured the boys must be out somewhere raising hell and getting up to no good, as they did sometimes when they started getting a little stir-crazy. He smiled as he thought about it, hoping they might return later on with another new brain donor or two. His hopes were high for good results from the work he'd done with the recent trio of test subjects, but more material to work with for future experimentation would always be welcome.

Jed had gotten to the open door of the bathroom before it dawned on him that he was stark naked. His clothes were still all in a haphazard heap on the floor in his room, discarded there in his haste to stick his throbbing rod in Meredith. Listening to Bubba Ray go at it with his girlfriends with such unbridled abandon had gotten him more fired up than usual, stirring his old libido to a state of agitation he'd experienced only rarely since his younger days. He'd been in such a frenzy of giddy excitement that, once it was over and his seed was spent, he'd been a little out of it.

He considered backtracking to the room to at least pull on his pants, but he'd come this far and figured it'd be easier to go on into the bathroom and take care of business. The boys were gone. Grandpap was probably asleep in his room. No one was around to see him walking around *au naturel*. He could sprint naked from one end of the house to the other, his low-hanging balls flapping and slapping about all willy-nilly, and it wouldn't matter. Not that he felt even the slightest inclination to do such a thing. He was still drained from the fuck-fest and, truth be told, his days of sprinting anywhere without paying a high physical price for it were just about over. Chasing that spirited filly through the woods the other night about did him in.

In the bathroom, he took a long piss, then dangled his dick over the sink to wash it off with warm water. He'd previously slathered it with numerous gobs of spit to slide it into the dead gal's dried-up cooze. He was rinsing off when he heard a loud crash followed by a cry of pain from down the hall.

Jed ran out of the bathroom. "Grandpap!"

The door to Grandpap's room was closed and locked, but the old door was as feeble as the old man behind it and the lock was rudimentary. It yielded instantly when Jed rammed a shoulder into it, swinging wide as he stumbled into the room and came to a sudden, swaying stop. His eyes popped wide as his gaze flicked from the floor to the bed and back again.

What in blazes?

Jed wasn't the only naked man in the foul-smelling room, which reeked from a brimming portable toilet way past overdue to be emptied and cleaned. On the bed was a partially inflated plastic sex doll of an ancient vintage.

Grandpap was sprawled on the floor next to the bed. One of his ankles was red and swollen, having landed at a bad angle. At a glance, Jed didn't think it was broken, but it was badly sprained at the very least. The old man didn't appear to have suffered any other obvious injuries. He was clawing at the dusty floor and mewling like a newborn, tears running from his eyes in a way that disturbed and sickened Jed.

This man was the Mitchell family's patriarch.

He'd been revered as a figure of strength and indomitable will for many decades. Seeing him reduced to a quivering, pathetic wretch was almost more than Jed could take. His body, shriveled and wasted-looking, was covered in age spots, moles, and other lesions, some of which were slow-leaking a clear fluid, one of the more obvious symptoms of an accelerating physical disintegration. His skin looked like rotting tissue paper, with every piece of his skeletal frame starkly outlined against it in ghastly fashion. He looked so insubstantial, like he was most of the way dead already.

Jed felt tears sting his eyes.

He rarely saw the man fully exposed like this, and it was bringing home the true extent of his frailty in a way his mind couldn't avoid. When the man was clothed, it was possible to hide from—or just plain ignore—the grim reality of his dire physical state. Seeing him like this, Jed could no longer seek refuge in the land of denial.

He sniffled and swiped at his tears. "Jesus Christ."

The new batch of brain-shine he'd started was a week away from being ready, at minimum. Now he wondered if the old man would even make it that long. The visual evidence suggested his body might up and quit on him any day now. Jed didn't want to believe that. It would mean all the experimentation he'd been doing was a waste, that all the gals who'd involuntarily donated their gray matter had died for nothing. Well . . . maybe not *quite* for nothing. Their brainless shells did function nicely as sperm repositories for a time.

But other than that . . .

Jed gave his head an angry, adamant shake.

No. He wasn't ready to give up yet. And he wouldn't, not so long as Grandpap was still drawing breath.

He knelt on the floor and, with great care and tenderness, drew the old man into his arms, cradling him against his chest. As he rose to his feet again, the man's physical insubstantiality became even clearer. He felt nearly as weightless as an injured bird. The old man groaned in a creaky, raspy way that made him sound like a centuries-old mummy stirring to feeble, reanimated life. His head, which looked too big for his withered body, rolled around as Jed carried him back over to his bed, his unfocused glassy eyes staring blankly up at the ceiling.

Jed swept the partly inflated sex doll to the floor before laying the old man out on the thin, piss-stained mattress. As he extracted his arms from beneath his delicate body, the man reached out with a shaky hand before Jed could back away. At first he believed Grandpap meant to pat him on the arm as a gesture of gratitude and affection, but instead his hand went to Jed's ball sack and squeezed.

"Ain't had no dick in a while," he said, wheezing.

Jed's heart froze in his chest and he was briefly incapable of movement or thought. His brain felt like it'd blown a circuit. He remained as still as a statue until the old man gave his sack a second, somehow even more grotesquely intimate squeeze.

Then he started pulling on it.

Jed gasped as his brain rebooted and reconnected with the sickening reality of the situation. He smacked the old man's hand away from his junk and staggered backward, his legs flying out from under him as he flopped to the floor, landing hard on his ass. Pain jolted up his spine and his teeth clacked together, drawing a bead of blood from the tip of his tongue. Tears blurred his vision as he cried out in sudden misery. He tried rising from the floor but decided against it when an even more agonizing lance of twisting pain tortured his spine.

Nothing felt broken. He had feeling in his extremities and could wiggle his toes. Once the initial state of panic over his well-being passed, his mind flashed back to the alarming thing that had precipitated his spill. Not just the old man's attempted molestation of his grandson but what he'd said.

Ain't had no dick in a while.

What Jed couldn't help fixating on was the "in a while" part. In his half-century of knowing the man, there'd never been even the slightest indication of him having any inclinations in that direction. Not that Jed cared. He had no hangups in that area. Whatever people did with their private parts was fine by him, except for in certain, limited cases where it was just plain wrong.

Like this one.

Groped by my dear old Grandpap! Jesus Christ!

A shiver of revulsion went through him again at the thought of it. Much of that time on the floor was spent trying to determine how to even move forward in the wake of something so traumatizing. In the end, the only thing that made sense was to try his damnedest to forget it'd ever happened.

There were bigger issues to contend with anyway. Unless Jed could come up with a solution, the old man's time might well be running out sooner than anyone had expected. That was more important than some random, weird incident that was without known precedent in the man's long life, a meaningless blip that, for all he knew, was a symptom of some undiagnosed brain disease.

Jed took a sober mental inventory of the scene in the room, knowing how it might look to anyone happening upon it. Two naked grown men in a bedroom. A blowup sex doll on the floor. God only knew what any of his kin would think if they happened to walk in.

More jabs of excruciating pain assailed his back as he got to his feet, but he pushed through it, knowing he shouldn't waste more time than he already had. He didn't know where everyone had gone off to, but he couldn't count on having the house to himself much longer.

Scooping up the old sex doll with the intent of burning it in the pit out back, he started toward the door but stopped short when the old man let out an unnervingly loud wail of distress. Jed glanced that way and gasped in alarm upon seeing that Grandpap was leaning over the side of the bed and flailing about with an outstretched hand. He was attempting to speak but all Jed could make out at first was some continuous nonsense mush.

It sounded like he was saying, *Orra-orra-orra-orra.*

Jed squinted in confusion a few moments longer.

Then he felt a renewed sense of surprise and disgust.

The old man wasn't saying "Orra" over and over.

He was saying "Norma."

While reaching desperately for the limp sex doll, which Grandpap seemed to have named after Jed's late wife.

Another thing Jed didn't want to spend much time thinking about, lest it stir up certain bad memories and feelings. He shoved the sex doll into the old man's arms, then pushed him back toward the center of the bed to head off another potentially disastrous tumble to the floor. He then stepped quickly back, careful to stay out of ball-grabbing range.

After admonishing the old man to take it easy, he hurried out of the room and moved quickly down the hall to his room, where he wrapped the dead girl up in her blanket and returned her to her spot under the bed. He then pulled on his clothes and went out to the kitchen, opened the refrigerator, and removed two jars.

One was filled with shine, a leftover from the last batch.

The other contained the portion of whisked brains he'd held back from the new batch of shine he'd started earlier in the day. He remained steadfast in his conviction that the new batch with the brains infused into it as part of the distillation process would ultimately prove more potent and effective, but this cruder way of crafting brain-shine would have to do for now. Grandpap's survival depended on getting help sooner rather than later.

Jed would see what he could do about that. An extra level of creativity in terms of additional ingredients might be in order.

He set the jars on the counter and started opening cabinets.

EIGHT

THE CHEAP PLASTIC HALLOWEEN MASK was too tight on his face. Bubba Ray didn't like how the attached rubber band cut into his skin. The urge to rip it off and cast it aside was strong, but Loretta would raise all kinds of hell if he did.

She'd dragged him all over Montclair in search of what she said they needed for the experiment she had in mind. Taking up space in the trunk of his lime green 1980 Chevelle were several used car batteries they'd swiped from the junkers behind Floyd's Auto Repair, some jumper cables, multiple long heavy-duty extension cords, a couple of industrial-grade power strips, and a portable transformer liberated from a hardware store with the assistance of a meth addict employee who did it in exchange for a promised line of credit with Loretta's meth cook dad. Whether she'd be able to deliver on the promise was questionable, but the important thing was the addict believed she could.

Bubba Ray had no faith in the viability of the film-inspired reanimation plan she'd concocted. Movies, especially old horror movies from the black and white days, were full of all kinds of crazy ideas.

DEPRAVED HALLOWEEN

He was no college boy, but even he knew the science behind most of those ideas was dubious in the extreme. Expecting to duplicate in real life what some made-up dude in a movie from almost a hundred damn years ago did was plain loony. True, the same could be said of his uncle Jed's quest to create a strain of magic moonshine rich with restorative powers, but Bubba Ray didn't have much faith in that, either.

Not that he'd ever say that to Jed.

They'd acquired the cheap-ass Halloween masks at the dollar store, the final stop on Loretta's supply-gathering agenda. They were each wearing one as they hunkered down behind some bushes at the edge of a cliffside clearing right on the edge of the county line. This was Coogan's Point, a once popular prototypical lover's lane spot. Cars used to line up all along the cliffside, the young lovers inside them steaming up windows with their amorous activities. This went on for many years, becoming a treasured rite of passage for local kids.

Until, that is, the Lover's Lane Murders started. Six teenagers were brutally slashed to death by a still unidentified madman with a butcher knife over the course of three weeks in the spring of 1989. Though a full generation had come of age since then and the murders had never recurred, the old lovers' spot never recovered its former popularity. It wasn't all about the murders, of course. The world had changed. Even here in the rural south, the social habits of the young had evolved.

Not that Bubba Ray had a lot of firsthand knowledge where these things were concerned, not being a town kid. Hell, at twenty-three, he wasn't a kid at all anymore, but even if he'd still been in his teens, odds were he'd still be out of touch with local youth culture. He'd been home-schooled, like all his siblings and cousins, which meant he'd barely been schooled at all. It was a miracle he could read or write. Some of his kin could not.

Montclair town kids were worldly sophisticates compared to the younger generation of rural Mitchells. They were like aliens to Bubba Ray. Loretta was backwoods trash like he was, but somehow her knowledge of the social habits of their townie counterparts was vastly greater than his own. According to her, Coogan's Point did still attract a small number of adventurous young souls this time of year. The spooky season made them want to see the place where the mysterious Lover's Lane Slasher did his bloody work all those years before they were even conceived. Tomorrow night, on Halloween, the spot might be almost busy, which wouldn't serve their purposes at all. There'd be too many potential witnesses, as well as too many ways things could go wrong and land them in real trouble.

But the night before Halloween?

That was perfect for what they had in mind. Or, rather, for what Loretta had in mind. Bubba Ray still put little stock in her deranged scheme, but it was far too late to extricate himself from it without incurring her wrath, something he did not want. He'd weighed the possibility of killing her as a way out, believing he could probably get away with it. In the end, he couldn't bring himself to do it. She was blood. Kin. Murdering her merely as a means of saving himself some bother didn't strike him as justifiable cause for betraying blood.

Bubba Ray shifted from kneeling on one knee to the other. He pushed the plastic mask up, leaving it atop his head as he wiped sweat from his face. "How long we been up here? An hour? We could have gone out to Eakin County and snatched a couple drunks from the parking lot of Big Roy's by now."

Big Roy's was a rowdy roadhouse in a neighboring town, sort of similar to Harley Toad's Juke and Puke on the rural outskirts of Montclair. Sloppy drunks wandered in and out of Big Roy's all hours of the night. The ones leaving in the wee hours of the morning were often too shitfaced to be wary of their personal safety. Bubba Ray and the boys had grabbed a few of them over the last couple years. It'd been easy each time and none of it ever came back on them. These incidents predated Jed's brain-shine experiments. Mostly they took people for fun and sometimes meat from the bodies made its way into the kitchen at Jed's house.

Loretta turned her head and looked at him through the holes of her mask. "Be patient, tubby. I'm telling you, someone will show up. Some couple keen to have the spot to themselves instead of mixing with the Halloween crowd. Besides, I'm fired up about carrying on the family tradition."

Bubba Ray frowned. "Uh-huh. What, uh . . . tradition is that?"

She snorted. "Oh, come on. Ain't you ever heard the family gossip? The Lover's Lane Slasher was one of our own."

Bubba Ray had, as a matter of fact, heard an offhand remark to that effect at some point in the dim past, but he'd figured it was horseshit. One of the many long-standing Mitchell clan traditions was telling tall tales. He'd assumed the Lover's Lane Slasher thing fell into that category, but now he wondered, acts of random, vicious murder being another time-honored Mitchell tradition.

He scratched his chin. "Huh. Well . . . who was it?"

She shrugged. "I ain't got anything like ironclad proof, but I always sort of figured it was Jedidiah. He was of an age the year those killings happened that he could have done it, and of course the clincher is what we all saw him do at Thanksgiving years back."

Bubba Ray's frown deepened.

She was talking about the infamous family holiday get-together where Jed, drunk and angry about some unknown thing he'd been simmering over all day, snapped and impulsively murdered his wife in spectacularly gory fashion. Right there in the dining room in front of everybody. Even for a clan of hardened backwoods folk accustomed to a certain brand of casual depravity, it was a stunning display. They were all a while getting over that. Pretending to be okay with it was a collective family effort of digging deep enough into denial mode to convince themselves Norma had it coming.

Maybe Loretta was on to something.

He sighed. "I guess it's possible."

She made a sound of exaggerated, sarcastic disdain. "No shit. I'm telling you, fat boy, he's the one who did it. Full goddamn stop. And you know what else?"

"What?"

She laughed. "I think it's cool as hell."

Bubba Ray didn't know what to say to that so he didn't say anything. He still missed his Aunt Norma sometimes. She'd been a sweet lady who was always kind to him. Hell, she'd even given him his first hand job.

Hard not to be sentimental over something like that.

Loretta reached out and pulled his mask back down over his face. "Hear that? Someone's coming. Keep the mask down, bitch."

The constant insults made Bubba Ray want to swat her. Maybe he couldn't kill his kin over some minor bullshit, unlike his scary uncle, but he could for damn sure put her in her place. Though he was always wary of her determination to avenge even the smallest slight, he couldn't let her keep walking all over him like this. If she kept taking so many liberties and disrespecting him, there was no telling how far it'd go. He was maybe a second away from reaching out to wrap a hand around her throat when his head snapped toward the clearing.

She was right.

Someone was coming.

The sound of an approaching engine was audible even before headlight beams appeared in the darkness, growing brighter by the moment as a car came up the narrow road and into the cliffside clearing. Instinct caused Bubba Ray to hunker down even lower in the brush. Loretta scooched in close next to him and put a hand on his knee, squeezing it in her excitement. The physical contact triggered another tingle of arousal, the first Bubba Ray had experienced since embarking on this probably misguided quest with his cousin.

Leaving aside the whole dubious matter of reanimating days-old corpses, maybe she was right about this part.

It might be fun.

The car stopped short of the cliffside. It was a black Mustang convertible, maybe a decade old. As they observed from the brush, a whirring sound signaled the retraction of the top. A young couple rose from the front and climbed into the back of the vehicle, disappearing from sight. Standard sounds of necking ensued, soft little moans and squeaks that enhanced Bubba Ray's arousal.

Loretta squeezed his knee tighter. "Let's do this."

Bubba Ray nodded and licked his lips behind the mask.

Loretta pushed through the brush and emerged into the clearing. Bubba Ray followed and stayed close to the ground as they moved fast toward the car, with their tools in hand.

NINE

ONE MOMENT SHE WAS IN a state of gauzy semi-consciousness, aware of nothing in any concrete way, and the next her eyes were open, registering the sight of a white-tiled floor. She was lying face-down on the floor, with her hands bound behind her back. Since being removed from the cruiser, the handcuffs had been exchanged for heavy-duty manacles attached to a chain. An additional manacle encircled each of her ankles. The ankle manacles were attached by chains to brackets on the wall behind her. At first she was puzzled by the use of separate manacles for each ankle as opposed to the set of double manacles holding her wrists together, but then the obvious horrible reason dawned on her. It was for easier access, so her legs could be pulled apart to facilitate sexual assault.

Jessica still had no intention of letting that happen without a fight. Even with her hands secured behind her back, she believed she was more than capable of making it close to impossible for an assailant to enjoy violating her. No way in hell would she simply relent and let the man who'd taken her do as he wanted with her without fiercely resisting. If he wanted to successfully commit the act of rape, he'd have to render her unconscious every single time. This wouldn't offer her much in the way of genuine consolation, but it'd be better than nothing.

A fuzzy memory of having awakened once already emerged from the slowly dissipating fog still clouding her thoughts. It'd happened before being brought to this room, shortly after being carried into the deputy's spacious log cabin-style house. She'd opened her eyes to find herself laid out on a comfy sofa. The first thing she saw was a hunting trophy, a deer's head mounted on the wall opposite the sofa. Then the deputy was looming over her again, this time with a syringe in his hand. Whatever was in the syringe was a far more powerful sedative than the chloroform-soaked rag, the effects of which had lasted no more than a few minutes.

Raising her head off the floor, Jessica maneuvered herself into a sitting position and took a look around. The clothes she'd been wearing were gone, replaced by a black leather bra and panties. The bra had silver metal tips at the nipples. She appeared to be in a basement the deputy had converted into a private dungeon. The walls were plain, unadorned. In a corner far to her right, well beyond the full extension length of the chains, was a staircase leading to a closed door. Against the back wall was a cafeteria-style table, upon which were items of a disturbing nature. These included ball gags, dildos, leather S&M hoods with zippered mouths, an implement that was either a riding crop or type of cane, an assortment of gleaming knives, and more than one kind of whip. Hanging from pegs above the table were a double-bladed axe, a sledgehammer, and a machete, the latter with a small strap attached to the handle. On the floor in front of the table was a gas-powered McCulloch chainsaw.

The table, of course, was as out of reach as the staircase.

Also, Jessica was not alone in the room.

Chained to the wall opposite her was another woman. She was unconscious, lying slumped against the wall. Filthy long brown hair obscured much of her face. The woman looked young but was skinny nearly to the point of emaciation. Her otherwise pale skin was marred by several welts and bruises, and her swollen feet were an alarming shade of red. It looked to Jessica as if the deputy had pulverized the woman's ankles with the sledgehammer. This ugly visual proof of her captor's capacity for brutality sickened her. It also made her consider taking extreme measures to avoid a similar fate.

She didn't want to die, but she also didn't want to be mutilated or brutally tortured for an unknown time. The emaciated woman looked like she'd been here a long while, long enough to be starved to a point far beyond what even an extreme case of anorexia might yield. The endless tortures she'd likely endured throughout her lengthy imprisonment must have been hellish. She'd probably wished for death often.

Jessica wondered if the slack in the chains would allow her enough maneuverability to ram her head into the wall. She'd need to do it with sufficient force to fracture her skull and cause a fatal brain injury. The alternative would be to behave in so troublesome a way as to provoke the deputy into killing her sooner rather than later. Each of these strategies was rife with potential pitfalls. A fractured skull might kill her or it might not. She might instead end up incapacitated but cursed with a level of diminished mental capacity, rendered powerless to fight off the deputy's sexual exploitation of her body. There was little doubt she could provoke the man into assaulting her in ultra-violent ways, but he might not kill her. He might do something similar to what he'd done to her sister-in-chains, use that sledgehammer to demolish her ankles and knees.

If it came down to it, she supposed she'd go with the head-ramming option, as it was the marginally less horrendous of the two bleak possibilities.

The woman opposite her made a groaning sound followed by a snort. Her chest heaved as she coughed. She seemed to be trying to come out of her slumber. Her chains clinked as she tried sitting up higher against the wall. Perhaps because of the hair hanging in her face, she appeared not to have noticed yet that she was no longer the sole prisoner in the basement.

Jessica cleared her throat. "Hello."

The woman ceased her physical efforts, going still. She stopped groaning. The subtle rise and fall of her chest as she breathed in and out also stopped. A coiled tension was evident in the taut muscles of her withered body. For a fleeting instant, Jessica panicked, wondering if by speaking she'd somehow frightened the woman enough to send her into cardiac arrest. She didn't want to believe that was possible, but perhaps the extent of the other prisoner's weakened condition was even worse than it seemed.

Then the woman sucked in a big breath and made another attempt to sit up higher on the wall. Unlike Jessica, her manacled hands were bound in front of her. She raised them to push some of the stringy, filthy hair out of her face. Her bleary eyes blinked slowly as she gazed at Jessica in incomprehension for a silent moment. The structure of her face suggested she'd been pretty once, but her beauty was marred by cuts and ugly bruises. A crust of dried blood adhered to each of her nostrils. Her lips parted, revealing several missing teeth. The ones that remained were aligned with perfect straightness, suggesting the rest had been knocked out of her mouth.

Or removed via some other means by the cruel deputy.

Jessica tried her best to make her voice as gentle and soothing as possible. "My name's Jessica. Who are you?"

The woman's mouth dropped open as she stared at her in astonishment for another silent moment.

Then she whimpered and spoke in a low, creaky voice. "You're real."

Jessica managed a smile she didn't feel and nodded. "Yes."

The woman looked like she was close to hyperventilating as her chest started going rapidly up and down. Her bleary eyes widened to the size of golf balls.

Then she started screaming.

Jessica winced in surprise and glanced toward the closed door at the top of the staircase, part of her expecting it to immediately fly open, the deputy descending to the basement to punish the screaming woman for the noise. She stared at it for several seconds, but it remained shut. The woman's screaming grew louder and shriller, almost deafeningly so. Unless the basement was soundproofed, she couldn't imagine the deputy ignoring the commotion much longer.

Jessica scooted forward on her knees, getting as close as the chains allowed while making urgent shushing noises. "Hey, it's okay. Just be quiet, okay? You don't need to be afraid of me."

The screaming did not stop.

Instead, the terrified woman again tested the limits of her vocal cords, generating a punishing volume that made Jessica grimace and clench her teeth. The sound was like a red-hot needle going straight through the middle of her skull. An unkind part of her she normally didn't like much began to wish she *had* frightened the woman to death.

She unclenched her teeth and made one more attempt to calm the woman down, raising her voice enough to hopefully penetrate the wall of ear-shredding noise. "Listen, you have got to stop. I know you're scared. I'm scared, too. But if you want to get out of here, you've got to be smarter than this."

The woman abruptly stopped screaming.

She gaped at Jessica in seeming disbelief for a moment.

Then tears started streaming down her face. "Get out of here? No one gets out of here."

Then she started screaming again.

Jessica sighed, bowing her head in defeat. "Jesus Christ."

A distant click signaled the opening of the door at the top of the stairs, a sound followed by the slow thumping of descending boot-heels. The other woman ceased screaming the instant she detected the sound of the deputy's approach. Her back stiffened against the wall as she began crying and moaning instead.

Jessica raised her head and looked at the muscular deputy as he moved through the center of the room. In addition to his boots, the man was wearing a black thong-like garment. And nothing else, though his nipples were pierced. His sleek form was shorn entirely of hair save for that atop his head. The five o'clock shadow he'd sported when last she saw him was gone. He met Jessica's gaze and winked but did not break his stride as he continued to the back of the room, where he lifted the double-bladed axe off the wall.

After kissing the edge of each axe blade and lovingly caressing the handle for a moment, he returned it to the wall and chose the sledge-hammer instead. He was smiling as he hefted it in both hands and turned away from the wall.

He moved into the space between Jessica and the distraught, weeping other woman. "This loud bitch is being a bit of a nuisance, wouldn't you say?"

Jessica shook her head. "Don't. Please."

The deputy laughed.

Then he lifted the sledgehammer off his shoulder, reared back with his arms, and brought it around. The heavy head of the sledge-hammer impacted the woman's withered chest with crushing force, breaking several ribs at once. From the gruesomely contorted look on the woman's face, it was clear the pain was devastating, but the placement and effect of the blow made additional screaming impos-sible. Instead, she wheezed and started sliding sideways to the floor.

Jessica cringed at the sight of the deep cavity in the middle of her chest, which was ugly-looking, but perhaps the most shocking thing about it was the blow had not killed her on impact. She imagined being struck with such force would be more than sufficient to induce instant death in most people in a similar state of advanced emaciation, whether by heart attack from the overwhelming trauma of it or any number of critical internal injuries. In all likelihood, she was in her last seconds of life, but for the moment, a thin, wheezing breath continued to issue from her lips.

The deputy shifted position and lifted the sledgehammer over his head again, bringing it down on one of the doomed woman's swollen feet, a blow that made the fever-red foot explode like a smashed grapefruit. Even as someone who'd witnessed far more than her fair share of genuine atrocities, this act of extreme cruelty inflicted on a person already on her way out of this world was shocking to Jessica. She gasped at the horrible sight and instinctively scooted backward, putting more distance between herself and the madman.

The pain was immense enough to rouse the woman one last time, causing her to lift her torso off the floor for a moment, long enough to twist around and start crawling away. The pulpy remains of her ruined foot described a bloody trail across a few feet of the white-tiled floor while the deputy watched her and belly-laughed. The laughter ceased as the woman began slowing down, her body close to expiring.

Still, the deputy did not allow her the flimsy grace of a peaceful last few seconds of life. He raised the sledgehammer over his head again and brought it down, smashing one of her bony shoulders. Shattered shards of bone protruded through the tissue-thin skin as the woman managed a final miserable whimper of pain and died.

A trembling Jessica spoke before she could think better of it. "You fucking bastard."

He smirked as he glanced at her. "You know why she was making all that noise, right? It was because of you."

Jessica shook her head, not wanting to believe this. "No. That doesn't make any sense."

The deputy laughed. "Oh, but it does. It makes perfect sense, in fact. She screamed because she knew I always keep only one of you bitches in here at a time. Make a note of that, blondie. You ever wake up and see another dumb cunt chained up across from you, that means your time has come."

Jessica sniffled.

She didn't want to cry and show weakness in front of this monster, but she hadn't been this terrified of anyone or anything in a long time.

The deputy touched the head of the sledgehammer to the underside of her chin, lifting it so she had no choice but to look at him. "Don't you worry, though. This bitch is dead, but our time together is just beginning. You're gonna be here a long, long time."

Jessica's bottom lip trembled as she struggled not to utter the shameful pleading words a part of her traumatized psyche yearned to say.

Perhaps mistaking her tears for weakness, the deputy touched one of her wet cheeks with the back of a hand, a gesture that was a mockery of actual tenderness. In another moment, as he her bottom lip continued to tremble, he pushed one of his fingers into her mouth.

Her eyes rolled up to look at him and he smiled as they made eye contact. "Suck it like it's a dick, bitch."

Jessica briefly contemplated another course of action, but she knew biting his finger off—or attempting to—wouldn't get her out of these chains. She made herself relax as best she could and closed her mouth around his forefinger. As she swirled her tongue around it, she watched as a growing erection stretched the fabric at the crotch of his bikini bottom. She told herself if he tried to put that thing in her mouth, she *would* bite, consequences be damned.

She was still fellating his finger when the door at the top of the stairs opened again and a woman's voice called down. "Dalton, honey, dinner's almost ready."

The deputy's gaze stayed on Jessica as he grinned and called back his reply, "Be up shortly, honey doll. Just gotta finish up something here. You let that tasty stew simmer a bit."

He spoke with what sounded like genuine affection, a tone matched by the woman as she said, "Will do, hon. Love you."

"Love you."

The door closed again with a click.

Dalton, the deputy, extracted his finger from Jessica's mouth. "That's my better half, as I reckon you already guessed. She's a proper lady. Doesn't curse. Doesn't sass her man and knows her place. Goes without saying, but she wouldn't have lifted a finger on your behalf if you'd tried calling out for help."

Jessica said nothing, having already figured as much.

Dalton returned the sledgehammer to its place on the back wall and picked up the chainsaw. He directed another winking grin at Jessica as he approached the recently deceased woman's pitifully thin form and stood over it. "Don't you look away now. I want you to watch every bit of this. If I look over there and see your eyes are closed, I may have to put off my dinner a little bit longer, if you know what I mean. Nod if you understand."

Fresh tears rolled down Jessica's face.

She nodded.

Dalton fired up the chainsaw and began the messy work of disassembling the lifeless body of his latest victim.

Jessica watched it all.

TEN

THE NATURE OF THE CHALLENGE at hand, as Jed saw it, was doing whatever he could to make this improvised dose of brainshine as potent as humanly possible. This meant it would need ingredients beyond just the shine and the remaining portion of whisked brains.

Spread out on the kitchen counter was an eclectic selection of potential new additions to the concoction. Some he'd pulled down from cabinets in the kitchen, while others he discovered by conducting a thorough search of the house. In the part of the search that involved entering the large room shared by four of his sons, the process was more akin to a ransacking. The boys slept in bunkbeds with filthy sheets that hadn't been changed at any point in recent memory. He pulled the sheets off and turned the grossly stained mattresses upside down, pulled up loose floorboards and shined a flashlight into tight, dark spaces squirming with bugs and rodents, and dug his fingers into every other nook and cranny he suspected might be a hiding place for various forms of contraband.

Under one of the loose floorboards, he found a rotting old true crime magazine of the lurid sort that once were commonly found on grocery store newsstands. It featured a combination of real crime scene photos and staged recreation photos showing scantily clad female models posing as corpses with fake blood all over them. He spent a few moments wondering where one of the boys might have found such a moldy old thing. Then a dim memory filtered in, reminding him the magazine was his. He'd stashed it away here back in the long-ago days when he'd shared this room with an earlier generation of Mitchell boys. A smile pulled at the corners of his mouth as more warm, fuzzy memories came drifting back while he leafed through the faded pages, some of which possessed a suspect stickiness. He kept going until he arrived at a story near the back of the magazine, one that made his breath catch in his throat.

A story about murders at a popular make-out spot in the rural south.

This was why he'd purchased the magazine all those long years ago.

He got so caught up in reading the story and gazing at the accompanying photos he lost track of time. The one actual crime scene photo especially transfixed him. It showed the lovely slender arm of a dead girl hanging out the open door of a car, a thin gold bracelet hanging loose around a delicate wrist. For a time, Jed felt incapable of averting his gaze from the image, not snapping out of it until he heard another pitiful wail of misery from down the hallway.

"Coming, Grandpap! Just give me a few more minutes!"

After rolling the old magazine up and shoving it into a back pocket, he completed his search of the boys' room, which even by the low standards of the household in general was in disgusting condition. There were hog pens less nasty, but in the end, the search was worth it. Only one discovery from the room was of potential brainshine use, but it was a doozy, a small baggie of what he was pretty sure was cocaine.

The baggie now sat on the counter, spread out with the rest of the items he'd selected. Among the other items were various types of vitamins, steroids, and an assortment of other pills of different shapes and sizes. Some of the pills were leftovers from ancient, unfinished prescriptions, some of the labels of which were faded to the point of being unreadable. Whatever those were, he figured adding them to the concoction couldn't hurt. They were medicine, right? And regardless of the particular ailment they were prescribed for, they were all formulated to restore health in various ways. Of these pills, any individual one might not do much, but stirred all together with the brains and the shine?

Well, who knew, but they might do *something*, which as every damn fool with half a brain in his head knew was better than *nothing*. He only wished the steroids were more along the lines of the powerful performance-enhancing type used by cheating professional athletes, but alas they were a lower grade prescribed for clearing up skin conditions and such-like.

Then there was the Viagra.

According to the label on the bottle, the prescription was for a gentleman named Kristopher Keene.

Whoever the hell that was.

One of the boys might have taken the bottle off someone they'd robbed or killed. Or maybe they dug it out of a dumpster behind one of Montclair's two drugstores. They did that kind of low-end scum-rat scavenging a lot. Whatever the case, it was going into the brain-shine along with the rest of this shit.

Using the bottom of a spoon, he mashed all the pills into a fine powder. Some of the pills were harder to grind down than others, requiring him to work at it. The process was time-consuming, and while he was engaged in it, more pitiful wails emerged from the hallway. It might have been his imagination, but he perceived each moan as progressively weaker-sounding than the one that preceded it. The conclusion was inescapable.

Grandpap was running out of time.

Pushing himself to work faster, he mashed harder and harder at the pills, screeching in frustration on occasion. When one shot out from under the spoon from the extreme pressure he was exerting and went flying across the room, he decided he'd done enough. By that point, he'd created a multi-hued, multi-ingredient powder pile of impressive size, a high percentage of which was boner dust. Considering it was his former virility that Grandpap missed the most, Jed had to figure it was one of the most crucial ingredients of all.

He took an empty Mason jar down from a shelf and poured in a portion of straight shine. After mixing in some of the whisked brains, he began the process of stirring in the powder with the spoon he'd used to mash the pills. The shine was clotted with thick beads of clumped powder at first, but this dissolved as he stirred. He kept at it until he was sure the entirety of the powder was reduced to fine granules, though there was too much of it for the cloudy shine to turn clear. On impulse, he added a generous pinch of cayenne pepper and several large dollops of habanero hot sauce for a little extra oomph, to make the taste more palatable. He considered jacking off into the shine, reasoning that the testosterone in his sperm might add another needed extra kick (as well as some creaminess), but the thought of the old man gargling his cum in the wake of the weird ball-tugging incident made him slightly queasy, so he refrained. Instead, he topped off the half-filled jar with another portion of shine and recommenced stirring.

Once he was at last satisfied with his work, Jed decided the time had come to serve the concoction to Grandpap, but then he had another brainstorm. In a lot of the comic books he'd read as a kid, the origin stories for many superheroes involved mishaps with radiation and atomic weapons. He didn't have access to anything resembling a nuclear reactor, but he did have a goddamn microwave oven.

Jed popped the jar of turbocharged brain-shine into the microwave and nuked it for thirty seconds. He worried doing it any longer than that might adversely affect the potency of the ingredients, as well as making it too hot for Grandpap to safely imbibe.

Then he went back down the hallway and into Grandpap's bedroom, where the old man was between the spread legs of the partly inflated sex doll, wheezing and whimpering as he made a pathetic attempt to hump the plastic whore with his floppy limp dick. A sad little puff of air escaped through an unseen hole in the doll each time he thrust his spindly frame against it.

Jed grimaced. "Dang it, Grandpap, you ain't in no shape for them kind of shenanigans, but I've got somethin' here that might help."

The old man scowled as he slowly turned his head toward his grandson. "Ain't had no good pussy in a while. Not since the last time I fucked your wife. You remember that, don't you, boy? Right at Thanksgiving, that was. Remember?"

Jed remembered.

It was something he'd tried hard to put out of his mind over the years, but now that the memory had stirred, it came screaming back to life in his head in vivid fashion. The old man was feeble even back then, seven years ago, but amazingly his dick had still worked. Jed had returned home earlier than expected from a trip into town to find the two of them going at it with surprising passion, Norma moaning and saying all kinds of filthy things she never said when Jed was putting it to her. He stewed and fumed over it all the rest of that day and into the next, until he snapped and killed her in front of everybody.

Thanksgivings had never been the same since then, all the remaining womenfolk who'd lived in his house taking refuge with other branches of the clan. His house became even more of a degenerate boys' club after that, a factor in some of the more lowlife cousins moving in with him and his sons. It wasn't quite accurate to say he and his boys were shunned by other Mitchells after that. Relations between all the Mitchell men of his generation remained cordial, at least on a surface level, but they never received any invites to holiday dinners.

Which, fair enough.

He didn't like it, but he understood it. In truth, he knew he was lucky no one had exacted retribution for the deed in all the years that followed. A lot of that was because those who might have had the courage to take him out refrained out of fear of starting a war within the family. Still, it'd been years before he stopped looking over his shoulder. Even now, every once in a long while, he still got a little case of the jitters over it, especially when he'd catch one of his sons looking at him a little too funny.

Jed's hands trembled as he gripped the Mason jar tighter, almost overcome by a brief but powerful urge to throw the concoction in the old man's sneering, smug face. The echo of hurt and betrayal possessed him with a volcanic intensity for a few seconds, but he took some calming breaths and soon was able to let it go.

He'd long ago gotten his pound of flesh for the transgression, after all.

A pound and then some.

Jed smiled as he set the jar down on an end table and began the sloppy and irritating work of disentwining the old man from the floppy limbs of his plastic lover. The old man protested and tried swatting his hands away, but Jed imposed his superior strength in a way he rarely did with his Grandpap. After tossing the doll to the floor, he turned the old man over and arranged him in a slumped semi-sitting position against the headboard. Then he tied a bib around his neck and sat down next to him with the jar of brain-shine.

He held the jar close to Grandpap's mouth. "You need to drink this."

The old man gave the jar of cloudy liquid a sneering glance of disapproval. "What in tarnation is this mess?"

Jed smiled. "It's the brain-shine, Grandpap."

"Don't look like no brain-shine I ever saw. That Cajun stuff was clear as hi-test gasoline, so pure it was beautiful."

Jed kept smiling as he suppressed a sigh of frustration. "This may not look like the brain juice you remember from way back in the long ago, Grandpap, but I promise you it's just as strong. Drink this down and you'll feel like a new man in no time."

In truth, he had no idea how effective the potion would be. For all he knew, it'd do nothing at all. Or it might make him so sick it accelerated his demise by causing him to puke his miserable guts out. Without more time to properly test the stuff, there was no way to know. Getting the old bastard to drink it was a hell of a risk, but one Jed was convinced was necessary.

The old man snorted. "Aw, hell with it, I don't care no more. If there's even one chance in a million this gunk puts some iron back in my pecker, it's worth a shot."

Jed nodded as he moved the jar closer to Grandpap's mouth. "Just think of all the fun you'll have if it works. I'll have the boys go out and snatch as many girls as you can handle."

The old man waggled his bushy gray eyebrows in an almost playful way and drew the straw into his mouth, slurping up the brain-shine with increasing gusto as he went along. He downed at least a third of it inside of a minute. The rapid progress shocked Jed. He'd been prepared for disappointment, thinking the old man would only manage a few feeble sips, a larger percentage of it dripping onto the bib rather than going down his throat. Instead, he took the jar in his own hands, wrenching it away from Jed.

Jed thought he'd probably end up dropping it, but that didn't happen. The loud slurping continued, his sucking on the straw growing ever more frantic as he inhaled the rest of the stuff at an incredible rate. Before long, the straw was sucking at the dry bottom of the jar.

Grandpap thrust the empty container at him with a scowl. "More."

Jed shrugged. "Sorry, Grandpap. That's all of it for now."

Grandpap sneered. "You useless piece of shit."

He smashed the empty jar against the side of Jed's head, an attack that happened with a swiftness he wouldn't have believed the man capable of a few moments ago. A shard of glass opened a gash down the side of his jaw, a slice that brought forth a steady stream of blood.

Jed cried out in pain as he rose from the bed and staggered

backward. He slapped a hand over the cut and held it there, gaping in disbelief at the mean old man he'd persisted in loving despite all the horrible ways he'd been cruel to him over the years.

Tears filled his eyes. "You hurt me."

The old man laughed as he pushed away from the headboard and swung his legs over the side of the bed. Though he looked the same as he had before consuming the brain-shine, shriveled up and decrepit, he moved with a speed and ease he hadn't exhibited in many years.

"That's right, boy, I did. And you think you're hurting now?" He snorted in loud disdain as he stood and rose fully to his feet, standing straight and tall without a hint of shakiness, not even reaching for his cane or walker. "That ain't nothin'. Get ready to hurt like you ain't never hurt before."

Jed continued backing toward the door, his eyes wide with terror and recognition of a stunning truth.

The new brain-shine recipe he'd whipped together . . . *worked*. How?

Who the hell knew, but it did. Jed didn't have much in the way of formal learning, but he'd always had an uncanny knack for figuring out complicated things. Much of this was intuitive, some a product of relentless trial and error. He was stubborn and willing to keep working at a thing well past the point where others would simply give up. In this case, that stubbornness paid off, yielding spectacular results with the right blend of ingredients, a unique formula no one else on earth had ever thought to put together.

A shuddery breath escaped his lips. "Holy shit."

I'm a goddamn backwoods Einstein.

It was a heady realization, but the superstitious part of him wondered if that was all there was to it. This being the night before Halloween, might there also be a bit of spooky magic in the air?

Before he could contemplate that unlikely-seeming aspect of it any further, the old man reached out to him with hands that no longer looked quite as gnarled and bony as before. "Come here, boy. Come take *your* medicine."

Jed gaped at him a moment longer.

Then he turned and ran out the door.

ELEVEN

AS THEY NEARED THE BACK of the Mustang, Bubba Ray and Loretta veered apart, creeping up on it from different sides. They rose slowly and peered into the back of the vehicle, where the young couple was squirming around on the seat, going at each other with passionate abandon, moaning and gasping, completely oblivious to the sinister audience that had arrived. The boy and girl looked like they could be high school seniors, but certainly no older than that. Not old enough to buy beer or a pack of cigarettes, but more than old enough to die.

They were no one Bubba Ray recognized, which didn't mean much because they were obviously town kids. Their clothes were too nice and they looked too healthy to be anything else. The boy was handsome in an airbrushed way and had an athletic build, while the girl was gorgeous with creamy, perfect skin and lush blonde hair like something out of a shampoo commercial. Bubba Ray had never attended a day of regular school in his life, but to him, they looked like star quarterback and homecoming queen material. The girl had a hand down the boy's unzipped pants while he pawed at her breasts.

DEPRAVED HALLOWEEN

Bubba Ray yearned for a look at the girl's naked titties. Her top was off but she was wearing a lacy white push-up bra that made them look delectable. The sight of them made his mouth water, while also making him feel like a damn fool for his earlier lack of enthusiasm for Loretta's plan. He still doubted anything worthwhile would come of the crazy resurrection experimentation she had in mind. Her knowledge of all things scientific was as limited as his own, which was somewhere in the vicinity of wholly nonexistent, but so what? She might not be able to restore his dead girlfriends to life, but that was okay because he intended to have plenty of fun with this here living girl before turning her into a dead one.

On the other side of the car, only Loretta's head was visible above the level of the door. Following her lead, Bubba Ray maintained a similar position on his side. The moaning young lovers hadn't yet noticed them, but that was likely to change soon. All it would take was one of them inevitably sparing a moment of attention for the world around them. Bubba Ray grinned behind his mask, wishing it would happen soon, anxious to hear their panicked sounds of terror. He wanted to rise and lean over them, let them sense the shadow of doom looming above, but he knew how angry Loretta would be if he didn't wait for her to make the first move. He was getting fidgety, though, and he knew he'd feel more settled if not for Loretta's mask. If he could see her face and read what she was thinking, he might not feel quite so impatient.

The relief he felt when she at last began to rise out of her squatting stance was a glorious unburdening. His grin spread wider behind his mask as he stood and leaned over the back seat as he'd envisioned.

It was the girl who noticed them first, looking up from her position beneath her boyfriend. At first she looked confused. Then she turned her head and saw there was not one but two masked strangers staring down at her. The boy remained oblivious for another moment, still kissing her neck until she took her hand out of his pants and started swatting his shoulder and shouting his name.

"Brad! Brad! Stop!"

Brad took his mouth away from her neck and peered into her wide eyes, frowning when he saw the look of alarm there. He turned his head to see what she was looking at, gasping when he saw the masked faces looking down at them. A reflexive look of fear passed quickly, giving way to scowling indignation.

He twisted his torso around and rose some, jabbing a finger at

Bubba Ray. "Get the fuck away from us, you fat hillbilly perv!"

Loretta cackled with glee. "Boo! Trick-or-treat, motherfucker! And go fuck yourself, you fat-shaming piece of townie shit!"

Bubba Ray was taken aback. Not by the initial insult, but by his cousin's response to it. She'd been flinging weight-related gibes at him all night, making her words now unexpected, to say the least. Of course, he knew she was just fucking with the kid, but a secret part of him he kept at a distance most of the time was touched by what she'd said nonetheless.

Brad shifted on the seat again, sitting up a little higher. "You redneck assholes need to take off before I get really mad."

Loretta squealed laughter. "Oh, yeah? Whatcha gonna do if'n we don't, boy? Cry for your momma?"

Brad sneered. "I'll kick your hick asses, that's what I'll fuckin' do!"

Loretta made a sound of mock dismay. "*Both* of our asses? But I'm a girl."

The homecoming queen made a scoffing sound. "Yeah, but not a *real* girl. You're just worthless hillbilly white trash." She touched her boyfriend's arm and smiled sweetly. "Baby, you have my permission to stomp them both into the ground."

Brad was squinting at Bubba Ray, confusion shading his features as he tilted his head. "There's something so familiar about that mask, but I can't place it."

Bubba Ray's fingers flexed around the handle of the machete he was hiding behind his back. He was eager to bring it out into view and see how fast the smug looks on the faces of these stuck-up town kids changed to expressions of terror. Once again, he was deferring to Loretta, waiting to see what she did, but he had a secondary reason for hesitating, which was that he was also curious about what exactly his mask was supposed to represent. He'd asked Loretta earlier, but she hadn't known either, having dug the matching set out of a bargain bin filled with random old masks at the dollar store.

Then the homecoming queen giggled. "Oh, my God. They're from that old movie my dad likes."

Brad was still squinting at Bubba Ray. "What old movie?"

The homecoming queen's giggles became bubblier as her amusement grew. "Holy *shit!*" Her voice rose in pitch, taking on a squealy tone that set Bubba Ray's teeth on edge. She smacked her boyfriend in the arm. "You remember! The so-called comedy about the 80s rock guy dorks. It had the famous scene where they're all singing that

Queen song in the car."

Brad broke out in a big grin as he started laughing along with the girl. "Oh, yeah." He made a devil horns sign with his fist. "Party on, dude."

He said the last three words in what Bubba Ray figured was supposed to be a dumb guy voice.

The homecoming queen squealed more laughter and mimicked her boyfriend. "Party on!" Then her laughter dried up with jarring abruptness. "If you hicks think those stupid things are supposed to be scary, you're even dumber than I thought. I bet you white trash idiots scavenged that crap from the town dump."

Brad chuckled. "Babe, they probably *live* in the town dump."

The homecoming queen erupted in laughter again.

Bubba Ray and Loretta looked at each other from opposite sides of the car. Though her face was still hidden, Bubba Ray could tell a drastic shift had occurred in her demeanor, one that should have served as a chilling warning to the kids in the car, but they were oblivious, lost in their amusement. Her body language was different, her posture stiffer, not as relaxed. She was breathing harder, each exhalation loudly rattling the flimsy plastic of the cheap mask. The lack of an immediate humorous comeback was the most telling sign of all.

Then she grunted and said, "I'm sorry you think our masks aren't scary. Let me know what you think about this."

She brought out the butcher knife she'd been hiding behind her back and, after unleashing a loud shriek of primal rage, whipped her arm around, dragging the sharp blade across the side of the boy's head. The blade sliced deep, cutting his ear in half and flaying open a cheek. Blood spilled from the wounds, pattering the homecoming queen's face beneath him. The boy screamed in pain and reared backward, his body squeezing into the narrow gap between the front seats. This was mere instinct, a reflexive retreat from the source of the pain, not a conscious attempt to climb up front and try to get away.

In another instant, the homecoming queen's moment of shocked, disbelieving silence came to an end, her mouth opening wide to emit an earsplitting scream. She slapped a hand against the backrest of the rear seat and tried to sit up, but Loretta leaned further in and slashed downward with the knife, driving the sharp tip straight through the center of the splayed hand, pinning it to the backrest. The girl screamed again and Loretta punched her in the face with her free hand, splitting open her bottom lip.

Brad made a belated attempt to come to the homecoming queen's aid, but by then Bubba Ray figured it was high time he got his own hands dirty. A lot happened all at once in the next moment. With her free hand, the homecoming queen reached for the blade stuck through her other hand, closing it around the blade itself rather than the handle gripped by Loretta. Brad reached for the knife in the same instant, but his attempt to help his girl was thwarted by Bubba Ray's first swing of the machete, the blade of which clipped through the top joints of the middle three fingers on his left hand. He reeled backward again, blood jetting from the stubs of his shortened digits, a lot of which spattered against Loretta's mask as he waved his injured hand around in disbelieving terror, streaks of crimson trailing down the white plastic like bloody tears.

The homecoming queen tightened her grip on the blade and tried pulling it out of her trapped hand, but Loretta held the knife firmly in place, causing the blade to slice deep into the girl's palm as she pulled on it. She squealed in pain again as blood spilled from her sliced palm, a fast-rushing stream that described a bright red trail down the underside of her pale, slender forearm. Bubba Ray raised his machete high overhead and brought it straight downward this time, the blade punching deep, splitting the boy's injured hand wide open straight down the middle, creating two halves of a hand that fell away from each other. A lot more blood gushed from this latest wound, and the boy's subsequent scream was even louder and shriller than the one his girlfriend had unleashed moments earlier.

There was a lot of screaming in general throughout the next several violent moments. The majority of it emanated from the victims, but not all of it. Loretta did some screaming of her own, but it was of a different quality, more exuberant, a wild expression of sadistic joy. Bubba Ray had never seen her this way and he was quite taken with it, seeing his cousin in a whole new, much more exciting light. He responded with a lot of whooping and hollering, her enthusiasm spurring him on as he brought the machete down in a straight arc again. This time the boy leaned backward just in time to avoid having the blade chop straight through the top of his head. Instead it clipped off the tip of his nose. Bubba Ray couldn't help grinning at the gruesome transformation the kid's formerly handsome face had undergone, every trace of the airbrushed magazine quality erased. With his sheared-off nose and flayed-open cheek, he now looked more like something out of an NC-17 horror show. The flap of cheek meat was hanging to his jawline like a piece of glistening wet, peeling wallpaper.

Loretta wrenched the butcher knife out of the homecoming queen's pinned hand and climbed into the back of the car with the doomed couple. She jabbed the tip of the blade into one of Brad's eyes when he turned his ruined face toward her, pushing it in hard enough to make ocular fluid squirt out around it. Then she pulled it out and slammed the blade into the homecoming queen's exposed stomach, eliciting another of those earsplitting screams. Loretta cackled wildly as she twisted the knife in the wound. The homecoming queen reached feebly for Loretta's face, pulling at the mask in an apparent attempt to dislodge it. Loretta swatted her hand away, yanked the knife out of her stomach, and slammed it back in, giving it an even more vicious twist.

She put her masked face close to that of her victim and screamed at her. "*How do you like that, you fucking whore!? This scary enough for you? Huh, bitch!?*"

The homecoming queen whimpered as blood gurgled from the corners of her mouth. She sniffled as tears filled her eyes. "Please," she said weakly, raising a trembling hand again. "I'm sorry."

Loretta reared back and pushed her mask up to the top of her head. Her face was radiant with deranged glee as she looked at her cousin. "Can you believe this bitch? How fucking pathetic." She laughed and gave the knife yet another twist. "What are you apologizing for, you dumb cunt? You're the one getting fucking murdered. Stupid townie bitch."

Bubba Ray wasn't always the best at reading people, but he sensed a lot of long-suppressed rage being released all at once. There was so much more fury here than the situation merited. He had no love of town snobs but harbored no specific hatred for them either. Engaging in bloody mayhem for the simple fun of it was one thing. He could understand that. The lacerating venom in Loretta's voice was something else, though.

Still holding the knife inside the crying girl's stomach, she said, "You got that head-bracer thing your uncle made?"

The device was on the ground at Bubba Ray's feet.

He nodded. "Yeah. You wanna pop their skulls open now? Shouldn't we finish them off first?"

The homecoming queen squealed upon hearing these bloodcurdling questions, a sound that prompted an answering moan of misery from her boyfriend.

Loretta laughed. "Hell no, we'll take them back to your place. Why cut our fun short? And we're only popping the boy's skull open." She gave the girl beneath her a leering glance, waggling her eyebrows. "I've got something else in mind for this smart-mouthed bitch. Hop up front and drive us down to your car."

Barely more than a minute later, after putting the car's top up, Bubba Ray drove them away in the Mustang, and a deathly silence once again fell upon the desolate and haunted lover's lane.

TWELVE

AT LEAST AN HOUR HAD passed since Jessica's last glimpse of the sadistic deputy. Since then she'd alternated between wishing she'd somehow never see him again and wanting nothing more in the world than to stare into his eyes as the last spark of life faded from them, going to his grave with the bitter knowledge she'd been the one to defeat him. Not seeing him again didn't feel like an even remote possibility, unless he was struck down by some unlikely fatal accident.

She knew she was capable of taking his life, having killed men bigger and stronger in the past. Some of those men she'd killed from a distance, with weapons that gave her an advantage, but other times she'd done it utilizing nothing other than her physical fighting skills. She wasn't above fighting dirty, if it was the only way to take down a particularly imposing opponent. The deputy's chiseled physique put him firmly in the category of the legitimately imposing, but she remained certain she could easily defeat him in a situation where she wasn't caught off-guard. The opposite, in other words, of what had gone down at the gas station.

Unfortunately, right now, chained up like an animal in this

basement, the odds of getting an opportunity to square up against him in a fairer rematch were depressingly low. She was strong, tough, and capable, but she wasn't stronger than heavy-duty steel. She couldn't break chains like Hercules. The manacles holding her wrists together behind her back had no give at all. Her hands might as well be encased in concrete.

She was helpless.

Powerless.

She was trying to stay calm, just as she'd done so often during years of active mercenary work when facing life-and-death situations, but her edge was gone after the years of inactivity. Her psyche had softened, leaving her more vulnerable to things like fear and anticipation of pain and suffering. The prospect of being raped and tortured by this horrible man made her want to scream, but she couldn't because of what he'd told her before leaving the basement.

This was after he'd finished cutting the other woman's body to pieces with the chainsaw. After he'd wrapped all the pieces of the corpse in plastic and sealed them in a black garbage bag. He squatted in front of her, addressing her in the patronizing manner of a parent scolding a misbehaving child or puppy, emphasizing that she was not to scream or make noise of any kind whenever she was left alone in the basement. If she were to violate this decree, he warned her, she would suffer greatly for it.

He didn't leave it at that.

He got unnervingly explicit about the things he would do to her if she "disappointed" him.

Then he patted her cheek. "I'd hate to have to ruin your face or body prematurely. That would be such a waste. You're a little older than I normally like my girls, but lord, your body is like a gift from God. It's truly out of this world."

He fell silent a moment.

Then he patted her cheek again, a little harder this time. "I'm complimenting you. You should say thank you."

Though it repulsed her to do so, she forced the words through her lips. "Th-thank you."

At that point, he rose out of his squat and went to the table against the back wall. In a few seconds, he returned, squatting before her again, showing her a padded sleep mask. "I'm leaving you for a while now. I have to take out the trash." He chuckled. "Then I'll take a shower and have my dinner. While I'm gone, my wife will come down here to clean up the bloody mess on the floor. You are not to speak to her. Not one word. Do you understand?"

Jessica's mouth moved, but no words came out. She tried to say she understood, but a fresh surge of fear rendered her tongue-tied.

Dalton slapped her. "Do you understand?"

She sniffled. "Y-yes."

He smiled. "Good. Remember, bitch. Not one word. If you say anything at all, my wife will tell me. She won't respond to you, she knows better, but she'll tell me. And after that, you'll never speak again."

With that, he slid the sleep mask over her head, adjusting it until he was satisfied she couldn't see anything. A miniscule amount of light did bleed around the eye pads' edges, but that was it. Then, after repeating his previous warnings, he gave her another hard pat on the cheek. The next thing she knew he was moving away from her, the heels of his boots clomping across the floor and then up the stairs. She heard the door open and click shut.

A shuddery breath escaped her lips the instant she heard the door close. The relief she felt at no longer having him right in front of her was profound. Her skin had crawled at his every touch. The guy oozed a malignant sickness of the soul. She had a hunch this was something he was adept at hiding in normal social situations, but in this setting, shut away from the judgmental eyes of the outside world, he was free to be the monster he was. Even when he wasn't touching her, she could feel it, a pulsing aura of evil. She felt tainted by it whenever he was close, could almost feel it seeping into her skin like poison gas.

So much time passed after his departure that she began to wonder if his wife really was coming. She knew nothing about Dalton's woman save for one thing, which was that she was continuing to share a life with him despite knowing exactly what kind of monster he was. This suggested a few different possibilities. She could be living with him under duress, another prisoner of sorts, albeit not one being kept in chains. Not all chains were forged of steel, though. His hold on her might instead be psychological. She might have been cowed into compliance for a long period, instilled with such an all-encompassing terror of him that physical restraint wasn't necessary. People without firsthand experience of similar situations might scoff, but Jessica knew it was quite common in cases of extreme long-term abuse.

Or there might be no coercion involved at all. There were several well-documented cases, some quite infamous, where women involved with sadistic sexual predators were willing accomplices to their vile deeds, sometimes taking great delight in participating in the torture. Women like this weren't as common as those beaten or terrified into obedience by their partners, but they did exist.

In either case, violating the edict of silence would come with great risk. Any attempt to win over a violently abused woman in a setting like this was likely to be difficult verging on impossible. A woman like that would be living in constant terror of the consequences of even one minor misstep, might even be eager to report the transgressions of a prisoner to curry favor with the man, thereby warding off violence that might otherwise be directed at herself.

Whereas the dangers inherent in daring to speak to a willing female accomplice were pretty self-evident.

Because she had no way of knowing which of these categories Dalton's woman fell into, Jessica figured her safest course of action would be to keep quiet as she'd been instructed. Then again, she was in a dire situation with little hope of escape or rescue. Taking a big risk might be her only viable way out.

She went back and forth like that over and over.

Thinking in circles.

She was running through the whole debate for what felt like the hundredth time when the door at the top of the stairs clicked open. Grunts of physical exertion accompanied the sounds of someone descending the stairs. That this person was not Dalton but his wife instead was clear both from her lighter tread and the timbre of the grunts, which were not mannish at all.

The woman set something heavy on the floor. Jessica guessed it was a large bucket from the sound of sloshing water. Moments later, she heard the woman's footsteps moving away again. She clumped back up the stairs and redescended moments later, depositing some more items on the floor in the vicinity of the bucket. One of those items was probably a mop, judging from what sounded like the clatter of its handle striking the floor. The woman went up and down the stairs two more times before commencing her cleanup work.

Jessica sat with perfect stillness as she listened to the woman work, hearing the splash of the mop going into the bucket and then the sounds of dribbling water as it was wrung out. Next came the heavy, wet plop of the mop head strands smacking the floor, followed by more grunts of exertion as the woman moved the mop back and forth across the blood-spattered tiles.

As she worked, she did not indicate paying any attention to Jessica, seeming to focus entirely on the work. She didn't hum or mutter anything to herself. This could either be a reflection of fear along with a grim determination to adhere to her husband's rules about silence or simply an indication of intense focus on the job at hand.

It was, after all, a big job.

Dalton's work with the chainsaw had spread a massive volume of blood over quite a wide area.

She worked at cleaning it all up in near-total silence for a long time, plunging the mop back into the bucket and wringing it out numerous times. Late in the process, it was clear she was becoming tired, her grunts of exertion growing louder. Occasional brief pauses preceded more mop plunges into the bucket. At last, it seemed she was finished with the mop, pushing the bucket out of the way before commencing the next phase. To Jessica, who'd continued listening with keen attentiveness the whole time, it sounded as if the woman was now on her hands and knees, scrubbing hard at the floor with rags or towels. This also went on for a significant period. When she was finally done, she sat up with a heavy breath and began dropping things in a trash bag.

A strange silence ensued when she was done with that part of it. For the first time, Jessica had the sense of being actively observed by the woman. There was a palpable sense of deep contemplation. The debate over whether to speak sparked to life inside her again. She felt her mouth drop open, her tongue moving like it wanted to form words. The words trembled on the razor edge of existence, waiting to bleed outward into the tension-fraught air hanging between them. They yearned to take shape, to create the lifeline that might pull her out of this hell and back out into the regular world.

Instead, she closed her mouth and tried not to tremble under the scrutiny of this woman she'd still not even glimpsed. That period of silent examination went on for at least several minutes, during which Jessica became convinced the woman would soon gather up her cleaning equipment and depart the basement.

Her body tensed in apprehension as she instead sensed the woman approaching her. She squared her shoulders and sat up straighter, her spine stiffening in a way that made her feel as if a rod of steel had been inserted into her back. Her mouth closed as she clenched her teeth tight, no longer trusting her tongue not to betray her, to defy her better instincts.

The woman lowered herself to the floor, kneeling in front of her. Her breathing changed, became heavier in a way that indicated either excitement or fear. Perhaps both. She scooted a little closer and Jessica felt her warm breath on her face. The heaviness of the woman's breathing became more pronounced. Jessica had the sense she was working herself up to something.

Maybe gathering the courage to defy her husband's will and speak? Jessica sure hoped so.

Then she gasped in surprise at the prodding of the woman's fingertips against her flesh. Her hand was on Jessica's left breast, the part of it not covered by the black leather bikini top. She trembled as her breathing turned ragged, wondering where this was going. It was difficult to take this as anything other than a bad sign. A daring attempt at communication would have filled her with hope, but now she only felt dread.

The woman pushed her fingers inside the bikini cup, breathing even more heavily as her hand acquired a firmer grasp on Jessica's breast. A smaller sound issued from the woman's lips, a muted sound of pleasure. She leaned closer still, until her face was no more than an inch from Jessica's face. Her fingers squeezed and groped the breast, the action accompanied by a longer groan of pleasure.

Jessica's mouth opened again, more tentative words straining to form, a promise of even greater pleasure she could deliver if only given the chance. If this was what the woman wanted, if it was some secret, forbidden thing she'd yearned for all her life, Jessica could give it to her, providing delights she'd only ever imagined. Though her preference was firmly for men, she had, after all, had ample practice in this area during her time in prison.

But then the woman leaned back and her hand came away from Jessica's breast.

Jessica took a deep breath, once again waging war within herself, urging herself to find the courage to say something before Dalton's wife left the basement. Before she could do that, she tensed again, sensing movement toward her face. The woman's fingers slid beneath the pads of the sleep mask and pushed them up. Her vision was bleary at first, until she squeezed them shut for a moment, blinking rapidly as she reopened them.

The world came into focus.

DEPRAVED HALLOWEEN

She gasped in dumbstruck horror at the twisted visage looming in front of her. The woman's nude body was slender and lovely, but her face was lumpy and misshapen, a result of many fractures from countless beatings that had healed poorly without proper medical care. The various parts had a strange, segmented appearance, as if they were pieces of a jigsaw puzzle that had been taken apart and jammed back together the wrong way. There were also numerous scars, some still with old stitches in them.

Dalton's wife looked like a reject from Dr. Frankenstein's laboratory.

This was the woman who'd called so sweetly down to him about dinner being ready?

Jesus fucking Christ.

A lump formed in her throat as she felt closer than ever to speaking, but then the brutalized woman shook her head and lowered the sleep mask back into place.

She stood and moved away from Jessica, beginning the task of hauling the heavy trash bag and her cleaning supplies back up the stairs. In a few more minutes, she closed the door and did not return. Not then. In the long and aching lonely silence that followed, Jessica surrendered to bitter despair, her shoulders quaking as endless tears spilled down her face.

THIRTEEN

CLETUS LEANED HIS HEAD AGAINST the passenger side window of Ol' Rustbucket as his brother Beau guided the ancient F1 pickup truck along one of Montclair's bumpy back roads. Ol' Rustbucket was a name their Grandpap had bestowed on the truck long ago, decades before he or any of his brothers were even a twinkle in their daddy's eye. Grandpap bought the truck brand new in 1951, so the story went, but probably many years went by before the nickname was applied. A lot of years of Grandpap banging down all these same back roads, getting up to the devil's business, as he always put it. The "devil's business" mainly consisting of running moonshine along with all the usual rambunctious shenanigans of good old boys juiced up on strong outlaw booze.

It was weird to think of Grandpap driving the old truck at all, let alone ever being that young and active. In the twenty-one years he'd been alive, Cletus had only ever known him as a broken-down collection of old skin and bones. Despite what everyone called him, he wasn't grandfather to Cletus and his brothers, more like great-grandfather, maybe even great-great-grandfather.

Cletus wasn't too sure on that count. All he was certain of was the man was older than dirt. Sometimes he seemed like he must have been alive when the earth itself was created, more an elemental force arisen from primordial ooze than anything like an actual human being.

And he was mean as hell.

He'd rarely ever lifted a finger against Cletus or his brothers, being too physically brittle by the time they were birthed into the world, but he'd beaten the shit out of Jedidiah, Cletus's daddy, on the regular when he was young. This wasn't something that got talked about in the open, but it was common knowledge in the family. Back when his mama was alive, he sometimes heard the stories. He always got the feeling mama didn't like daddy much, that she maybe even hated him a little. Maybe more than a little.

Maybe for good reason.

Cletus didn't hate his daddy, but he didn't hero-worship him the way he had when he was younger, either. That bloody Thanksgiving several years back had changed everything forever, but mostly he tried not to think about that awful day. It was "old business," as his daddy always put it, best forgotten.

Right now, as they were en route to a remote roadhouse, he didn't care much at all about old times. What his mind kept coming back to was that lady they'd run into at the Pump N' Go, the one who'd given Dalton all the trouble he could handle before he was able to wrestle her into his cruiser.

Cletus had enjoyed taunting her before the deputy's arrival. Acting like a weirdo was about the only way he could get ladies of that caliber to acknowledge his existence. After years of being treated like a freak by townies *and* outsiders, as something to be shunned and avoided, he'd concluded he might as well lean into the gut perception people had of him. He refined his inherent creepiness to an art form and became something people crossed the street to avoid. Whether he was unmasked or wearing something over his face didn't matter, the result was always the same. People looked at him and cringed. Sometimes they said things like "Oh my God" and "Jesus Christ," the sight of him evoking a level of revulsion so primal it triggered instinctive appeals to heavenly entities. They almost always tried to get away from him as fast as humanly possible, evincing little in the way of self-consciousness about showing what cowards they were.

Not that they didn't have good reason to be afraid.

The lady at the gas station was different, though. He'd creeped her out, too, he could tell, but she hadn't been afraid of him. She'd stood her ground and made threats. Even after Beau came out of the store, she hadn't backed down. To the contrary, she'd only gotten more belligerent. The same behavior in another person—just about anyone else, really—might have come off as a terrified bluff, but Cletus had sensed she wasn't bluffing at all. Her demeanor was sheer confidence, and something in the way she moved told him she might actually have been able to deliver on her promise to knock Beau's teeth down his throat. He liked to think that if he and his brother had worked together, they might have been able to take her, but he wasn't sure about that either.

She might have wiped the floor with both of them.

Still, he couldn't help fixating on what might have been if Dalton hadn't come along, if he and Beau had somehow managed to corral the woman and take her back home, where they could do whatever they wanted with her. He pictured her naked and trussed up, squirming and crying, powerless as he ran his hands all over her beautiful body, sliding his fingers into her holes and giggling at her squeals and expressions of terrified disgust.

He liked it when they squirmed.

Unfortunately, it wasn't meant to be, thanks to Danny Trimble, the man who owned the Pump N' Go. Any chance they had at claiming the bitch for themselves went out the window the moment he got on the horn to Deputy Dalton, his cousin.

"Stupid assholes."

"What was that?"

Cletus sat up a little straighter and turned his head to look at Beau through the eye slits of the pumpkin. "Huh?"

Beau shifted his gaze from the road to Cletus. "You said something. What was it?"

Cletus hadn't realized he'd voiced his opinion of Danny and his cousin out loud. "Nothin' important. Can you pull over? I gotta piss somethin' fierce."

Beau took an open beer can from between his legs and swigged deeply from it. "Goddammit, boy, we stopped not five minutes ago, now you gotta drain the lizard again already?"

Cletus shrugged. "Beer."

The one word was explanation enough as far as he was concerned. One or two and he was okay, could go a while without needing to piss too awful bad, but once he got up to nine or ten, he started need-ing to go maybe every fifteen minutes. If he had twelve or more, as he sometimes did when out horsing around with Beau, he started thinking it might be a good idea to have a hose connected to his pee hole, one that would empty into a big plastic jug or bag he could later empty at his convenience.

Beau sneered. "Hell." *Hail.* "You ain't had no more'n I've had, and I ain't havin' to go half as much."

Cletus shrugged again, raising his current beer to slide a straw through the mouth of the pumpkin. He slurped on it a bit, draining the last dregs from the can of Milwaukee's Best. "Reckon you've got some kind of super liver. I gotta pee real fuckin' bad, brother. Just might piss my pants if we don't stop soon."

After dropping the empty on the floor, he popped the top on a new can and inserted the straw, taking an immediate deep slurp.

Beau scowled. "Well, we can't have that, I suppose." He eyed his brother's fresh can of beer and shook his head. "What I can't figger out is why you don't put a plug in the drinkin' until after you empty yourself out some. Ain't you just makin' things worse for yourself?"

Cletus sipped more beer through the straw. "Yep."

Beau grunted. "I suppose I could pull over, but we're only about a mile away from another gas station. Reckon you can wait that long?"

Cletus took a bigger slurp of beer. "Gas station sounds good. Can you get me some tater chips? The hot kind?"

"Why? We're goin' up to Harley Toad's right after."

Harley Toad's Juke and Puke was the roadhouse they'd come out this way to visit. Hidden away from an easy view in the woods, it was a down-and-dirty outlaw joint frequented only by those who lived in the less developed parts of Montclair. There was live music on week-ends and a carb-heavy menu of greasy and delicious bar food.

Cletus nodded. "I know, but I got an awful strong hankerin' for hot chips. Can you get them for me? Please?"

Beau sighed. "Fine. Don't say I never done nothin' for ya."

They pulled up in front of the gas station, another Pump N' Go location. There were three in Montclair, all operated by different members of the Trimble family. Beau went into the store to grab the hot chips while Cletus staggered off to the bathroom around the side of the building.

Rusted hinges squeaked as he pulled the door open and lurched inside. The bathroom was a small space, with only one urinal and one stall. A pair of feet was visible through the open space at the bottom of the stall. Too bad. Cletus preferred to use a stall whenever possible, even if he didn't have to go number two. He didn't much care for having people stare at him while he did his business. Sometimes if a stall wasn't available, he'd wait until one was, even with an open urinal present. In this case, he didn't feel like he could wait. His bladder really did feel like it was at the absolute outer limits of maximum capacity.

"Motherfucker," Cletus muttered.

He stumbled over to the urinal, opened his pants, and took out his dick. Piss pattered on the floor and all over the side of the urinal before he at last managed to direct it to the right place. The forceful stream continued jetting out of him as he stood there and wobbled in place for over a full minute, his head lolling about like a balloon bobbing at the end of a string. He felt a touch dizzy and it was all he could do to remain upright as he waited for his stream to slow to a trickle. It was still dribbling out when he heard the person in the stall flush the toilet.

A moment later, the stall door opened with an even louder squeak than that produced by the outer door's hinges. Someone stepped out and soon he heard footsteps behind him. At the same time, the one working light bulb above the sink flickered and went out, bringing total blackness to the interior of the bathroom.

Cletus didn't think to be scared right away. This was in part because he was on what he thought of as home territory, well away from the center of Montclair, among that small percentage of the population that didn't automatically treat him like a pariah on sight. He did start getting a little scared when he sensed the presence right behind him, so close the hairs on the back of his neck tingled.

A deep, penetrating coldness had seeped into the room since he'd staggered through the door. He felt it in his bones and teeth, a resonant ache that unnerved him. The sinister presence soon felt even closer. He imagined it as a vampire or some other kind of monster from the movies. His balls shriveled as an image formed in his mind of the creature, whatever it was, leaning close to take a bite out of him, or to draw him into its arms in a killing embrace. He thought he should scream or run out of the bathroom, but he couldn't get his legs to cooperate. He just stood there, shaking and whimpering, sensing the thing behind him was reveling in his fear. More than that, *gloating* over it.

DEPRAVED HALLOWEEN

Cletus opened his mouth and managed to squeak out a single whispered word: "Please . . ."

Something touched the back of the pumpkin, making him flinch. He had the impression of a hand of unusual size cupping the pumpkin, long fingers stretching wide to grasp it fully, like a softball held in a normal-sized hand. The connection made Cletus squirm and feel dirty, as if some dark and oily malignant substance was invading all the pores of his body.

Then the light flickered back on and the strange presence behind him was gone. He whirled drunkenly about on the piss-wet floor to confirm this, heaving a big breath of relief upon seeing that he was alone. The stall door was standing wide open. He peeked inside to be sure. No one was in it, but the toilet bowl was filled with a foul black sludge that was like no form of human or animal shit Cletus had ever seen. He backed out of the stall and pulled the door shut, thinking he should run out of the bathroom right there and then, now that he was no longer being held in place by . . . whatever that thing was.

Instead he went to the mirror and stared at his reflection, thinking about the way that thing had gripped the pumpkin with its long, skinny fingers, a powerful dark energy flowing out of them. Some instinct made him want to look away, but he gripped the edge of the sink and held himself right there, forcing his eyes to keep facing forward.

At first he could discern nothing out of the ordinary. Relatively speaking, as a person walking around with a pumpkin on his head. Then, as he stared a little longer, he began to perceive a change in the texture of the pumpkin. A quality that looked almost . . . fleshy. Plus, it seemed to have shrunk by some small degree, appearing to adhere more tightly to his head.

Cletus leaned closer to the mirror, wondering if these things might only be a trick of his imagination, which after all was clouded by the influence of a high blood-alcohol level. After another moment of uncertainty, he leaned closer still, studying the reflection of his eyes.

He let out a panicked gasp, whimpering again.

His eyes . . . they were *orange*.

He grasped the pumpkin and tried lifting it off his head.

Cletus shrieked in fright.

The pumpkin wouldn't budge.

It was part of him now.

FOURTEEN

AFTER RUNNING FULL-TILT OUT of Grandpap's room, Jed came to a panting stop in the middle of the parlor. He stood bent over for a minute, struggling to regain his composure. A part of his mind wanted to shift right into denial mode. On one hand, he recognized this as silly, because he'd seen what he'd seen and knew it'd been no hallucination. Knowing this didn't stop that rogue part of his brain from striving to reject the reality of what had transpired.

He'd pursued the attempt to replicate the brain-shine from the old man's stories in full earnestness, with the hope it might have some genuine restorative properties, perhaps enough to prolong his life for years to come. What he'd envisioned was a concoction that would halt or at least slow the man's decline while also providing a boost of energy and strength. At no point had he believed it might actually reverse the aging process. What he'd witnessed was something he could not have imagined, a rejuvenation he could visually gauge as it occurred, something that simply shouldn't have been possible.

What concerned him now was the question of how much additional improvement might still occur. If the brain-shine functioned like any ordinary healing medicine, the expected result would be a cumulative effect accrued through regular doses. What he was hoping for now was a slowing of the restoration process following this initial amazing result. The benefit of one jar, he theorized, should achieve a plateau level and progress no further without another dose.

He sure as hell hoped so, anyway.

Based on what he'd said prior to Jed fleeing the room, a Grandpap fully restored to youthful vigor might present a significant danger to his well-being. The worst part of imagining such a scenario was he had no idea how far he might take the conflict. He hoped the old man wanted nothing more than to give him a brutal beating, the way he had so many times when Jed was a child, but his fear was Grandpap wanted to kill him.

To finally avenge Norma.

He wished he could go back to the past and change what he'd done, find some other way to vent the rage that had eaten him up in the wake of his wife's betrayal. He felt the same pang of bitter regret he always did when he imagined the alternate world in which his unthinking act of blind fury hadn't splintered the family unit. A world in which there were still women in the household, treasured sisters, aunts, and nieces who provided that crucial balancing influence. In all the intervening years since that Thanksgiving, he hadn't had one willing bed partner, just corpses and temporarily alive outsider females he either had to tie up or beat into consciousness to penetrate them.

Jed gasped as he heard Grandpap's footsteps in the hallway. He wasn't moving fast, but the absence of the familiar clump-clump of the walker or cane indicated he was walking unassisted for the first time in many years.

"I'm coming to get you, boy," the old man called out to him. "Coming to put paid to your old debt. You know the one I mean."

Jed knew from listening to him that the process of rejuvenation had not stopped. His voice was stronger and clearer, no longer the low, phlegmy wheeze it'd degenerated into in recent years. Also, it seemed his walking pace was accelerating. Hearing this, Jed began having serious regrets over his fevered last-ditch effort to brew up some strain of brain-shine potent enough to stave off the old man's demise, which no longer seemed nearly so imminent.

Should have poisoned the old son of a bitch instead.

Despite his growing fear, Jed almost laughed.

It was funny because it was true, but it was a truth imbued with a deep vein of bitterness.

All this work, all the risks I had the boys take in snatching all those bitches, and this *is the thanks I get?*

"Fuck you, old man," he mumbled. "Fucking ungrateful bastard."

The old man laughed. He was almost to the end of the hallway. "I ain't ungrateful. Hell, I'm plenty grateful. But you're a bad man, Jedidiah, and it's time to pay the piper."

His hearing was getting better, too.

Jed took his side-by-side shotgun down from its place over the mantel, cracked it open, and fed a shell into each tube. The old man was in the parlor now, moving faster by the moment. Jed turned away from the fireplace and brought the double barrels around in time to aim at Grandpap's chest.

The old man came to an abrupt stop, although he was no longer actually old, at least in appearance. His body had undergone such a radical change it was akin to shapeshifting. He was taller and more filled-out, the bones beneath the skin firmer, his skin healthier-looking, almost entirely absent of the age spots and lesions that had marred it. A short while ago, only a few wispy strands of white hair had remained on his spotty scalp, but now he had a full head of dark-brown locks. He also appeared to still be aging in reverse, the few remaining blemishes fading before his eyes, his nude physique turning more muscular.

In a way, the man standing before him was a stranger, a version of Grandpap he'd never seen outside of a few blurry black-and-white photographs. Indeed, it was hard to think of this man as "Grandpap" at all. This was John Mitchell, how he'd looked long before enduring for nearly a century, before advanced age shrank and enfeebled him, rendering him unrecognizable.

He scowled when he saw the shotgun. "You piece of shit. Face me like a man, not a coward."

Jed grunted. "Go to hell."

The shotgun boomed and a red hole opened in the center of John Mitchell's chest, blood and tissue leaping from the larger exit wound in his back. He took a staggering step backward but did not topple over. Jed moved in closer and fired again.

This time John did fall over.

Jed felt numb as he spent the next few moments staring at the man's unmoving form, half-expecting to see it rise again, like some unkillable monster in a horror movie. It was a notion he'd scoff at any other time, but he'd already seen a human being age in reverse at astonishing speed. Was the idea of a corpse getting up and walking around again more preposterous than that?

Jed moved closer and knelt next to the corpse to check for a pulse, pressing his fingers into the man's neck. Though John was still warm, it was apparent he was indeed dead. He could tell by the body's absolute stillness and unblinking eyes. The lack of a pulse confirmed it.

He felt a hitch in his breath as his eyes misted with tears, the enormity of the unalterable thing he'd done hitting him with staggering force. All the years spent loving this man and desperately trying to get him to love him back, to save him, only for it to come to this, another moment of bloody, impulsive reckoning. He felt a hole opening up inside him, a deep wound of the spirit so raw and aching he briefly felt like a man standing on the brink of an abyss, teetering on its edge, waiting for that last little nudge that would send him plunging into it.

There were still more shells in that box on the mantel. Just one was all he'd need. So many things had gone wrong in his life, and he'd fucked up in so many ways. Maybe suicide was the only good move still left to him, the only way possible to atone for all he'd done.

After some moments spent visualizing that, Jed could feel himself edging away from that self-obliterating inner blackness. His emotions were still raw, but he was self-aware enough to know he prized his safety and survival above all other things. Hard thing though it was, he'd done the only thing he could do under the messed-up circumstances. These raw feelings would fade with time.

He returned the side-by-side to its spot above the mantel.

The corpse still hadn't moved when he looked at it again. He wondered how long it'd be until his weary psyche stopped expecting anything else. Probably not until the body was out of his house and under the ground. Because that was his first thought when he was able to get past the blunt emotion of the moment and start processing things rationally again—what he'd need to do to cover up what he'd done.

He was fortunate in one way, in that no one else was home when this happened. The sooner he got John Mitchell's body out of the house and disposed of, the better off he'd be, because any or all of the boys might return at any moment and then he'd be in a hell of a mess.

He was less than thrilled by the daunting amount of work ahead of him. Dragging the body deep into the woods for burial was one part of it. Even with it out of the house, abundant evidence of a violent incident would remain. The old parlor rug, which was older even than Jed himself, was stained with the dead man's blood, quite a lot of it, and there was more blood and scattered bits of tissue on the floor beyond the edge of the rug. The floor he could scrub clean, but the rug was more of a problem. Rolling it up and getting rid of it, possibly burying it deep beneath the ground with the body, might be the easiest solution, but it'd be hard to explain. The boys would wonder about the sudden absence of something that'd occupied a place of prominence in the house their entire lives. None of his boys were especially bright, but they weren't completely stupid either. The rug and John Mitchell disappearing on the same night would arouse suspicions.

None of which changed the bottom line, which was that something had to be done and soon. He was right on the verge of beginning to move items of furniture off the rug in order to roll the body up inside it when the light bulb moment of inspiration arrived out of nowhere. It was an idea so stunning in its audacity it almost made him laugh.

Maybe the answer to his problems was he didn't have to do anything at all.

In terms of physical work, that is.

The man on the floor truly bore no discernible resemblance to the Grandpap the boys had known. In addition, those few blurry old photos of the young John Mitchell that Jed remembered had never been on display in the house. He'd only ever seen them while shuffling through a shoebox filled with loose old pictures when he was a boy.

A shoebox that was long gone, taken away by one of his aunts during the exodus of womenfolk from his house. There seemed little chance at all any of the boys could guess the dead man's identity. Therefore the solution to Jed's dilemma was simplicity itself.

In the story he would tell, the man on the floor was not Grandpap. He was instead some unknown stranger, a crazed intruder who'd burst into the house in search of meth. No meth was cooked on the premises, but locals knew some of the boys sold meth made by Jed's brother, Moss Mitchell. He could suggest the intruder was an addict from town who'd confused his house for Moss's house. As for the dead man's unclothed state, that could be chalked up to his drug mania. Jed could say he'd come in from tending the still to find the man ransacking the house. The mess he'd made in the kitchen while making the brain-shine could now be written off as part of that, as further evidence of the mystery man's desperate quest for not only meth but any potential mind-altering substance he could get his hands on.

Jed could also say he struggled with the man in an effort to boot him from the house, a confrontation that ultimately led to his death by shotgun. Then, once he was sure the man was dead, he'd raced down the hallway to check on Grandpap in his room, only to find him missing. Jed would theorize the old man had fled the house in fear of the intruder, only to become disoriented and lost in the woods. He'd have the boys conduct a thorough search of the surrounding area, one he'd join them in for as long as it took to convince them he was as in the dark regarding the old man's fate as the rest of them.

Feeling much lighter of spirit, Jed went into the kitchen and took a bottle of Coors out of the refrigerator. After spinning off the cap and flicking it toward the trash can—which it missed—he put the bottle to his mouth, tilted his head up, and took a long drink. Beer rather than shine seemed a good idea. It would provide the pleasant warm flush of alcohol without fucking him up too bad. He'd do his best to keep his wits about him over the next day or two, however long it took to get past this crisis, then he'd blow off steam with a good old-fashioned bender.

After finishing the beer and dropping the bottle in the trash can, he returned to the parlor intending to look out one of the front windows, see if there was any sign of the boys returning. He'd passed through the archway into the parlor when his gaze was drawn to the bloodstained spot on the rug.

His mouth dropped open. If the bottle had still been in his hand, it surely would've slipped from his fingers. A sick feeling deep in his gut brought a tickle of nausea to the back of his throat.

John Mitchell was gone.

FIFTEEN

WHAT THEY DID WAS THEY transferred the bleeding high school kids from the backseat of the Mustang to the trunk of Bubba Ray's Chevelle. Because they were still alive, there was some resistance, but they were so weakened from the multiple wounds it didn't amount to much. The girl came the closest to squirming free for a moment, not that it would've helped her. Loretta subdued her by pushing her fingers into one of the holes in her belly before she could slip away, reaching deep to prod hard at something extra sensitive, giggling at the way she screamed.

This was all done in a matter of minutes at the spot down the road where they'd stowed the Chevelle before their walk through the woods. There was, of course, a risk of someone coming along and glimpsing the bloody business they were up to, but Bubba Ray wasn't too worried. The road to the bluff saw little traffic even during the daytime. No other vehicles passed by in the time it took them to get the job done. The blood-spattered Mustang was left at the roadside as they drove away in the Chevelle.

Shortly after they got moving again, Loretta jerked a thumb over her shoulder. "Ain't that the sweetest music you ever heard?"

Bubba Ray was briefly confused, but then he realized the pitiful moaning and whimpering of the high school kids was audible from the trunk. He supposed there *was* something musical to the way the separate moans constantly modulated up and down, like a Satanic chorus in some black metal song meant to evoke ultimate evil.

Loretta leaned over and reached a hand between his legs, gripping his crotch. "That shit get you as hot as it gets me?"

Bubba Ray's crotch swelled against her squeezing grip.

She laughed and squeezed harder, the physical response the only answer necessary. Her hand stayed right there and continued to manipulate him through the fabric of his pants. She did it so well he began to have trouble concentrating on his driving. It was a good thing they wouldn't need to deviate from any of the lightly traveled back roads on their way back to Jedidiah's house.

Given how intensely she was turning him on with her ardent, gasping ministrations, it amazed him to think this was the same meth-damaged girl he'd always sought to avoid, finding her off-putting in so many ways. Despite fucking her once or twice in the past, he'd never found her all that attractive. He had better-looking girl cousins and sometimes they were willing to give him a tumble so long as he wore a condom to ward off the embarrassment of getting knocked-up by one of "Jed's boys," never mind that he wasn't one of the man's actual sons. As far as many were concerned, he was tainted by association, and that was without most people even knowing about some of the more fucked up shit they got up to sometimes.

Loretta groaned. "What the fuck's wrong with you?"

Bubba Ray blinked. "Huh? What are you talking about?"

She sneered. "Well, for one thing, you've gone soft all of a sudden, but also you're driving on the wrong side of the road."

Bubba Ray had traveled up and down and all around these back roads so often he sometimes drifted into doing it on autopilot while his mind wandered off in other directions. Once in a while he got so lost in his head he'd have a close call, snapping out of it in time to avoid a collision with another vehicle.

This was one of those times.

His eyes went wide as, still in the wrong lane, he took the Chevelle around a bend and saw a bright pair of headlights pop up right in front of him. He screamed and Loretta cackled as he wrenched the wheel hard to the right, veering back into the correct lane in time to avoid disaster.

From their perspective, at least.

The driver of the other vehicle veered hard in the opposite direction, skidding off the road and plowing into a tree with a loud crunch of truncating metal.

Bubba Ray gasped in shock as he glanced at his rearview mirror. "Holy fucking crawdaddy shit!"

Loretta laughed again.

Then her demeanor abruptly changed, her expression turning grim as she twisted in her seat and looked out the rear window a moment before glancing at Bubba Ray. "Turn this fuckin' car around."

Bubba Ray's face registered confusion. "What? Why?"

The request flew in the face of everything he knew about his demented cousin. He'd never known her to be concerned about the well-being of anyone at all, not even her closest kin. Why would she care to offer aid to some random injured stranger?

She punched him in the shoulder. Hard. "Turn around, goddammit. Now."

Once again, Bubba Ray rankled at the liberties she was taking with him. The ceaseless barrage of insults. The physical aggression. He was resigned to putting up with it instead of killing her because she was blood, but at a certain point his pride would demand some form of retribution.

Regardless, he did as she demanded, slowing the Chevelle and executing a wide, looping turn to head back in the direction of the crashed vehicle.

He shook his head, his temper still simmering. "This ain't like you. Wanting to help somebody."

She laughed. "That ain't it, shit-for-brains. I recognized that car."

Bubba Ray frowned.

The near-miss with the other vehicle had happened in a flashing instant, too fast for anything about it other than those looming headlights to register in his brain. He wasn't sure how Loretta had discerned more than that, but if she was right, he supposed they might need to check it out.

It didn't take long to arrive at the crash site, as they'd traveled no more than another quarter mile down the road. They got out of the Chevelle after he pulled over on the shoulder of the road, Bubba Ray popping the trunk open to retrieve a flashlight. The volume of the moans emanating from his human cargo increased as the trunk lid raised. He smacked aside fluttery hands that reached for him as he groped around for his Maglite. After he found it, he couldn't resist sticking a finger in one of the homecoming queen's stab wounds, remembering how she'd screamed so nicely when Loretta did it. The one she unleashed this time didn't let him down. He sure hoped the girl would still be alive by the time they finally made it back to Jed's house, just long enough to make her scream some more.

Loretta punched him in the back hard enough to make his knees buckle. "Stop fooling around with that whore, lardass. We've got work to do."

Bubba Ray slammed the trunk lid shut, grimacing in pain and frustration as the suffering young lovers loudly lamented the renewed blotting-out of the outside world.

That's it. I can't take it no more.

He brought a huge, clenched fist around as he turned toward her, sliding in the gravel at the side of the road when she dodged the blow. After righting himself, he got turned toward her again in time to receive a kick in the balls, the heel of one of Loretta's cowgirl boots mashing them hard enough to elicit a high-pitched shriek of pain. Bubba Ray dropped the Maglite as he fell to his knees and moaned.

Loretta scooped it up, flicked the beam on, and stepped off the road, moving through a shallow ditch and up a slight rise to the line of trees. Bubba Ray watched as she directed the beam at a steaming wreck. Through his tears of pain, he glimpsed the crumpled front end of an old powder-blue Cadillac. As soon as he saw it, he knew his cousin had been right from the start, not that it made him any less pissed off at her.

"This is Maureen Trimble's car. I fuckin' knew it," Loretta called out to him, confirming what he already knew. "Get up off your ass and come on over here. I think she's still alive."

Bubba Ray whimpered in anticipation of the fresh flare of pain he knew would come with attempting to stand. "Just gimme a sec, bitch. I think you done gave me an involuntary vasectomy. Pretty sure I ain't ever gonna be able to procreate."

Loretta chuckled. "I reckon that's my one contribution to the betterment of society out of the way for this year. Now quit your whinin' and get over here like I told you."

As Bubba Ray lurched to his feet with a twisted grimace of pain, he heard a low murmur of conversation coming from the direction of the wrecked car. Loretta was bent over and talking to someone—

Maureen, presumably—through the open window of the mangled driver's side door. Given the condition of the car, it was amazing anyone inside hadn't died on impact.

The Cadillac's hood had folded in the middle from the force of impact, hanging above the ruined, steaming engine like an inverted V. The grille was obliterated, what remained of the front of the car curling around the wide base of the tree that had brought it to a crunching stop. When Bubba Ray got to within about six feet of the wreck, he was finally able to glimpse Maureen's face in the glow of the flashlight beam. She was whimpering softly, glistening tear tracks intermingling with the froth of blood bubbling from her red-painted lips. Her eyes looked glassy and her head was listing about in a way that suggested she was barely clinging to consciousness. Or life itself.

Maureen was a cousin to the Trimble siblings who owned and operated all the Pump N' Go stations in town. The Trimbles were an old family, with Montclair roots stretching back into the nineteenth century. They didn't go quite as far back as the Mitchells, but no one did. None of the old families quite qualified as rich, but the Trimbles were close. They cashed out of the moonshine-running business way back, using their money to buy property and operate businesses that were at least semi-legitimate.

Bubba Ray began to get anxious, glancing out at the road in fear of another vehicle coming along. The Trimbles were the one group of people in Montclair he never wanted to cross.

"What are you waiting for?" he asked his cousin, dropping his voice to an urgent whisper. "Hurry up and do it and let's skedaddle before someone sees us."

By "do it" he meant cut her throat.

Loretta smirked as she glanced back at him. "Ain't gonna be necessary. Bitch is already on the way out. She ain't talkin' to no-fuckin-body. Come check this shit out. It's fuckin' intense."

Bubba Ray's anger started to rise again, but he tamped it down because he knew arguing with her was pointless. He'd get out of here faster by doing what she wanted. That didn't mean he had to pretend to be happy about it. He grumbled and cursed as he trudged the rest of the way over to the crumpled car.

Now that he was complying, Loretta's former look of leering, morbid delight returned. She glanced into the car one more time before moving out of the way and waving Bubba Ray in for a better look. He bent down and stuck his head in through the window.

After a moment of silent appraisal, all he could say was, "Damn."

Loretta laughed. "You can say that again. Them old waistline seat-belts are killers. Bitch should've known better. Hell, she might've survived a trip through the glass. But this . . ."

Bubba Ray let out a low whistle and shook his head. The crash impact was of such tremendous force the seatbelt had come close to cutting Maureen in half. It was embedded deep in her body at waist level, bits of lacerated organs visible through the gash in her flesh, including a tangle of guts sliding out onto her bloody legs.

Maureen was somewhere in her early to mid-forties, but she looked as good or better than a lot of gals half her age. She was dressed in the standard redneck sexpot outfit of a skimpy halter top and denim cutoffs. He licked his lips as he observed the magical way her big, juicy knockers strained the thin fabric of the top. The impulse to reach out and squeeze them was strong. He'd lusted after Maureen for much of his life but he'd never hit on her because he'd always known she'd shoot him down and laugh at him for trying. The Trimble ladies all thought they were above the likes of him.

Loretta leaned in close, her voice hot and breathy against his ear. "Go on and do it. You know you want to. Hell, *I* want you to."

So, after swallowing a lump in his throat, Bubba Ray did it, a nice, long, luxurious grope of each of the dying woman's breasts. It was exactly as glorious as he'd imagined. Still, he knew they needed to get moving. They'd already lingered here far too long.

He pulled his head out of the window. "Let's go. Last thing I want is to get implicated in the death of a Trimble."

A smile of dangerous mischief tugged at the edges of Loretta's mouth. "Let's take her with us."

Bubba Ray frowned. "Say what again?"

Her smile got bigger, more infused with lunatic glee. "I'm serious. Let's take her."

Bubba Ray gave his head an adamant shake. "We ain't got time. We already been here too long. For real."

He started to turn away, but she gripped him by the arm. "Hey, think about it. Look at her again. She's almost half a woman already. You're big and strong. I bet if you tried, you could pull the top part of her right out."

Bubba Ray gaped at her. "Damn. And people call me crazy. I ain't got shit on you."

His cousin giggled. "Got that right. Go on. Don't even think about it. Just reach in and do it."

Bubba Ray was still confused. "But why?"

She shrugged. "All kinds of reasons, all of 'em fun as hell. You can fuck them big ol' titties once we get her back to Jed's place, then we can take off her head with the hacksaw."

Bubba Ray didn't ask why she wanted to do the latter, figuring it was likely the same reason she wanted to saw off the homecoming queen's head.

"Fuck it."

He turned back to the car, leaned in, and slid his hands under Maureen's arms, getting a firm, hug-like hold on her. She mewled softly in his arms as he began to pull at her, somehow still alive despite the massive trauma to her body, but Bubba Ray knew she was down to minutes or perhaps even seconds left in this world. He tightened his grip and pulled harder, for a moment wondering if he had the strength to do as Loretta suggested, but then he heard a muffled crack, probably the sound of her mangled spine giving way, and the top half of her came away from the bottom half with shocking abruptness, causing Bubba Ray to bump his head against the roof of the car on his way out.

As he pulled Maureen clear, Loretta jumped up and down and clapped her hands, that expression of demonic glee lighting up her face again. "Goddamn, holy shit, you really did it! I'm proud of you, Bubba Ray."

He felt oddly touched. "You are?"

"Hell, yeah. Now let's fuckin' boogie."

She turned away from him and moved fast toward the Chevelle.

Bubba Ray hurried after her as fast as he could. Well, as fast as he could while hugging half a dying woman's body against his chest. Amazingly, she still hadn't fully expired as he stepped through the ditch, more organ pieces and loops of intestine spilling out of her along with more blood.

Loretta popped the trunk open for him.

Bubba Ray looked in at the crying teenagers. "Here's some company, kids."

He dumped Maureen in and slammed the trunk shut, smiling at the renewed loud squeals of horror.

Moments later, they were back inside the Chevelle and driving away.

SIXTEEN

THE DOOR AT THE TOP of the stairs opened again and Dalton descended to the basement. Jessica could tell it was him by the slow, thumping tread of his booted feet on the wooden stair planks. He was taking his time and being extra noisy about it, his way of letting her know it was he who was coming to see her this time and not his wife. The slow descent was also about allowing her dread of his return to build and build, anticipation as a psychological torture technique.

Somewhere around thirty to forty minutes had passed since the departure of the deputy's wife. In the interim, Jessica had scooted backward to rest her back against the wall. Because her hands were bound tightly behind her, the reduction in her physical discomfort level was marginal, but it was better than nothing. As she sat there and listened to the man's heavy footfalls, she wondered if the moment had finally arrived when he would attempt to rape her.

That he would try it at some point, probably sooner than later, was a given. Her determination to make it as difficult as possible for him remained, but in the end, she knew, he would take what he wanted. An existential coldness took root inside her at the prospect, all she'd done and fought against in the fifteen years since Hoke raped her only to end up in the same goddamn position, just as vulnerable as back then.

Hell, more so.

The clomping of his bootheels was even louder as he crossed the white tiles. Then the heavy footfalls stopped and after a few moments, he said, "Come forward."

Jessica pushed away from the wall and waddled awkwardly forward on her knees until Dalton told her to stop, which she promptly did. She'd given fleeting consideration to ignoring the command, rejecting the thought almost right away as pointless because she knew how it would go if she disobeyed. He would threaten her, bark louder, angrier commands at her. Then he'd compel obedience through some painful act of physical violence against her. Better to get on with it and let him do whatever he was going to do anyway.

A brief silence elapsed after Dalton ordered her to stop. Then he stepped closer, stopping right in front of her, close enough for her to feel the heat emanating from his body. He was maybe a foot away and she could tell from his breathing he was all worked up about something. She figured a command to open her mouth and accept the insertion of his cock was imminent.

Then she flinched in surprise when she instead felt the touch of his hand at the top of her head. He began gently stroking her hair, repeating the motion several times, petting her like a dog. When he finally stopped doing this, he put the back of his hand against her mouth.

"Kiss it."

Jessica kissed his hand.

Again, this was a case of surrendering to the inevitable, complying to reduce the overall level of hurt. She had no doubt he intended to inflict pain before he was done with her this time around. There was no getting away from that. Any way she could diminish the extent and severity of that pain might help her later.

So she hoped.

He chuckled, patting her head. "Good girl."

Then he stepped back and raised his voice to shouting level. "Callie! You got that slop ready?"

His wife, Callie, called back her response, her voice the same bright, cheerful tone Jessica had heard before. "Yes, dear!"

"Well, bring it on down here, and be quick about it."

"Coming!"

Seconds later, the sound of the woman's lighter, more rapid footfalls came from the direction of the stairs. From the sound of it, she was wearing either slippers or socks, or she was barefoot, her feet a whisper across the tiles.

When she drew close, her husband said, "Set it there."

Callie's only response to this was a meek sounding, "Yes, sir."

She approached Jessica and set something on the floor directly in front of her. The metallic *clink* it made when it touched the floor provided a strong clue as to what it was.

A dog food bowl, Jessica was pretty sure.

You got that slop ready?

The deputy grumbled in irritation before saying, "You incompetent piece of garbage. I told you just to brown the meat. You've fucking cooked it through."

Callie whimpered in fearful anticipation. "I'm s-sorry. I—"

A loud *thwap* rang out, the meaty sound of a hand whipping across a face. This was followed by Callie crying out in pain as she tumbled to the floor. She cried out again as he hauled her back to her feet and administered three more hard slaps in rapid succession.

The deputy screamed out in rage and made a percussive noise that Jessica needed a few seconds to identify as the man beating his fists against his chest like some kind of deranged caveman warrior.

He then directed more shouted commands at his wife. "Go on back upstairs, you idiot. I'll have to make do with this well-done shit, though it sure would've been a lot more fun with raw meat."

Callie sniffled. "I'm s-s—"

Dalton groaned in impatient annoyance. "Yeah, yeah, whatever. You're so fucking sorry." He snorted angry, ugly laughter. "If you were really sorry, you wouldn't fuck up simple shit so damn often. You need a time-out. Go up to the attic and sit in your cage until I come fetch you."

The woman whimpered and made a sound like she was trying to speak, probably to once again say she was sorry. Jessica cringed in anticipation, itching to yell at the woman to stop and run upstairs while she still could. Jessica's fear of the man remained, had increased, but her righteous rage was flaring up again as well. She strained at the tight manacles around her wrists, again desperately wishing she had the superhero-level strength necessary to tear out of them.

The trembly words of apology again spilled from Callie's mouth.

This time they were followed by a heavy smack that drove the woman back to the floor. A flurry of additional heavy blows followed. Dalton screamed throughout the assault on his wife, who eventually did find it within her to restrain the fear-driven instinct to apologize. Shortly thereafter, Jessica heard the sound of the woman's soft footsteps going back up the stairs, though she moved much more slowly now.

After her departure, Dalton heaved a big breath. "Sorry about that. She forgets her training sometimes. Now then . . . where were we? Oh, yes. I have a question for you. Are you hungry?"

Jessica sighed. "Not really."

"Are you sure? You've been locked up down here for hours. Surely you're feeling at least a little peckish."

Jessica shook her head. "I'm really not hungry."

She thought of the snacks she'd purchased at the Pump N' Go along with the cans of Red Bull. While she hadn't felt quite ravenous at that point, she'd desired food enough to grab two small bags of typical gas station snack food. Now it was hours later and she still hadn't eaten. Under ordinary circumstances, she would be hungry enough by this point to make doing something about it a priority, but, having spent these last few hours being terrorized and held captive, her appetite was in a state of suppression. That would change, of course, if she was deprived of food for any significant length of time. Right now she wanted no part of whatever had been set before her, but by tomorrow? Or the next day?

By then she might be ready to partake of the unnamed "slop," at least enough to sustain her strength a little longer. She had a feeling she knew what the slop was and it repulsed her, but at a certain point grim pragmatism would take over, compelling her to ingest what she was pretty sure was human flesh.

Dalton came closer and pushed the sleep mask up to her forehead. He clamped his hand tight around her jaw, forcing him to look up at his sneering face. "Where are your manners, bitch? My loving little wife thoughtfully prepared this meal for you, and you *will* eat it, whether you're hungry or not. You can either do it willingly, or I can force it down your throat. Which is it gonna be?"

The pressure around her jaw tightened, becoming painful, but she managed to squeeze out a reply. "I'll eat."

He showed her a grin of leering triumph. "Damn right, you will." He shoved her to the floor and moved out of the way. "Now get to it. Don't make me get out one of my special toys to force obedience.

Or are you the kind of sick fucking whore who'd like something like that?"

Bound and helpless or not, Jessica did not care for being addressed with such sneering, dehumanizing contempt, especially from someone as vile as this man. The urge to respond with an equal measure of verbal venom was surging again, getting close to the point where it might soon overwhelm her desire to ward off physical harm. This detestable man in his stupid boots and spandex bikini bottom was not her equal. He was the one deserving of contempt, not her, and she longed to put him in his place.

That place preferably being a shallow grave with that ridiculous crotch-hugging garment shoved down his throat.

She flinched when he screamed at her again and stamped one of his booted feet on the floor. "*Eat!*"

Biting back the acidic words she yearned to spew, Jessica got herself positioned in front of the bowl and glanced up at the deputy, who was grinning and rubbing his crotch. The front of the bikini-style garment was immensely swollen. No surprise there. This piece of shit's whole thing was getting off on terrorizing and belittling women. A range of possible scathing insults related to this floated through her head, but this time she more easily restrained her tongue. Despite her rage, she didn't want to get hurt if she could help it.

Resigned to this next stage of degradation, she eyed the pile of minced meat in the bowl, which looked a little different from ground beef purchased from a grocery store. It'd been cooked to a shade of dark brown. She supposed she could at least be thankful to Callie for that. It caused her to wonder whether the woman had defied her husband's instructions on purpose, knowing she'd pay a price for it. She doubted it. Dalton's wife was a thoroughly cowed slave. The idea she'd willfully disobey him was absurd. She'd made a mistake, nothing more, her attention possibly lapsing during the cooking process. Also, lest she forget, the woman had taken advantage of Jessica's helplessness in her own way. It was unlikely she had any greater level of sympathy for her than the previous woman held captive in this room. Or the one before her. Or the one before that one.

She bent forward, lowering her face to the bowl and doing her best to ignore Dalton's louder grunts of sexual arousal. She opened her mouth to take the first bite but hesitated as a wave of last-second nausea came over her, forcing her to choke back bile. A twinge of shame colored her lingering rage when she heard Dalton chuckle in response to her moment of difficulty. This was not the first time she'd been held captive by a sadist, but she'd rarely ever felt quite this humiliated. Her dwindling pride felt like it was circling the drain. At this rate, it wouldn't be long before she was kissing his feet and beseeching him for mercy, becoming another of his pathetically submissive slaves.

Jessica opened her mouth and tried again.

This time she took one of the freshly cooked morsels of dark brown meat between her teeth and began to chew. The actual taste wasn't terrible—it'd been seasoned—but knowing the source of the meat was enough to prevent her from deriving any enjoyment from it. She was grateful for that, because otherwise the stubborn vein of humanity she'd managed to hold onto through all her tribulations over the years might finally have shriveled up and died.

Dalton screamed, making her flinch again and nearly choke on the chewy morsel in her mouth. She wasn't eating fast enough to satisfy him, it seemed, so she endeavored to consume more of the meat more quickly, but it wasn't easy. The meat wasn't like anything she'd ever purchased from a grocery store. It was harder to chew. After forcing the first few bites down her gullet, the sickening possibility of enjoying the meal on some base instinct level diminished because there was no way she could fool herself into thinking it was no different from animal meat. The taste was *off* in some essential way that continued to fuel nausea and repulsion even as she made herself keep gobbling it down.

She ate so much of the meat in a short time that she had to force herself to slow down again to avoid choking on it. At one point, she had to stop and cough hard enough to expel a particularly lumpy piece, which landed on the floor instead of going back into the bowl. This prompted some of Dalton's loudest screaming so far. She was "disrespecting" him by soiling his floor. He ordered her to clean up her mess immediately unless she wanted him to start breaking her fingers.

Jessica shifted around slightly on her knees and bent her head to the floor, snatching the lumpier morsel off a white tile with her teeth. She chewed it more carefully this time, making it small enough to finally force down her throat without choking. The whole time Dalton was screaming at her, louder and louder, more unhinged than ever. She let her eyes flick upward once and saw veins bulging at his temples, his face flushed an alarming shade of bright red. This was one seriously psychotic motherfucker, way crazier even than she'd already imagined. Maybe the craziest motherfucker she'd met in a depressingly long line of crazy motherfuckers. Recognizing this filled her with despair.

I'm never getting out of here, she thought. *My chance to get loose and smash his fucking brains in is never gonna come.*

The glance up at him further inflamed his arousal. He took his swollen, veiny cock out and began frenziedly pumping it. She watched him do this until he screamed at her to resume eating, which she promptly did. Gladly did, at that point. Funny thing, consuming the flesh of another terrorized woman was preferable to watching this monster masquerading as a man pleasuring himself. As she resumed the vile meal, she was annoyed by how much of it there still was. She wouldn't have thought it possible to get this much edible meat off such an emaciated body. Of course, she was only assuming this meat was from the woman who'd been chained up in the basement with her when she awoke earlier. It might have come from an earlier victim. This didn't seem likely, but Jessica wouldn't put it past this lunatic to have a storage freezer filled with packages of human flesh.

Dalton's moans of pleasure became higher-pitched the deeper into the meal she got, the pumping of his hand more and more frenzied. His eyes rolled back in his head as he swayed on his feet, and in between the moans, he mumbled things about what a worthless bitch she was.

Then he let out a loud gasp and leaned forward on the tips of his toes, thick white ropes of semen hitting her face and dripping into the bowl. Jessica was so disgusted, she instantly tried rising to her knees again, but the deputy dropped to his knees and gripped her by the neck, forcing her head back down to the bowl. Her face sank into the remaining pile of meat. She tried resisting, but he increased the pressure on her neck, commanding her to eat.

Just as she was sure she would have no choice but to ingest a semen-coated bit of human flesh, Dalton let out a small gasp of surprise and relaxed his grip on her. He rose shakily to his feet and slapped weakly at his neck. Jessica sat up and watched in surprise as he wobbled away from her for a few feet before crashing unconscious to the floor.

She glanced up and then to her right, eyes widening upon seeing the ruined face of the deputy's meek, submissive wife.

Who maybe wasn't quite so submissive anymore.

Clutched in the fingers of her right hand was an empty hypodermic needle.

SEVENTEEN

THE REJUVENATED OLD MAN WAS gone, but a blood trail leading from the rug into the dining room provided a clue. Jed again retrieved his shotgun from its place above the mantel, fed a fresh shell into each barrel, and slipped more into the front pocket of his shirt.

Keeping the double barrels aimed in front of him, he followed the trail of smeared blood into the dining room, continuing past the table where he and the boys took their meals and on toward the door that opened onto the rear of the property.

The door was standing open, and a bright smear of blood was on the doorknob.

Jed shook his head in disbelief.

The visual evidence told a pretty clear tale. Despite being shot twice at close range, John Mitchell had summoned the strength to drag himself across the floor and open the door. How he'd managed to do that without making a sound, Jed could not imagine. It shouldn't be possible for a man that badly wounded to do such a thing. He'd be in a tremendous amount of unbearable pain that would only be amplified by the physical effort necessary to get to the door and beyond. At the very least, he should have been whimpering and crying out the entire way, if not outright screaming. Instead, somehow, he'd slithered away as soundlessly as a snake.

All this was strange enough, but then there was the matter of the man being *dead* to consider. There'd been no doubt in Jed's mind on that count, at least not until now. He'd checked the pulse. There wasn't one. He hadn't been breathing. He'd looked into his still, unblinking eyes. Jed knew a dead man when he saw one, and John Mitchell, last he saw him, was as stone-cold dead as any he'd ever seen.

He stopped short of the open door, his breathing quickening as his mind scrambled for an explanation. A number of wild notions occurred to him, the most unsettling of which were related to the brain-shine. What if, in addition to facilitating a rapid reversal of the aging process, the potion could restore life in the recently deceased? It seemed a crazy idea but not, he reckoned, any crazier than what he'd already witnessed.

Was it possible he'd rendered his old Grandpap immortal?

Jed grimaced at the thought.

Oh, lord, please no.

A John Mitchell who could return to life no matter how many times he was shot was his worst nightmare, but surely there must be a limit to the amount of damage he could absorb. Drastic action might be required once Jed caught up to him. He was thinking of the burn pit out back. Soaking the old bastard with a can of kerosene and setting him ablaze might be the best option. Reduce him to a pile of ash and scatter the ashes all over the goddamn county.

He smirked.

Try coming back from that, *you son of a bitch.*

Another idea occurred to him, and in its own way, it was as unsettling as the notion of John Mitchell's resurrection. Perhaps someone else had entered the house while he was in the kitchen, someone who'd dragged the dead man outside. That could explain the trail of blood and the lack of agonized screams from a man shot twice in the chest with a shotgun.

On the surface, this was a far more rational explanation than the idea that, through a process of mixing an assortment of random-ass ingredients into a jar of hi-test moonshine, he'd somehow crafted an elixir capable of bestowing immortality.

Who, then, was the theoretical silent intruder? *If* one existed, the most likely candidate would be one of his boys, but if that were the case, why hadn't they come looking for him? Why hadn't they cried out in shock upon finding the corpse of a naked stranger sprawled out on the parlor rug?

These were all questions without obvious answers for the time being, and Jed knew he was stalling. The fearful part of him found it easier to mull over all the various angles than to do what was really necessary, which was to step through that door and go find his answers.

He took a big breath and stepped out onto the back stoop, flipping a light switch on the way out that lit up the area between the back of the house and Bubba Ray's mini-camper. The lights were out in the camper. That was enough to tell him it was not Bubba Ray who'd returned home early. Even when he was home, that boy was always up deep into the night, drinking and carrying on.

Farther back were the two sheds on the property, the one for moonshining and the larger one used for storing old tools and all kinds of random junk, including, sometimes, people. Even now a girl was hanging from a rafter in there, one who'd been dead and rotting a little too long. Jed had been meaning to get after the boys to take her down and get rid of her for a while, but it kept slipping his mind. Things had been slipping his mind more often lately. If he could get this business settled without too much bother, he might try recreating a batch of the super brain-shine for himself. The idea of once again being as young and randy as his boys was thrilling. If it worked, he might even start joining them on their nightly rambles, or he might go out a-prowling on his own. That could be fun.

He might even get to relive the bloody thrills of 1989.

Jed smiled at the thought.

I was such a naughty boy back then.

The torture shed was the farthest back of the two, its dark outline barely perceivable at this distance. The moonshine shed was off to the left of the mini-camper and set back maybe twenty feet to its rear. This proximity was why Bubba Ray's loudly amorous antics with his dead girlfriends had caused Jed such consternation earlier in the day.

A razor-thin vertical slit of light was visible leaking from the door of the moonshine shed.

Gathering his courage, Jed reached back inside the house and turned off the exterior illumination, then stepped off the stoop to the ground. He kept the shotgun aimed in front of him as he began his approach to the shed. Whether the person (or persons) in the shed had seen the track lights come on was debatable, but if they had, he wanted them to think he'd gone back inside. The tactic might not work, but it was worth a shot.

He approached the shed with as much stealth as he could manage. Even without the track lights on, he could see well enough in the moonlight to avoid unseen obstructions on the ground. The closer he got to the shed, the more his hands wanted to shake, and he compensated by clenching them tighter on the shotgun, though he was careful to keep his finger outside the trigger guard. Any tactical advantage he might have gained by striving for a quiet approach would, of course, be wiped out if he accidentally fired off a round because he couldn't keep his damn nerves steady.

By the time he was within ten feet of the shed, he'd become aware of a sound emanating from it, a low moaning or whimpering. Upon hearing it, his alternate theory of John Mitchell's body being dragged away by one of the boys did a slow fade in his mind. This was a sound of suffering. The sound a badly wounded person might make.

Now he wondered if Grandpap had somehow faked his death. Jed had seen old movies where secret agent types, either through ingesting a drug or by some exotic form of training, were able to do that, regulating their heartbeat to a point where it was so slow it was undetectable. He guessed maybe he could buy that part of it, at a really extreme stretch of credulity, but the other stuff was harder to believe. The not blinking or seeming to breathe, for one thing, but the real clincher was the two shotgun shells fired into the center of his chest, in the vicinity of his fucking heart.

Nah, no way.

That man was dead for real, one-hundred and ten percent, the last time Jed set eyes on him. Were these sounds from that same man, somehow reanimated, restored to life?

He was about to find out.

He was within a few feet of the door. One more step would take him there. The low moaning was still audible, but now he detected a different quality of the sound. There was a weakness to it that matched the initial perception of suffering, but he now thought what he was hearing was more akin to . . . *suckling*.

What the goddamn hell?

Jed took that last step toward the door, lowered the shotgun's double barrels, and pressed an eye to the thin crack. What he saw inside the shed surprised him so much he was unable to suppress a loud gasp. The person in there moaned louder on hearing the sound but did not turn toward Jed as he pushed the creaking door open and stepped fully inside.

Jed let out a shaky breath. "Holy guacamole."

John Mitchell was indeed in the shed, and it appeared he had been restored to some semblance of life, though he did not look much like the man who'd confronted him in the living room. His eyes were glassy and his head was lolling to one side with long strings of drool dangling from each corner of his mouth. He held his hands limply in front of him, and they made occasional weak little movements, like those of an infant taking milk from its mother's teat. This was because a disconnected end of the still's copper tube was now inserted in his mouth. He was trying to suck the brain-shine mash out of the beer keg.

Jed was at first at a loss to deduce a reason for any of this, but it came to him that John's steady moaning made him sound lobotomized. He considered what little he knew about the medical realities of death and soon hit upon a nugget of an idea. If enough time had passed between the moment of the man's expiration and the moment of his reanimation, his brain might have become too damaged to function as it had before. Perhaps he'd retained enough cognitive ability to know any hope of restoring his faculties was dependent on receiving another infusion of miracle brain juice. Though the specific concoction Jed had whipped together for him in the kitchen was gone, the contents of the still might yet provide some helpful measure of augmentation.

Or so whatever remained of John inside his degraded brain possibly hoped in some gray, vague fashion. The impulse was understandable, but Jed remained unconvinced John would achieve the desired result by this method of infusion. The mash had not yet been turned into shine, for one thing. Then again, the man's return from the dead wasn't anything he'd expected either, meaning they'd entered a realm where anything seemed possible. Jed experienced a fresh stirring of dread. A fully restored John Mitchell could spell a lot of trouble for him.

There was only one sensible course of action here.

He raised the shotgun again as he moved closer to the still, aiming the double barrels at John Mitchell's head. This came with a reflexive pang of emotional torment, an echo of what he'd felt after shooting the man the first time, but the feeling slipped away within seconds. Having done this once already, he knew he could do it again, *had* to do it again. This unnatural reversal of the man's real death was wrong, an obscene mockery of the proper way of things. Sending the man back into the great beyond would be doing him a favor. If, as Jed suspected, the undistilled brain mash failed to restore his intelligence, condemning the man to some strange half-life as a drooling ghoul would be a far more terrible thing than putting him down again.

He moved closer, slipping a forefinger inside the shotgun's trigger guard. John Mitchell's dull gaze shifted toward the looming double barrels, and while his brain wasn't functioning at anywhere near normal capacity, some trace instinct within him recognized the threat the weapon presented. The steady moan became a whimper of fear as he shrank away from Jed. One of the limp hands flicked at him in a weak go-away gesture that made Jed smile. All token moralizing aside, a larger part of him relished being granted one last opportunity to terrorize the enfeebled shell of a man threatening him a short while ago.

He sneered. "See you in hell, Grandpap."

The copper tube slipped out of John Mitchell's mouth as he turned his head and raised his hands in a pathetic shielding gesture that only made Jed grin wider. A squeeze of one of the side-by-side's triggers yielded a big boom and obliterated part of one of those trembling hands in addition to pulping the crown of the man's skull. John pitched over onto his side, leaking blood on the floor as his body twitched and trembled.

Jed moved closer for a kill shot. The first shell had missed its mark slightly but had done enough damage to negate any mild threat the man might still have presented. The glimpse of bloody, convulsing brain pulp visible through the ragged hole at the top of his skull seemed to offer conclusive proof on that count, but Jed wasn't taking any chances. Blasting out what remained of John Mitchell's brains seemed the safest course, the only way to be absolutely certain he wouldn't become a problem again.

He took a fresh shell from his shirt pocket. One still remained in the side-by-side's other barrel, but he wanted to be able to press the weapon against the side of the man's head and give him both barrels at once. That would empty his skull of the rest of his scrambled brains and hopefully finish this business for good. Before he could open the shotgun and insert the second shell, the door to the shed banged open behind him.

Dropping the shell he'd plucked from his pocket, he whirled around and fired on instinct. His eyes went wide upon seeing that he'd shot Jed Jr., his youngest son. J.J., as he was called, fell back against the open door with his hands clutched around his throat. Blood gurgled out between his fingers as he tried and failed to speak, more blood streaming from the corners of his mouth. With his back against the door, he slid to the floor, still gurgling and trying to talk for another few moments as Jed watched in dumbstruck horror. Then the boy's hands came slowly away from his throat and flopped against the floor. Seconds later, his head drooped to one side and the gurgling sound ceased.

Jed Jr., who'd turned eighteen only a month ago, was dead.

Jed stared at him uncomprehendingly for the next few moments, his grip on the shotgun going slack as the barrels dipped toward the floor. His mouth moved, but no words came out, which was fitting as there were no words that could set this right. Tears welled in his eyes as he struggled to make sense of what had happened. He didn't want to believe it was real, *refused* to believe it at first because it'd happened with such shocking, unexpected swiftness. Mere minutes ago, he'd been convinced he was alone on the property with John Mitchell. There'd been no sound of an approaching car heralding the return of any of the boys. Unless, that is, it'd been masked by the roar of the previous shotgun blast.

That must be it. He'd happened to squeeze the trigger at the exact wrong moment. His son, hearing the blast, had come rushing in to investigate, fearful, perhaps, for the safety of his father or brothers. Because Jed Jr. was the youngest of them, he'd not had to bear the brunt of his father's rages as often as his older siblings. Jed didn't know if any of the boys still loved him without reservation, but if any of them did, it'd been J.J.

The grief rising inside Jed was beginning to intensify when he heard the sound of footsteps running fast across the ground outside the shed. Forcing his eyes away from J.J., he saw another of his younger sons running through the open doorway. This time it was Carl. The nineteen-year-old was his next youngest boy. His arrival on the scene at this moment made sense, given that Carl and J.J. palled around together more than they did with the other boys. Where you got one, you almost always got the other. This time was no different.

Unfortunately.

Carl slapped a hand over his mouth and reeled backward in shock when he saw his dead brother. An instant later, he dropped to his knees at J.J.'s side. Jed perceived some of the same denial he'd experienced in the boy's demeanor. Carl made useless attempts to rouse his brother, as if he'd only fallen asleep or fainted, anything other than the grisly truth told by the large and ragged wound to his throat.

As the full, grim import of that truth registered at last, Carl turned a face shiny with tears toward his father. "Daddy, what happened?"

The raw, razor-edged anguish in his voice was a painful thing to hear. "A terrible accident is what happened," Jed said, his voice flat as he shook his head. "I was dealing with this son of a bitch." He indicated Grandpap's still weakly trembling but de-aged form with a tilt of his chin. "This crazy man broke into our house and scared off Grandpap. I cornered him in here and . . . and . . ."

Carl's face was a study in confusion, but he was hanging on his father's words. "And what happened then, Daddy?"

Jed didn't bother telling the boy it was pretty damn obvious what had happened next. He'd had an idea, one he would deem a symptom of sheer insanity on just about any night other than this one.

There was no more of the super brain-shine he'd whipped up for Grandpap, but what if its reanimating properties could be harnessed another way?

Jed began to smile. "I think we can bring your brother back to life." He held up a hand to stifle the boy's confused protests. "Never mind how. Run on back to the house and fetch me a knife, the sharpest you can find." He scooped up the bucket he'd used for mixing the mash earlier in the day and thrust it into the boy's hands. "And rinse that out while you're at it. We'll need it to collect the blood."

EIGHTEEN

ELISE PETERSON WAS HAVING A hard time accepting the reality of her grim predicament. All the available evidence strongly suggested she was nearing the end of her life and given that she was a Christmas baby and not yet eighteen, this felt fundamentally unfair. It went against all she'd thought she understood about what was right and good in the world. All her life she'd held fast to an unwavering belief that God would always protect the innocent and pure of heart, thereby making her safe from the bad people of the world.

Tonight had disabused her of that notion.

She wanted to believe her brain was torturing her with some terrible nightmare, one generated by the horror movie she and Brad semi-watched while making out in his bedroom earlier in the day. There were times when she was quite capable of existing in a pocket of denial to cope with things that annoyed her or made her uncomfortable, like that time as a small child when she'd accidentally discovered her macho father's secret stash of gay porn, or that other time last year when she'd been touched inappropriately by the cute history teacher she'd had a crush on.

In each of those cases—and quite a few others besides—she'd managed to banish memories of the disquieting incidents to corners of her mind so remote that returning them to the forefront of her consciousness was unlikely, barring some direct inciting event that dragged them out of the murk. This didn't mean she'd scrubbed the memories entirely from her mind. It just meant they were so effectively submerged she was able to pretend those uncomfortable things hadn't happened. At worst, they were likely to faintly recall dreams of another life.

She didn't think she'd be able to do that this time, and the reasons for this were plentiful, the aching pain from her multiple stab wounds being foremost among them. All she had to do was think of that big blade plunging into her abdomen and the horrible sensation of the steel lodged deep inside her body returned full-force, as if it were happening all over again. That was bad, horrendous, but the way the hillbilly girl had twisted the knife inside her had ignited an agony almost beyond comprehension, a pain so spectacularly intense it blotted out her brain's ability to form coherent thoughts, rendered speech impossible, leaving her only able to scream and scream in reaction to it. Almost as bad was the way both of the hicks later stuck their fingers inside the wounds, sending her agony to new heights while probably also filling her with all sorts of nasty germs, given that they both smelled like they hadn't washed in weeks.

The wounds to her hands were less directly life-threatening, she supposed, but each was searingly painful in its own right. If she hadn't been stabbed multiple times in the gut, the pain from her wounded hands would undoubtedly qualify as the worst she'd ever experienced. She couldn't clench the hand that'd been stabbed straight through without triggering fresh waves of unbearable throbbing agony that made her wish for a full-body anesthetic. The deep slice across the middle of her palm was nearly as bad, the exposed nerve endings of the flayed flesh sensitive to every little movement she made, forcing her to hug it to her chest and try her best not to move at all.

Unfortunately, the jostling motion of the old car as it traveled fast over bumpy back roads made staying still impossible. Even worse, she knew any faint hope of escape would depend on her being able to push past the pain. At present, she couldn't imagine any feasible way escape could be affected, but if some unlikely opportunity did present itself, she'd have to use her hands, probably a lot.

For now, however, she was trapped.

DEPRAVED HALLOWEEN

Not just trapped, but enclosed inside a suffocatingly tight space with a half-corpse of some lady she didn't know and her boyfriend who, if anything, was even more badly wounded than she was. She couldn't see anything inside the trunk of the Chevelle, but in her mind she kept seeing the grisly ruination of Brad's face and his gruesomely bisected hand. The halves of the hand had flopped around in a way that made them look more like the appendages of some outer space creature than anything human.

She'd tried speaking to him a few times since the start of their time in the trunk but had not yet received anything like a coherent verbal response. He was only capable of the occasional faint whimper. The periods between whimpers rendered her almost helpless with anxiety. She kept thinking he was either already dead or about to die, a prospect that incited a panicked sense of dread inside her. Not just because she loved him, but because she couldn't bear the thought of facing whatever was still to come alone. She needed the comfort of his company, paltry though it was in his debilitated condition. Her sweetheart since sophomore year, he was her strong protector, the captain of the wrestling team. She'd always felt so safe in his presence.

But Brad's days of protecting her were over.

Though any hope of escape seemed slim verging on utterly impossible, a stubborn part of her continued to cling to the idea of being able to slip away once she was out of the trunk. It was probably a foolish idea, but she couldn't let go of it, not so long as there was still breath in her body. Yet, even in her wildest imaginings, she could not conceive of any viable scenario in which she was able to slip away with Brad in tow.

I can only save myself. I'm sorry, baby, but it's true.

And that meant her time with Bradley Harding as a vital, integral part of her life was coming to an end. It also meant all the elaborate visions of their future together she'd spent so many bored afternoons daydreaming about in school would never become anything more than that.

They wouldn't get married.

Or have kids.

In more immediate terms, they wouldn't be graduating from high school, nor would they be enrolling at Auburn University come next fall. She wouldn't get to pledge a sorority or have all the other amazing college experiences she'd been looking forward to for so long.

No! Stop thinking like that.

She'd lapsed into including herself in the fatalism she felt where Brad was concerned, which frightened and infuriated her, so she fought back against it with all the internal fierceness still available. Her fate wasn't sealed, not yet. Her wounds probably wouldn't be fatal if she could get to a doctor in time. She was breathing without issue and no major arteries had been severed. Though it would be hard at first, she would forge a new life if she survived, find someone else to love. More than anything else, she would savor and appreciate her life more than ever before, never taking it for granted again.

The Chevelle slowed and took a turn down a road bumpier even than all the previous ones. It felt like it wasn't a paved road at all. After that, the car picked up a bit of speed again, but it no longer moved at anywhere near the prior breakneck pace. Elise figured all this must mean their abductors were close to wherever they were going. Her breathing quickened at the thought, panic rising inside her again. She tried to fight against it, psyching herself up to act without hesitation when her golden moment came, that one that might lead to her salvation. There would only be one such moment, she was certain, and she was determined to be ready for it.

The car traveled a winding path through what she imagined was a more heavily wooded area. That was scary, but it also made sense. Her mind flashed back to the bizarre verbal exchange between the guy and the chick. It'd been difficult to lock in on what they were saying amid her pain and terror, but some of their words penetrated, stuff about decapitation and possibly something about brain removal. It all sounded completely insane and the purpose of it all wasn't anything she could fathom on any level, but the thing to keep in mind was these were crazy people. Their minds worked in strange ways and their motivations were unknowable without more information. What Elise did know was they would want some reasonable assurance of privacy before initiating the next phase of whatever mad scheme they were pursuing.

The car slowed some more, almost to a crawl now.

The moment that would determine her fate was imminent.

It'd been a while since she'd felt Brad move around or make a sound. She could no longer hear his slow, labored breathing.

"Brad?" she said, keeping her voice low. "Can you hear me? Are you still with me?"

Several silent seconds passed, then she heard a small moan, soft and short in duration, almost inaudible. He was still with her, but from the sound of him she doubted he would be for much longer. After shoving the half-corpse of the mystery woman further toward the back of the trunk, she tried twisting around and reaching out for him, and he grunted in pain when she accidentally kneed him in the groin.

"Sorry, baby," she said, sniffling as she found his hand and squeezed it. "I need to tell you that I love you so much. Whatever comes after this, I'll always remember you. You'll always—"

She went silent at the sound of a key sliding into the trunk lock.

She shifted around again, getting into a low squat, priming herself to leap, to—

PART II

RISE OF THE
NIGHT THINGS
(PIERCING THE VEIL)

NINETEEN

BUBBA RAY TOOK THE KEY out of the lock and raised the lid of the Chevelle's trunk. As the lid came up, the girl he thought of as a homecoming queen rose on her knees and tried crawling out of the trunk over the body of her boyfriend, who looked like he might already be dead.

Bubba Ray grinned at how hard she was trying despite her serious wounds and overall weakened condition. He liked it when they showed even just a little bit of feistiness. Never really helped them much in the end, but it did make things more interesting sometimes, as in when they'd chased that college gal through the woods a few nights ago.

That'd been a hell of a time. Flashing back to the memory of mounting that gal's primo corpse in the woods got his ding-a-ling all a-tingle.

The girl in the trunk looked up at him with shiny, pleading eyes.

She reached out to him with one of her damaged hands, the one with a hole right through the middle. "Please. I'll do anything . . ."

Bubba Ray chuckled and leaned close, intending to shove his

thumb right through the hole in her hand.

Loretta shoved him out of the way and stabbed the girl in the throat, a gusher of blood erupting from the vertical hole when the blade retracted from her flesh. His cousin grabbed hold of the homecoming queen by her hair and hauled her out of the trunk, dumping her face-down on the ground.

They'd pulled around the back of Jed's house, parking in front of the mini-camper. Bubba Ray had noted the outdoor lights in the back were already on and that the back door to the house was standing open. That was a bit odd. Most times Jed raised holy hell if anyone left a door wide open like that. What's more, lights were on inside the moonshining shed. He normally wouldn't have been able to tell due to the blacked-out windows, but the door was open a tiny crack.

Bubba Ray glanced back and forth between the back of the house and the shed. "Wonder what's goin' on here?"

Loretta grunted. "Who the hell cares?"

The girl on the ground was still barely clinging to life. Loretta gave her a few savage kicks in the side, eliciting a soft groan of pain. "How ya like that, townie bitch? Want some more? Here ya go."

She kicked the dying girl somewhere in the neighborhood of ten more times, which even Bubba Ray considered a tad excessive. It was clear the girl was no longer capable of resisting. Hell, even holding her hand over the hole in her throat like she was doing, she wouldn't be capable of anything much longer. More blood dribbled from the corners of her mouth when she coughed and spluttered.

Loretta reached into the Chevelle's back seat and came out with the hacksaw, smacking it against Bubba Ray's chest. "Take that."

Bubba Ray's fingers curled around the hacksaw's handle. It was a rusty old thing, one of a handful of tools they'd grabbed from the torture shed before embarking on tonight's mission. "What am I supposed to do with this?"

Loretta snorted. "What do you think? We're cuttin' this dumb cunt's head off. You'll do the sawin' 'cause you're stronger 'n me. I'll hold her fuckin' still."

She approached the homecoming queen and dropped down to straddle her back. On impulse, she unhooked the girl's bra, tearing it away from her body in a way that caused her hand to come away from her throat. The blood from the hole flowed thickly for a few seconds before the girl managed to close her hand over the wound again.

Loretta again put her hands on the girl's shoulders and pressed down hard, glancing at Bubba Ray. "Well, whatcha waitin' for? Get to sawin', bitch."

Bubba Ray got himself positioned above the girl's head, taking a moment to hitch up his saggy jeans before easing his hefty bulk to the ground. Because his knees were right up against the top of her head, he scooted backward a bit to give himself more room to operate. The girl turned her head far enough to one side to look up at him with wet, bleary eyes. She looked like a scared puppy anticipating a stern reprimand from its master for some misbehavior. For a moment, he felt a flickering pang of something almost like regret, an echo of the kind and innocent boy he'd been before a long, forced immersion in blood and violence by his elders. The feeling didn't last long because he'd come too far and done too much to ever be that person again.

He moved her long dark hair away from the back of her neck, enjoying how soft and clean it felt against his fingers, the polar opposite of Loretta's tangled rat's nest. It had a faint but pleasing fragrance as well, a hint of something that made him think of fresh-cut flowers, and it was tempting to put his face in her hair and take a good, long whiff. Only the prospect of Loretta's sneering derision kept him from doing so.

"Sorry, doll. You're outta time."

Bubba Ray turned her head so that her face was again pressed against the ground, keeping it there with one hand pressed hard against the back of her skull.

Loretta made a sound of disgust. "Don't apologize to this bitch, tubby. She don't deserve no pity. The townie whore deserves this. They all fuckin' do."

As a general rule, Bubba Ray wasn't fond of sweeping blanket statements against any group of people. While it was true a lot of town folks were snooty assholes, he'd met a few he liked, people who didn't automatically treat him like he was lower than dirt because of his background, but this wasn't the time for a debate. Besides, this girl's fate was already settled. Even if some part of him wished he could spare her, he couldn't do it, not after all she'd seen.

He placed the rusty edge of the hacksaw blade against the nape of her slender neck, taking care to avoid the thin gold chain draped around it. She mewled and squirmed when she felt the touch of the jagged steel, and he pressed down harder against the back of her head to keep her still. The crying and squirming got his thoughts moving in a different direction, one about as far removed from the fading vestiges of his tainted conscience as possible, his excitement growing as he remembered why they were doing this in the first place. This girl's life was ending, but that didn't mean he was done with her, not even close.

His grip on the hacksaw's handle tightened as he began to bear down with the blade. The girl summoned a last reserve of energy and strength and tried bucking Loretta off her, but the effort was unsuccessful. Loretta laughed and shifted her weight atop the girl, pressing down harder on her shoulders and taunting her with more profane insults.

A line of blood appeared at the back of the girl's neck as Bubba Ray began to saw. The girl's constant mewling turned into a louder cry of pain as the sawing blade went back and forth, digging deeper into her neck. Her body twitched as it went even deeper and nicked her spinal column.

At that moment, Bubba Ray, distracted by a creaking sound somewhere behind him, paused in his sawing and turned his head toward the sound. He frowned as he saw his uncle come out of the moonshining shed. Before Jed closed the door again, Bubba Ray glimpsed two things that roused his curiosity, a wide pool of blood on the floor and a flicker of movement. At least one other person was in the shed, but he hadn't gotten a clear look at whoever it was.

The look on Jed's face was hard to read as he slowly crossed the twenty feet of ground between the shed and the spot where they had the girl pinned down. It seemed to convey a mixture of things, including annoyance, curiosity, and perhaps even a touch of wariness. The latter struck Bubba Ray as a tad strange, as this was a man accustomed to acts of murder and perversion being committed on his property, acts in which he was often an eager participant. That tinge of wariness couldn't be because he was disgusted or unsettled by what they were doing.

So what was it?

Bubba Ray was at a loss.

Jed's expression shifted some as he drew closer, becoming more neutral, and Bubba Ray had the impression this was a forced change. He had the sense the man was trying not to give away something, something that had to do with whatever was going on in the shed. The blood he'd glimpsed implied certain things. There seemed a high degree of likelihood someone had been killed in there, though he couldn't guess why his uncle would be secretive about that. This was, after all, the same man who'd once chopped his wife to death in full view of his whole family.

"What's going on here, boy?"

Bubba Ray shrugged. "Not much. Just cuttin' this gal's head off."

Loretta giggled. "We're doin' some Dr. Frankenstein shit. Her head's gonna go on some other gal's body."

Jed grunted. "I see. Well . . . y'all have fun with that. Just stay out of the shed. I've got some delicate work shit goin' on in there."

He started to turn away from them.

"Uncle Jed?"

A flicker of annoyance again crossed the man's face as he glanced back at them, there and gone in the blink of an eye, that more carefully neutral look replacing it so quickly Bubba Ray wondered if he might be misreading things.

"Yeah, boy?"

Bubba Ray hesitated a moment, wondering if he should let the matter drop. "Um . . ."

His uncle scowled. "Spit it out."

Bubba Ray felt a touch of heat color his cheeks. He prided himself on being a man who didn't scare easily, one who wasn't intimidated, but that sense of something wrong radiating from his uncle made him uneasy. "Um . . . I was just wonderin', uh, there, uh . . . any of that leftover pot roast still in the fridge?"

Jed squinted at him. "The pot roast?"

Bubba Ray's face reddened some more. "Yessir. I could eat a bit, I guess." His eyes flicked briefly toward the dying girl on the ground. "I mean, like, after we're done with this business." He forced a grin. "You know how I always work up an appetite after some killin'."

Jed snorted. "Boy, you work up an appetite just rolling out of bed in the morning. You'll have to check on that pot roast yourself." He again started to turn away from them, then immediately stopped and lifted a finger to point in their general direction. "Heads up. Y'all got a live one still in the trunk."

Jed started moving toward the shed again.

Bubba Ray glanced back toward the Chevelle in time to see the homecoming queen's boyfriend spill out of the open trunk and to the ground. The sound of his body landing right behind her dragged a startled yelp of fright out of Loretta. She sprang up off the homecoming queen's back and turned toward the Chevelle as the boyfriend was rising to his feet. A rusty old tire iron of significant heft was clutched in his left hand, the only still-functioning hand he had. He lurched toward Loretta and took a weak swing at her, one she was able to dodge with ease. He shifted his grip on the tire iron and lurched toward her again, attempting an even weaker swing. The boy was weak in general from the numerous wounds inflicted on his flesh, but Bubba Ray had a hunch the ineffectualness of his swings had a different explanation, which was that his ruined hand was his formerly dominant one. His attempts to lash out at Loretta were so feeble she mostly just laughed at him, barely needing to move as she dodged the lazy arcs of the tire iron.

After observing this comically macabre dance for a few moments, Bubba Ray rose to his feet with a loud grunt of exertion and wobbled closer, putting himself between Loretta and the boy. When Brad tried swinging at him, Bubba Ray plucked the tire iron out of his hands and cracked it over his head. The blow from the heavy tool was sufficient to open a fissure of significant size in the boy's skull. Blood came burbling out of the crack as the boy first swayed on his feet and then dropped to his knees. Bubba Ray grabbed hold of his shirt, heaved him up to about waist level, and cracked the tire iron over his skull a few more times.

Loretta stamped a foot on the ground. "Stop it!"

He glanced at her. "What's the problem?"

She made an exasperated sound and rolled her eyes. "You're gonna ruin that boy's brain. It's already damn near useless for reanimatin' purposes."

Bubba Ray took a moment to appraise the latest drastic changes wrought to the shape of the boy's skull by the tire iron. "Huh. I see what you mean. It's kind of leakin' out. Whoopsie daisy."

Another screech from Loretta briefly made him believe she was still upset about the mess he'd made of the boy's head, but then he turned and saw that the homecoming queen was up on her feet and stumbling away from them. She appeared to be heading toward the line of trees that started at the back of the clearing behind the house. Bubba Ray wasn't overly concerned. The girl's movements were slow and uncoordinated, herky-jerky, as if the different parts of her body no longer knew how to work together. Bubba Ray remembered the way she'd spasmed when the hacksaw blade nicked her spine and figured that might have something to do with it.

Loretta laughed. "Goddamn, it's like watchin' a puppet operated by a blind baby with a brain defect."

She retrieved the butcher knife she'd used earlier and went after the homecoming queen, taking her time about it, giggling at every lurching sideways step. The girl got as far as the side of the moonshine shed, falling against it as Loretta caught up to her and rammed the big blade into her lower back. She leaned into the girl, pressing her against the side of the structure as she held the blade inside her body. Bubba Ray watched as she put her mouth to the girl's ear and whispered something he couldn't hear.

Then she took the blade out and rammed it in again.

And then again.

After the third time, she slowly extracted the blood-painted blade and stepped back, smiling as the girl's lifeless body dropped to the ground.

Bubba Ray stepped up next to her and looked down at the dead girl. Her face was frozen in a look of slack surrender, her glassy eyes no longer reminding him of a scared puppy, if only because she was beyond being scared of anything now.

Loretta nudged him with an elbow. "Look at them tits."

Bubba Ray grunted. "I see 'em."

Loretta chuckled. "Not bad for a homecoming queen, but she ain't got shit on the tits of that half-bitch."

She started walking away.

"Grab that whore and drag her back over here. We've still got work to do."

TWENTY

THE DEPUTY'S WIFE WAS HAVING a hard time. Her petite build was less than ideal for dragging the dead weight of a big man's unconscious body from one side of the spacious basement to the other. After a lot of loud grunting and straining, she was only about halfway there. It was pretty obvious what her intentions were—at least in part—but the remaining captive in the room had concerns.

Jessica cleared her throat. "You know, I may not look it, but I'm pretty strong. Take a minute to cut me loose from these chains. With my help, you'll get that done in no time."

Callie had a two-handed grip on one of her husband's wrists and was walking backward with her knees bent low, which was not the most effective way to move the body of a musclehead like the deputy. She looked up and leveled a look at Jessica that might have been a scowl of annoyance, though the grotesque reconfiguration of her face made it difficult to read any expression.

"I believe you were told to stay quiet."

The surprising words triggered a fresh feeling of unease in Jessica, who'd taken the other woman's risky act of rebellion as a sign that her own liberation was imminent. "I'm just trying to help."

Callie grunted. "You can help by shutting the fuck up."

Hearing the unfriendly edge in the woman's voice did a lot to douse what remained of Jessica's resurgent hope. She had the sense Callie might not restrict herself to venting her long-suppressed feelings of rage against the obvious target. Speaking again in the face of that rage would be risky, but Jessica felt she had no choice but to do so one more time.

"I'm worried about the strength of that sedative you used. He's a big man. If it's the same dose he uses on much smaller women, he might wake up before you can get him in those chains. If that's what you're planning, I mean, and it sure looks like it."

Callie dragged her husband across another couple inches of the floor before screeching in frustration. She relinquished her grip on the man's wrist and stood straight with a huff. After glaring at Jessica, she marched toward the back of the room and retrieved something from the table littered with the deputy's toys and tools of sadism. She came right back at that same rapid, angry marching pace, veering away from the unconscious man on the floor this time.

Jessica sucked in a big breath and shook her head. "No. Don't. Please. I just want to help. Please let—"

Callie tore off a strip of gray duct tape from the roll and pressed it over Jessica's mouth. After casting the roll of tape aside, she cracked a hand across her face, whipping her head to the side.

There was strength in that blow. More than Jessica would've guessed.

"Be fucking quiet or you won't like what happens next."

She returned to her husband and resumed her two-handed grip on his thick wrist, getting back into that backward, hunched-over position. The loud grunts of exertion also resumed, but this time her focus wasn't solely on the hard physical task at hand.

She looked at Jessica. "You must think I'm stupid. I prepare the doses for him. Would you have guessed that?" She snorted. "Probably not. But it's true. Trust me, I've got plenty of time to work with."

She nonetheless made an obvious attempt to redouble her efforts, grunting even louder and pulling much harder at the man's unconscious form, a sheen of sweat appearing on her weirdly segmented face. One or two inches of floor covered at a time became three or four at a time. Still slow, but better, though still not fast enough to set Jessica at ease. The woman's attitude toward her was troubling, but the prospect of the deputy waking up before Callie could lock him in those chains worried her a lot more.

If nothing else, a safely bound Deputy Dalton wouldn't be able to stick his dick in her. Even if she died in this room, which she hoped didn't happen, she would take some comfort in knowing the monster had been denied his pleasure.

A low moan from the deputy's mouth made Jessica's eyes go wide, her breath quickening behind the duct tape. "Hurry!"

Callie glanced at her, scowling at the muffled utterance.

Then came another moan, not quite as weak as the one before it.

Callie cursed and let go of the deputy's arm again. This time she turned and ran for the stairs, her bare feet ascending the wooden planks with an almost spidery silent swiftness. She launched herself through the open door at the top, disappearing from sight.

Jessica groaned in despair.

She feared she was being abandoned to whatever grim fate the deputy might choose for her when he woke up to find his wife had run away. The drugged man still sounded pretty out of it but, unencumbered by chains, he would be free to do as he wanted with her when he did regain consciousness. She had a feeling that once he fully understood the potential ramifications of his changed situation, he might discard his original plans for her in favor of putting a bullet in her head, after which he'd probably flee the area, possibly even try to leave the country. A man as organized as the deputy probably had a bug-out plan in place, one he was prepared to put into motion at a moment's notice should knowledge of his crimes ever come to light. A plan that almost certainly wouldn't involve dragging a captive woman along with him, particularly one who'd already displayed ample ability to make trouble.

The deputy moaned again.

Then he made a snorting noise and coughed, after which he mumbled a brief something that was incoherent. One of his hands lifted an inch off the floor, the fingers shaking. Seeing these signs of stirring semi-consciousness made Jessica's heart race. She feared she didn't have much longer to live. Her nostrils flared above the strip of duct tape, her breathing quickening as she cursed the man's stupid, selfish wife, who easily could have saved her after knocking out the deputy with the sedative but had not. A scream of anger and frustration began building up inside her. She was on the verge of unleashing it when she perceived motion in her peripheral vision.

Jessica turned her head and saw Callie again descending the stairs in that same almost preternaturally swift and silent way. She came bearing another syringe presumably filled with the same drug as before. A gasp tore out of her when she saw Dalton struggling to lift his head. She ran across the floor and dropped to her knees at his side, swatting his shaking hand aside as he reached for her.

Then she jabbed the needle into his neck, straight into the jugular, and pushed the plunger down.

Jessica's body sagged in relief. "Jesus."

Callie glanced at her, her lumpy features shifting and forming what was either a smirk or a smile. She nodded at the dog food bowl still on the floor in front of Jessica. "I see you have not finished your meal. That's unacceptable." Her features shifted a little more. More a smile than a smirk, Jessica now figured, but a mean one. "We'll deal with that in good time. Meanwhile . . ."

She cast aside the spent hypodermic and got to her feet, then she resumed dragging the deputy toward the opposite wall. This time he did not stir as she completed the job, securing his wrists and ankles with the manacles and chains. A lot more grunting and straining went into getting his back propped against the wall. She then adjusted the chains, shortening them through the brackets so that his splayed arms were held flat and tight against the wall. Next she adjusted the chains connected to the ankle manacles, spreading his legs apart.

Seeing this, Jessica couldn't help smiling behind the tape. Dalton was now as helpless as she was. More so, maybe. She wished for freedom with even more fervency than before, longed for the chance to go over there and give the sadistic deputy a taste of his own medicine. Her wrists twisted against the manacles behind her back. To her chagrin, she still had not magically become stronger than steel. The only thing she was accomplishing was making her wrists hurt. Her only hope still lay in somehow winning over Callie.

Satisfied at last with her adjustments, the woman stood and appraised her work. After nodding in satisfaction, she turned away from the snoozing deputy and approached Jessica, bending slightly to rip away the strip of duct tape.

Jessica heaved a breath. "Thank God. Listen, let me help you with him." She lifted her chin at the deputy. "I know a thing or two about torture myself. Was trained in it by experts, actually. Swear to God." The smile that came to her lips was not forced in the least. "I'd love nothing more than to—"

Callie slapped her. "You don't listen well, do you? Be fucking quiet." She raised a hand as if to strike her again. "Do you understand? If so, nod."

Jessica nodded.

The woman's mangled lips moved, forming another of those mean smiles. "I'm going back up to fetch some things. While I'm gone, I expect you to finish the meal I worked so hard on. If you don't, I'll whip you until you bleed." The smile widened. "Just for starters. Nod if you understand."

Shivering, Jessica nodded.

"Be right back!" the woman said, in a brighter, jauntier tone reminiscent of how she'd sounded when calling down to Dalton earlier.

She went to the stairs and flew up them again with her characteristic swiftness. Jessica experienced another intense pang of longing as she stared at the open door.

Then she sighed and eyed the dog bowl, her face twisting in revulsion at the layer of meat still at the bottom and its glaze of semen. She didn't like the idea of having to swallow it, seeing it as a passive, secondhand way of Dalton continuing to taint her with his vileness even after being negated as an active threat. The problem was, she believed Callie's threats were sincere. Her theory was the woman was suffering from a variation of bullied child syndrome. She was so damaged by severe abuse that she could only make herself feel better by heaping that same abuse, or worse, on anyone she could.

Getting this moment of repugnance over with was the only viable option available to her. At least she'd eaten most of the sickening meal already, powering through it at Dalton's command. She would do the same again, as fast as possible, endure one awful moment of supreme grossness, and then it'd be done.

Callie might be back any moment.

The bowl needed to be empty before then.

Jessica leaned forward and pressed her face into the bowl. She worked hard to force back the bile rising into her throat as she gobbled the remaining meat down, her gag reflex betraying her as the slimy morsels slid down her gullet. The gag reflex kept working even after the bowl was empty, and she endured several minutes of miserable struggle before finally getting it under control.

By then Callie had returned to the basement. Though still barefoot, she'd changed into a tiny green dress. She also came bearing a small plastic sewing kit, which she opened as she knelt at her husband's side. After threading a needle, she placed the tip of the needle at a spot below a corner of the deputy's bottom lip. Then she pushed the needle into the flesh, pulled the lip back, tugged the needle through, and drew out a long length of thread. Next she pulled his upper lip away from his gum and slipped the needle inside the lip, once again pushing it through the flesh. After again pulling the long length of thread all the way through, she placed the tip of the needle at a spot beneath his bottom lip perhaps a centimeter distant from the first hole she'd created. Again, she pushed it through the flesh, pulled back his bottom lip, and drew the thread taut. On and on the process went, the pattern of upper and lower lip punctures continuing until she'd sealed his mouth. Little dots of blood appeared with each new puncture, slowly painting a sloppy red smear across the middle of his face that made him look a little like a deranged clown.

When she was finished, she picked up her sewing kit, got to her feet, and approached Jessica, kneeling to wave the needle in front of her face. "If you can't be quiet like you've been told, I'll sew your mouth shut, too. Do you want that?"

Jessica shook her head.

Callie flashed another crooked smile. "Good, because I'd rather not. I will if I have to, but it's not my preference. I have some other ideas in mind for that mouth of yours."

Callie laughed.

Jessica shuddered.

The truth was, her situation hadn't improved much at all.

Callie stuffed the needle and thread back into the sewing kit, zipped it shut, and patted Jessica's face, her hand lingering on her cheek. "You belong to me now. My possession. My puppet. My pet. I'm going to have fun playing with you."

She stood up and walked out of the basement.

A moment later, Jessica heard the click of the lock.

TWENTY-ONE

The rest of what Jed got up to before Bubba Ray and Loretta returned was this . . .

JOHN MITCHELL WAS STILL CLINGING to life as Jed and Carl worked together to raise him from the floor and position him over the plastic bucket. This was important because his beating heart would stimulate blood flow, making it easier to drain a large quantity. He moaned and drooled as they wrestled him into place, not resisting their physical manipulations but not exactly cooperating either. The damage to his brain from the shotgun blast meant he probably was not cognizant of what was happening, at least not fully, but a few times the quality of the moans issuing from his mouth changed in a way that indicated annoyance.

This didn't concern Jed, who attributed it to a vague sense of bother on the old man's part. He didn't know what was happening to him but knew he was being handled and some instinct made him dislike it. Though he made no active effort to get loose, there was some squirming that made their work harder. When they finally got him into the optimal kneeling position in front of the bucket, they were able to make him bend at the waist with his neck stretched out right over the top without too much trouble.

Carl was then able to hold the man in place without resorting to any extraordinary measures, keeping his hands braced on his shoulders as he eyed Jed and said, "We really not know who this guy is, Pa?"

Kneeling on the opposite side of the bucket with the knife in his hand, Jed cocked an eyebrow at the boy. "Does he look familiar to you?"

Carl frowned. "I don't think so."

Jed nodded. "That's good, don't you think?"

Carl's expression turned thoughtful for a moment, his smooth features scrunching up before he shrugged and said, "I reckon. It's better when we don't know them. That's what you've always said. Makes sense to me."

Jed nodded again in approval. "That's right, and that's because killing folks we have no connection to is safer, less likely to get any of us in trouble with the law. This man here, for instance, ain't likely kin to us or any of our neighbors. We'd have seen him around before."

Carl grunted. "I guess that's right, but . . ."

Jed felt a twinge of apprehension. "But what? Spit it out, boy."

Carl sighed. "Aw, it's nothin', really. He definitely don't look much like nobody I ever seen, but . . . he's got those blue eyes like Grandpap."

Jed fought back a grimace. "Lots of folks with blue eyes, son. It's common."

Carl shrugged. "I know. It's just a little . . . spooky." His frown returned. "Shouldn't we be trying to track down Grandpap? You said he wandered off into the woods when this fella broke in, right? He's apt to hurt himself stumbling around out there in the dark."

Jed again called on inner reserves of patience and did his best to arrange his features in a smile of reassurance. "He'll be fine. Don't let that man's age fool you. He gets around better than he lets on. First things first. We gotta let this man's blood out so we can help J.J. That's the priority. If we don't work fast, we might not be able to bring him back."

Gripping a bloody thatch of the wounded man's hair to lift his head with one hand, he placed the sharp edge of the hunting knife against his throat with the other. His muscles tensed as he tightened his grip on the knife's handle, preparing to bear down and slice deep.

John Mitchell's squirming became a touch more agitated, though he wasn't difficult to handle. Carl planted a knee in the middle of the man's back and pressed harder on his shoulders.

"You really think this man's blood can bring J.J. back to life?"

This time Jed was unable to suppress a groan of irritation. This boy was full of questions. What made it worse was he understood the nature of his inquisitiveness. In the boy's place, he'd be seething with skepticism. The story he'd spun about a mysterious drug-crazed intruder was about as believable as a fairy tale. He saw that now, after having given voice to it. It'd sounded better in his head, but there was no taking it back now, nor could he further embellish it without a high risk of tripping over the made-up details he'd already provided. All he could do was stick to it and hope the desperate scheme he'd hatched worked. The only reason he wasn't completely losing his mind was he sincerely believed there was a chance it might. Maybe a slim one, but it was better than no chance at all.

It will *work*, a strident inner voice told him. *It will because this might be the end of everything if it doesn't.*

Jed rebuked the part of his psyche responsible for the thought. He didn't really believe his whole world would come crashing down if the miracle he was hoping for eluded him, but it might become fundamentally altered. He could too easily envision a scenario in which most of his five remaining boys abandoned him, moving out to take up with other, less sordid factions of the Mitchell clan. Bubba Ray, too, maybe. Cletus might not leave regardless because he was too weird to function out in the world on his own, but the rest of them?

Well, they just might.

With that thought galvanizing him, Jed began to push the serrated blade into John Mitchell's throat. Just as the steel started cutting through his skin, a gagging sound emerged from his mouth followed by a mumbled, indistinct utterance.

Indistinct, at least, to Jed.

"Pa!"

Jed kept sawing side to side with the blade, pushing it in deeper to widen the gash in John's flesh. Blood began to pump out at an impressive rate from the man's jugular, pattering against the bottom of the bucket like water from a tap.

Carl leaned over and grabbed hold of his wrist, stopping him. "Pa!"

"Goddammit all!" Jed glared at his son. "What in tarnation is it, boy?"

The boy's face was a study in live-wire urgency, his eyes bulging and his features contorting as his grip on Jed's wrist tightened. "Didn't you hear that? He said my name. Right as you started to cut."

A half-inch of the blade was buried in John's throat, blood continuing to patter out around it. It was coming out fast but was not yet the gusher that would occur when Jed finished the job, which would have happened already, if not for his boy's unexpected act of interference.

"You heard no such thing," he said, struggling to bite back rising fury. "Now, you best take your hand off me or I'll give you a whipping like you ain't never had before."

Carl made a sound of exasperation. "But Pa—"

"Remove your fucking hand from my goddamn person this instant," Jed told him, voice crackling with a level of black, searing menace he'd last leveled at a blood relation seven years earlier. "*Now.*"

Carl, who'd been at that fateful Thanksgiving dinner, reacted to the tone instinctually, gasping in fright as he jerked his hand away. "I'm . . . I'm . . . s-s-s . . ."

Tears gushed from the corners of the boy's eyes as he started to shake all over.

Jed sneered, shaking his head. "Look at you. Crying like a bitch. You've always been kind of a pansy, haven't you?"

"I don't . . . I don't . . ." Carl took his knee off John's back and started to rise. "Daddy . . . what's going on?"

Shaking his head in disgust, Jed took the knife away from John's throat and rose to his feet as well.

Carl backpedaled a few steps before reversing course and making a break for the door. Jed acted on impulse, lurching to his right and striking out with the knife in a slashing motion. The blade cut through the boy's shirt and sliced into the side of his body. He cried out and stumbled but somehow managed to make it to the door before Jed caught up with him, grabbing hold of him with an arm wrapped around his body. The boy struggled with wild abandon, arms and legs flailing, but Jed held him fast, pulling him against the front of his body. Then he reached around and plunged the big blade into his son, three quick, deep jabs that made the boy wheeze in helpless pain and go limp in his arms.

John looked up from the bucket, the gash in his neck still dribbling a fast, thin stream of blood. Despite the dull look in his eyes, it was impossible not to read a note of accusation in his expression.

Jed sighed.

He stabbed Carl three more times, each thrust of the knife more savage than the last. When he relinquished his grip on his body, the boy tried clinging to him, but Jed heaved him aside. Carl dropped to the floor, wheezed once more, and rolled onto his back. After that, he didn't move, his sightless eyes staring at the shed's ceiling.

Jed spent the next few moments staring in numb disbelief at the boy's lifeless form. That was two of his sons he'd murdered in one night. In the space of less than an hour. One purely by accident, granted, but the result was the same. It was a surreal, mind-bending thing, and a part of him wanted to believe he was hallucinating, that he was sick in his bed, trapped in some suffocating fever dream of blood and horror. Too quickly, the moment passed, denying him the frail comfort of delusion.

He'd done it again.

That thing he'd done seven years ago when the rage inspired by his wife's transgressions had overwhelmed him. Killing outsiders was nothing, no different from hunting and skinning wild game. A different line was crossed when a man killed family. Looking at Carl's fresh corpse, he wondered if the darkness inside him might finally be taking over for good. There'd been one other time when he'd toyed seriously with the notion of allowing the darker side of his psyche full, permanent rein over his actions—that glorious Halloween season of 1989, his all-too-brief reign as the Lover's Lane Slasher.

That wondrous time came to an end because the older Mitchell men of the era figured out he was responsible for the killings and decided to put an end to it. Not because they were such great detectives but because he'd been stupid. Shortly after the trophies he'd taken from his victims were discovered in the room he shared with his brothers, the elders took him out into the woods and gave him a brutal ass-thrashing the likes of which he hadn't experienced before or since then.

After it was over, he was given the sternest possible warning. The problem was his victims were all town kids. It didn't matter that they weren't from rural old families. They were still locals, meaning they were the furthest thing from ideal candidates for wanton murder. It was the kind of thing that could bring heat on them all. He was strongly advised to never kill any innocent local people again, and if he felt like he simply had to kill *someone*, he should do it somewhere far from Montclair. Should he fail to heed this advice, it was strongly implied he would be taken back out into the woods, only instead of a beating he'd be buried in a deep hole. Jed had known it was no empty threat, but the galling thing about it was not one of those men was a saint. They'd all gotten their hands bloody one way or another at various points in their own lives.

Several of the men who'd beaten him that day were dead, including his daddy, who'd never liked him as much as his other kids. The ones still alive were elderly and creeping toward senility. In the more than a third of a century that had passed since his Halloween killing spree, awareness among his kin of what he'd done had receded. None of the men who'd assaulted him had breathed a word about it again, at least not in his presence. The whole affair was all but forgotten as far as Jed could tell.

Except by Jed, of course.

He also hadn't forgotten the role of John Mitchell in the beatdown. Though he had not participated in the actual beating, being old already even back then, it was he who'd decreed that it should happen. He told the men what to do and how to do it, including the specific threats that should be made.

The only reason Jed didn't end up hating him was because he later learned the punishment the man devised was a substitute for the execution some of the other men favored. Over time his sour feelings for the man softened back into something resembling love. Even catching him with Norma hadn't changed that.

Now, with a moaning John Mitchell leaking a line of blood down the front of his torso as he swayed on his knees in front of the bucket, Jed wondered if perhaps he should've been as unforgiving with him as he'd been with Norma.

He smiled, nodding to himself.

Yes, fuck you, old man.

Jed again seized the bloody thatch of hair at the top of John's head and this time drove the hunting knife deep into the hollow of his throat. Instead of guiding him back toward the bucket to direct the subsequent jugular geyser into it, Jed removed the knife, pushed the man to the floor, and clamped his mouth over the gushing wound. This was done on impulse, one triggered by a vestige of his earlier, now discarded plan to attempt a resurrection of J.J. with John Mitchell's blood. Until that moment, he hadn't known he wouldn't be trying to bring back either of his dead kids. The awareness that he no longer cared was just there, seemingly out of nowhere, though later he'd realize it was just a natural consequence of deciding to unleash his inner darkness.

Meanwhile, so long as there remained some remote chance the blood contained restorative properties, there was no reason to let it all go to waste. So he kept his mouth over the wound, slurping deep, big swallow after big swallow, feeling like a vampire as he continued to suck at the hole even when the spurts of blood became less powerful with the slowing of the dying man's heart. John made weak attempts to clutch at him with his trembling fingers, but soon his hands fell limp to the floor. John sucked harder at the wound, drawing more blood out of the ragged vein, craving every precious drop because what he wanted more than anything was a second chance. A chance to be young again. To become the career serial slasher he'd wanted so desperately to be as a teenager.

When he was at last satisfied he'd drawn out as much blood as he could, he sat up and wiped his mouth with the back of his hand. Then he took a look around at the tableau of carnage the shed had become. One son with his throat blown open by a shotgun, another stabbed numerous times, and his great-grandfather with his throat torn open. Blood all over the floor. More blood smeared all over his face. Unless he planned to blow town right away, this could present a problem.

Then he thought of another possible problem.

He frowned, studying the slack features of Grandpap's face, remembering this was technically the second time he'd killed the man tonight.

If he'd come back once, could he come back again?

Jed had no idea, but he figured the safest solution was probably to destroy the body completely. What he needed to do was run out to the torture shed and fetch back either the chainsaw or an axe and do it fucking fast before the dead man could rejuvenate again. Or, no . . . kerosene. Yes, that was the answer. Douse the shed in it and burn up all the evidence.

He was still thinking about it when he heard the sound of the approaching car engine. It kept getting closer and louder, and he soon realized it must be Bubba Ray's old Chevelle. He was the only one of the boys who made a habit of parking his vehicle around back of the house.

Goddammit. Just what I needed.

Out of all of them, he'd fully expected Bubba Ray to be out much later into the night, but instead he was back, arriving at the worst possible moment. If the boy came into the shed, he'd have to kill him too.

Grabbing a rag from a nearby table, Jed wiped blood from his face and went to the door, opening it a tiny crack to peek outside.

BRYAN SMITH

TWENTY-TWO

NO MATTER HOW HARD HE tried to remove it, the pumpkin would not come off his head. Cletus gave it his best effort, attempting to dig his fingers under the bottom edge, but it'd drawn tight around his neck, like a noose pulled by an invisible hand. At first his mind rebelled against his initial impression that it'd become part of his flesh by some supernatural process. Though he'd never been in love with the face he'd been born with, having had every word synonymous with ugly directed at him countless times, at least it was his own, natural face. Until tonight, it'd always been his choice whether to show or hide it, but it seemed that was no longer the case and it terrified him.

There was irony in this because a part of him had always longed to be a monster like in the movies. Not just some ordinary killer, as he already was one of those, but a strange and fearsome creature with uncanny abilities. A forest-dwelling thing of legend that emerged into populated areas to stalk and take human prey when it needed to feed. A thing forever hunted but never captured, sort of like Bigfoot, but way freakier. This fantasy stemmed, in large part, from already being treated like a monster much of the time. If he couldn't make people, especially ladies, love or desire him, he wanted to at least be able to scare the bejesus out of them.

That didn't mean he wanted some mysterious ghoul altering his DNA with dark magic. A fantasy was just a fantasy, a temporary flight of fancy, something he could take comfort in when feeling low. He could put it out of his mind whenever he grew tired of it, as he sometimes did.

This was different.

It felt permanent.

At last he was forced to accept that the hole he'd cut in the pumpkin days ago to slide it over his head no longer existed because it'd fused with the flesh of his neck. In frustration, he banged a fist against the mirror in the Pump N' Go's bathroom, creating several new cracks in the already fractured reflective glass. He made one last attempt to pull it off, straining with every bit of desperate strength he could summon, but it was as useless as all the previous attempts.

"*Fuck!*"

The pumpkin was no longer a removable foreign object. It was a part of his head, a new outer layer of rippled orange flesh with strangely shaped eyes and large, jagged teeth. He tried moving his mouth and in the broken mirror glass saw the pumpkin teeth go up and down, at which point he realized the shape of his mouth had also changed.

Cletus felt like crying.

His brothers had already teased him about the pumpkin, calling him nasty for continuing to wear the rotting thing over his head day after day nearly a week after he'd carved out its insides. How much worse would the ribbing get if he couldn't remove it? Even more concerning, what would happen when they finally realized it'd become a part of him?

Shit, he knew the answer to that.

They'd probably cut his head off.

The worst part about it was he wouldn't be able to blame them. How could anyone live comfortably with a supernatural monster in their midst? Who knew what he might do or how else he might change?

Cletus jumped when the door to the bathroom creaked open and Beau peeked in at him.

He gave Cletus a squinty, puzzled look. "You about done in here?

Was startin' to think you fell in the damn toilet."

Cletus laughed nervously. "I'm comin'. Think that was the longest piss of my life."

Beau gave his brother a longer look of confused appraisal. His eyes were bleary from all the beer and he was leaning on the doorframe in part to hold himself up, but even drunk as hell, it seemed he could tell something wasn't quite right with Cletus, something beyond even the usual stuff.

"Why you lookin' at me like that?"

The question popped out and Cletus regretted it right away, believing it'd only enhance any fuzzy impression of something amiss.

Beau gave him the same confused look again, then pushed away from the doorframe with a groan of drunken exertion. "No reason. Let's get on down to the Juke and Puke. Thought I'd pass out in the damn truck waitin' for ya."

And with that, he turned and lurched away from the open door.

The feeling of relief that swept through Cletus ran so deep it briefly made him feel lightheaded, forcing him to grab hold of the sink. He walked out of the bathroom as soon as he felt he could do so without falling over.

Beau had Ol' Rustbucket in gear and was already starting to roll away from the front of the gas station even as Cletus was climbing in. They'd gone not even the length of a football field down the road when Cletus realized the time he'd spent freaking out in the bathroom was long enough for his bladder to start feeling the strain again. He squeezed his legs together and did his best not to squirm. Harley Toad's Juke and Puke wasn't far. He could hold it until after they got there. Asking Beau to pull over again was emphatically *not* an option this time.

In a weird way, the persistence of this basic biological function comforted him. It was proof that despite the change he'd undergone he was still essentially human. As best he could tell, the transformation was limited to the pumpkin becoming part of his head.

Another source of hope was an idea that came to him as they neared the roadhouse. Was it possible his transformation was temporary? Something this weird and spooky happening right on the cusp of the clock ticking over to Halloween was a mighty big coincidence. Maybe after Halloween the spell, or whatever, would revert itself, restoring him to a fully human state. He had nothing solid to base this supposition, but he saw no good reason not to hope for it.

Grabbing another beer from the floor, he popped the tab on it and tried his damnedest to put the matter out of his mind, telling himself he should only worry about it if Halloween came and went with no hint of reversal occurring. He inserted his straw and started slurping the warm brew down, draining most of it by the time Beau steered the old pickup down the narrow road in the woods that led to Harley Toad's Juke and Puke.

Less than a minute later, they arrived at the roadhouse. Out front was a big parking lot. It was around two-thirds full. Inside was a large bar area with adjacent spaces for billiards and live music performances. The performance stage had chicken wire nailed up around it to shield musicians from bottles and cans chucked at them by inebriated patrons. Above the entrance was a custom neon sign of a giant toad. The neon lit up in a repeating pattern that made the toad look like it was vomiting up some load of toxic yellow goop over and over.

Beau parked the ancient F1 a couple of rows back from the entrance. Before getting out of the truck, he did a sloppy line of cocaine off the back of his hand, snorting it up with a rolled-up dollar bill. He offered some to Cletus, who declined by holding up his nearly empty can of beer to indicate his preference. He feared having a pumpkin for a head might make the mechanics of inhaling the powder difficult in a way he wouldn't be able to explain. Not without revealing what he'd become, anyway.

Beau didn't give a shit.

Not having to share meant more for him.

He did another line and they got out of the truck, then started staggering toward the front of the building, seeing evidence of the joint's well-earned reputation for wanton debauchery before they were inside. Off to Cletus's right, a blonde woman with big titties was going at it with two men between two giant late-model pickup trucks. One man was giving it to her from behind while the woman was bent over and sucking the dick of the other man in front of her. This was not an unusual sight in the parking lot of the Juke and Puke.

Another man, the next row up, was splayed out on the ground. His face was bloody and there was broken glass on the pavement in the vicinity of his head. At a glance, Cletus couldn't tell whether the man was dead or unconscious. Either way, he didn't care. All he gave a shit about was getting inside the Juke and Puke where his first order of business would be to take another long-ass piss. After that he would recommence the serious work of getting as sloshed as humanly possible.

Once inside, no one paid much mind to the unusual headgear that was also now his actual head. This was because he was here often wearing some form of face or head covering. People recognized him by his tall, lanky build. He was a Mitchell, and in this part of Montclair that meant he was not to be fucked with in any egregious way if you had aspirations of remaining above ground.

After Cletus drained his bladder again in the bathroom, he returned to the bar area and located the table Beau had claimed for them. There were two young women with him. One was a lady in tight jeans and a buckskin fringe jacket Cletus recognized as Deanna Burton. Deanna was sitting in Beau's lap with one arm slung over his shoulder. Beau had a hand up high on one of her thighs, which she didn't seem to mind.

This was curious because Deanna, while a rural local in good standing at the Juke and Puke, was a higher-class gal than Beau was ordinarily able to corral. Her flowing mane of glossy black hair that hung almost to her waist was especially striking. While Beau wasn't the ugliest son of a bitch ever to walk the earth—compared to Cletus he was a dreamboat—his lax attitude toward personal hygiene meant he normally got stuck with ladies on the lower end of the attractiveness spectrum. The little smear of white powder under one nostril struck Cletus as a good clue as to how he'd lured in Deanna and her friend.

The other woman sitting on the opposite side of the little round table was at least Deanna's equal in the looks department. Cletus had never seen her before, either here in the Juke and Puke or anywhere else. He was positive because this was not the kind of woman you could glance at and forget. She was a leggy blonde in tan cotton shorts and a lacy black top. A lot of jewelry adorned her slender wrists and fingers, more rings and shiny bangles than he'd ever seen any single person wear at one time. She had a face of such pronounced prettiness it stirred an instant feeling of unease in Cletus as he approached the table. This was exactly the kind of woman who crossed the street to avoid him.

His normal impulse upon encountering a lady of such high quality was to go into his freaky creep routine, but he had a hunch Beau would be none too pleased with him if he were to try anything like that now. The stern look on his brother's face confirmed this.

The stern look turned into a smirk. "Boy, you sitting the fuck down or what?"

Deanna tossed her head back and laughed like she'd never heard anything so funny. She took a swig from a longneck bottle of Pabst Blue Ribbon and gave Cletus an amused once-over, eyebrows raised as she looked him up and down. "Little early for Halloween dress-up, ain't it?"

"It's practically Halloween now," the other woman put in. "Midnight isn't far off."

Deanna rolled her eyes as she took another swig of PBR. "Yeah, technically, but the Spook Bash ain't until tomorrow night." She gave Cletus another pointed, eyebrow-waggling look. "Dumb to show up in your costume before then. It's like the party version of premature ejaculation."

Beau sighed. "Hey, now, come on, be nice. You know the boy's kinda . . . special. He's been wearing that thing for days." He chuckled but eyed Cletus in that stern, warning way again. "Boy, I done told you to sit your ass down."

Until then, Cletus was not fully aware of having come to a complete stop just short of the table. The way his pumpkin face flushed with heat might have served as another source of embarrassment, but he was pretty sure the new dark orange shade of his flesh hid the blush. The thing was, he didn't know how to act around women like these two when they weren't trying to run away from him.

Seeing that Beau was about a second from rebuking him in a more aggressive way, Cletus pulled out the only remaining empty chair at the table and plopped down in it. He was on the same side of the table as the woman he didn't recognize, with only a few feet of separation. It came as no surprise when she leaned away from him, putting as much distance between them as she could without actually moving her chair.

Cletus dug his crumpled drinking straw from his hip pocket, the same straw he'd been using all night, and inserted it in the bottle of Miller High Life Beau had ordered for him while he was in the bathroom. He inserted it between the jagged teeth of his pumpkin mouth and began to slurp beer.

The blonde woman gave him a look that conveyed confusion mixed with mild disapproval. The bangles on her wrists jingled when she scooted her chair a few inches farther away from him. "Why are you drinking beer through a straw?"

Cletus shrugged and said nothing.

He slurped more beer.

The blonde gaped at him a moment before exchanging a wordless look with Deanna. A second later, both women gathered their purses and rose from the table. Beau looked close to blowing his top when that happened, leveling a look of simmering rage at his brother for possibly scuttling his chance at scoring with top-shelf pussy. Then Deanna bent down and whispered something in his ear. Whatever it was appeared to soothe Beau because he immediately broke out into a big smile, then reached around and clapped her on the butt, which elicited a yelp and a giggle. Deanna then made a sniffing gesture with a finger held against one side of her nose.

She also raised an eyebrow.

Beau patted the front pocket of his coat. "Got ya covered, doll. Hurry back and we'll keep this party goin'."

Deanna gave him a peck on the cheek, then she and her friend waltzed off, disappearing into the throng of rowdy drinkers.

As soon as they were out of sight, Beau leaned across the table and spoke in a low, urgent tone. "Look, man, I know you can't altogether help it, but try to dial the awkward shit back a notch or two. That other gal's an out-of-towner. Dee found her in a bar in Birmingham last night. She's a college gal there."

Cletus frowned as he slurped more beer. "What's a lady from Birmingham doing way to hell and gone in Montclair?"

Beau smirked. "Dee used her powers of persuasion. Raved all about the annual Spook Bash, how it puts any big city Halloween party to shame."

Cletus nodded. "And she got suckered right in."

Beau grinned. "That's about the size of it. Dee talked up the Juke and Puke, making it out to be a bucket list kind of thing for those in the know, the kind of place that has to be experienced at least once in a lifetime, especially on Halloween."

Cletus smiled.

For a high percentage of out-of-towners, once in a lifetime was all they ever got when visiting the Juke and Puke.

They'd finished their beers by the time Deanna and the college lady from Birmingham returned from their trip to the bathroom. Beau sprinkled another sloppy line of white powder on the table and shared it with Deanna. The college girl declined at first when offered some but acquiesced after only a token bit of badgering from Deanna and Beau. Cletus declined the inevitable offer that came his way, once again to avoid closer scrutiny of the changes he'd undergone.

Several more rounds of rowdy drinking ensued, with everyone at the table loosening up as it continued. This included the college girl, whose name turned out to be Eleanor.

The booze-up went on in the same good-natured fashion until Beau finished a glass of whiskey-soda and spoke directly to Deanna's guest. "What do you say, Elle, you like this place? Gotta be kind of . . . rustic for a big city gal such as yourself."

Eleanor responded with loud, sloppy laughter. "I wouldn't call Birmingham a big city."

Beau snorted. "It is compared to the likes of Montclair."

Eleanor gulped more of her vodka slushie drink. "I guess. It's bigger than I expected. Pretty wild, too, though I don't know if it's quite as Sodom and Gomorrah as Dee made it out to be. Little disappointed on that count, to be honest. I was picturing nonstop orgies."

Beau was still looking straight at her. "Well, now that we know you're cool, I'll let you in on a little secret."

Cletus felt his pumpkin smile curve and widen slightly.

Here we go.

Eleanor's brow furrowed. "Oh? And what would that be?"

Beau leaned closer and dropped his voice to a conspiratorial whisper. "The real party's happenin' downstairs. It's invite only. Exclusive access. You think it's wild up here? This shit's naptime at the old folks home compared to what's goin' on in the Sin Den."

Eleanor frowned. "The Sin Den? Seriously?"

"That's what they call it."

She pursed her lips. "Okay, so what goes on in the Sin Den?"

"The craziest shit you could ever imagine," Deanna chimed in. "Stuff like you ain't never seen, not even in a movie."

Eleanor's eyes flicked toward Deanna for a second, then a small smile tugged at the edges of her mouth. "Well, I'm down, assuming you're not pulling my leg."

Beau cackled, leaning back in his chair. "Someone might pull your leg tonight, doll, but it won't be me."

Eleanor laughed, too, in that loud, sloppy way from earlier.

It would be one of the last times she ever laughed at anything.

TWENTY-THREE

THE WORK OF PUTTING IN motion Loretta's ambitious foray into experimental corpse reanimation took a while. First they had to remove all the equipment they'd acquired earlier in the evening from the Chevelle and get it all arranged according to her plan. This involved getting the car batteries connected via the industrial-grade power strips and running multiple heavy-duty extension cords into the house.

Then came the remainder of the surgical work with the corpses. The focus of the first stage of this process was removing the head of one of Bubba Ray's dead girlfriends with the hacksaw and replacing it with the fresher head of the homecoming queen. Sewing severed heads onto bodies to which they did not originally belong required far more finesse than Bubba Ray could manage even when he was stone sober. At this particular juncture in time, he was a dozen beers deep, and so it was a given that the job of suturing the body pieces together would fall to Loretta.

Bubba Ray's cousin wasn't sober either, but her fingers were smaller and defter and she did have some small level of skill with a needle and thread. She was a far cry from anything like an expert in the area of repairing human bodies, but she made up for her lack of knowledge with a high level of enthusiasm. To her credit, when she pronounced the first head transplant finished, the homecoming queen's head did appear solidly connected to the body of the girlfriend Bubba Ray had selected for the procedure. That's not to say her head looked natural on the body of the dead college girl, who'd been older than the homecoming queen by a few years. It did not. For one thing, the homecoming queen was freshly demised, whereas the college girl was three days dead. The contrast in flesh tone was stark. Also, while the homecoming queen had been pretty, the juxtaposition of the head of a girl in late adolescence attached to the body of a fully grown woman was a bit jarring. Not that this would put Bubba Ray off fucking her Frankenstein-ed brains out, because it emphatically would not.

At Loretta's direction, Bubba Ray stretched the body of the first of his reconfigured girlfriends out on the picnic table near the minicamper. Because he'd been away from her all night, he allowed himself a few moments to refamiliarize himself with the terrain of the already well-explored body. His hand roved all over the beautiful torso. He felt the expected tingles of arousal but it was tempered by the presence of more bugs crawling on the graying flesh than he'd noticed earlier in the day.

His confidence in Loretta's ability to restore life to this body remained low. He wanted to believe it was possible, but he couldn't see how because his lack of formal learning didn't mean he was a total idiot. There were obvious flaws in his cousin's scheme. She had sewn flesh to flesh. It was a thing almost anyone with the stomach for it could do with enough patience. What Loretta could not do was reconnect or repair delicate arteries and nerve endings. She couldn't fuse spinal columns. Hell, under these primitive conditions, performing all the intricate microsurgical work necessary would be beyond the skills of even the world's finest medical professionals.

On the other hand, she wasn't relying solely on her crackpot version of science to bring about resurrection. The real impetus behind this endeavor boiled down to magic and superstition. Bubba Ray was pretty sure that thinning of the veil between worlds on Halloween business was something she'd heard on some TV show. Maybe it derived from actual supernatural lore, but that didn't make it credible. Not that his lack of genuine belief mattered much. He was just along for the ride. If by some wild chance this insane exercise in weird science produced the desired results, well, that'd be one hell of a trippy bonus.

The original plan called for popping the brain of the homecoming queen's boyfriend into the skull of the second of Bubba Ray's two dead girlfriends, but that aspect of it fell to the wayside following the boyfriend's failed attempt to come to the homecoming queen's rescue. It was Bubba Ray's fault for bashing the boy's brains in with a little too much enthusiasm. Loretta briefly considered using a portion of the scrambled gray matter, but in the end she deemed the lumpy, bloody bit that remained unsuitable to their purposes. It'd been "compromised," rendered "unviable."

Where an elementary school dropout like Loretta had learned a word like "unviable," lord only knew. Maybe it was another TV thing.

Whatever the case, she was dead set on seeing her resurrection scheme through to the end. The ruination of the boyfriend's brain was only a minor setback, because having taken Maureen Trimble's torso away from the site of the wreck meant they already had a Plan B candidate to fall back on.

The second of the night's head transplant operations involved sawing off the heads of Maureen and dead girlfriend number two. Removing Maureen's head with the hacksaw turned into quite an interesting experience. Loretta had stripped the half-woman's top from her torso, exposing the large, luscious breasts. She took them in her hands, gripping the dead flesh tight and pressing down while Bubba Ray worked with the saw. By the time he got to the halfway point of cutting through Maureen's neck, Loretta had a mischievous grin on her face. Bubba Ray paused in his sawing as he watched his crazy cousin lick and suck on the dead woman's nipples. His dick got so hard he thought it might bust through his pants. He began to rise with the intention of removing them to free his throbbing boner. Whether to stick it in Loretta's mouth or titty-fuck the half-woman, he did not know, but he really wanted to stick it *somewhere*.

He'd assumed Loretta would be down for that, knowing her taste for sick and perverted shit in general, but she slapped him and yelled at him to get back to work, saying they were running out of time. She said he could get his freak on later, swearing it would be worth the wait. While he wasn't sure what she meant by running out of time—they had all the time in the world, as far as he could tell—he decided once again to restrain the urge to lash out at her. Maybe later, after all this crazy shit was over, he'd finally put her in her place.

Or not.

Because another thing he was struggling with was that a part of him kind of liked the aggressive demeanor she evinced toward him, maybe even found it . . . exciting. So he muttered a curse and got back to work with the saw. At the same time, Loretta resumed her necro-erotic manipulations of Maureen's impressively large titties. While he continued to saw as instructed, her actions again proved quite distracting. He was able to finish removing the half-woman's head, but his cut wasn't quite as straight and clean as what he'd managed with the homecoming queen.

While Loretta busied herself with sewing Maureen's head onto the body of dead girlfriend number two, Bubba Ray took the severed heads of both of his dead girlfriends into the mini-camper to store them in a cabinet. While he understood the concept of needing viable brains for the reanimation attempt, he lamented the loss of his girlfriends in their original form. Their bodies were beautiful, but so were their faces.

Once he was inside the mini-camper, he couldn't resist taking the opportunity to spend some quality time with the heads before storing them in the cabinet. He reclined with them on his bed, alternating making out with each of them, which was as enjoyable as he'd anticipated, despite the occasional need to spit out a bug. He got so worked up he again felt tempted to take out his throbbing dick and rub it all over their faces, refraining only because he knew Loretta would not approve. She wanted him to save his ardor for when the time was right, whenever the hell that was. In the meantime, he was getting the goddamnedest case of blue balls he'd ever experienced.

He jumped in surprise when Loretta screamed at him to come on back outside. One of the heads slipped from his grip and thumped to the floor. He was bending over to scoop it up when Loretta screamed at him again, sounding angrier than the first time.

"All right, hold your damn horses!" he yelled back at her.

Giving each succulent pair of blue lips one last kiss, he stored them in the cabinet and went back outside, noting that Loretta appeared to have finished attaching Maureen's head to body number two. The symmetry was a bit more off in this case, owing in part to his sloppier cut with the hacksaw. It was also because Maureen had been a woman proportionately larger than girlfriend number two, taller and bigger-framed. Evidently a fair amount of flesh stretching had gone into making it work (to the extent that it did). Even with a surgically precise cut, the older woman's head would not have looked quite right atop its new body. Instead, the head was attached at a weirdly cocked angle, an unfortunate perception that became more prominent when, at Loretta's direction, Bubba Ray propped girlfriend number two up in a sitting position.

A sneer of disgust curled Loretta's lips. Then she sighed and shook her head. "Bitch looks like she broke her neck slam-dancing. Whatever-the-fuck. Best I can do. Get her up on the table with the other one, tubby."

Bubba Ray did as instructed, laying her out on the surface of the picnic table alongside the body of girlfriend number one, arranging the bodies so they were pointed in opposite directions.

After that, they went about the work of connecting the car batteries to the corpses with multiple sets of jumper cables, using two sets of cables for each body. They attached one set of cables to the ankles of each body, while the second set was clamped to the industrial-sized screws driven into each side of the necks of the reattached heads. The screws were a nod to the inspiration for Loretta's experiment, the old film version of *Frankenstein* starring Boris Karloff. Because the batteries were already charging, they started sending a current of electricity to the bodies as soon as the cables were attached. The low current was priming the bodies for the big jolt still to come.

Once she was satisfied with the preparations, Loretta fished two dripping-wet cans of Coors Light from the Styrofoam cooler Bubba Ray kept outside the mini-camper. She tossed one to him and popped the tab on the other, taking an immediate big swig as foam dribbled out around the opening. That first swig was followed by a longer, deeper one, her throat moving as she guzzled with her head tilted back. She continued until she'd drained the entire can, at which point she crushed the empty, tossed it over her shoulder, and belched like a frat boy at his first kegger.

Bubba Ray hadn't even opened his can yet.

Loretta scowled as she snatched it from him. "What's the matter, pussy? Don't feel like drinkin'?" She popped the tab and downed the beer nearly as quickly as the first one, smirking as she tossed the second empty over her shoulder. "What about fuckin' me? Ya feel like doin' that?"

Bubba Ray gulped. "Yes, ma'am."

Her laugh then had an edge of mockery. "Are you sure? You don't wanna play hard to fuckin' get like usual?"

He shook his head. "I do not."

More of that mocking laughter. "Well, too bad, bitch." She waggled an admonishing forefinger at him. "No pussy for you until after the main event."

Bubba Ray groaned. "Well, shit, what are we waiting for? Go on and throw the switch."

Loretta took two more cans of Coors Light from the cooler and again tossed one to Bubba Ray. "Because it ain't time yet, tubby."

Bubba Ray opened his beer. "When's it gonna be time?"

The mocking twist to Loretta's features gave way to an expression of surprising earnestness. "We'll want to do it right at the stroke of midnight," she said, glancing at her wrist like a person checking the time, only there was no watch there. "That's just under twenty minutes from now."

Bubba Ray frowned.

He considered saying something about the invisible watch but decided not to open that can of worms. That she wasn't right in the head was something he'd already known. If she was seeing things that weren't there, it could hardly be called surprising.

"This have anything to do with that veil between the worlds thinning business you were on about earlier?"

She nodded, sipping beer. "Yep. I know you think nothin' will happen, but you'll see for yourself soon. When the midnight hour arrives and we flip that switch, the dead will rise. I guarantee it."

Bubba Ray grunted. "How can you be so sure?"

She shrugged, spreading her hands. "I've been taught some things, but it's also the kind of thing that can't be properly explained with words. You have to see. You have to *feel*. I can already feel that dark energy that gets strong at this time of year gathering around us, ripening to its maximum potential as the evening cools and the minutes slide toward midnight."

Bubba Ray gaped at her, not knowing what to say.

He'd never heard her talk like that. She sounded almost like a stranger, like some wayward spirit inhabiting his cousin's body.

They sat at the picnic table with their backs to the stretched-out bodies, lapsing into silence as they sipped more beer and waited for the final minutes before midnight to slip away. The wait was still going on by the time Bubba Ray finished his beer, which he'd been nursing. He was right on the verge of going to the cooler to fetch another when Loretta abruptly jumped to her feet and said, "It's time, motherfucker."

Bubba Ray didn't ask for clarification. She could only mean one thing. He got to his feet and hovered in the vicinity of the picnic table while Loretta took up a position next to the portable transformer and again checked the nonexistent watch on her left wrist. Her mouth moved soundlessly for a few moments as she continued to stare at it.

Then she pointed at Bubba Ray and said, "Count back from ten."

Bubba Ray hesitated only the barest fraction of a second before beginning the count. The instant it reached zero, Loretta flipped the switch on the transformer, triggering a palpable sizzle of energy accompanied by an audible hum of powerful current. In another moment, the screws embedded in the necks of their subjects began to glow a steely blue. Shortly after that, the bodies started to visibly vibrate. Bubba Ray's heart raced as he watched this happen. Loretta was right about at least one thing, he could feel the shift of energy in the air, a building charge that had started even before she'd switched on the transformer.

Something was happening, something beyond the mere flow of electrical current. A presence had arrived, passing through that thin veil into this world, imbuing the thrumming current with dark magic.

Then, in the precise same instant, both bodies on the picnic table sat bolt upright.

Bubba Ray gasped aloud in startled fright and stumbled backward, tripping over his feet and dropping heavily to the ground.

Loretta spread her arms wide and turned her head to the sky, cackling with mad glee.

From the cracked door of the moonshine shed, Jed Mitchell observed with keen interest.

TWENTY-FOUR

THE THINGS JED SAW HIS nephew and his brother's daughter get up to that night astonished him. As a man who'd stumbled into creating a powerful age regression potion earlier that same evening, this was no small feat. A potion, by the way, he'd created with the noble intention of extending the life of a beloved elder family member, a man he later killed. Twice. A man whose blood he'd greedily slurped from his severed jugular like a ravenous vampire.

In other words, he'd seen some shit.

Some real fucked up shit.

And yet still, he was taken aback by much of what he witnessed while spying through the cracked door of the moonshine shed. First there'd been the messy way they'd gone about murdering the young couple they'd abducted. They were fortunate one or both of them hadn't managed to slip away into the woods. If he hadn't been out there to warn them of the boy coming out of the Chevelle's trunk with that tire iron, things might have gone south in a hurry. They were able to avert disaster, but just barely.

Having returned to the shed by that point, Jed felt compelled to continue observing them in hopes they would soon finish their business and retire to the mini-camper. He had serious matters of his own to sort out and was impatient for the chance to get on with it. The problem was that as long as Bubba Ray and Loretta were around he wouldn't feel comfortable leaving the shed unattended long enough to retrieve the items he needed to get started. He could order Bubba Ray not to poke his head in for a look-see and the boy would probably respect this decree. He was rambunctious and sometimes a source of great irritation, but he'd always been good about adhering to the few rules Jed imposed as a condition of keeping his mini-camper parked on his property.

Loretta was another matter entirely.

She was the definition of a wild card. If she heard Jed tell Bubba Ray to stay out of the shed, she'd almost certainly bust in as soon as he was out of sight. In that event, all bets would be off. Bubba Ray would wonder why his uncle had sought to keep the grim fate of his cousins hidden. The mere act of trying to hide it would severely erode the believability of any cover story he might concoct.

No, he was stuck.

He had to remain right where he was until they were gone, keeping them out by bodily force if necessary.

His aggravation grew along with his astonishment as he continued to watch them. He'd figured the removal of heads and reattachment to different bodies would be the extent of the "Frankenstein shit," but it turned out that was only phase one of a far more insane overall plan. He began to get the bigger picture once they attached the jumper cables to the bodies. They meant to jolt those days-dead corpses back to life with electricity, or at least attempt to do so.

Jed couldn't help chuckling at the stupidity of it all. If the reanimation of corpses was that simple, people would've been doing it for centuries. That these two weren't the sharpest tools in the box wasn't a revelation. The good news, as he saw it, was their Frankenstein experiment would soon fail, at which point they'd hopefully go off and do something else.

What he hadn't counted on was the strange shift in the atmosphere outside. It happened as the deranged duo took a long break following the completion of their reanimation preparations. As the minutes dragged on and they talked and drank, Jed's frustration grew exponentially worse. The rage built to such a point he entertained the idea of killing them. He could march back into the house real fast-like, grab a few more shells for his shotgun, then come right back out and blow them away.

He hadn't contemplated yet more acts of family murder up until that point, but the idea held no small amount of appeal. What the hell, he'd already killed three of his kin in one night, so why stop there? He could go off on a whole spree, slaughtering as many other Mitchells as he could. A once unthinkable notion, but, again, why not? He'd been an object of scorn among such a large faction of the clan for a long time.

Maybe the time had finally come around to make some people pay.

To make *everybody* pay.

The idea was abandoned as soon as he felt the charge of strange energy in the cooling air outside. That it was a product of something not quite natural was obvious immediately. It was palpable even from his hidden position behind the door.

When they turned the transformer on, he felt the hum of strong electric current deep in his bones, but that was of minor significance compared to the growing occult energy. Jed had done a lot of, let's face it, morally questionable things in his time, including many acts of brutal, sadistic murder, but that was the work of a man imposing his will over another human being. It was of the natural world. This unknown power his niece and nephew were tapping into felt like it was from somewhere beyond this world, and it scared the hell out of him. By the time the corpses on the picnic table sat up, he was not surprised.

In paranoia, he cast a glance behind him, half-expecting to find the corpses in the shed with him also reviving. The relief he felt when he saw they were not was immense.

By that point, it was clear to Jed his time of lurking in the shed was far from over because Bubba Ray and Loretta were only just beginning to play with their new toys.

~

When Elise Peterson opened her eyes to again look upon the world as a living creature, it was as if only seconds had passed since the fadeout of her consciousness. In reality, more than an hour had passed. Where she had gone during that time, she did not know. After the fadeout, there was nothing, at least not that she remembered. She'd gone into that nothing with the knowledge that she was dying, feeling the bleak, terrible reality of it right down to her core, in every atom of her body. Her life was ending. Blackness took her and she was gone.

Now, somehow, she was back.

The last moments before that black nothing came back to her with horrifying clarity. Being pinned against the outside of that shed by that meth-crazed hillbilly bitch, feeling powerless, too weak and wounded to fight back any more than she already had. The knife inside her, that big wedge of solid steel, going in and out of her flesh three final times, each deep penetration feeling like it was going all the way through her body. That girl's mouth warm against her ear, tongue teasing the inner part of it as she whispered that awful madness about how as her killer she owned her soul and would not allow her to go down to hell like she deserved.

"You're coming back as my slave, whore," was the last thing she heard.

Elise hadn't believed her.

She was being murdered and there was nothing she could do about that, but she'd gone into the dark confident the hillbilly's psychotic ravings were a pile of baseless nonsense. Only now it seemed she'd been dead wrong because she was back in the little clearing behind the backwoods house. Everything was as she remembered, except instead of bleeding out onto the ground she was sitting up on a picnic table. Her hillbilly tormentors were standing nearby, eyeing her with grins of sadistic glee.

At first she thought these images were a tiny blip, a surreal and illusory last false glimpse of the world conjured by a failing brain fighting against its imminent loss of viability. A literal brain fart that would vanish in another second or two, after which the dark nothing would reclaim her.

After several more seconds passed with no hint of anything of the sort happening, she began to panic. She had died, really died, and now she'd returned, just as the crazy hillbilly chick had promised. The cool air against her face was real, not illusory, as was the breath going in and out of her body and the seemingly thunderous beating of her heart. At first she was glad to be alive again despite still being in the clutches of her killers, but then she realized something was . . . off.

She frowned as she glanced down at her chest and saw that her breasts were unquestionably bigger than they'd been before her death. Much of the terrain of her body in general was unfamiliar, seemingly more fully developed, more like that of a sumptuously proportioned grownup woman. Her face twisted in terrified confusion as it came to her that the body she now inhabited was not her body. Even more disturbing was the gray shade of the flesh, which somehow seemed to be alive and decomposing at the same time.

Dead/alive, she thought, *dead/alive!*

As disorienting as this revelation was, it was a mere prelude to what was coming because in the next instant she at last sensed the presence of another person next to her on the picnic table. She turned her head and saw the face of the forty-something woman the hillbillies had pulled out of the car wreck. The older woman's head was also connected to a body that was not originally her own. In fact, it appeared to have been imperfectly attached to the body of a much younger girl, a body that looked a lot like . . .

Elise gasped in horror.

Like mine. It looks like my body because it is my body.

She opened her mouth wider and screamed.

The woman who now had her body also screamed.

The hillbillies slapped their thighs and laughed in uproarious fashion. In between the gales of delirious laughter, they pointed at the resurrected women and made mocking remarks. Elise's brain railed at her as she watched this unhinged display of grotesque, inhuman derision

Run! Do it now, while you still fucking can!

She swung her legs over the side of the table and lowered herself to the ground. Her legs felt weak and unsteady as she took a few halting steps, the jumper cable clamps tugging at her ankles and at the sides of her neck before coming loose. It wasn't just that her legs felt weak, though. While she had sensation in her partly decomposed limbs, the feeling was distant. Dead nerve endings were reawakening, but they were taking their time about it. It was a thing she feared could hinder any attempt to run.

As it turned out, her will to flee was a non-factor.

The hillbilly bitch stepped close and uttered a single word in a tone of absolute, undeniable authority: "Stop."

Elise stopped.

She didn't want to, tried her damnedest to make her new, longer legs keep moving, but she couldn't. That feeling of numb distance in her limbs continued to fade as sensation slowly returned, but that one word had immobilized her.

Elise sniffled, shaking her head. "No. No, no, no."

The hillbilly girl smiled. "Yes. You're my slave, just like I said you'd be. Now drop to your knees in front of me."

Elise dropped to her knees

The girl laughed. "Shit. It really fuckin' worked. That old witch lady from Hopkins Bend told me it would, but I don't think I believed her until fuckin' now."

Her boyfriend—or whatever the big guy was to her—showed her a confused look. "What old witch lady?"

The girl waved this off. "It don't matter. What does matter is the tons of motherfuckin' fun we're about to have."

And that was the beginning of a long night of humiliation and degradation for both Elise Peterson and Maureen Trimble. The hillbilly couple forced them to participate in seemingly every possible sexual combination three women and one man could manage together, the range of which went far beyond anything Elise would've imagined prior to her death. It went on for hours, with the guy allowing himself some recuperative periods to go at them again. During one of those periods, the hillbilly couple compelled Elise and Maureen to enthusiastically sixty-nine each for at least an hour. While that was happening, the rednecks guzzled more beer and indulged in more cruel mockery.

All the while, Elise told herself she had to make it through the night, to outlast the boundless appetite for sexual sadism her captors possessed. They were drinking so much it was bound to catch up to them sooner or later. If they didn't finally lose interest in humiliating them first, eventually they would pass out, possibly leaving Elise free to walk away.

Unless . . .

No.

She didn't even want that thought in her head, out of fear that allowing it to form might also lend the notion of a substance detectable to these vile people who held so much power over her.

Deep into the wee hours of the morning the degenerate couple at last began to run out of steam. There came an increasingly frequent series of deep, jaw-cracking yawns from each of them. After going at Maureen for at least a half-hour toward the end without managing to cum, the big male hillbilly pulled out and announced he was done for the night. His girl's response was another epic yawn. By then she was reclined on one of the picnic table's bench seats, her eyes looking all glassy as her head rolled about, an almost empty beer bottle on the verge of slipping from her fingers. She looked at her boyfriend—or whatever—and nodded. "Yeah, I'm done, too. Let's hit the fuckin' hay."

Elise again tried her best to suppress any conscious-level awareness of her intentions, but in the end it turned out the girl was pretty sharp in a way that was unaffected either by her obvious derangement or her epic alcohol consumption. She'd already had a plan in mind for what to do with her during any inevitable period of unconsciousness. The one called Bubba Ray took Maureen into the mini-camper to spend the night with them, contemplation of which sent a shudder of revulsion through Elise, who was surprised to find that even after all she'd endured, she could still be grossed out. That was still her body Maureen's weirdly tilted head was attached to. Seeing it walk up into the mini-camper with a naked Bubba Ray made her want to scream.

The hillbilly girl led her out to the back of the clearing where she tied her to a sturdy tree with a rope. Her breath smelled like an explosion at a brewery as she belched and leaned in close to whisper in her ear again, a grotesque intimacy that was a painful echo of the final moments of her original life.

"Stay right where you are," the girl whispered, slurring her words. "Don't you move from this fuckin' spot until I come fetch you come daylight."

Then she stumbled away and went into the mini-camper with Bubba Ray, shutting the door behind her.

Elise's eyes spilled over with tears as she soon realized she could not defy the spoken will of her new mistress. It was maddening because her bonds were not tight. Had she been in control of her own will, she believed it'd be easy to free herself and leave.

But she could do nothing but sit on the ground and weep.

She was still wide awake as the full dark of night began to shift toward gray dawn. This hyper-alertness functioned as an extra level of torment. With escape impossible, sleep would be welcome. She longed for a period of mental retreat, of faded awareness, but it stubbornly eluded her. This state endured for so long she began to wonder if she might no longer even be capable of sleep in this rejuvenated form. The notion horrified her.

She was still thinking about it when she became aware of the unnatural presence somewhere very close. Turning her head, she looked into the woods and saw a tall, slender form standing a few feet back.

DEPRAVED HALLOWEEN

Humanoid in form, but not human at all. This was something else, an elemental thing, a strange visitor from the other side of the veil between worlds. The creature was vaguely male in appearance, but even that she couldn't determine with any certainty. He stood so perfectly still Elise wondered if her eyes were playing tricks on her.

Then he came forward, moving out of the darker shadows of the woods and into the gray dawn. She looked up at him with a gasp of surprise, realizing at once that he was even taller than she'd imagined, eight feet or better. His frame was skeletally thin, and his smooth and hairless head was bulbously large at the top, his face long and almost featureless, tapering away to a pointed jaw. The creature's hands were more than twice the size of a normal man's hands, with long, tendril-like fingers. Elise belatedly realized they also had more than the normal allotment of fingers. A strange black cloak concealed much of the top half of his body. The material wasn't anything she recognized, though it resembled the Spanish moss she'd seen hanging from trees in Georgia. Only not green, obviously.

Elise rose to her feet and looked up at the creature as he came even closer, feeling nervous but strangely unafraid.

"Who are you? What are you?"

His mouth didn't move as he communicated his thoughts without speaking. Those thoughts entered her mind not as recognizable words, but as images, concepts, and feelings. These were arranged in such a way that she understood him perfectly despite the absence of traditional language. He was the God of Halloween, and he was here to give her a new purpose, a new shadow life as a night thing, but only if she desired it.

Elise was a little scared, finally, by that point, but she nodded as fresh tears welled in her eyes. "Yes, please. I'll do it. I'll do anything."

The creature's blank expression never changed as he raised one of his freakishly large hands and placed it over her face, curling those long, tendril-like fingers around her head.

TWENTY-FIVE

THE SMELL OF SOMETHING BURNING brought her out of a dream where she and Deputy Dalton were young lovers on the run. In the dream, she was in her late teens or early twenties, close to two decades younger than she was now. Her dream self looked exactly as she remembered from back then, that hot young thing who couldn't go anywhere without drawing tons of male attention, most of it unwanted. Dalton was also younger than his current age. He was better-looking, too, gifted with that almost unreal, plastic handsomeness of a daytime soap opera star, his hair lusher and wavier than in real life. The dream was about them being chased by professional assassins hired by her father, who wanted to shut them up before they could spill scandalous government secrets to the press.

Or something like that.

It was a dream. The whole thing got more jumbled up and incomprehensible as it went along, the way dreams so often do. As it ended, the assassins were on the verge of catching up to them. They'd run into a dead-end alley with no way out. There was a sound of gunfire and then blackness.

DEPRAVED HALLOWEEN

Jessica's nose twitched at the burning scent as she began to rise out of her dream state. It did not alarm her at first because she was preoccupied by fuzzy thoughts of confused angst. Tears came to her eyes at the thought of her lover possibly dying in a hail of gunfire, but the sense of anguish was undermined within seconds by the jarring recognition that she didn't actually love Dalton.

In fact . . . didn't she hate him?

Her nose twitched again as her eyes began to flutter open. Blurry light intruded, another indication that something had changed while she slept. That she'd slept at all was surprising given the physical discomfort of her bonds. The last she remembered, she'd been lying on her side in the dark, a helpless prisoner in more ways than one. As that silent time in the dark stretched on, she couldn't get away from her thoughts, which remained so frustrating and circular in nature, but it seemed that at some point her mind became overwhelmed and simply shut down. That her dreaming mind had cast Dalton as her tragic romantic interest in some twisted version of a Lifetime network TV movie was both upsetting and understandable. The real Dalton was a monster she would not hesitate to kill given the chance, but there was no escaping the uncomfortable truth that she'd been strongly attracted to him at first sight. Some lizard part of her sleeping brain still was, it seemed.

Squinting as the last foggy dregs of sleep cleared from her head, her vision came into focus and she got her first glimpse of the source of the burning smell. In the middle of the white-tiled floor was a small portable grill. It was filled with glowing charcoal. In addition to the burning smell, there was a sharp tang of lighter fluid in the air. Protruding from the coals was the handle of a fireplace poker.

A clacking of high heels preceded Jessica's sudden awareness of a shadow looming over her. She turned her head and looked up, saw Callie's nightmare face leering down at her. The deputy's rebellious wife had changed out of her simple green dress and into an outfit of tight latex, which included a shiny, form-fitting blue skirt and a black top with plunging cleavage. She also wore lace-up platform boots that made her look like a giant.

She smiled in her usual crooked way. "There you are, sleepyhead. Happy Halloween! Did you have sweet dreams?"

Jessica grimaced. "Not really."

Callie grunted. "Good. You don't deserve happy dreams."

Jessica didn't bother responding to that. She'd never done

anything to harm this woman or cause her offense. There was no logic behind the scorn and hostility, and she'd already been given ample reason to avoid any attempt to reason with her.

"Sit up, bitch. Be quick about it if you don't want to get stepped on." She stomped one of her platform boots on the floor and laughed. "Or maybe you'd like that, hmm? Some people do, you know."

Jessica groaned and sat up.

In the process of doing so, she realized something. Her hands were no longer behind her back. They were still locked in manacles, but now they were at the front of her body. The deep frown that came to her face at the moment of recognition made Callie giggle.

The confusion Jessica felt at this development troubled her for a moment. Even amid deep sleep, the physical manipulation necessary to switch the manacles from back to front should've awakened her, but she'd been entirely oblivious.

Then she realized the puzzle had an obvious solution. She'd been drugged, either via the disgusting meal she'd been forced to fully ingest or by needle. She felt rested the way she did after a full night's sleep, an insight that led to another revelation. This was no longer later in the evening on the night of her abduction. It was now the next day. That explained the exuberant "Happy Halloween" greeting, though with a face as wrecked as Callie's, every day was Halloween, in a way.

She kept that observation to herself.

Callie smirked. "Feeling more comfortable now?"

Jessica sighed. "I guess."

It was true enough in one sense. The position of her body was no longer so awkward. On the other hand, having been in the basement a while at this point, she needed to pee pretty badly, but that wasn't the worst of it. The worst was the tight, overstuffed feeling in her guts, a result of her forced venture into cannibalism.

Shitting out the digested remains of the woman she'd partly consumed was a thing that would have to happen soon.

Callie stomped a boot on the floor again, making her flinch. "I better hear some gratitude out of you." Her mangled smirk became more pronounced. "Or else."

Jessica suppressed a self-defeating impulse to say something mean about the woman's messed up face. It'd feel nice in a nasty way for a second, but she knew she'd be made to regret it almost instantly. "I do feel more comfortable now. Thank you."

Callie chuckled. "That's better. Now how about some compliments?" She struck a model-like pose. "Do you like my outfit? Do you think it's hot?"

Jessica nodded. "Yes."

Callie's fractured expression turned noticeably more severe as she came a step closer. "Yes you like it, or yes you think it's hot?"

"Both."

Callie tilted her head. "You're not just saying that, are you? Because I hate liars."

Jessica cleared her throat and spoke in the most earnest tone she could manage. "You have a nice body. I think you know that. Shiny, stretchy latex looks incredible on it."

A muffled outburst from the opposite wall intruded on their interaction. This sound was followed by a metallic clanking. Then even more muffled, indecipherable words.

Dalton was awake.

Jessica leaned slightly to one side to gaze at him, unable to help the little twitch of a smile that came to her lips. Her former tormentor's eyes were bugged open in an almost cartoonish way. The muscles in his arms and legs stood out like jittering live wires. He grunted and strained against his bonds but there was no give to them at all. The adjustments Callie had made to his chains prior to Jessica's long period of unconsciousness had not changed. His limbs were still splayed outward, his legs spread, arms flat and tight against the wall.

Callie flashed Jessica what might have been a playful smile before turning to her husband. "Oh, good, you're awake. How'd you sleep, honey? Did you have sweet dreams?"

Though her interaction with the reawakened deputy began as a replay of her exchange with Jessica, it soon unfolded in a drastically different direction as Callie donned leather gloves, grasped the fireplace poker by its handle, and removed it from the portable grill. The poker must have been embedded in the coals for a good while because its ornate head was a bright, glowing red. She touched its tip to the white tiles and dragged it along on the floor as she approached her husband in a hip-swaying strut. The tip of the poker etched a black, smoking line through the tiles.

Jessica's smile widened as she saw the man's eyes bug out even more cartoonishly. The temptation to taunt him in some cruel way was strong, but she resisted for the same reason she'd refrained from insulting Callie. This was her domain now and she was in charge. Any taunting that occurred would be done only by her.

The man's muffled protests of rage and terror grew louder as Callie stepped between his widely splayed legs. He continued frantic efforts to jerk free of his bonds, but they remained as ineffective as ever. Callie nudged his genitals with one of her platform boots. Jessica held her breath a moment, excitement building in her as she anticipated the woman rearing back and kicking him. She could almost hear the muffled squeal of agony he'd make. His dick and balls were flat against the floor, in perfect kicking position. Jessica was sure that was why Callie had arranged his limbs that way.

She was wrong, as she was about to find out.

Callie giggled. "There they are, your pride and joy. You've had so much fun using them on me and other women, mostly against our will. Well, honey, playtime has been canceled. You're done with all your fun. Forever."

She shifted position and dragged the glowing poker closer, more little wisps of smoke curling as it seared the tiles. The ornate loop of iron inches above the sharp point stopped less than an inch from the tip of the deputy's penis. The man's muffled screaming was louder than ever. He was screaming so hard it was stretching the thread Callie had used to sew his mouth shut.

Jessica understood now.

A slight wince creased her features, primitive sympathy instinct, but it was gone in an instant, her excitement building again in anticipation of bearing witness to maybe the most fitting case of pure, righteous justice she'd ever seen. She smiled as she studied the apocalyptic terror twisting the man's features. His chest was heaving and his face was turning red. Jessica's only worry was he might die of fright before his punishment could be administered.

Once again, she was wrong about that.

Callie pressed the point of the poker against the tip of her husband's penis. The deputy's next scream was his loudest by far. His face was now nearly as bright red as the poker itself. A couple of the thread sutures popped from the force of his screaming, a little trickle of blood spilling from the corner of his mouth. A smell of cooking meat wafted across the room. When Callie took the poker away, Jessica saw that the tip of the man's penis appeared to have melted to the floor. It now looked like a black nub of gooey tar.

Callie wasn't done.

DEPRAVED HALLOWEEN

She knelt down and slid the poker under what remained of his flaccid penis, triggering a fresh round of shrill screams as molten iron again touched flesh. As she lifted it off the floor, strands of the burned head stretched away like taffy. Another strong whiff of burning meat made the fine hairs in Jessica's nostrils tingle. The length of Dalton's smoldering cock drooped against the shaft of the poker, the flesh turning black at the edges. Callie held the poker in that same position for several more moments, glancing back at Jessica with what was unmistakably a grin of sheer delight. The emotion shone through so clearly that for a fleeting instant it was almost possible to see how pretty she'd been before Dalton had gone to work on her.

Jessica matched the expression.

Good for you, Callie. I mean it.

She did, too.

A time might soon come when her feelings about Callie would transition back to dread and terror, possibly even hatred, but at that moment, Jessica only thought of her as a perfect avenging angel.

More gooey threads of blackened flesh came away as Callie removed the poker from the underside of Dalton's cock and applied it to the top. Dalton was still screaming, but the sound was hoarsening from the sheer force of extreme vocal exertion. As his penis continued to cook and melt, he soon became incapable of screaming, reduced to a continuous, pitiful sobbing. His head lolled and his eyelids fluttered. He looked close to passing out from shock.

Then Callie used the point of the poker to pry his blackened cock free of his scrotum. His eyes snapped open again and he managed a gurgling scream as Callie stood up and swept the burnt remnant of his penis away from him. It went sliding across the white tiles, coming to a stop near where the now absent dog food bowl sat the previous evening. Jessica couldn't help grimacing at the closeup view of the little twist of smoking flesh. It looked like melted rubber. Her overstuffed guts clenched and she felt a sour tickle of bile in her throat.

Blood came gushing out of the new hole in Dalton's scrotum. Jessica thought he'd probably bleed out, but it turned out Callie still wasn't done with her husband. She pushed the poker into the hole. The cooking smell returned, along with more wisps of pungent smoke. Dalton sobbed and strained uselessly against the manacles holding him in place. Callie maintained the pressure of the poker against the scrotum, turning it this way and that as the process of cauterization continued. Once the hole was sealed, she applied the poker to his balls, maintaining firm pressure for several minutes with each one. The sac of ugly, wrinkly flesh took more time melting than the now destroyed shaft of his cock, but it did soon yield to the extreme heat. The blackened, gooey mess that remained when she was finished was scarcely recognizable as anything that'd once been a set of human genitals.

Callie raised the poker higher and touched the point to Dalton's mouth, making him squeal in fright. A nonstop stream of tears poured from his eyes as she carefully used the very tip of the tool to melt away the remaining bits of thread she'd used to seal his mouth. As soon as they were gone, instinct caused the deputy to gasp and open his mouth wide.

His wife smiled and rammed the poker in.

Dalton's body went instantly rigid as the molten length of iron invaded the interior of his mouth, his limbs twisting and twitching like those of a man in an electric chair after the switch had been thrown. Callie laughed as she watched him spasm and weep uncontrollably. She moved the poker around inside his mouth, making him hack and gag as streams of blood intermingled with drool and melting flesh spilled past his lips.

The whole time, she laughed and laughed, relishing every second.

Then, as her husband began to noticeably weaken, she gripped the handle of the poker in both hands and gave it a hard, upward shove, driving it into his brain. His body spasmed a final, violent time, then he went still.

Deputy Dalton was dead.

Jessica let out a breath she hadn't known she'd been holding. "Wow."

Callie left the poker lodged inside his mouth as she turned away from the corpse of her husband and strutted back over to the opposite side of the room. She didn't stop until she was standing directly above her one still living captive, so close the tips of her boots were touching Jessica's knees, forcing her to lean her head backward to peer up at her.

"Enjoyed that, did you?"

No point in lying.

"Yeah."

Callie grunted. "I get why, but I imagine you've guessed by now that I'm not letting you go."

Jessica didn't say anything to that. There was no need.

Callie stripped the leather gloves off and gently touched Jessica's face with the back of a hand, a gentle gesture that was an uncomfortable reminder of the way the woman's late husband had petted her like an animal the night before. "You belong to me now. Hearing about how fiercely you fought him and almost got away was the start of this, you know. The turning point. The reason I finally fought back. When he told me about that, I knew I needed to claim you for my own. You're also the most beautiful of all the women he kept here over the years, and there have been many."

Then Callie knelt in front of her. "I'll tell you a secret or two. Dalton tormented me without mercy for a long time. He was especially brutal in the early years, and for a long time, I dreamed of escape. I dreamed of being rescued. Dreamed of Dalton being punished, sent to jail forever, maybe even sentenced to death by a court of law. I hated him with every fiber of my being, and I had such pity for the other women he tortured here. Over time, though, he involved me in the cruel things he did to those women, made me an active participant in all of it. At first I did it only to survive, to keep from being hurt more than I already had, but, funny thing, after years of helping him torture women, I came to genuinely enjoy it. Maybe even more than him. See? Isn't that funny?"

Jessica didn't respond.

Callie raised a hand as if to strike her. "I asked you a question."

Silence wasn't an option this time, but Jessica chose to respond with honesty rather than obsequiousness. "I don't think it's funny at all."

She looked directly into Callie's eyes, holding her gaze without flinching.

Callie nodded. "You're right. It's not even a little funny. It's actually pretty fucked up, but it's the truth. Something else you should know. I was going to keep this a surprise, but since we're being honest and shit here, what the hell. I can't keep you."

These words caused a fresh stirring of unease. That was a statement that could imply anything from freedom to execution. Callie being what she was, Jessica wasn't inclined to believe it portended anything positive for her.

Callie chuckled. "I can almost see your thoughts. Here's the thing. Dalton was awful, but he gifted me with a great passion for a hobby I have no intention of abandoning. Unfortunately, I won't be able to keep doing it here in Montclair. Dalton wasn't just a cop, he was a member of one of the most powerful families in these parts. He can't just disappear. People will come around looking for him. Trying to pin his death on you is pointless because it'd involve revealing everything he was and that would be dangerous for me. Way too many ways of possibly incriminating myself without meaning to. The potential pitfalls are fucking limitless." She shook her head. "No. I have to leave town. Forever."

Jessica became exasperated as she listened to this. "Okay? So just fucking let me go." She huffed a breath. "There's no good reason you can't. I won't tell anyone about any of this shit. Look at me. Listen to my voice. After all you've done, I think you can tell when a person is lying. I have my reasons to stay silent, reasons that have nothing to do with anything you've done. I'm something of a fugitive myself. I've got people I'm trying to avoid. It's in my best interests to slip away and disappear. I swear to God, Callie."

Callie studied her face for a few silent moments.

Then she nodded. "Yeah, okay. I believe you. You're right. I can almost always tell when a person is lying. But it doesn't matter. I can't let you go because you're my ticket to a new life somewhere else."

Jessica frowned. "I don't understand."

Callie rose out of her crouch and again loomed directly above Jessica. "That's because you're not from around here. Later tonight I'll take you to the Spook Bash. That's the annual Halloween party at a lowdown sleazy roadhouse called Harley Toad's Juke and Puke. Halloween is the one night I can go out in public looking like this." She passed a hand over her face. "They'll think I'm in costume like everyone else. Anyway, the Juke and Puke is a cesspool, but there's a secret part of it that's even worse. A literal underground part. That's where I'll cash in my ticket."

Jessica tilted her head way back to meet Callie's gaze again. "What exactly does that mean?"

Callie placed the heel of a hand against Jessica's forehead. "It means you'll be my entry in the Bitch Fights."

"The fucking *what?*"

Callie laughed and pressed her hand a little more firmly against Jessica's forehead. "The Bitch Fights, an old tradition going back decades at the Juke and Puke. Or, more specifically, in the Sin Den, the underground part. That's where you, being *my* bitch, will fight another bitch to the death. Possibly many bitches. For every fight you win, I'll also win. Win money, that is. Lots of it. I'll use some of it to have a

DEPRAVED HALLOWEEN

black-market plastic surgeon fix my face enough to at least function in society. The rest I'll use to build a new dungeon in some other part of the country."

Jessica frowned. "If I win every fight, do I get let go?"

Callie snorted cynical laughter. "Maybe. I don't know. You'll have to take that up with whoever I sell you to at the end of the night."

She leaned forward, giving Jessica's head a hard shove, making her flop onto her back. Then she took up a position above Jessica's face and began to peel up the hem of her tight latex skirt.

TWENTY-SIX

THE SOUND OF SCREAMING DRAGGED Bubba Ray up out of sleep. He'd been dreaming he was the star of one of those creature feature flicks from the golden oldie days. For a fleeting instant, he wondered where on earth his brain had conjured up that sort of thing. Being the kind of guy he was, a murdering sexual predator and necrophile, he was prone to sleepy-time visions of blood and sex, but usually they were not imbued with this level of creative flair.

Then his eyes opened and he saw the woman in bed next to him. The face belonged to Maureen Trimble, a local lady he'd known in a casual way his whole life. She looked to have been through a lot since last he'd seen her, though. Her body didn't look right and . . .

It all came slamming back into his head in a single instant, the origin of his fun and freaky dream suddenly becoming crystal clear.

Maureen groaned behind the dirty bandanna Loretta had inserted in her mouth as a gag. She tried reaching toward Bubba Ray but her hands were wrapped tight with twine. Her body didn't look right because it wasn't her body at all. It was the body of a high school girl with Maureen's head sewn onto it.

Bubba Ray pushed her bound hands away and reached out to tweak her nipples, giving each a rough twist that made her groan again. His penis twitched when he did this and he considered spreading her legs and helping himself to a restorative morning fuck. In his extensive experience, there was nothing better than an orgasm for relieving the pain of a morning-after hangover, and the throbbing in his head was pretty bad. It was as good an excuse as any, he supposed, not that he needed one. As he'd learned last night, Maureen and the other girl were helpless to do anything other than obey their every command. They were slaves to their will, animated sex puppets.

He was just starting to push Maureen's legs apart when the screaming that had awakened him started up again. The first time he heard it he'd assumed it was part of his dream because it'd stopped almost as soon as his eyes opened. As he heaved his body over and struggled to a sitting position, he realized that wasn't the case because now it was going on and on. There was something familiar in the timbre of the sound. It wasn't the vocal expression of unbridled terror he'd become accustomed to hearing throughout his years of committing brutal, bloody murder. The distinguishing characteristic of *this* scream struck him as far more akin to volcanic rage.

Bubba Ray swallowed a lump in his throat.

Shit.

It was Loretta.

A quick survey of the mini-camper's cramped and cluttered interior confirmed this was no false impression. She was gone. Also, the camper's door was slightly ajar. He figured she'd gotten up not long before he did and had slipped outside to find a spot to piss. While out there, she discovered something that upset the holy hell out of her.

There was a pause in the screaming.

Then it resumed again.

Bubba Ray sighed and rolled out of bed with a grunt of exertion, reaching out to scoop up a pair of boxers from the floor. The throbbing in his head worsened from bending over, throwing him off-kilter as he tried inserting a foot through one of the garment's leg holes. His foot got caught up in the fabric and he ended up crashing heavily to the floor, igniting more flares of pain in all sorts of places.

"Goddammit," he said, rolling over and putting a hand to his forehead as he whimpered in misery. "You know what, Maureen? I may have myself a wee bit of a drinkin' problem."

Maureen groaned.

Bubba Ray made a similar noise in response. "Tell me about it."

The racket from outside came to an abrupt end. A blissful feeling of relative peace ensued as Bubba Ray lay there and watched a spider of disturbing size crawl across the mini-camper's ceiling. Any other time he might have looked for something to smack it with, but at present he didn't have the energy. A part of him wanted to stay right where he was for another hour, maybe longer, however long he needed to start feeling semi-human again. This desire conflicted with a burgeoning need to get outside and piss about ten gallons. The situation would come to a head soon enough because if he didn't manage to get off his ass and stagger outside, he'd end up pissing all over the floor of the mini-camper.

He was about to try sitting up when the door crashed open and Loretta came stomping inside.

She stood over him, glaring down. "She's gone!"

Bubba Ray squinted at her, sweat forming on his brow as the need to unleash the Kraken intensified. "Say what now? Who's gone?"

Loretta shrieked.

Then she reared back and kicked him super hard. "The fuckin' homecoming queen, you idjit. Who the fuck else?"

Bubba Ray moaned in agony and shifted his weight to the side opposite of where she'd kicked him. He felt like a cannonball had been launched into his gut from close range. "Oh, lordy," he said, whimpering pitifully. "I think you might've ruptured somethin'."

She knelt over him and screamed into his face, painting his cheeks with a froth of spittle. "*I'll rupture your motherfuckin' skull right fuckin' now if you don't get off your fat fuckin' ass and help me find that bitch!*"

Bubba Ray had actual tears in his eyes by that point. "All right, damn. You don't have to be so fuckin' mean about it."

She scowled. "I mean it, tubby. If you're not outside in ten seconds, I'll have your balls for dinner."

Then she was gone, flinging the door wide hard enough to make it smack against the wall and slowly swing almost shut again. After descending the cinderblock steps to the ground, she remained in the general area right out front. He knew this because he could hear her counting to ten through the crack in the door. That spurred him into motion, finally. He didn't think she was serious about dining on his balls, but where Loretta was concerned, you could never really tell.

He rocked himself over onto his side and then got to his hands and knees, clenching his teeth against the detonation of fresh pain the effort set off in his gut. Outside, Loretta was still counting and was already most of the way to ten, her voice increasing in volume with each number she spit out. Bubba Ray scurried to the door on his hands and knees and used the handle to haul himself up. Loretta's ten count ended two, maybe three seconds before he was able to haul open the door. He stood panting and slightly hunched in the small frame, sweat streaming down both sides of his flushed face as he pulled up the boxers.

Loretta gave him a withering look. "You didn't make it in time. That means balls are on the menu tonight, tubby. The only way that changes is if you find that bitch for me."

Bubba Ray sighed as he lumbered his way down the cinderblock steps. "We'll find her. She can't have gotten far on foot."

Loretta snorted. "Oh, is that fuckin' so? We were conked out for *hours*, you plus-sized sack of flaming monkey shit. There's no tellin' how long ago she got loose and took off."

Bubba Ray scratched his head and glanced around, taking in the abundant gruesome evidence of what they'd been up to the night before. Among other things, this included the body of the homecoming queen's boyfriend, Maureen Trimble's headless partial body, and the decomposing corpse of his other girlfriend, the one they hadn't reanimated. All the components of the jerry-rigged reanimation apparatus were still hooked up and buzzing. The loud hum of an electric current was disconcerting enough to send Bubba Ray staggering over to the transformer to shut it off.

He grunted. "We might oughta think about cleanin' up this mess. We don't get prying eyes out here often, but leavin' a bunch of fucked-up dead folks lyin' around out in the open don't seem like the best idea."

Loretta made hooked claws of her hands and waved them about as she screeched in frustration. "Goddammit, Bubba Ray, we ain't got time for all that. We got to commence lookin' for that uppity zombie whore right the fuck now. We need to find her before she starts blabbin' to the cops." She snorted, sweeping a hand around at the evidence of carnage. "You and I both know this ain't but the tip of the goddamn iceberg. How many bodies and parts of bodies are concealed in and around this fuckin' house? Dozens? More than that?"

Bubba Ray hadn't thought about that.

If the homecoming queen tipped off the authorities and they came out poking around, they'd find enough evidence to send them all to the penitentiary forever. That was only if they didn't get sent to the gas chamber, which seemed probable. Thinking about it, he started to become concerned. There'd always been an unspoken assumption that at Jed's house he lived in a sort of protective zone outside the reach of the law. Whether that was true was something he was suddenly a lot less certain about.

He sighed. "Shit. We gotta find her."

Loretta rolled her eyes. "Gee, ya think?"

Bubba Ray ignored her sarcastic tone as he continued casting his gaze around. Something else he couldn't quite put his finger on was starting to trouble him, something creeping in like black poison around the edges of his conscious mind. Something dreadful right on the cusp of perception. He kept turning about in front of the mini-camper. His gaze swept past the moonshine shed more than once before locking in on it. Seeing that the door was open a crack made him think back to last night. He'd seen Jed go back into the shed after stepping out a minute to talk to them, but he hadn't seen him come back out.

He turned back toward Loretta. "That girl . . . you just left her out here before comin' to bed?"

"I tied her to a tree back yonder with an old rope." She pointed toward the line of trees at the back of the clearing behind the house. "See it on the ground there? She got loose somehow during the night."

Bubba Ray nodded in a distracted way, his gaze still trained on the shed's slightly ajar door rather than the tree where Loretta claimed she'd left the homecoming queen. He figured she was telling the truth about that because he didn't think she was talented enough an actress to believably fake this level of enraged distress.

So, okay, yeah, she left the girl tied up back there, presumably along with a command to stay put. Based on his boozy recollection of the evening's events, that should've been enough to keep her right there, yet there was no denying she was gone now. It was puzzling for sure, but he could think of two possible explanations for the girl's absence. Either the compulsion to do as she was told by her resurrectionists was a temporary thing that faded away after a few hours, or . . .

His feet started carrying him toward the shed before he'd even made a conscious decision to check it out.

Loretta fell into step beside him. "What are you doing?"

His gaze stayed on the shed as he continued moving toward it, a feeling of dread building inside him with each step. He couldn't yet guess what awaited him on the other side of that door, but his gut was telling him it was something bad. A few steps closer, he was seized by the conviction that everything was about to change forever, that opening the door would be like stepping through a portal out of the past and into a profoundly uncertain future.

He shivered in the cool morning air. "Just somethin' I gotta see. Might be nothin', I dunno."

Halfway to the shed, Loretta grabbed him by the arm, stopping him cold. "Don't you think I already checked the sheds? Bitch ain't in neither of 'em. If Jed took her, which I know is what you're thinkin', they went somewhere else. Ain't in the house either."

Bubba Ray turned toward her, frowning as he studied the look on her face. "What are you not telling me?"

Loretta groaned as she let go of his arm. "Goddammit. Was hopin' not to have to deal with this now, but . . ." She tossed up her arms in exasperation. "Shit, fuck it, might as well get it over." She marched ahead of him and put her back against the door. "Look, Ray-Ray, what's in here is gonna upset you. Maybe take a minute to chew on that and get yourself ready."

Her words only confirmed what his gut had already told him. Something bad was in there. Tears misted his eyes as he thought about how she hadn't called him by his childhood nickname in a whole bunch of years, since she was just a tiny thing. A rare instance of sensitivity from the murdering wildcat she'd become only made him dread what he was about to see even more. When she moved out of the way, he went to the door, hesitated a final moment, and pushed it open.

His mouth dropped open as he took in all the shocking details. A naked man he didn't recognize was dead on the floor, his head, arms, and legs severed from his body. A gruesome sight to be sure, but not something that, in itself, fazed him. This was an outsider, presumably, dead and mutilated on a patch of land where that sort of thing happened to people like him with regularity. It was expected, common. Bubba Ray knew this because he'd helped send his share of such people to their graves.

What truly shocked him was the lifeless bodies of his two young cousins, one with his throat cut, the other shot to death. He spent the next several moments shaking his head at the scene, his mind temporarily incapable of processing any of it. Once his beleaguered brain started creaking back into gear, he tried picturing how this unlikely slaughter might have occurred. He could only assume Jed had killed these boys, because why else had he tried to hide what had happened in the shed? If not for that, Bubba Ray would've pegged the chopped-up stranger as the culprit.

His mind flashed back to the bloody Thanksgiving dinner of seven years ago, a watershed moment that created a permanent rupture in their branch of the family, the one ruled by Jed and his brothers. That the man hadn't been handed over to the law after that was something Bubba Ray understood. That was not how the Mitchells had ever done things. There was such a thing as backwoods justice, though. *Family* justice. Yet for reasons he'd never understood as a boy, Jed's brothers had opted against putting him in the ground. Well, maybe the time had arrived to take matters into his own hands. He'd long felt gratitude toward Jed for allowing him to park his mini-camper behind his house, but the sight of these dead boys canceled that right the hell out.

In the normal course of things, Bubba Ray wasn't a sentimental guy, but he'd liked these kids. They'd been like little brothers to him, replacements for the actual brothers he never saw much anymore due to being kicked out of his own daddy's home for being caught messing around with his sister. Now, though, he'd been robbed even of this substitute.

Loretta yammered away as he stood there taking in the scene. She'd started in seconds after he stepped through the door, but in those first shocked minutes the sense behind her words was lost to him, becoming an indecipherable background drone. Her tone was urgent and nagging as her words began to come back into focus, cutting through the buzz of festering rage in his head.

She smacked his arm. "Are you listenin' to me? I'm sorry as shit this happened. I liked them boys, too. But we have to catch up to the homecoming bitch before she brings the hammer of fuckin' justice down on our sorry asses."

She grabbed him by the arm and tried tugging him toward the door.

What happened next was an unthinking impulse that was the combined result of his terrible hangover and the traumatic experience of encountering the corpses of his cousins. The deep aggravation of being relentlessly hectored by Loretta since early yesterday evening was a not insignificant contributing factor.

He hauled off and hit her as he turned toward her, knocking her down with a blow hard enough to lift her off her feet for an instant before she crumpled to the floor. She looked up at him with an expression of stunned disbelief followed by the briefest flicker of fear. Then a corner of her mouth began to curl in a way Bubba Ray found disturbing. Even before the shift in her expression, he was assailed by regret. She was annoying in a lot of ways, but he'd had a hell of a time with her last night, setting aside all the verbal abuse. He'd even started to look forward to having more wild times with her in the future.

She sat up and got to her feet. "Are you gonna help me find the homecoming bitch or not?"

Bubba Ray tried a placating tone. "First off, I'm sorry I hit you. I'm just whatchamacallit . . . overwhelmed. I didn't mean to do it."

Loretta's blank expression didn't change. "Don't bother apologizin'. That's pussy shit. You did what you meant to do."

Bubba Ray sighed. "Believe what you want. I really am sorry as hell. Look, if Jed has that girl, one thing we don't have to worry about is her talking to the po-lice. Knowin' him, she's good as dead again already and nothin' to worry about."

Loretta shook her head. "We don't *know* he has her, dumbass. For all we know, she got loose some other way. Either fuckin' way, we have to find her to know for sure."

An idea popped into Bubba Ray's head. "How about we split up? You go look for the girl while I hunt around for Jed. We'll cover more ground that way."

Loretta grumbled, a look of sullen disdain darkening her features. "Whatever."

Bubba Ray groaned.

He was done arguing with her. He felt grief-stricken and weary in general, but behind all that was the new thirst for righteous vengeance. Doing something about that was his new number-one priority. Well, first he'd need to finally empty his goddamn aching bladder and take a fistful of painkillers, but *then* it would become his top priority.

Shortly after walking out of the shed, he pulled his dick out of his boxers and began urinating on the ground.

Just as he at last began to feel a little bit of physical relief, the blade of the axe slammed into his back.

TWENTY-SEVEN

WAKING UP WITH A HANGOVER was nothing unusual for Leroy Beauregard Mitchell, as he went to bed with a belly full of beer and whiskey more often than not. He'd averaged a single sober day every week for a lot of years, and the only reason those days happened was because his body required them to recuperate and promptly steamroll right into another week of debauchery and law-breaking. It was the entrenched cycle of his existence, as familiar to him as his taste for cocaine and the stench of rotting corpses.

He was less accustomed to waking up in bed after a night of drunken shenanigans next to a woman as attractive as Deanna Burton. Waking up next to a woman of any type wasn't exactly a common occurrence in Beau's life. It did happen from time to time, but seduction and romance weren't his bag. He was more the type to pay a meth whore for the privilege of choking on his hog. Not one of those gals was anyone's idea of a beauty queen, but they did the job well enough most of the time. Sometimes when they failed to satisfy him, he switched to doing the choking with his hands. Though he wasn't as deep into the necrophile thing as his daddy and his cousin Bubba

Ray, he did indulge on occasion, and the last woman he woke up with was not among the living.

It was therefore an amazing thing to open his eyes, turn his head, and see the exquisite nude form of Deanna stretched out next to him in her bed at the back of her little single-wide trailer. She was lying on her side with her back to him. The comforter and sheets had been swept from the bed amid their frenzied lovemaking at the end of the night, which was deep into the wee hours of the morning. The rays of sunlight filtering in through the window blind bathed her flawless body in dazzling light, making her look like a golden goddess.

Gazing upon her beauty, he was taken by an unfamiliar feeling, one that brought a frown to his face. It hit him that there were nice things out there in life, beautiful things, and those things had always been out of reach for him because he'd wallowed for so long in the ugly side of existence. He'd gotten so deep into that ugliness that he'd allowed it to infect him like a sickness. It was why he rarely bathed and was content to walk around in garments that were filthy to the point of being putrid. Genuinely attractive women who were not meth whores did not tend to want to spend time in the company of lowly scumbags such as himself. The only reason it had gone differently on this one occasion was Deanna was already drunk by the time he lured her in with his ample supply of Bolivian marching powder. That was easier than he'd ever imagined it would be due to her deep love of the drug. Now, in the aftermath of their wild night of boozing and drugging at the Bitch Fights down in the seediest depths of the Juke and Puke, he felt on the verge of something revelatory.

The clarity of this rare moment of honest self-reflection stirred a desire to transform his life. Many aspects of his existence would be hard to shake. A man with his lack of formal schooling and non-existent traditional work history faced certain limits in terms of what he could do to change things. It might not be possible to stop thieving and killing altogether, at least not in the beginning, but he did have the money to buy himself some new clothes. He could burn all the putrid rags he owned and dress more respectably. That was doable. He could also bathe and shave off the unkempt, bushy beard that made him resemble a big city skid row bum. Looking the part of a man who didn't look out of place next to someone like Deanna would be at least half the battle.

Deanna remained asleep for several minutes after he woke up, snoring softly as he lay there enraptured by what felt like the most profound vision of loveliness he'd ever encountered. At one point, she groaned and stretched her body, flexing her toes and twisting her back in a way that gave greater emphasis to the round ripeness of her perfect ass. When she did that, he thought she was on the verge of waking, and he held his breath, expecting the rapturous spell he'd been under to break at any second. Then the soft, almost inaudible snoring resumed.

Beau wriggled a little closer to her, taking care to move in a way that would not jostle the mattress. He didn't want her waking up yet. When he was close enough, he reached out and lightly cupped one of her buttocks with the palm of his hand. The feel of her warm, soft flesh against his rougher, calloused skin caused another stuttering intake of breath. His cock stirred and he felt a little dizzy. Fucking her when they were both six sheets to the wind was one thing. It was nice. But he was sober now, his every nerve-ending seemingly far more alive and sensitive. Touching her now felt like tapping into a little slice of heaven.

His hand roved all over her ass for at least a minute before beginning to slide down the backside of one of her shapely legs. She moaned softly in her sleep and did a smaller stretch. Those things triggered more than a twitch of his cock. He became so painfully hard he knew he'd have to insert it in her whether she was awake or not. His incipient desire to become a better version of himself did not, it seemed, extend to refraining from his baser urges. He wriggled a little closer, getting the tip of his throbbing cock into position to slide between her legs from behind.

Then she woke up with a yawn, stretching her arms as she groaned and began to roll toward him. The peaceful look on her face froze as her eyes fluttered open. Her features then slowly shifted into a look of repulsion, and she cringed when she spied his erect, dripping penis inches from her flesh. Her reaction inflicted a massive amount of damage on his psyche in an instant, piercing the rapturous spell like a bubble, popping it out of existence with a hurtful finality that made him want to cry. He'd never cried over a woman in his life. Well, except for when his daddy chopped his mother to pieces right in front of him, but that was different. He was a grown man now and this hurt in a different way. He knew right there and then his dream of becoming a different kind of man was just that. Only a dream. Now and forever.

Deanna made a sound of distress as she quickly wriggled closer to the opposite edge of the bed. She then sat up with a loud gasp of alarm, putting her hands to the sides of her face. "Oh my God. Oh, dear Jesus." She glanced at Beau, cringing again. "We didn't really fuck, did we? That was just a crazy drunken dream, wasn't it?" A sound of whimpering distress passed her lips. "Please say it was. Oh, God. Oh, Jesus."

Beau sat up with a scowl, unhappy about the way his penis was no longer happy, wilting fast from the harshness of her words. "It weren't no dream."

Deanna ran her hands through her hair, whimpering again. "Oh, my fucking God." She made a gagging sound. "I might be sick."

Beau's scowl deepened. "Layin' it on a little thick, ain't ya? You seemed to enjoy it last night. Hell, you were the one who started it." He snorted. "I think we did every position in the damn book. You were like a porn star."

Deanna made more sounds of distress.

Then she gasped again, showing him a horrorstruck expression. "What about that weirdo brother of yours? He didn't get in on it, did he?"

Beau shook his head. "Hell, no. I'm not sure the boy's ever fucked a woman with a pulse. At least not one that had a choice about it."

Deanna narrowed her eyes, tilting her head in a contemplative way. "You're not saying what I think you're saying, are you? I mean, I've heard stories about Jed's brood but never knew how serious to take them."

Beau stared at her.

Deanna's gaze went to the closed bedroom door. "He's not still here, is he? He must have gone home at some point, right?"

Despite his hurt feelings, Beau laughed. "You gotta be joking. That boy's not right in the head in more ways than one. He can't drive himself anywhere. Ain't got the knack."

Deanna made a scoffing sound. "He can't *drive*? Jesus, how pathetic. What a piece of shit. Y'all should've euthanized him like an animal when y'all realized how useless he was."

Beau frowned. "Might want to keep your voice down." He nodded toward the door. "If he's awake, I'm sure he already heard you. Your trailer ain't exactly the fuckin' Taj Mahal."

Deanna leaned over the side of the bed, snagged the bedsheet, and pulled it up to her chest as she sat up again, tucking it in beneath her arms to hold it in place. "I'll say whatever the fuck I want about whatever the fuck in my own goddamn home." She flicked her hand in a dismissive wave. "You had your fun last night. Now it's time to git." She did the hand-wave thing again. "Go on, what are you waiting for? Get your shit together and get out of here with that fuckin' weirdo so I can take a shower and wash the filth off of me."

Beau glared at her in silence for a moment.

Deanna must not have liked something in his expression because she rose from the bed and made a dash toward the door. Beau launched himself at her, catching up to her at the door. She had a hand on the knob and was starting to turn it when he tore her away and tossed her back onto the bed, where she landed facedown. She tried to rise again, but Beau pinned her to the bed with his body. As she wriggled and flailed beneath him, he savored her terror in the same way he always did when they tortured female captives at the homestead. His cock started to stiffen again, but at that point he knew he couldn't take the time to do what he wanted with her. She'd already screamed once and he could feel her building up to unleash another one.

Though they were in the rural part of Montclair they considered home turf, that didn't mean they were free to take liberties with whoever they pleased. This was a local girl liked by many. Redneck but not trash, an important distinction in these parts. Killing Deanna in her trailer park home in broad daylight would not be an optimal development. It would be the precise opposite of that, but Beau also knew he couldn't allow her to keep screaming. He was also intensely angry, cut deep by her scathing words and further wounded by her attitude toward his brother, who couldn't help being the way he was.

He clamped a hand over her mouth to muffle the screams.

Then he shifted position above her and got an arm wrapped around her neck. When he felt he had the firmest possible hold on her, he gave her neck a hard, brutal twist, snapping it. He smiled and sighed in satisfaction as he felt her twitch and then go still beneath him.

After lying upon her for several more minutes, he sat up and spent some more time admiring her body, which remained every bit as lovely as before. The only flaw was it was now sapped of all its future potential. He felt he could keep staring at her forever. He could also picture every stage of her slow decomposition. It was, after all, a process he'd seen happen countless times.

Staring at her forever, as enjoyable as that would be, was not a realistic option. He needed to rouse Cletus and get the two of them out of here, preferably with Deanna's corpse in tow, if he felt they could sneak her out somehow with none of her neighbors noticing. He put on his clothes and went out to the trailer's living area to wake his brother.

Cletus was already awake.

He was sitting in a dining chair positioned in a corner of the living room facing the previously closed bedroom door. His legs were spread wide and his fingers were clenched on his knees. Beau intended to rouse his brother into urgent motion, but he stayed silent at first, struck by a sense of something off about the boy's posture and demeanor.

But, no . . . it was more than that.

He didn't look right.

Those fingers clenched against his knees looked longer and thinner than they should be, almost like . . . talons. He was wide awake and staring at Beau through the slits in the rotting pumpkin. Only the pumpkin no longer quite looked like it was rotting. The texture of it had changed. It appeared to have shrunk, to almost have melted, adhering to his skin like a second layer of thick flesh. And his mouth . . . those jagged teeth carved from the rind no longer looked like an imprecise imitation of living teeth.

They looked functional.

The mouth stretched wide in a hideous, profoundly unsettling grin, the orange pumpkin flesh shifting and stretching like real skin because it *was* real skin.

Cletus rose slowly from the dining chair, the top of his pumpkin head bumping against the ceiling of the trailer. A lump formed in Beau's throat as he realized his brother was now at least a foot taller than he'd always been. And those fingers were quite a bit longer now. The pumpkin grin widened and widened. Beau didn't get how it could get so wide without tearing the strange orange flesh.

Beau felt water running down his leg and realized he was pissing himself.

His brother wasn't his brother anymore.

He'd become a monster.

Beau whimpered.

He was overcome by the feeling he wasn't ever getting out of this trailer. Only moments ago he was consoling himself with the knowledge that the necessity of killing Deanna, while regrettable, also came with the benefit of making off with her ample share of their winnings from the Bitch Fights.

That was all out the window.

Cletus took a step toward him.

Out the window.

Beau's eyes widened in sudden epiphany.

He couldn't go out the front door because that would mean having to go past Cletus, which now felt like it'd be tantamount to suicide, but maybe he *could* go out the bedroom window. He'd started backing into the room before he'd even made a conscious decision to do it. Once he realized he was in motion, he committed, turning around once he was inside the room and making a dash toward the window. He had to hope he'd have enough momentum to crash through it, because he knew he wouldn't have time to open it.

Cletus caught up to him before he could get there.

Beau whimpered and pissed himself again as he felt his brother's long fingers close tight around his neck, making him wheeze as they cut off his breath. A fountain of blood erupted as Cletus made a wrenching motion with his arm, tearing Beau's head off his body. Some of the blood splashed against his pumpkin face and more of it hit the ceiling.

After allowing Beau's corpse to drop to the floor, Cletus turned and spent some moments observing Deanna's unmoving form. He tilted his head far to the side in imitation of the intentionally creepy move he'd often made when he was still human.

Then his mouth widened and widened again as he went to the bed and took Deanna into his arms. His mouth kept widening as he bit off her head, spat it out, and began to drink deeply of the blood gushing from the stump.

TWENTY-EIGHT

WHEN BUBBA RAY OPENED HIS eyes, he was flat on his back and staring up at an overcast afternoon sky. Hours might have passed since his last moment of consciousness. The passage of time interested him in only the most fleeting way. Mostly what he felt was surprise that he was waking up at all.

The last thing he remembered was the brutal pain of a large and heavy object punching deep into his back. He'd dropped to his knees an instant before flopping facedown to the ground. Then someone stepped on his back, gripped the handle of the axe, and began wrenching it up and down to pry it loose. Though he felt none of it now, the memory of the explosion of searing, brain-frying agony remained.

He also remembered a grunt of exertion from somewhere above him, a sound he now realized was his attacker raising the axe high overhead again. An instant later, the blade came down again, this time with a greater level of force as it punched deep into his back a second time. The pain that time was so bad it made him cry out for his mama, a woman who'd always scorned him, who once told him her biggest regret in life was not selling him for drug money. His attacker tore the axe loose again and brought it down a third time, and the blackness took him after that.

He had no doubt he'd been killed, but now he was back.

It didn't take him long to come up with the likely explanation for this turn of events. Loretta, who'd also been his attacker, had hooked his corpse up to the resurrection apparatus and put it to use again. He hadn't seen her come at him with the axe, nor had she said anything during the attack. It was theoretically possible someone else had done it, but Bubba Ray knew that wasn't the case. There'd been no one else around at the time. No one else alive, that is. He experienced a faint flicker of emotional pain at the memory of seeing the bloody corpses of his cousins. It still bothered him, but in a more distant way, as if it were a tragedy that had transpired years ago instead of only last night. It was a strange thing, but he figured the feeling was related to having been killed himself.

Another thing that didn't take him long to figure out was *why* she'd attacked him. The attack was retribution for hauling off and hitting her. That'd been a real punch, too, a hard blow that landed square to her jaw. It was delivered with the same force he'd use when trading blows with a man in a bar fight. He'd regretted it right away, apologizing profusely, but evidently that had not been good enough for Loretta, who'd also been upset with him about not treating the matter of the missing zombie girl with the appropriate level of concern. He figured she'd acted on impulse, grabbing the axe and coming at him during a surge of rage. Then, in a spasm of regret, she decided to restore him to life. Though he wasn't happy about having been murdered, he supposed he should be grateful it'd worked again.

He frowned as he thought about it, beginning to focus more intently on how weird it was that his resurrected body wasn't again writhing in agony from the massive damage done to it. Vague suspicions of having been drugged or anesthetized struck him as unfounded. He could feel the ground beneath him and had sensation throughout his body. Also, the gaping wounds in his back felt like they were no longer there. He initially told himself this must be a false impression, but he was less able to believe it with each passing second. It made him wonder if Loretta had done some pre-resurrection work on his body before jolting it with electricity. She might have sutured the wounds or used the surgical stapler on them.

But, no, that didn't feel right either.

He should still feel the damage done to his flesh.

As he was thinking about it, he lifted a hand off the ground and brought it to his face to scratch an itch at the side of his nose. He'd started to scratch when he noticed something that made his eyes go wide in distress. It was so strange he thought he must be hallucinating. He took the hand away from his nose and lifted it higher above his face to study it more closely. In particular, he was most entranced by the sight of the chipped red nail polish decorating his long fingernails. It was the same red shade worn by his other dead girlfriend, the one whose corpse they'd not resurrected the night before. The hand was also much smaller than it should be, the wrist slender and almost delicate-looking, with a thin silver bracelet around it.

Bubba Ray gulped. "Oh, shit."

This was why his body didn't feel right. It wasn't his body at all. He felt a rising sense of panic as his hands went to his chest and he cupped his breasts. The same pleasantly plump breasts he'd fondled with such amorous abandon for days inside the mini-camper. The same dead breasts he'd titty-fucked several times. He reached a hand between his legs to check for his willy wing-wang, but it was gone, his fingers instead finding the folds of a vagina.

He sat up with a gasp as he gave his new body a more thorough examination, overcome with shock as he was soon made to face an inescapable truth. His head was now attached to the body of the other dead girlfriend. This wasn't some waking nightmare. It was real. He couldn't close his eyes and count to ten to will it away. The radical scope of the change in his essential reality made his brain feel close to exploding.

Somewhere nearby, someone was cackling.

Bubba Ray's head turned toward the sound.

Loretta was sitting at the picnic table with a plate in front of her and two cans of cold Coors Light. She waved and beckoned him to join her. "Get your ass on over here, cutie."

Cutie.

Not tubby, but cutie.

This was the opposite of a welcome change. Before being murdered, he'd not been fond of Loretta's penchant for relentlessly fat-shaming him, but now he'd give anything to flip the script back to the original paradigm. He loved the bodies of women, but from the perspective of one outside the gender, as objects existing primarily to provide sexual satisfaction to a man. All his life he'd been an enthusiastic appreciator of the feminine form. It was one of nature's great wonders, even when the beautiful body he was appreciating was lifeless, probably especially then. Now he'd had the ability to experience that pleasure stolen from him.

Loretta thumped a fist against the picnic table, making him flinch. "Goddammit, when I speak, you do as you're fuckin' told. Now get up off your ass and get over here."

Her harsher tone sparked his prompt obedience as he rose to his feet and started toward the picnic table. As he did this, he couldn't help noting how he moved so much more easily than he had when attached to the bulk of his former body. He hadn't been able to get up from a flat position on the ground like that with so little effort since early childhood. It felt good to move like this. Given that this new flesh suit was a rejuvenated version of a corpse that had lain dead in his mini-camper for days, that was quite the indictment of the inhibited functionality of his old form. Didn't make him miss his manhood any less, but it was an interesting consideration.

On his way to the picnic table, he spotted his headless original body on the ground nearby. The white boxers he'd been wearing at the time of his murder had been stripped away, leaving the flabby form entirely nude. His groin resembled a pile of bloody raw beef. Seeing this ruination of what he'd once been was a jarring counterbalance to the instinctive appreciation of inhabiting a lighter vessel. A breath hitched in his throat as tears welled in his eyes.

Loretta again slapped a palm on the picnic table. "*Bubba Ray!*"

Jumping again at the sound of her angry voice, he hurried over to the table and stopped to peer at her from the opposite side. She had a shiner from where he'd punched her, a sure indication of the passage of at least several hours since his murder. When he realized what was on her plate, he experienced a moment of lightheaded queasiness.

Loretta pushed one of the beer cans across the table to him. "Sit yourself down, you stupid bitch. *Now.*"

Bubba Ray again reacted promptly to her command, seating himself on the bench across from her. It came to him then he was now experiencing the same compulsion to obey he'd observed in the women they'd resurrected last night. The rejuvenated heart that was now his stuttered at the startling thought. He could think of few things more unsettling than having no choice but to obey Loretta's every deranged whim.

Loretta pointed at him with a fork. "Pop open that beer, bitch."

DEPRAVED HALLOWEEN

Bubba Ray opened the beer.

Loretta sneered. "You're gonna need that to wash down your meal."

"My what?"

Loretta set the fork on the plate and pushed it across the table. "I told you balls were gonna be on the menu if you didn't help me find the homecoming bitch. Only I've decided you're eatin' instead of me."

It appeared she'd cooked his cock and balls on a skillet. His junk was blackened and had shriveled to about half its normal size, yet because he'd been hung like a horse, it still constituted a significant hunk of meat. There was a reason Loretta had always come around begging for it. Also on the plate was a little steak knife and a pile of ketchup.

"Eat it. Every damn bite."

Bubba Ray experienced another moment of fluttery queasiness. This time the feeling was so strong it brought sweat to his brow and a flush to his cheeks. He scratched at his neck and whimpered in pain when he almost pulled one of the large screws out by accident. It felt scorched from the large amount of electricity that had flowed through it during his resurrection.

Loretta again slammed a fist against the table, this time hard enough to rattle the cutlery. She didn't say anything. By this point, it wasn't necessary. He knew what she wanted him to do. Also, while he was capable of slight hesitation, he was not capable of rebellion. The compulsion to do as she said was a writhing thing inside him, a worm squirming in his brain, making his throbbing head feel uncomfortably warm and thick. He instinctively knew obedience would be his only means of relief from this feeling.

He picked up the knife and fork and began the process of cutting his cooked cock into bite-sized pieces. Once he'd done that, he forked every piece into his mouth as quickly as he could, taking a second to dab each bite with ketchup before ingestion. When he was finished, he went to work on his shrunken testicles. This meat was tougher to cut. It was tempting to swallow each severed testicle whole, but he persevered and eventually managed to reduce them to more acceptable portions. These pieces were crunchier when he chewed, with a surprising juiciness. If it hadn't been his genitals he was eating, he might have deemed it a halfway tolerable meal. The beer can was empty by the time he finished with a small belch nowhere near as robust as his usual.

Then again, *he* wasn't as robust as he'd been a short while ago.

He started crying.

Loretta laughed. "Punch yourself in the face as hard as you can, you fuckin' piece of shit."

Bubba Ray punched himself.

His new, daintier fist didn't pack the same force as his old one, but he managed to deliver a blow to his cheek hard enough to hurt. "Ow."

Loretta smiled. "Do it again. Right in the fuckin' teeth this time."

Bubba Ray punched himself in the mouth.

He started crying again.

Loretta cackled. "Aw, poor baby girl. So sad."

Bubba Ray wiped some of the moisture from his eyes and looked at her. "Y-y . . . you . . . killed-ed me."

Loretta nodded. "That's right, I did, and I ain't about to apologize for it. You had it comin'."

He sniffled and went on crying.

Loretta watched him with an expression of scornful disdain for several minutes without saying anything.

"Now that you've got that out of your system," she said at last, once his tears finally began to dry up, "here's the plan for the rest of the day. We're gonna have a little more fun with Maureen, then after that, you and me are headin' up to the Goodwill on Patterson Road."

"What for?"

She smiled mischievously as she came around to his side of the table. "Why else, cutie? So we can buy you a pretty outfit for the Halloween Spook Bash at the fuckin' Juke and Puke tonight."

Bubba Ray frowned. "But what about the girl who got away? Why ain't you still fired up about finding her?"

Loretta shrugged. "Half the day's gone by already. I figure we're safe now. You were probably right about Jed taking her. And if not? Well, fuck it. The cops come, I'll melt away into the woods, disappear like I do sometimes." She grinned. "They'll never fuckin' find me, I can promise you that."

Bubba Ray didn't bother disagreeing with his feral cousin.

Hell, she was probably right.

She took him by the hand and led him into the mini-camper.

TWENTY-NINE

CALLIE WAS GONE FROM THE basement for hours after informing Jessica of her unsettling plans. Unlike previous occasions when she'd been left alone for extended periods, the lights were left on, something Jessica considered a mixed blessing. In the dark, it was sometimes possible to pretend she was somewhere else, but the harsh overhead track lighting dampened her mind's ability to disconnect from reality and lose herself in fantasy.

She was trapped in a place where countless women before her had suffered miserably, without anyone ever coming to rescue them, with all their prayers unanswered, except for ones in which they eventually pleaded for the sweet release of death. Caught between four plain white walls that brought to mind the sickly repulsive sterility of a hospital. Hospitals were never as clean as they seemed at first glance, nor as safe and nurturing as many imagined. They were places where the screams of the suffering resonated behind closed doors, where vomit was expelled and liquid shit gushed from straining assholes, along with all the other excretions of the sick and dying masked by the odor of industrial cleaning agents.

Not much different from this place in certain ways, really, except that no one with a genuine interest in her well-being was coming around to check on her regularly. Instead of receiving healing medicines, she was being threatened, tortured, and subjected to sexual abuse. It depressed her to the point of despair and beyond, and the worst part remained her inability to do anything about it.

Staring for so long at the mutilated dead man sitting slumped against the opposite wall wasn't doing much to elevate her mood either. At first she'd gloated over his demise, enjoying every sweet second of his suffering. It was hard to imagine a more agonizing way of shuffling off this mortal coil, and Jessica figured he'd gotten exactly what he deserved. Then all those hours alone with only the dead man for company stretched out, with his ruined physical shell slowly becoming an incredibly repulsive sack of dead meat. Whatever made him the monster he'd been had departed that shell, leaving behind only the ugliness of violent death.

Sometimes she kept her eyes shut for minutes at a time to blot out the sight of him. It was an easy thing to do but only effective for limited periods due to the intrusive pressure of the bright lighting against her eyelids. At one point, she turned away from him and sat facing the wall to which she was chained. Unlike the dead man, she'd been allowed enough slack in her bonds to maneuver to that degree. This was another thing she was grateful for at first, but then she became annoyed by the closeness of the wall in front of her face. When she couldn't take that any longer, she stretched out on her back and stared at the ceiling.

She was still on her back much later when the door at the top of the stairs finally opened. The whisper-soft sound of Callie's bare feet descending the stairs was barely audible. Jessica sat up and twisted around in time to see she'd traded her outfit of high-heeled platform boots and shiny latex for shorts and a T-shirt. She'd closed to within a few feet of her by the time Jessica glimpsed the syringe held upright in the fingers of her right hand, a tiny bead of clear liquid visible at the tip of the long needle.

Jessica tried scooting backward. "No. Don't."

Callie didn't say anything and the expression on her jigsaw face changed in no discernible way as she caught up with her and pushed her onto her back again, straddling her. With her manacled hands trapped beneath the woman, Jessica could only shake her head hard from side to side in a hopeless effort to avoid the sting of the needle.

Callie pressed a hand against a side of Jessica's head and pushed her face to the floor. The needle went in at a spot below her jawline. She whimpered as she felt Callie slowly depress the plunger.

Just like the other times she'd been drugged in this place, her consciousness embarked on a distressingly fast fade. When she opened her eyes again, she was again staring up at the white ceiling. She tried sitting up, but she found she was now restrained in a new way, one that inhibited her range of motion far more severely. She was no longer able to move her hands and arms at all. During her latest period of unconsciousness, the manacles had been removed from her wrists, but her entire torso was now wrapped up in a suffocatingly tight BDSM restraining garment modeled from the straight-jackets common to an earlier, less-enlightened era of mental health treatment.

And that wasn't all.

A studded collar was cinched tight around her neck, irritating the way it cut into her skin. Jessica was not surprised to see Callie holding a black leash when she again loomed into view above her. She waggled the metal lead at the end of the leash. "I'm going to attach this now. I trust you realize how pointless it is to resist, but in case you're thinking about being stupid, just know that I've decided to severely punish any further acts of disobedience. If you give me trouble, I'll cut off your nose. It'd reduce your value somewhat, but your body is nice enough that I'm confident you'll still sell for a considerable sum at the end of the night." She laughed. "If you survive, of course."

Jessica sighed, relaxing her body. "I won't give you any trouble."

Callie nodded. "Of course you won't. Because I've broken you, haven't I?"

Jessica didn't bother responding to that, but she bowed her head, figuring there might be something to gain from allowing the woman to believe it.

Callie had changed outfits again while Jessica was unconscious, swapping the shorts and T-shirt out for a tiny black and orange dress and sheer black tights with a pattern of spooky Halloween images woven into them.

Jessica deduced from this that several more hours had passed.

It was now Halloween night.

Callie attached the lead to Jessica's collar and stood erect again, tugging hard at the leash with both hands as she hauled her up off the floor. Because of the tightness of the restraint garment, she was unable to offer any assistance in this effort. The pain caused by the collar redoubled as it dug harder into her neck. Callie kept pulling harder and harder, her fractured countenance twisting in what was either a grimace of effort or an expression of rapturous pleasure.

Or both.

Relief of some degree arrived once she was finally able to get her feet beneath her and use her leg muscles to drive herself upward. Once she was on her feet, Callie pressed a finger against Jessica's lips. "Now I'll remove the chains from your legs. Stay still as I do this, refraining from any urge to execute any crazy Ninja moves. I'm sure you're capable of such things, but in this case they will not help you. You will not be able to overpower me, nor will you be able to free yourself from the slave jacket. Do we understand each other?"

Jessica winced as she cleared her tender throat. "Yes."

Callie tapped the forefinger against Jessica's lips. "Good. Now stay quiet while I work. Or else."

Jessica did as she was told, keeping her mouth shut while Callie freed her ankles from the chains and manacles. The relief she felt as they came away from her flesh was considerable. So was the urge to defy the woman's edict against giving her trouble. She was right, after all. She did have an arsenal of dangerous and even deadly moves at her disposal, some she could execute with just the power of her legs. At full strength, even in the restraint jacket, she was more than capable of knocking this psycho bitch out with a perfectly executed roundhouse kick to the head. The problem was she *wasn't* at full strength, not after so many hours of uncomfortable chain restraint.

The matter was settled when Callie pulled a gun from a bag on the floor and pointed it at Jessica's face. "I'm sure you're still weighing your options despite what I've told you. You'll stop that now."

A statement, not a question.

Jessica nodded.

Callie's features shifted in a way that managed to form the clearest semblance of a smile she'd yet managed in Jessica's presence. "That's good. I'd hate to have to disfigure or kill you before we even get to the Spook Bash. I haven't been in a long time, since before Dalton ruined my face, but it was always such a good time. I can't wait. What about you?"

Jessica grunted. "I guess."

Callie laughed. "Come on, girl. Where's your Halloween spirit?"

"In the fucking graveyard, with all the other dead things."

Callie laughed again. "Haha. Good one. We're leaving now."

She tugged at the leash, leading Jessica toward the stairs. They paused at the bottom long enough for Callie to move into position behind her.

"You go up ahead of me. If you try anything funny, I shoot you in the back. Understood?"

"Understood."

Jessica started up the stairs.

Because she was still a little wobbly from being chained up, she had to lean and brace a shoulder against the wall from time to time to maintain her balance. Once or twice, she felt precariously close to losing her footing, but each time she managed to avert taking a tumble. Each time she wondered if maybe she should've let it happen, especially the last time, when they were three-quarters of the way up the stairs. Toppling backward into Callie from that high up might result in a disabling injury to the woman. The problem was, she might break her own neck in the process. She kept ascending the stairs and in a few more seconds arrived in a spacious, modern kitchen.

At Callie's direction, they moved through the kitchen and a large and nicely appointed great room. Moments later, they went out the front door and into the cool night air. Jessica sucked in a big breath of it, reveling in the wide-open space, so wondrous after her period of confinement in the stultifying basement.

Two vehicles were parked in front of the big cabin. One was Dalton's sheriff's department cruiser. The other was a big black SUV with tinted windows.

Callie steered Jessica toward the latter.

She opened one of the middle doors and shoved Jessica inside.

Jessica had to do some fierce wriggling on her own to get into the vehicle.

Callie was peering in at her once she was able to sit up and turn her head toward the open door. "Not that you could try them, but the child locks are engaged." She indicated the screen of thick mesh netting between the front and back seats. "That barrier's not law enforcement grade, but it'll easily do the job against a woman in your position. You won't be able to get loose and you won't be able to get to me or disrupt my driving. I recommend you stay still and quiet throughout our drive."

She slammed the door shut and got in behind the wheel of the SUV, starting the engine up and putting the vehicle in gear. Seconds later, they were driving down the long, winding private road that functioned as the cabin home's driveway.

As Callie drove, she put on some music, a Halloween playlist. It started with "Monster Mash" by Bobby "Boris" Pickett. That was followed by "Every Day Is Halloween" by Ministry and "Ghouls Night Out" by the Misfits.

And so on and so on in that vein to the Juke and Puke, with Callie dancing enthusiastically in her seat the entire ride.

THIRTY

BEFORE FLEEING HIS HOMESTEAD SHORTLY after dawn, Jed spent a lot of time musing on the subject of dark magic. Though the old families of the rural part of Montclair were largely god-fearing, some small factions of that population were witchier, more inclined toward pagan beliefs and practices. After covertly observing Loretta's successful midnight attempt at corpse-raising, he revisited an idea he'd entertained earlier that evening, namely that the souped-up version of brain-shine he'd concocted to rejuvenate Grandpap only worked because there was a spark of Halloween magic in the air.

After thinking about it much of those early morning hours while hiding in the shed, he came to believe this was closer to the truth than he originally thought. Much as a part of him yearned to believe the concoction succeeded purely as a result of his genius, a seed of doubt intruded and soon overtook his thinking on the matter. On the surface, the events he witnessed that night and into the next morning, on Halloween itself, practically demanded an explanation rooted in the fantastical.

The real clincher came at dawn after he awakened from an unplanned lapse into sleep while still inside the shed. At first, his big concern was, once again, fear of discovery. Bubba Ray barging in to find him dozing peacefully in the presence of his murdered sons would be a disastrous thing. After rousing himself, he went to the door to peek outside. At that point, faint light was beginning to tinge the sky. Dawn was coming, which meant he hadn't merely been dozing. He'd been soundly asleep for hours. He was rebuking himself for this blunder when something drew his attention to the tree line at the back of the clearing. Opening the door a bit wider, he squinted in that direction until what he'd glimpsed in the gray early morning light came into focus.

The resurrected girl Loretta and Bubba Ray spent so much time playing with after they revived her was tied to a tree back there. She was sitting on the ground but looking up at something in an attentive way, as if she were carefully listening to something someone was telling her.

Only no one else was there.

It was just the girl, possibly driven mad by all she'd endured.

That perception began to change as he watched the girl get to her feet, still seeming to look up at something, either a very tall person or something curious up in one of the trees. Jed thought she was in the grip of some delusion when something invisible closed around her head. Though he couldn't see whatever it was, he could tell this was happening by the way it mashed her facial features and flattened her hair. He saw her body go rigid for a moment before beginning to shake all over as if in the grip of a seizure. While this was happening, Jed was at last able to discern the hazy outline of some other presence out there with her. A strange creature of tremendous height. His hunch was he could only see this because a transfer of powerful energy was occurring. It was reminiscent of what he'd felt at the moment of the midnight resurrection event, but the quality of this energy had a subtly different feeling to it. A darker one. When the girl stopped shaking, the outline of the creature's form disappeared.

Then something even stranger happened.

The girl tore free of the rope binding her wrists with shocking ease, as if it were no more substantial than a fraying length of string. She didn't appear to have changed in any obvious outward way, but that display of unnatural strength was unnerving. Jed stood shaking behind the door, fearing what might happen if the girl turned her attention his way. She did glance briefly at the shed as well as at the mini-camper, but instead of approaching either, she turned away and walked into the woods, soon disappearing from view. The extra strange part of that was he didn't simply lose sight of her amidst the trees. Her physical form instead turned hazy before vanishing like an evaporating mist.

At that point, Jed made a momentous decision. He was done with this place. The house he'd called home all his life, but not just that. He was done with Montclair and his whole damn family. The weight of so many years of being scorned by so many among his kin all at once felt like it was too much. He had a good amount of cash squirreled away, more than enough to live on simply for quite some time. He would take it and go someplace far away, be a drifting killer on the road like in that one old song, but his first order of business was getting away from this house and the demons he thought might be haunting the woods behind it.

He stepped out of the shed and closed it behind him before scampering across the clearing toward the back of the house. Once inside, he worked fast, throwing some clothes and other necessities into an old hard-shell suitcase, just the bare minimum to get started somewhere else. He packed nothing in the way of personal mementos, wishing to shed all reminders of this previous life like dead skin. He pushed his bed aside and pried up floorboards to retrieve his stash of cash. On his way out, he spared one last longing glance at Meredith, wishing he could take that sweet dead pussy for one last glorious spin, but there wasn't time for it. He gave a moment's thought to taking her with him and decided against it, knowing he'd soon have opportunities to create brand new dead girlfriends.

A few minutes after he started throwing things in the suitcase, he tossed it in the trunk of his Buick and drove away from his house for the last time. Soon thereafter, he decided he'd not yet slept enough to spend an extended time driving down unfamiliar highways, so he got himself a big bottle of Jim Beam and drove to a lakeside park area. He spent some time drinking on the boat dock while staring out at the rippling water, finishing nearly half the bottle before returning to his car to stretch out in the back seat.

When he woke up again, he was annoyed to find most of the day had melted away. He'd been more sleep-deprived than he'd realized. The booze likely hadn't helped matters either. What most bothered him about this was he'd counted on having a full day ahead of him to drive while the sun was out, minus a couple of hours at the start for some shuteye.

Well, that was out the fuckin' window, at least for now. He decided he'd stay in town one last day and aim for a fresh start in the morning.

He got out his bottle of Jim Beam and decided to spend some time driving around town, taking in a few of the familiar old sights before leaving it all behind forever. On impulse, he drove up to Coogan's Point, site of the Lover's Lane Murders from 1989. He thought it'd be nice to spend some time there reminiscing over old days, recalling the screams of his victims and the warm spurt of young blood against his skin. To his great surprise, the area was blocked off by police vehicles. In a panic, he turned around and drove off as fast as he could, checking his mirrors for signs of pursuit, his abrupt departure possibly being construed as suspicious, but he was not followed.

As the sky began to darken slightly, he was still driving aimlessly up and down the back roads of rural Montclair, swigging from his diminishing bottle of Jim Beam all the while. This continued until he spied a car stopped at the side of the road. The car was some spanking new thing with out-of-state plates. A pretty young woman in a flowery dress was standing outside the car with a phone to her ear, visibly upset as she talked to the person on the other end animatedly, with lots of hand gestures.

Jed pulled up behind her and got out of the Buick, glancing up and down the curving road in each direction before approaching her. "What seems to be the problem, miss? Anything I can do to help?"

She gave him a look of sneering annoyance as she continued talking to someone who was probably either a boyfriend or husband from the sound of it. How she'd ended up in this unlikeliest of all places, Jed did not know, but he could tell she did not belong in any part of Montclair, not even among the somewhat more forward-thinking denizens in the more developed part of town. She was too sophisticated, too redolent of smug big-city slickness.

As she yammered on, Jed studied her vehicle a little more closely and soon deduced it was one of those electric vehicles favored by save-the-planet types. The shiny contraption's motherboard had suffered some type of glitch, whatever the hell that meant. Even if Jed had stopped with the sincere intention of offering mechanical help, which he most certainly had not, he would have been powerless to do anything for her. He could work on any old car from the days before they all became rolling computers, but with these newfangled ones, he was at a total loss.

Again, he did not care.

He glanced up and down the road one more time.

Then he showed the woman a shark-like grin as he plucked the phone from her fingers and flung it into the woods. She could only gape at him, shocked into frozen silence by what he'd done.

He laughed. "Didn't expect that, didja?"

She sucked in a breath and started to back away from him, but he seized her by the neck before she could take more than one step. He compressed his hands tighter around her neck as she started to scream, cutting off the shrill noise. She flailed at him with her hands, scratching nails raking across his face and drawing blood. He turned her around and slammed her face against the edge of her vehicle's trunk lid. Once, twice, three times, until she stopped flailing. She was still conscious, groaning weakly as he dragged her into the woods beyond the side of the road.

Once he had her out of sight of anyone who might pass by, he hurried back to the Buick, where he opened the trunk and removed a hunting knife from the suitcase. After another quick check of the road, he hurried back into the woods, moving fast because he knew this impulsive act was highly ill-advised. Though it was starting to get a little dark, there was still good light in the sky. Things could get seriously complicated, maybe even messy beyond his ability to handle, if someone else came along and stopped. He could get apprehended if a lawman came along, maybe sent to jail for a long time.

Or killed.

He had to be quick as hell about this, no doubt.

What also was not in doubt was his desire to do it despite the risk. He was in the grip of a frenzy unlike anything he'd experienced in a long time. The kills he'd participated in at the house with his boys were different, a more controlled thing. Things did get a little crazy a few nights back when they had to chase Meredith through the woods, but that incident was a rare exception rather than the rule.

This, though . . . this was like 1989 all over again. It felt infused with the electric promise of becoming one of the greatest moments of his life.

He went into the woods and stopped her with a foot on her back as she tried crawling away. After letting her squirm beneath the pressure of his boot for a moment, he dropped to his knees and flipped her over, cutting open the front of her dress with the knife. He cut apart her bra in the middle and pulled the cups aside, exposing her breasts. She squealed in terror as he showed her that shark-like grin again.

Then he stabbed her in the chest.

He yanked the knife out and raised it over his head as blood gushed from the wound he'd created. Right as he was about to slam it down again, something strange happened to her face. It appeared to shift like putty, the features rearranging and reforming in seconds, showing him the countenance of a woman who'd died seven years ago.

Norma.

His heart almost seized in his chest at the sight of her.

He heaved a breath. "No. No. There's no way. This ain't real."

He closed his eyes, telling himself that when he opened them again the face of his dead wife would be gone, revealed as an illusion.

He opened his eyes.

Nothing had changed.

Blood was still gushing from the deep puncture wound in the woman's exposed chest. The body the blade had violated still looked like the body of the sophisticated city woman. A woman whose presence here was so inexplicable, except that perhaps she'd fallen victim to something—some force—that had muddled her thoughts, steering her off her intended path.

But it was still Norma looking back at him.

The thing with Norma's face smiled. "The veil is thin. Some of your kin is eager to see you again."

In his astonishment, Jed had lowered the hand gripping the knife.

She plucked it from his hand and rammed it into his throat.

Norma, or the thing that looked like her, shoved him off her and rose easily to her feet, showing no indication of being weakened by the gaping wound. She took the dying man by the wrist and dragged him deeper into the woods, pulling him along as easily as a child would drag a rag doll. His last fading conscious thoughts were tinged with acidic bitterness, an intense sense of resentment that with so much strange magic floating around, none of it was benefitting him in any fashion. All that blood he'd consumed from Grandpap, all of it presumably imbued with such great power, and yet he felt no stronger than he had days ago, before the God of Halloween passed through the veil to visit Montclair.

Not fair, he thought, as his vision blurred and his thoughts turned fuzzy. *Just no fuckin' fair at all.*

In a lifetime of being shunned and treated with scorn, it was like a final, spiteful kick in the nads from the universe.

No one ever saw Jed alive again, and his body was never found.

PART III
THE SPOOK BASH

THE FINAL CHAPTER

THE SIN DEN WAS ROCKING as Eleanor Mountbatten rose shakily to her feet and walked away from her defeated opponent. Her knuckles were sore and slick with the blood of the woman she'd just killed. The many rings adorning her fingers afforded her a punching force advantage that had helped see her through three successful fights since her forced induction into bitch fighting late last night. The brutal underground competition was metastasized misogyny at its most grotesque and reprehensible. Though she naturally despised everything about it, she participated because the only other option was death.

At the back of the square-shaped arena was an elevated stage at least twice the size of the stage used for live music performances upstairs in the Juke and Puke. The fighters, all women, were kept in dog crates stacked three high at the back of the stage. Burly armed guards were stationed at the sides of the stage and in front. Their job was to ensure the caged women behaved and to discourage the unruly and often spectacularly drunk spectators from climbing up to the stage to get at them. Eleanor had assumed the size of the guards and their weaponry would be more than sufficient to dissuade anyone from trying anything so crazy, but in the space of less than a full day of captivity, she'd already witnessed a handful of failed attempts. The drunken assholes who tried it, all men, were all given severe, bone-crunching beatdowns. She was pretty sure at least one of those men had perished in the attempt. What would possess anyone to try something so clearly impossible given the safeguards in place, she did not know, but she figured sheer brain-damaged stupidity on an epic scale was the largest part of it.

Though those guilty of the most egregiously cretinous behavior were of course all men, a significant percentage of the audience was female, which at first she found shocking. She couldn't understand how any woman could cheer the debased brutalization of other women as if it were no different from any other spectator sport. Some among them were swilling booze and raising hell in nearly as unhinged a fashion as their male companions. She tried to rationalize it, hoping it was coerced or performative behavior to pacify men who might hurt them if they voiced disapproval, but quite a few of the women appeared to be here unaccompanied by a male. The only explanation she could think of was that it was indicative of a deeper moral and social rot ingrained in a large swath of the local white trash population.

These people were *bad* to the core.

Not just bad, though.

Evil.

The elevated octagonal fighting cage was situated in the center of the arena's floor area. It looked like the MMA fighting cages she'd seen on TV, with an outer catwalk ringing the slightly slanted cage walls. A frat guy she'd dated a couple of semesters back loved watching that stuff. At the time, she'd only rolled her eyes at it, never for a second imagining she'd one day be forced to fight for her life over and over again in a similar setting.

A tall but portly gray-haired man entered the octagon through one of the multiple cage doors and approached her with a triumphant grin on his face. This was the man who'd purchased her from Deanna and her repulsive hillbilly friends at the end of the previous night's competition. She still couldn't believe she'd been duped so thoroughly by that deceitful bitch, who'd somehow managed to put forth a convincing impression of a normal and civilized woman before revealing her true intentions.

A lot of the caged women were vulnerable unfortunates from the seedy fringes of society. Some had needle marks and bruises on their arms. Others were skinny to the point of starvation. Still, others displayed all the typical hallmarks of meth addiction, including oozing facial scabs and missing teeth. Many were bottom-rung whores that had been snatched out of the streets, broken women hardly anyone would ever miss. Quite a few weren't local, having been trucked in like cattle from other states.

There were also a handful of women from much higher social stratum. Eleanor was in this category. She and the women like her were procured by people like Deanna, who ranged far out of their home territory to hunt for them. Unlike the scrawny meth whore she'd just beaten to death, Eleanor assuredly *would* be missed. Not that it would matter, because she suspected Deanna was an old hand at this and had covered her tracks well. As an attractive missing blonde, her disappearance would probably be a big story on at least the local news for a while. Then it would slowly fade from media prominence as time passed and she was never found.

The tall gray-haired man took one of her hands in his and raised it above his head, sparking another raucous eruption of cheering, hooting, and clapping from the spectators, who filled bleacher seating on three sides of the octagon. Many stamped their feet on the aluminum bleachers, rattling them so hard the din soared to an almost deafening level. Eleanor was not a star basking in applause and adulation. She was a terrified prisoner, and she knew they would cheer just as hard for whoever finally defeated her, if not harder.

After her two victories at the end of the previous night, the man holding her upraised hand took her into a back office and informed her he was her new owner. He then had his way with her under threat of violence while two cigar-smoking associates of his watched from a decrepit leather sofa. After that was over, he told her he believed she might have what it took to break the Sin Den's consecutive victories record for bitch fighting. The record was nineteen straight successful fights to the death. It was a mark that had stood for nearly two decades. If she could break it, he would take her out of the Sin Den and give her a place in his home. He wouldn't be able to release her for obvious reasons, but she would have a life of comfortable enslavement in a nice house.

It wasn't the future she'd hoped for—far from it—but Eleanor did not want to die. A life as this man's pretend wife and sexual slave was better than no life at all, yet she would not delude herself. The task ahead of her would not be an easy one. She already felt battered and sore all over from her first three fights. It was hard to imagine feeling any way other than unrelentingly miserable after twenty, even spread out over some time. Her three opponents so far were all pathetic wretches who fought hard and got her bloody, but she ultimately defeated them without ever feeling like her life was in danger. If they kept feeding her crack whores in the cage, she'd get to twenty wins for sure.

But then there was the not-insignificant factor that victory was dependent on killing your opponent. There was no such thing as a draw or a judge's decision in bitch fighting. Breaking the record would require killing twenty human beings, a staggering number, a staggering concept. The idea of doing it made her feel hollow inside. Each death at her hands would scrub away another piece of her soul.

She hated that.

But not so much that she wouldn't do it.

You've killed three already, she told herself. *That line's already been crossed. At this point it's just about driving up that number.*

The cheering of the drunken crowd slowly began to ebb, and it was soon replaced by a murmur of excited conversation as the house lights were dimmed and a spotlight was trained on two figures marching down an aisle toward the fighting cage. It was two women, one of whom looked like she might be wearing an especially ugly Halloween mask. They continued up the aisle and past the bleachers, continuing toward the steps leading up to the fighting cage. The woman possibly wearing a mask was leading the other one by a leash.

The woman on the leash was bound in a straitjacket.

~

The parking lot of the Juke and Puke was jam-packed for the Halloween Spook Bash. On most nights, lot capacity ranged from a quarter-full to half-filled. Sometimes it was higher than that, but only on special occasions was it like this, damn near impossible to find even a single open space. Even along the edges of the lot, cars were parked bumper-to-bumper, with no room to squeeze in. The Juke and Puke was always a madhouse on Halloween, but based on what they were seeing, this year's Spook Bash was shaping up to be the biggest ever.

Bubba Ray's body thrummed with tension as Loretta drove them up and down the packed rows. He winced every time she slapped the Chevelle's steering wheel and snapped off another string of frustrated curses, though his nerves had nothing to do with Loretta's surliness. That was standard for her. Because she hadn't yet allowed him to don his new mask, he was in terror of being spotted by someone he knew. He couldn't imagine how he might explain the drastic change in his physical form in a way that wouldn't freak people out.

It'd been a bit since his last excursion to the roadhouse, almost a month, but that wasn't nearly enough time to have believably lost way more than half his body weight by any normal means. That was without even considering that, oh yeah, he had the body of a frickin' *woman* now, a fact made plain by the ludicrously sexy outfit Loretta had forced him into. Inwardly, he still identified as male and always would, but the perception of others was something he could do nothing about while in this absurd getup. He would've preferred some baggy and shapeless butch clothing that might obscure the feminine form he now inhabited, but Loretta had no interest in accommodating his feelings.

The outfit consisted of a backless black dress with a mid-thigh hemline and heels. He'd already made a stumbling fool of himself once in the heels. That was in the parking lot outside the Goodwill while Loretta watched and bellowed laughter. She made him practice walking in them until he was able to do so without teetering on the verge of falling over with every step. The whole time he'd felt mired in the same sort of terror gripping him now. A number of people had gone in and out of the thrift store while he practiced, some of whom glanced his way with dubious looks on their faces. This exercise in humiliation went on so long he was sure he'd be recognized, but by some miracle it didn't happen.

Now his anxiety was through the roof again.

He whimpered. "Can I please put the mask on?"

A corner of her lip curled as she glanced at him a second before returning her attention to her crawl through the parking lot. "Punch yourself in the face."

Dammit. Not again.

Bubba Ray punched himself in the face.

A car backed out of a space twenty feet directly ahead. Loretta gasped and gunned the Chevelle's engine, making Bubba Ray rock backward in his seat as the car shot forward. At the same time, a Subaru turned into the row from the opposite end. Its driver also hit the gas upon spotting the empty space, but the car pulling out of the spot turned in the direction of the Subaru, giving Loretta the opening to swoop in first. She punched the gas again and whipped into the open space, laughing maniacally as she put the Chevelle in park and twisted around in her seat to give the Subaru's driver a double middle finger salute. The driver shouted something indecipherable but fraught with anger and frustration before moving on.

Bubba Ray unclenched his fists and let out a breath. "Finally. Was startin' to think we'd spend the rest of the night circling the lot."

Loretta chuckled. "Nah. If that shit had gone on much longer, I would've been like, fuck this noise, time to abandon ship."

Bubba Ray frowned. "You mean ditch my car between the rows?"

Loretta did a bump of cocaine and sniffed a few times. "What the fuck else would I mean?"

"My car would be gone by the time we leave, towed away somewhere," Bubba Ray said, a hint of a whine in his voice. "Can you imagine me tryin' to get it back lookin' like this?"

Loretta laughed. "That'd be funny as hell. Anyway, it don't really matter." The flush of humor in her expression did a quick fade. When she spoke again, it was in a more somber tone. "Listen, cuz, there's something I need to tell you. You're not gonna be too happy about it, so get yourself ready."

Her words would have been unsettling enough on their own, but it was the way she said them that most bothered Bubba Ray. She sounded like a TV doctor about to deliver some heavy news to a patient waiting to hear their diagnosis.

As it turned out, that wasn't too far from the truth.

His eyes filled with tears. "You're scarin' me."

Loretta sighed. "I'm sorry, Ray-Ray, I really am. You and me have had ourselves a blast and a fuckin' half since last night, but all parties gotta end eventually. This right here." She nodded in the direction of the Juke and Puke. "This is our swan song. Come sunrise, the party will be over."

Bubba Ray wiped a tear from his cheek. "Wh-what's that mean?"

She put a hand on his bare knee and gave it a gentle squeeze. "The electric shock channeled the magic that brought you back, but it's only the magic that's sustaining you. It's Halloween magic, the type that only comes around once a year, when that dang ol' veil is thin." She squeezed his knee again. "The rays of tomorrow's sun will burn the last of it away."

He sniffled. "You mean . . . I'll die? For real this time?"

She nodded, said nothing.

Bubba Ray began to sob in earnest.

Loretta let him cry, sitting there in silence for a few minutes while occasionally patting his knee.

At last, Bubba Ray began to compose himself, wiping snot from his nose and rubbing the mucus on the upholstery. He even managed a brittle smile. "You know what? It's okay. I mean it." He indicated his new body with a wave of his hand. "I don't really want to go on like this anyway. It just ain't me. Not really. Do you think I'll go to hell?"

Loretta's usual sneering grin returned. "Oh, most definitely. You've earned that, don't you think?"

Bubba Ray didn't have to give it much thought.

He nodded. "I earned it and then some, I reckon."

Loretta slipped out from behind the wheel and crawled into his lap, giving him a long, lusty kiss on the mouth, slipping him quite a bit of tongue before breaking the clench with a grin. "You know I'll join you there one of these days, cuz."

Bubba Ray did a full-body shiver. "Lordy, if I still had a wing-wang, it'd be hard as a rock right now."

Loretta reached for the door handle, yanked it, and shoved the passenger door open. "Put on that mask. It's time to go kill it on the dance floor."

She slithered out of the Chevelle with Bubba Ray right behind her.

Some items were retrieved from the trunk.

Moments later, they started walking hand-in-hand toward the Juke and Puke.

~

The reality of the Bitch Fights was drastically different from what Jessica had imagined. She'd pictured it taking place in a much smaller space, for one thing. A large barn or basement, perhaps, with a small group of men standing in a loose circle around the combatants. A hot, dimly lit space, with clouds of drifting cigar smoke to make the atmosphere extra stifling, something a bit like the scenes of cock fighting she'd seen in old movies.

She'd gotten the drifting smoke part right.

The rest of it . . . not so much.

The Sin Den, the private access club beneath the backwoods road-house called Harley Toad's Juke and Puke, was at least the size of the sprawling roadhouse itself, if not larger. Instead of the low-rent affair she'd expected, she was confronted with a comparatively large-scale entertainment spectacle. The fighting cage at the center of the arena was not some homemade contraption. It looked like the ones used by professionals. Jessica figured it must have been purchased for a hefty sum from the same manufacturer that supplied legitimate fighting organizations. The cage was ringed by a stage and three sections of bleacher seating. There were even a few balcony box seats for whatever passed for a VIP in these parts.

At first, after threading their way through the crowd of costumed partiers in the Juke and Puke, it seemed that Callie might not be granted admission to the Sin Den. There was a heated initial discussion with the men guarding the entrance to the club. The crux of it was that she was not a recognized member, entry being restricted to members and those in the company of members. It also didn't help that she didn't know the current password. The tone of the exchange changed when Callie invoked the names of certain high-up Sin Den officials as well as that of her husband, a longtime member in good standing.

A call was made and one of the men stepped aside to talk to someone in hushed tones. He soon came back to them and handed the phone to Callie, who spent a few moments talking to the person on the other end. Callie's tone during that conversation was much different than any Jessica had heretofore heard her use, bright, animated, and friendly. She seemed to know the person she was talking to. After about a minute, she handed the phone back to the guard, who put it to his ear and nodded a few times while listening to the mystery person.

The man was smiling as he ended the call. "Sorry about that, Mrs. Trimble. We have to be careful, you know."

Callie might have smiled. She might have scowled. As always it was hard to tell. "Perfectly understandable," she told the man. "I'm sure your vigilance is appreciated."

The other guard ushered them down a set of stairs, through a door, and then down a long hallway to a back office. As Jessica was dragged by the leash through the hallway, she heard the muffled loud cheering from the fighting arena. That was her first hint of the actual scale of the operation.

In the back office, they were met by a tall fat man with gray hair. Two other men in cowboy boots and western attire were in the office with him, sitting at opposite ends of a worn-looking brown sofa. They smoked cigars and said nothing the entire time Callie conversed with the tall man.

Other people, subordinates of some type, poked in a few times to have a word with the man about some matter or other. From these interactions, Jessica gleaned that the tall man was alternately known as either Toad Jr. or Big H. Jessica then put her powers of deduction to work and concluded he must be the son of the original Harley Toad.

Though the man was at first taken aback by the state of Callie's face, he soon settled into an easy rapport with her, and Jessica gathered he'd known her well before Dalton stopped letting her leave the house. Knew her well and liked her, from the sound of it, and he was receptive to her desire to enter Jessica in tonight's already underway competition. All she had to do was pay the entry fee along with an initial wager, which she promptly produced.

After taking her money, Toad Jr. turned his attention fully to Jessica, eyeballing her up and down in a way that made her feel slimy. He grinned as he shook his head, making noises of appreciation and pronouncing her "one fine filly." This was not her first time being sized up like a cut of meat and she was able to project an outward stoicism while seething inside.

Toad Jr. did a bit of thinking and made a proposition.

Jessica would be pitted against his current champion at double the stakes. If Callie wanted to pit her slave against a lesser opponent, that could be arranged, with a win all but guaranteed. Her winnings, however, stood to be much higher if she agreed to terms with Toad Jr.

Callie agreed.

They decided to make a big production of it, with Callie escorting her fighter to the fighting cage under a spotlight. The stomping and roaring of the crowd as she was led down the aisle stunned Jessica. From what she'd been told, the tradition of Bitch Fights went back several decades. How this many people could know about it and keep it a secret this long was hard to understand. She couldn't even begin to wrap her head around it. This was blood-sport, institutionalized mass murder with countless victims. In all her explorations of many of the world's most corrupt places, she'd never encountered anything quite so appalling. She wanted to kill every single cheering piece of shit in the arena.

Inside the fighting cage, Jessica and her opponent stood apart from each other while Callie and Toad Jr. engaged in rabblerousing banter via the microphones each held. Each made boisterous claims about the prowess of their fighter, stirring the crowd to ever greater heights of frothing pandemonium.

Jessica's slave jacket was soon removed, leaving her attired only in the ridiculous black leather bikini top and bottom she'd been wearing when she woke up in Dalton's basement. As Callie and Toad Jr. departed the cage and were escorted to one of the VIP balconies, Jessica stretched and flexed her sore limbs while sizing up her opponent.

The other woman glared at her, the look on her face a mixture of wariness and hatred. Her hands were coated red with the still-wet blood of her previous opponent. She wasn't wearing a stitch of clothing. There was more blood on the floor padding inside the cage. The woman flexed her ring-adorned fingers and sneered.

"You're number four, bitch."

Jessica wasn't positive what that meant, but she had a good idea. She shook her head. "I'm sorry, but I'm not."

Several more minutes elapsed while those in the audience who wished to place bets were allowed to do so, passing slips of paper to ushers patrolling the bleachers.

Then the bell they'd been told to wait for sounded.

The other woman let out a screech of rage and charged forward the instant she heard the sound, her eyes open wide and blazing with the desire to kill.

Jessica relaxed her stance and stayed perfectly still until the screeching woman was within range. She then smoothly sidestepped and snagged the woman by a wrist, using her momentum to swing her around and fling her against one of the cage panels, which rattled with the impact. The woman bounced off the panel and flopped like a deadweight to the floor. She did not initially move, but Jessica thought she detected a faint groan of pain through the din of the roaring crowd. Some of the spectators—maybe even the majority— seemed to think the other woman was dead already. They weren't accustomed to seeing a move of that type executed with such vicious precision.

Then her opponent braced her bloody hands on the floor and started shakily raising herself, prompting another round of enthusiastic cheering.

This time it was Jessica who took a running start at her opponent, who'd risen to her hands and knees when a powerful roundhouse kick knocked her jaw out of alignment and sent her rolling back toward the side of the cage. The woman screeched in pain. The fight was won. Jessica knew that already. This lady might have thrived against some of the wretches kept in crates at the back of the stage, but she had no real fighting skills and was not a worthy adversary for someone of Jessica's trained pedigree. She doubted any of the women imprisoned here would even come close. Fighting her way through all of them wouldn't be a problem. The only question was what would happen to her at the end of the night.

The crowd, seeing that Jessica's opponent had no chance of rallying, started up a chant: *"Finish her! Finish her! Finish her!"*

At the start of her journey early yesterday, Jessica did a lot of reflecting about how happy she'd been to leave her former life of violence behind. She'd gone years without killing anyone and that was the way she wanted it. She hoped to never have to kill another human being again. She still held out some sliver of hope she might yet get free and return to that more peaceful path, but right here and now, on this most haunted of all nights, she would give these pagan celebrants the blood show they were thirsting for.

She stalked slowly over to where the other woman lay mewling and squirming on the floor. Standing over her with clenched fists raised overhead, she planted a foot on the woman's back and gestured toward the crowd, further inflaming their blood lust. The aluminum bleachers rocked and rattled harder than ever. She could see them *shaking*. It inspired her to continue inciting them in hopes of the bleachers collapsing from the strain.

After lifting the whimpering woman off the cage floor, Jessica ran into the center of the cage, executed another spinning move, and heaved her out of her arms. The woman's back smashed against a wall panel with even greater force than before. When she dropped to the floor this time, she didn't move or make a sound, but the bloody snot bubble that popped from one of her nostrils told Jessica she was still alive.

The crowd was in a screaming frenzy as Jessica grabbed her opponent by the hair and dragged her back toward the center of the cage. She hauled her up to her knees and held her there with one hand while waving to the crowd with the other. Some of the more drunkenly fired-up spectators came rushing down from the bleachers to jump up on the catwalk outside the stage. The wild cheering from the rest continued as baton-swinging guards rushed in and worked to remove them.

Jessica waited until a relative degree of order had been restored.

DEPRAVED HALLOWEEN

Then she took her opponent's head in both hands, gripped it tight, looked out at the crowd with a leering grin for a final moment of anticipation, and then she gave the defeated woman's neck a brutal twist, snapping it. She held onto the now very dead woman a moment longer, roaring in triumph, before letting go and allowing the corpse to drop to the floor.

She stood in the center of the cage, turning in a circle with hands raised overhead again, basking in the glory.

A shameful little part of her didn't fully hate it.

She cast her gaze upward and searched the balcony booths, smiling when she saw Callie on her feet applauding wildly. Toad Jr. was standing next to her. It was hard to be sure from this distance, but she sensed he was less than pleased with the outcome of the fight.

~

Bubba Ray's new rubber mask was doing a fine job of obscuring his identity. Loretta had picked it out for him at a party store in town after their trip to Goodwill. It was a depiction of a green-skinned zombie woman with an open scalp wound and bone visible where half of her face had rotted away. Loretta felt the fake skin tone sort of went with the gray tinge of Bubba Ray's slightly decomposed flesh. They didn't quite match, but she wasn't wrong. It was now possible to pass off the rotted flesh and the bolts in his neck as nothing more than other elements of his costume. The many appreciative comments he received within moments of walking into the Juke and Puke confirmed this beyond any doubt, while also functioning as unassailable evidence that no one would ever guess it was Bubba Ray Mitchell's face hidden beneath the mask.

The irony in the situation was that Bubba Ray now felt more uncomfortable than ever. This was in large part because of the leering looks that accompanied so many of those appreciative comments he was receiving, nearly all of which were from male patrons of the roadhouse. Out in the parking lot, all he cared about was not being recognized, but that was before finding himself surrounded by a bunch of highly inebriated men with lustful looks on their faces.

As he passed through the dense throng of patrons with Loretta's hand gripped tightly in his own, his ass was groped numerous times. The first time he was furious about it and longed to kick the offender's ass for daring to lay hands on him, but the tightness of the crowd and the dim party lighting combined to make it difficult to pick out who'd done it. Then he gave up and accepted that he couldn't stop people from groping him. His only consolation was in the cheap purse Loretta made him bring along. She had one just like it. In each one was a knife. Bubba Ray's fingers stayed inside his purse the whole time as Loretta dragged him through the crowd. If any of these assholes tried anything ruder or anything more violating than basic grabass, they'd be getting a nasty surprise.

Soon they arrived at the section of the roadhouse reserved for live music performance. The band playing behind the chicken wire tonight was not playing the southern rock or country fare that was the norm for the Juke and Puke. In place of cowboy hats and western gear, the musicians were all clothed identically, their outfits consisting of black capes with red inner linings, dark vests worn over puffy white shirts, and black slacks. Their faces were caked in white makeup, and each of them wore their dyed-black hair slicked back. They looked like what you'd get if Dracula made four clones of himself and they all formed a band together. As for their sound, it was about what you'd expect based on their look, a vaguely punkish strain of rockabilly with spooky lyrics.

The tables and chairs that were normally in this area had all been cleared out to make room for dancing. Dancing was a thing that didn't happen much on regular nights at the Juke and Puke, but tonight was no regular night. The floor was filled with gyrating costumed revelers. As Loretta pulled him out into their midst, Bubba Ray saw people dressed as pirates, devils, vampires, werewolves, sexy nurses, and more. Some wore complete head-to-toe costumes with lavish makeup while others wore only a mask with their regular clothes. With her party store hockey mask, Loretta fell into the latter category, because the rest of her outfit was still what she'd worn since last night, the raggedy Poison T-shirt and denim shorts. Bubba Ray wasn't sure she even owned any other clothes.

Once they were out in the approximate center of the floor, Loretta let go of his hand and commenced thrashing about in a wildly spastic way Bubba Ray supposed nominally counted as "dancing." She looked like she'd been possessed by a demon and for all he knew that was nothing less than the damn truth. On a few occasions, she abruptly stopped and shoved at him, urging him to dance with her. His hesitation to join in was rooted in two things. One, he'd never danced in his life, unless spinning around in the living room as a toddler while his daddy listened to old C&W records counted. The bigger reason was the goddamn heels. He'd managed to stay on his feet while

Loretta pulled him through the crowd, but he'd been in a panic the entire time, feeling like he was perpetually on the verge of a spill.

She shoved at him again, almost making him topple over. "*Dance, bitch!*" she said, shouting to be heard over the raucous music. Then she cackled. "*That's a fuckin' order, you sexy thing!*"

Behind the mask, Bubba Ray felt like crying. Once again, thanks to that loathsome obedience compulsion, he had no choice but to make an effort. He made a tentative attempt to start moving his feet while shaking his ass a bit. His movements felt awkward and clumsy, stiff and mechanical, devoid of any sense of rhythm whatsoever, but he kept at it because he had no choice.

As she often had since being magically bequeathed with this ability to control him, Loretta laughed like crazy, braying her amusement from behind her mask at such a volume he could hear it even through the loud live music. For the first time in a while, he yearned to haul off and hit her, but he refrained because he knew what a stupid thing it would be. He could do it. He wasn't fucking paralyzed. But she'd get back at him by making him punch himself in the face a bunch of times, maybe something even worse than that. The other big thing to consider was he was no longer strong enough to knock her out with his hardest punch.

Not even close.

So he kept dancing in his ridiculous herky-jerky way while Loretta kept on laughing. After a while, she stopped doing her weird, random flailing thing and started copying his movements. A few other dancers in the vicinity noticed and started doing the same. Someone dubbed it the "zombie dance" and in short order it became a whole thing, with at least half the dancing revelers doing some version of it. Even the band got in on the act, launching into a song the singer announced as "The Zombie Boogie."

Bubba Ray didn't know whether to feel flattered or embarrassed. He felt like he was being made fun of, but everyone seemed to be having a high ol' time. It wasn't until one of the dancing men tried to rub up on him from behind that he realized what was happening. He was stuck on his old, ingrained perception of himself, which was no longer relevant to anyone but himself. Except for Loretta, what the partying people at the Juke and Puke saw when they looked at him was a woman with a hot body in revealing clothes. He wasn't being ridiculed, at least not in a mean way. They were joining in because they perceived him as someone cool and exciting they wanted to be around.

It was fuckin' weird.

Disorienting, too, because Bubba Ray had never had the slightest inkling of what it felt like to be at the center of that type of attention. For a few fleeting seconds, he felt close to enjoying it.

Then the guy rubbed up on him.

Instinct sent Bubba Ray's hand into his purse. The guy was grinding away against him as his fingers closed around the handle of the knife. He'd begun extracting it from his purse when he happened to turn his head and catch sight of someone he thought might be Cletus Mitchell. Or maybe not. He wasn't sure, because this person was taller than his weird cousin by at least a foot. The build sure was similar, though, and he had that same rotting pumpkin on his head, except it looked a little different now. Fleshier. Or more rotten-looking. It was hard to tell because the person who maybe was and maybe wasn't his cousin was out in the main bar area, standing still as the thickening crowd flowed around him. The pumpkin head was slowly swiveling about, as if studying the sea of drunken humanity. A part of Bubba Ray's psyche was still telling him he needed to do something about this dude grinding his erection against his ass, but the pumpkin guy compelled most of his attention.

His height was such that he stood well above everyone out there. There was something distinctly eerie and uncanny about him. The longer he stared, the more certain Bubba Ray became that the clothes the pumpkin guy was wearing were the same garments he'd last seen Cletus wearing, only now they looked stretched and split at the seams. The ripped clothes made him look like a Halloween version of The Incredible Hulk.

Maybe that was on purpose?

It could be part of his costume.

And maybe he was wearing stilts to look super tall. Okay, that was ridiculous and Bubba Ray knew it, but how else to explain what he was seeing when he felt 99.9% sure that was his cousin out there?

As if sensing this thought, the pumpkin head swiveled in Bubba Ray's direction, the orange-tinted eyes locking in on him as if by some form of supernatural radar. An instant later, the jagged, blood-stained pumpkin teeth spread in a wide grin.

Bubba Ray shuddered.

That's Cletus. I don't know how, but it is.

The pumpkin face turned away from him ... and continued

turning, doing a full 360-degree revolution, jagged grin continuing to widen.

On any other night, faced with a sight like that, Bubba Ray would make getting as far away from it as possible his number one priority. Beyond the initial shock of recognition, what he mostly felt was a strangely deeper sense of kinship with his cousin, one that delved deeper than the bloodline they shared. Like Cletus, he'd changed, had become something new. He sensed deadly intent in Cletus, but that was okay too. For his part, he was already doomed. He'd be gone with the sunrise. Loretta had said it, and he believed her. As for the rest of these people, well, he reckoned he didn't give a single warmed-over shit about any of them.

Not anymore.

The guy behind him had his hands on Bubba Ray's breasts now. He was talking dirty, telling him all the things he wanted to do to him.

Bubba Ray's face hardened as he went cold inside.

That's enough.

He squirmed free of the man's embrace as he took the knife out of his purse, slashing outward with it as he whirled around on the heels. The wobble that occurred as he did this sent the slashing trajectory of his hand off-target slightly. Instead of cutting the man's throat, the sharp edge of the blade sliced across his face. Blood gushed from the slash across his cheek as the man recoiled in shock. He staggered backward, slipped, and fell to the floor.

Bubba Ray pounced on him before he could get up.

Behind him, Loretta whooped in celebration of the bloodshed. "*Hell, yeah!*"

When screams erupted from her general vicinity, Bubba Ray didn't have to look to know she'd drawn blood of her own. He raised his blade and brought it down, slamming it into one of the groping pest's bulging eyes.

From somewhere farther out, perhaps out there in the main bar area, many more screams of abject terror rang out, filling the air. On the stage, the band of rockin' Dracula impostors played on as the Juke and Puke descended into bedlam.

~

Down in the Sin Den, Jessica was removed from the fighting cage and escorted under armed guard to the same back office she'd been taken to earlier. A high percentage of the crowd came down from the bleachers and pressed in close as she was led down the aisle, cheering and straining to touch and grope her. Guards repelled them with batons and shock rods, bloodying faces of paying patrons and loosening more than a few teeth. Their unhinged enthusiasm amazed Jessica. They were acting like they were in the presence of a superstar athlete, not someone they'd never set eyes on prior to a half hour ago.

Callie and Toad Jr. were waiting for her in the back office. The same two men in Western wear still anchored their respective sides of the old sofa, puffing away on cigars and regarding her with unreadable expressions. Two guards with sidearms remained in the room with them while the others went out to the hallway.

Callie embraced Jessica like an old friend, slapping her on the back before breaking the clench and stepping back to shake her head, the features of her ruined face twisting to express something like awe. "My God, that was incredible. You said you had some skills, but I never imagined anything like that."

Jessica shrugged, said nothing.

Toad Jr. finished lighting a cigar and came away from the desk, jabbing a forefinger at Jessica. "What's your name, woman?"

Jessica didn't like his tone, but she knew better than to verbally joust with a man like this in a situation where she was at such a disadvantage. One wrong word from her, and he'd have his men chop her up and bury her in a deep hole. Callie might object, but she wasn't sure it'd make a difference.

She sighed. "Jessica."

He grunted. "What's your background, Jess? Where'd you learn to fight like a goddamn mercenary?"

Jessica hated it when people—men, especially—shortened her name. A part of her already burned with the need to cave in this man's stupid, jowly face. Again, she tamped down the bile rising inside her in the interest of staying alive.

"I'm ex-military. Black ops. A trained assassin."

Toad Jr. took the cigar out of his mouth, grunting and shaking his head as he glanced at Callie. "Did you know about any of this?"

Callie shook her head. "No, Big H. I swear. I just knew she had a little bit of fighting ability and thought, what the hell, might as well see if I can make some money off her."

Toad Jr. nodded thoughtfully after another puff on his cigar. His eyes had a predatory, assessing glint in them as he looked Jessica over. After yet another puff on his cigar, his gaze shifted back to Callie. "I'll make a generous cash offer for her right now. How does twenty-five grand sound?"

Callie didn't look happy. "I could make a lot more than that with the higher bout cuts I'd get as her owner. Even by the end of tonight, I'd make more."

A big grin spread across Toad Jr.'s face, but the expression didn't reach his eyes. He approached Callie, looming over her like the predator he was. "That's true, little lady, but what's also true is you sent a trained killer up against my best girl tonight. A gal I had high hopes for, for your information." Callie cringed and leaned away from him as he tossed his hands up in consternation. "Now that's all out the damn window. I'd like to believe you didn't pit this badass killer against my champion knowing in advance what she was capable of, but I don't think I do."

Callie's eyes misted with tears. "I swear I didn't know. You've got to believe me. I know how stupid that would be. I'd definitely tell you before trying to enter her in the competition."

A lengthy silence ensued as Toad Jr. glared down at the trembling woman. The air in the office felt thick with the promise of impending violence. Jessica believed the man was seconds away from taking Callie's slender neck in his big, beefy hands and strangling her.

Then he backed off as his big grin returned. "Where's your loving husband tonight? I'm frankly surprised to see you here without him." He snorted. "Hell, I'm surprised to see you here at all. It's been a while. A *long* while." He glanced at one of the cigar-smoking men on the sofa. "How long would you say it's been, Ambrose?"

Ambrose waggled a hand. "Three years or thereabouts."

His mirror image at the opposite end of the sofa nodded. "Yep. Three years and a few months."

Toad Jr. chuckled. "Sounds about right." Despite the chuckle, his expression was flat and humorless as he again made eye contact with Callie. "You still haven't told us where your better half is tonight."

Callie couldn't stop shaking. "He's out on puh-puh . . . patrol."

The tears welling in her eyes overflowed.

Toad Jr. backhanded her, knocking her to the floor. He set his smoldering cigar in a glass ashtray and massaged his knuckles, sneering down at the weeping woman. "I don't tolerate lying in women with faces like angels. What makes you think I'd take it from a cheating cunt with a face like a blender? I put in a call to the sheriff shortly after you showed up here. Do you want to know what they told me about Dalton?"

Callie wailed in despair as she curled up on the floor. She looked as defeated as any human being Jessica had ever seen. When she didn't answer the big man's question right away, he asked it again. Again, she didn't answer, just kept on weeping.

Toad Jr. sighed, shaking his head in disappointment. "What the sheriff told me, Callie, was they hadn't heard from your man since yesterday. I wonder why that would be."

His tone on that last part indicated it was a purely rhetorical statement rather than an actual question. He wasn't expecting any answer at all, much less an honest one.

Jessica figured she had nothing to lose at this point by interjecting with the truth. "She castrated him with a heated fireplace poker. Then she killed him by driving it through his brain."

Toad Jr. glanced at her, arching an eyebrow. "Damn. Seriously?"

Jessica nodded. "Send some of your guys out there to check if you don't believe me."

The big man grunted. "Oh, I'll send some men out there for sure, but I believe you, missy."

He held out a hand to one of the guards, palm up, indicating what he wanted by flexing his fingers. The guard's sidearm was already unholstered, likely as a precaution in the event Jessica gave any hint of trying some more of the moves she'd demonstrated in the fighting cage on the men in this room. He put it in Toad Jr.'s hand while giving Jessica a hard look meant to discourage her from trying anything now that he was armed only with a baton.

Jessica gave a slight nod to indicate she understood. Not that she had any intention yet of making a move. The other guard in the room still had his piece and the similar hard look on his face told her he was more than willing to use it at the slightest hint of anything hinky on her part.

The big man worked the gun's slide to chamber a round, then aimed it at the cowering woman on the floor, who started to rise when she saw the looming gun barrel. She started talking, making a last-ditch attempt to bargain her way out of the doom bearing down on her.

It was useless.

All anyone had to do was see the grim look on the club owner's face to know that.

"Shut the hell up," Toad Jr. told her. "You know as well as I do killing a Trimble is a death sentence in this town. I'm doing you a favor, doll. At least this way it's over fast."

He squeezed the trigger.

The bullet punched through Callie's forehead and sent a spray of blood and brains across the floor from the exit wound at the back of her skull.

Toad Jr. returned the weapon to the guard and shifted his focus to Jessica. "I reckon you know what this means, but in case you need it spelled out, you belong to me now."

Jessica had figured as much. "Okay."

The big man retrieved his cigar from the ashtray and got it going again with a Zippo. "We don't get gals like you here often," he told her, after expelling a cloud of smoke. "More like never, if I'm being honest. I expect you've told the truth about what you are, but I'd like to do some more digging into your background. If I like what I find out, maybe I could offer you a role in my operation."

Jessica frowned. "You mean, like, a job?"

Toad Jr. shrugged, chuckling. "Don't sound so surprised. I didn't get where I am by not recognizing a unique opportunity when I see it. The business I run here requires having some tough characters in my employ to make sure everything goes smoothly. I think you might be perfect for the gig. What do you think?"

Jessica glanced at the dead woman on the floor, then made eye contact with the boss. "What I think is it beats a bullet in the head any day of the week."

Toad Jr. cracked up at that, slapping a thigh as he leaned his ample ass back against the edge of his desk. "You're funny. I like you. Like I said, though, I'll need to do some checking first. I'm sure you understand. In the meantime, how do you feel about another fight?"

Jessica thought about the women in those cages out in the arena, how pitiful-looking most of them were. Even the ones healthier in appearance wouldn't present anything like a real threat.

She shrugged. "Why not?"

The boss pushed away from the desk, clapped his hands together. "That's the spirit!" He glanced at the guards. "Escort the lady back to the octagon. Tell Phil . . ." He paused to wink at Jessica. "That's the fight boss. Tell Phil to await instructions." He glanced at the floor, face crinkling in disgust. "And get somebody in here to clean up this mess."

~

Up in the Juke and Puke, chaos reigned.

The guy who'd rubbed up on him was dead within a few swings of the blade, but Bubba Ray stabbed him a few more times for good measure. All the nervous energy that'd been building within him all day as Loretta taunted, teased, and humiliated him vented outward in the form of an explosion of murderous rage. In the normal course of things, he wasn't prone to public episodes of unhinged violence. Sure, he liked to sometimes snatch folks and haul them back to Jed's place for extended torture and rape sessions, but that was violence perpetrated in a controlled environment. Unless something went awry with the snatching itself, a rare event, the risk was mostly quite low.

Pretty much the opposite of what was happening now.

After reeling out of the way in shock at the beginning of his attack on the groper, a few brave souls tried to intervene. When he sensed hands reaching for him, Bubba Ray yanked the knife out of the dead man's body and slashed outward in a wide arc, back and forth several times. There were screams and gasps of pain as the blade parted skin and drew blood. More attempts to intervene ensued, but by then he was on his feet, lashing out again and again while wobbling precariously on the high heels.

Enough people were around him that a group might have soon managed to come together and prevail against him, but even those who were willing were thwarted by the manic actions of Loretta. By then she'd already cut several people with her knife. Bubba Ray saw multiple bodies on the floor in her vicinity. Some were wounded, but he saw at least one slit throat belonging to a shaggy-haired man wearing a simple Zorro mask. People caught between these two clusters of savage violence occurring so close together became overwhelmed, uncertain of where they should focus their defensive actions.

Loretta was a whirling dervish of flesh-shredding, coked-up energy, spinning and spinning as she slashed and slashed, her limber arm whipping the blood-dripping blade around with reckless abandon. Fingers went flying from the upraised hand of a woman trying to shield herself. Gaping slash wounds opened across the faces of several unfortunates who didn't get out of the way quickly enough. Bubba Ray caught glimpses of this as he continued to move and turn clumsily in a desperate effort to fend off those still trying to get close enough to disarm him. What he saw of Loretta's annihilating assault on anyone stupid enough to get within range of her inspired awe inside him. He hated what she'd done to him—hated that his time on earth was near an end—but in those moments, he felt as one with her.

This was their night. Their time.

Kill it on the dance floor, she'd told him.

So be it.

He turned and shoved his knife into the throat of a musclebound man in a Captain Jack Sparrow costume. The man had crept up on him from behind, closing to within grabbing range, but he'd hesitated a millisecond too long. Bubba Ray couldn't help laughing at the look of surprise on his face when the big blade of the hunting knife plunged into his flesh. When Bubba Ray ripped the blade out again, blood jetted from the wound, spraying against his mask and the front of his dress. The man took a staggering step toward him with a hand extended in a final effort to grab for the knife, but the effort only earned him another ragged hole in his flesh.

By that point, the screaming on the dance floor and from out there in the bar area was louder than the driving beat of the psychobilly band on the stage. After persisting through nearly the length of an entire song while the multiple attacks on patrons were in progress, the band's performance came to a crashing, clanging halt. Loud voices raised in a tone of authority became audible as the last notes of the interrupted song died away.

Bubba Ray looked toward the bar area and saw men attired in the garb of security personnel working to push their way through the crowd. Some were headed for the dance floor, but the majority were trying to get to the tall man with the pumpkin head, who Bubba Ray was still certain was some mutated version of Cletus. In between lashing out with his knife to keep more would-be heroes at arm's length, he looked out toward the bar area and saw his pumpkin-headed cousin doing astounding things. He swatted at people with his long, talon-like hands, flaying open throats and faces, eviscerating bellies that spewed forth piles of steaming guts. Cletus tore off heads and flung them away, sending them spinning high out into the air like basketballs. One time Bubba Ray saw Cletus lift a man and stretched his jagged mouth wide enough to bite off the top of the man's head. He picked up dead bodies and whipped them around like human-shaped baseball bats, knocking down scores of people.

The stampede toward the exits was inevitable.

The guards trying to get to Cletus were stymied by the sheer press of bodies trying to get past them. In frustration, multiple security officers pulled their guns and fired at Cletus, but Bubba Ray's transformed cousin appeared impervious to them. The bullets had no more effect on him than Japanese Zeros strafing Godzilla with machine gun fire.

It didn't take long for the remaining people on the dance floor to realize they had bigger problems than a couple of maniacs with knives. Almost everyone dropped what they were doing and joined the attempted exodus from the Juke and Puke. Bubba Ray stood there huffing and puffing in the middle of the dance floor, watching the retreating backs of the fleeing patrons. At that moment, he believed he and Loretta were the only ones who'd stayed behind.

He kept thinking that until Loretta glanced his way and screamed, "Look out!"

But it was too late.

A solitary straggler who'd hidden in a dark corner of the dance floor throughout the assault had crept close enough during Bubba Ray's moment of distraction to snatch his knife from his fingers. Instinct caused Bubba Ray to turn toward a little man in a Batman outfit.

The pint-sized Batman plunged the knife into Bubba Ray's belly the instant he turned, driving it into the hilt. Bubba Ray tried grabbing at the man's hands to pull the blade out as his attacker held it there, twisting it inside him. An explosion of blinding pain made his knees go weak. A disconnected part of him marveled at how flesh that had been dead for days could experience pain so intense. It was a reminder of how powerful the Halloween magic Loretta had somehow harnessed was.

Unfortunately, as he already knew, it was not powerful enough to save him now.

Loretta arrived as Bubba Ray dropped to his knees, tackling the little Batman and driving him to the floor. The man screamed as shrilly as any woman Bubba Ray had ever had fun with in Jed's torture shed, but his screams soon yielded to wet gurgling as Loretta sliced open his jugular.

Bubba Ray took his hands away from the wound to his stomach and shivered at the sight of his blood-coated palms. As the last of his second body's strength began to drain away, he crumpled to the floor and rolled onto his back, staring through bleary eyes at the multicolored strings of crisscrossing party lights hanging from the ceiling. His vision came back into focus as Loretta's face loomed above his own. Her cheap party store hockey mask was gone, swept away when she knelt next to him.

She had tears in her eyes as she carefully removed his zombie lady mask and cast it aside. "Oh, Ray-Ray. I'm sorry your last party ended sooner than we thought it would."

He managed a whimpering final laugh as she caressed his face with a bloody, soothing hand. "It's okay. At least I went out in style."

His eyes fluttered as his voice weakened.

A last wheezing breath rattled from his throat as his thoughts faded to gray, then to black.

Loretta bent down to kiss him.

Then she dropped her knife and joined the mad rush to flee the Juke and Puke.

~

Jessica stood alone in the center of the fighting cage for at least ten minutes before she saw some men come out of the door she'd been marched through after being escorted from Toad Jr.'s office. The trio of men who emerged through it now consisted of two guards flanking a large bald man in a two-toned bowling shirt. As the door shut behind them, they headed toward the stage where the women in crates were stacked against the back wall.

Before this development, she'd waited passively in the cage, doing her best to show no emotion of any kind or otherwise react to the antics of the increasingly restless crowd. The sheer disparate range of things the drunken rowdies shouted at her during this period was almost impressive. Some of those things were professions of love and admiration. There was at least one marriage proposal, though how the guy meant to make that happen given her status as a possession of the man in charge was a mystery. It wasn't just praise being directed her way, though. There was a lot of ugliness, too. She was bombarded with a ceaseless stream of misogynistic insults. A few men in the crowd screamed at the tops of their lungs about how they wanted to see her stomped to death. She did her best to let their hateful words wash over her, but it did begin to get to her a bit, slowly but surely, so much so that it came as a relief when the man in the bowling shirt climbed the steps to the stage and directed the guards as they removed one of the women from a crate.

The prospect of killing another innocent wasn't something she relished, but she rationalized it with the knowledge that these women were doomed no matter what. This was far from the first time she'd been put in the position of killing people who didn't deserve it to preserve her own life. There was no way of getting around what a shitty thing it was, but that wouldn't stop her from going through with it. One more stain on an already blackened soul wouldn't make much of a difference at this point anyway.

As the woman they'd removed from the second row of crates was lowered to the stage, Jessica began flexing and stretching, readying herself to begin the process of brutally demolishing another human being. The woman on the stage grimaced as she tentatively stretched her scrawny limbs. It wasn't possible to fully assess her potential as a fighter from this distance, but from what Jessica could already discern, there wasn't much to worry about.

But then an interesting thing happened.

Another crate was opened and a second woman was pulled out onto the stage. From a distance, she looked marginally less physically wasted than the first woman, though far from the picture of good health. Then yet another crate on the bottom row of stacks was opened, and a brown-skinned woman who moved with the sinewy speed of a leopard shot of the crate, eluding multiple guards as she raced toward the side of the stage. She was soon cornered and subdued with shock rods, but for a second there Jessica thought she might manage to leap off the stage. Where she intended to go from there, Jessica did not know. There were too many of Toad Jr.'s people surrounding the stage. The woman would've been taken down no matter what, but it sure was a valiant effort.

The trio of women was led from the stage to the fighting cage, with the two skinny ones quaking in fear from the barrage of boos and jeers from the seething crowd. The brown-skinned woman, who Jessica saw was a Latina once she drew a little closer, showed no fear as she walked ahead of the others with shoulders and chin up.

Jessica frowned.

Depending on her training and abilities—if any—that one might be trouble.

Nothing had been said to her about how the next fight would proceed, but based on her first one, she'd assumed it would be another one-on-one bout. Instead, it appeared three women would be pitted against her at the same time. The frenzy level of the crowd ramped up again as many in the bleachers began to come to the same conclusion.

At first blush, this ran contrary to Toad Jr.'s expressed interest in bringing her on as part of his team. She believed she could easily prevail against any single one of these women head-to-head, even the stronger, feistier one, but as a group, it'd be a far more daunting task. Defeating all three at once was certainly doable. What she worried about was making some critical mistake at the wrong moment, one her opponents wouldn't hesitate to exploit. Jessica was highly skilled, but she wasn't some superwoman. Allowing them even the slightest opportunity to pile in on her at once could prove fatal. Victory would depend on fast action and creating enough space to keep them spread out.

Toad Jr. was testing her, seeing if she was what she claimed. It was the only thing that made sense. Well, she'd have to try her best not to let him down.

Once the trio of women arrived at the fighting cage, they were led up the stairs to the catwalk and then through a door into the cage. Two guards and the man in the bowling shirt entered behind them. Two of the women stared at Jessica with wary, haunted eyes, the third with a palpable thirst for cracking skulls.

The man in the bowling shirt—Phil, presumably—cleared his throat and spoke into a microphone: "Ladies and gentlemen, whores and sick fucking bastards, the Sin Den is proud to present a match sure to go down in the annals of Bitch Fight history as absolutely legendary, a battle—"

As Phil continued his spiel, Jessica noticed how the attention of all three of her opponents had shifted to the crowd. Even the stronger one was surveying the sea of screaming faces, standing proudly with her chin jutting defiantly outward, sneering like a genuine badass with no fear.

Jessica smiled.

Since her arrival in this den of debauchery, no one had spelled out any formal fighting rules.

Anything goes.

The volume of Phil's shouting into the microphone had increased along with the roar of the crowd, whose stamping of feet on the bleachers became so cacophonous it made them sound like an army of marching robots.

Moving fast, Jessica slipped in behind the Latina and got her in a chokehold. The woman was surprised but fought back with admirable toughness, nearly managing to shake free as Jessica wrestled her to the floor. Before she could do that, Jessica slid a hand around to the woman's face, spread her thumb and forefinger apart, and gouged them into the woman's eyes, grinding them into their sockets with every ounce of strength she could muster. The woman screamed and thrashed like a bucking bronco beneath her, demonstrating impressive strength, but Jessica managed to hold on and continue gouging away.

As she did this, she was dimly aware of the crowd's explosive eruption of outrage. A rain of bottles and cans struck the outside of the cage, and a few landed inside it. One crumpled aluminum can hit Jessica's back, but the soft impact was no more jarring than a fly landing on her. She continued pushing her digits into the struggling woman's eyes while Phil screamed into the microphone, demanding calm from the audience. The advice was ignored. More plastic, aluminum, and glass missiles rained down on the fighting cage. The woman was still screaming beneath Jessica, but now it was more in pain than rage. Jessica felt blood and fluid oozing out around her fingers. By the time the guards finally recovered from their shock and pulled her away, the most fearsome of her opponents was effectively blinded.

Jessica shook free of the hands holding onto her and thrust her arms triumphantly into the air, inciting another surge of rabid indignation. She grinned and made devil horns with her fists, shaking them like she was a fan at a metal concert instead of a coerced combatant at an illegal underground fight-to-the-death club. At this point, feeling more than a little unhinged herself, she was making a deliberate effort to drive them completely out of control. It was either an act of willful and aggressive self-destruction or a brilliantly risky survival strategy, she wasn't sure which. Phil screamed recriminations and threats, getting almost up in her face, but they were just words, useless fucking words, flowing over her body like water, draining away, fading, becoming nothing.

The two other women who'd entered the ring with the Latina had retreated and were cowering together at the bottom of one of the cage walls. Their eyes were full of tears, and they were looking at her like she was some kind of crazy woman.

Like she was a monster.

Maybe they were right.

Phil gesticulated wildly at the guards, ordering them to seize Jessica. She went into a defensive posture as they approached her, moving her feet as she sized up the one reaching for the gun in his holster. Was she crazy enough to try taking it from him in the middle of all this madness?

Maybe.

Just as the guard was starting to draw his weapon, a massively loud crash from the direction of the arena's entrance sent a shock through the crowd. Everyone in the cage turned toward the sound. The screaming of moments ago was replaced by gasps of surprise and cries of fear. Right on the heels of the first big crash, screams of agony and terror emanated from the same direction. Then came another tremendous crash, this one of floor-shaking ferocity.

Something made Jessica look up in time to spy the rectangular shape of a door spinning through the air high overhead. Her sense of adrenaline-fueled bravado deserted her as she watched the door descend, still spinning like a rogue helicopter rotor as it smashed into one of the bleachers near the top, taking out multiple rows of spectators in one fell swoop.

The tumult that ensued dwarfed all the preceding madness in a single instant. Surviving spectators came swarming down from the bleachers, running into each other in an instinctive effort to get far away from whatever was capable of ripping a door off its hinges and tossing it through the air as if it were no more substantial than a pack of tissues. The problem, for a lot of them, was they were running in the exact wrong direction, toward the entrance, the approximate location of whatever had done this. More screams of agony filled the stuffy air in the arena as those at the front of the surge neared the entrance. Numerous other people got trampled, crushed underfoot in the stampede of panicking humanity.

In a few more moments, Jessica perceived a strange shape rising above the crowd, impossibly tall and lanky, with a head shaped like a ... like a ...

Pumpkin.

Jessica shook her head.

No. No fucking way. It can't be.

But it was.

That fact became undeniable as the marauding pumpkin monster continued cutting an effortless swath of carnage through the crowd, ripping off heads, biting off heads, tearing dozens of human bodies apart as if they were made of matchsticks rather than flesh and blood.

It was the same guy—the same weird geek—who'd harassed her at the gas station shortly after her arrival in Montclair. She didn't know how it was possible, but she felt the truth of it deep inside.

Something had happened to him, some inexplicable supernatural transformation, but it was him. So much taller, larger, and stronger than before, but him, no question.

Phil and the guards who'd accompanied him into the fighting cage were as thunderstruck as anyone. Jessica took advantage of their distraction to glance around and note how unguarded the door leading to the back offices was. The guards who'd been there had either fled or had rushed forward to fight off the monster. The number in the latter category was likely small. These were mercenaries, after all, not dedicated soldiers. Most would care more about saving their own skin than anything else.

Taking advantage of his distraction, Jessica snatched the gun from the holster of the guard who'd been about to draw down on her a few short minutes ago. Before he could grab her, she placed the muzzle of the gun against the side of his head and squeezed the trigger. She shifted her aim fast and shot the other guard in the face before he could undo the buckle of his holster.

Phil shrank away from her, cringing in terror with shaking hands raised.

Another shot in the face dropped him.

Sparing a final glance for her intended fight opponents, she considered putting the blind, wailing woman out of her misery with a bullet to the back of the head. She chose instead to leave her to her fate, whatever that might be. Leaving the cage through an unlocked panel door, she hopped from the edge of the catwalk to the floor and ran for the door leading to the back offices. By that point, the crowd was beginning to surge back in the opposite direction. Jessica was just ahead of its leading edge and managed to slip through the open door ahead of the rest of them, pulling it shut and locking it from the inside. A dozen fists or more hammered against the other side of the door, rattling it in its frame, but the door was sturdy steel. She moved away from it and looked up and down the hallway. One way led to a dead end, the other to a staircase.

She ran toward the staircase.

Through an open door to her right was Toad Jr.'s office. She skidded to a halt and peeked inside. There was no sign of the boss man, but his cowboy friends were dead on the sofa, each with a bullet entry wound in the forehead. Behind her, the banging on the door grew louder. Fearing the fleeing spectators might have found something to use as a battering ram, Jessica resumed her flight toward the stairs, arriving within a few more seconds. She raced up them and ran through another open door into the gravel employees' parking lot behind the Juke and Puke.

Right away, she spied Toad Jr.

He was fumbling with his keys next to a cherry red Corvette, his hands shaking like those of a man who has seen his life flash before his eyes. So intent was he on the task of trying to grip the right key for his vintage automobile that his senses failed to alert him to the danger approaching until it was too late. His prodigious bulk turned toward her in the last instant, mouth opening to say words he never got to speak because Jessica fired a bullet straight into it.

Stepping over his fallen corpse, she ripped his keys from his dead fingers, found the right key, and got in behind the wheel. She fired the engine up and spent a moment revving it, savoring the muscular power in that 8-cylinder roar. Then she put the Corvette in gear, cranked the wheel, and drove over Toad Jr.'s splayed legs.

Driving around the side of the building, she came up on the closed gate of a tall aluminum fence. Instead of stopping to see if she could get out and roll the gate open, she pushed the gas pedal to the floor and blasted through it, ripping a gaping hole in the fencing.

She drove around to the front of the building, scanned the crowded parking lot for a moment, surveying the scene of wounded bodies lying all around. It appeared the rampaging pumpkin monster had cut a similar swath of carnage through the patrons of the Juke and Puke. She heard wailing moans and cries of anguish even above the throaty rumble of the Corvette's engine.

Heads were turning her way.

She had the feeling there were people here who recognized this car. They were all cut from the same cloth. Sneering locals, many of whom undoubtedly knew all about the dead boss man's evil underground business. Never in her life had she wished more for the power to call in a vaporizing airstrike to wipe a place from the face of the earth.

Once upon a time . . .

But that time was gone.

Jessica gunned the engine and sped away from the Juke and Puke.

~

In joining the press to escape the Juke and Puke, Loretta undertook a certain level of risk. Her knockoff Jason mask was gone and she'd stripped off her blood-soaked Poison T-shirt, but there was a chance survivors of the dance floor massacre might recognize her anyway, maybe by her hair or the shape of her body. Whatever. It didn't matter. All that mattered was getting away. She didn't know if the thing Cletus had become would harm her. Maybe it would, maybe not, but she wasn't about to walk up to the thing and put it to the test. Either way, she had other reasons to run, mainly in the form of a bunch of dead, ventilated fuckers who'd tasted her steel. There was a good chance she'd be identified as a suspect and she wanted to be long gone before the law pigs could show up and start asking questions.

The doors leading out of the roadhouse were all jammed with people. Behind the logjam was a writhing mass of other people jostling for position. Loretta felt the weight of all that body heat closing in on her like a suffocating blanket. Losing patience, she twisted her slender body and slithered through the narrow gaps between people, poking and jabbing hard with her sharp elbows to create spaces wide enough to continue slipping through until she was free of the knot of panicked, screaming humanity. She wound up in the bar area, the floor of which was littered with bodies and parts of bodies. The floor was awash with blood. So was the damn ceiling, for that matter.

Most importantly, Cletus seemed to have disappeared. That provided a fresh aspect of mystery until she detected more screaming from the direction of the Sin Den's underground entrance.

Stepping over bodies and trying not to lose her footing in all the slippery blood, she made it to the windows at the front of the roadhouse. The thing to do at this point was obvious. She was shocked no one else had tried it yet. Picking up a barstool, she smashed out one of the windows and crawled through it, out into the night, where she took a moment to breathe in the blessedly cooler outside air before beginning a dash across the parking lot. Some of the people who'd made it out first glanced her way as she ran by them, but no one tried to stop her. Either they didn't recognize her as one of the attackers or they were too relieved to still be alive to bother trying to intercept her.

Out in the parking lot, she had a panicked few moments of disorientation, during which she couldn't remember where she'd parked Bubba Ray's Chevelle. Soon, though, she realized she'd overshot it by a row and backtracked, heaving a huge sigh of relief when she finally spotted it.

She ran to the Chevelle and got in, firing the engine up as soon as she was able to jam the key in the ignition. Changing gears, she punched the gas and backed out of the parking space without checking her mirror. There was a heavy thump of impact as the back of the Chevelle plowed into someone on foot behind her. Someone nearby screamed. Loretta kept her foot on the gas and backed over the person she'd hit, another scream piercing the night as one of her rear wheels crushed the fallen victim's head.

Loretta didn't care.

She was home free, on her way out of here.

Spotting the screaming person, a woman distraught over the sudden death of whoever Loretta had run over, she gave the woman the finger. Then she changed gears, hit the gas again, and drove as fast as she could out of the Juke and Puke's parking lot.

She didn't begin to calm down until she was several miles away, racing down some of the same dark back roads she and Bubba Ray had traveled the previous night. After many paranoid glances at the rearview mirror, she finally accepted that no one was in immediate pursuit of her. The rapid hammering of her heart at last began to slow and fall back into a normal rhythm. She wiped sweat from her brow as her breathing slowly evened out.

Loretta wasn't a person who panicked easily, but that'd been one hell of a close call. She thought she was probably going to be able to get away with everything she'd done, but maybe it'd be a good idea to get out of town for a bit, lie low until the heat died down. She'd just need to swing by her daddy's place first and liberate some cash from the stash in his safe. Just enough to get by on for a few weeks. Or, hell, maybe she'd take the whole damn shebang and split town for good. What was there to keep her here anyway, other than a bunch of drug-addled relations who'd abused and neglected her all her life?

Not a fuckin' thing, that's what.

Loretta smiled, suddenly captivated by the idea of leaving, never to return.

With all that money, she could reinvent herself, become something better than she was.

She snorted.

Or worse.

Whichever seemed like it'd be more fun was what it would boil down to in the end, she knew. The truth was, she was an unrepentant hedonist at heart, and it didn't seem likely anything would ever change that.

She was still smiling when she glanced again at the rearview mirror and saw the dead girl sitting in the back seat of the Chevelle.

The homecoming queen. Oh, shit.

It was her, no doubt.

Only there was something off about her now. The shade of her skin was pale. So pale, in fact, it almost glowed in the gloom of the back seat. When she spoke, her voice was imbued with a strange ethereal resonance, a subtle vibration that pimpled Loretta's arms with gooseflesh.

"I've come to take you home, Loretta."

Loretta trembled. "Are you a ghost?"

The homecoming queen smiled again.

Then she leaned forward to point at something in the road. "Watch out."

Loretta frowned.

She hadn't seen anything, but now a good portion of the road was obscured by a swirling ground fog that hadn't been there seconds ago. As she drove on, the Chevelle's headlights picked out a tall, imposing figure standing amid the fog. A primal sense of terror and dark wonder gripped Loretta as she took in the creature's egg-shaped head with its tapering square chin, bulbous black eyes, and pointed ears.

"What the fuck is that?"

The homecoming queen's dead lips were against Loretta's ear now, whispering insidious words about night things and the sacred territory of the dead, through which they were now passing.

Territory that belonged to the God of Halloween.

Who was right in front of her, spreading his long arms, reaching toward her with his talon-like fingers. Looming behind him, shrouded in more swirling mist and even taller and scarier looking than he'd been mere minutes ago, was Cletus, whose leering pumpkin head had swollen to several times its original size. Like Elise, he was one of the Halloween God's night things now.

Loretta closed her eyes.

See you soon, Ray-Ray.

She wrenched the wheel of the Chevelle and it went sailing off the road. Her body smashed through the windshield as the car struck a tree. The top of her head hit the wide, solid trunk of the ancient tree dead-on, mashing it flat like a cheap can of beer.

~

Just as he had been when she pulled up to this place the night before, the clerk at the Pump N' Go was nodding off behind the counter as

DEPRAVED HALLOWEEN

Jessica directed the Corvette across the gas station's parking lot at full speed. The high revving of the engine woke him up an instant too late, his eyes fluttering open and his head turning toward the front windows as the front of the car smashed through the front of the store and kept coming, stopping only after it slammed into the sales counter. The impact knocked big Danny Trimble off his stool and threw him into the wall behind him.

Seconds after he collapsed to the floor, Jessica climbed out of the Corvette through an open window, leaned over the wreck of the counter, and pointed her gun at Danny's bleeding face. "Who's the stupid cunt now, asshole?"

He squinted up at her in amazement, stunned to see who had come crashing back into his life. "Please," he said, whimpering. "I'm sorry. I . . . I didn't . . ."

Jessica fired a round into the wall next to him. "I don't give a fuck. Shut your piehole. Where's my fucking car, bitch?"

Danny whimpered some more, but then he raised his trembling hand again and gestured vaguely toward the wall behind him. "Out back. Keys are under the visor. I didn't take nothin' from it. Please don't huh-huh . . ."

Jessica made a sound of disgust. "Oh, shut up."

She shot him through an eye.

Walking back out through the wreck of the store's entrance, she glanced toward the road, checking both directions.

No one coming.

Yet.

She hurried around to the back of the gas station and found her Versa right where the dead store clerk said it would be, parked next to a dumpster. The keys were also where he'd said they would be. She opened the trunk and did a quick check of her belongings. It was clear someone—probably Danny—had gone through her bags. Everything was in disarray, but as far as she could tell, nothing important was missing. Even her cash was still in its secret compartment. Probably thought he'd have a lot more time to dispose of her car and go through her things at his leisure. The thought brought a smile to her lips. It was always nice to disappoint those who underestimated her. She discarded the stupid leather underwear she'd been forced to wear and donned some of the clothes from her bags.

After pulling her car around to the front, she went back into the store and grabbed some drinks and snacks. She felt it was the least of what she was owed, after what she'd been through.

Back behind the wheel of the Versa, she popped open a tall can of Budweiser, set it in the cupholder, and drove out to the edge of the parking lot. Before pulling out onto the road, she paused a moment to let out a shuddery breath and shake her head.

"Jesus. Fucking small towns. Never again, I swear to God."

She pulled out onto the road and drove fast toward the exit.

AFTERWORD
Exploring Fresh Depravities

Probably the most surprising thing about this book is that it exists at all. As some of you may recall, when *Depraved 4* was released in 2020, I proclaimed it the final entry in the series. Over the course of four books, I figured I'd written enough about protagonist Jessica Sloan and her adventures and it was time to devote more of my focus to original ideas. I had every intention of sticking to that until not even three months prior to writing this afterword.

How it came about is a typical case of me having an idea for a thing that, once started, quickly grows far beyond what I originally intended. *Depraved Halloween* was originally conceived as bonus material for a planned reissue of my short novella *The Halloween Bride*. The intent was to beef up the length of that release with another Halloween-themed story, as *The Halloween Bride* was a little too short to release in paperback on its own. I thought this new story in the *Depraved* universe would be a quick little novella. In retrospect, I really should've known better. Once I started work on the project, it quickly became apparent I couldn't write about Jessica Sloan for the first time in four years without it turning into a full-length novel. When it became obvious what was happening, plans changed. *The Halloween Bride* was instead included in a collection of novellas called *Dread Ink*, while *Depraved Halloween* became a stand-alone book.

It's kind of a weird thing, really. When the original Leisure Books edition of *Depraved* came out in 2009, I hadn't the faintest inkling I'd still be writing about Jessica a decade and a half later, but here we are. One thing I kept at the front of my mind as I wrote this new book was to portray Jessica as an evolved, changed version of who she once was. Some of my favorite older mystery series (Ed McBain's 87th Precinct novels, for example) feature a cast of characters who somehow remain magically young over several decades. I love those books, but I couldn't do it that way. Jessica was somewhere in her mid-twenties in *Depraved*, but in this latest entry, she's portrayed as approaching forty. She's slowed down some. She's wearier and she's lost some of her edge, which is what lands her in such a vulnerable place in this book, but when the shit hits the fan and she needs to kick ass and be ruthlessly violent again, she can still do it. She ain't happy about it, but when her moment arrives, she seizes it.

I have to admit I was happy to end up writing about her again, after all. It was fun. It felt like coming home. It's a good thing I didn't do anything crazy like kill her off in the last one, eh? Though even in that case, I could probably have figured something out. This is the horror genre, after all, where pretty much anything is possible.

In talking about this book, I have referred to it as a "sequel in spirit" to the first one, and by that I'm partly referring to a return to a backwoods, rural setting, but I also wanted it to have some of the same kooky what-the-fuck wild energy of the original. I also wanted it to be a book newcomers could read without having read all the other sequels. This book isn't a reboot that negates everything that happened in those books. Those things are still part of Jessica's canon. It just doesn't refer to those events at all, except perhaps once or twice in the vaguest way early on.

Sharp-eyed long-time readers may have noticed that the underground fighting club in this book has the same name as the backwoods strip club in the first book. This was, of course, on purpose. The idea is that both are perhaps part of the same underground network of human traffickers. I didn't explore that explicitly here because it's incidental to the story I was telling, but who knows, maybe it'll come up again in a future book.

Finally, in the event anyone wants to debate the viability of the reanimation mechanisms engineered by Loretta and Jed in this story, specifically that there's no way in hell they would work even with some form of supernatural assistance, what I have to say to that is, NO SHIT. What I was striving for here was B-movie entertainment value, not scientific plausibility.

Anyway, I hope you enjoyed this book. I had a blast writing it. This time around I'm not calling this Jessica's last adventure. Maybe she'll be back again a bit down the road. We'll just have to wait and see.

Bryan Smith
July 20, 2024

BIO

Bryan Smith is the author of numerous novels and novellas, including *Depraved*, *68 Kill*, *Slowly We Rot*, *The Killing Kind*, and *Dead End House*. He's a two-time Splatterpunk Award winner, once for best novella (*Kill For Satan!*) and once for best collection (*Dirty Rotten Hippies and Other Stories*). He is also the co-author of *Suburban Gothic*, written with Brian Keene. A film version of *68 Kill* was released in 2017. He'll have a story in the forthcoming Simon & Schuster anthology *The End of the World As We Know It: Tales of Stephen King's The Stand*. He lives in TN with his dog Mac. Signed copies of his books can be purchased at https://bryansmithhorror.bigcartel.com/

PLAYLIST

https://open.spotify.com/playlist/4wwPCT5JGZmzU-LXsB2BuXX?si=706f0276542e4b2c

Other Grindhouse Press Titles